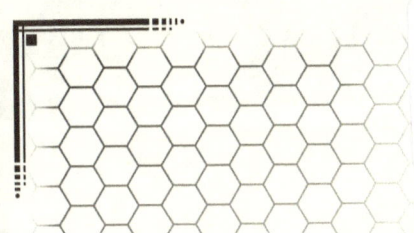

THE
PURIFICATION

THE EVARAN CHRONICLES

BOOK 3

ADAIR HART

Editing done by Laura Petrella

Cover done by Tom Edwards

Interior design done by Colleen Sheehan

Proofread done by Red Adept Publishing

Published by Quantum Edge Publishing

ISBN: 978-0-9967172-2-9

www.AdairHart.com

To get updates on new books and other notifications, sign up for my mailing list at:

www.AdairHart.com/MailingList.aspx

THE
PURIFICATION

THE STORY SO FAR

Dr. Albert Snowden and his niece, Emily, were abducted by an alien race known as the Krotovore. They were rescued by a space- and time-traveling being known as Evaran, who dropped them back off on Earth.

When Evaran returned to check on them, they asked to travel with him, and Evaran accepted. They have been on one adventure that helped the people of Fredoria, a planet of human ex-slaves, become a full trade partner with the Kreagan Star Empire, the local galactic superpower in Earth's region of the galaxy.

This book takes place after that adventure.

EVARAN'S TECHNOLOGY

Torvatta—his ship that can travel through time and space

Universal interface card (UIC)—a credit-card-sized device carried on his belt that allows access to any technological system

Augmented reality interface (ARI)—an interface that only he can see around him

Utility handle—a hilt-like device carried on his belt that can extend morphable matter in any shape, typically extended into a baton or staff; can also fire repulsion and stun beams

Illumination orbs—small orbs on his belt that provide lighting and can hover

Projection orb—an orb that allows projections to be sent to it from remote sources, such as Evaran's ring or the Torvatta

Ring—a ring that can provide holographic projection and also scan

PROLOGUE

The Purification must be stopped. The thought jumbled around in John Holington's mind as he sat at his desk, planning the next assault on the Purifiers. He had been fighting them for almost a hundred years, but their human supremacist movement had enveloped a large portion of the galactic region surrounding Earth.

Although his small spaceship had limited firepower, it was fast and well suited for the guerrilla tactics of his crew. Nonhumans were still around, but their numbers were low and scattered to aging ships like his. Still, he held hope that the tide would change in their favor at some point.

Lord Vygon, the deceased and former leader of the vampire house he belonged to, had entrusted him to deliver a message to a being known as Evaran. John had never seen this person or anyone that knew of him. It seemed hopeless, but he would honor it as long as he could. His attention turned to the doorway of his office.

"They're here!" said Miles O'Bannon.

John looked up from his desk at the large, pale man with curly red hair trying to catch his breath. "Who?"

"Evaran, Dr. Snowden, and Emily."

John's heartbeat raced. If it was true, then maybe this mission would finally be over. He scrambled out from behind his desk and slapped Miles on the chest. "I'll meet you in the command room. Assemble the others. Go."

Miles nodded and took off.

John walked over to a steel panel on the wall and tapped it twice. A reflective surface appeared. He smoothed out his short, straight black hair and stared at the mirror, where his silver eyes stood in stark contrast to his dark skin. Looking at his form, even after a thousand years, never got old. With a final glance, he double-tapped the panel, causing it to shut down the surface, then headed to the command room. It took him several minutes to get there through the cramped hallways.

The quiet hum of the ship echoed around the room as he scanned his crew of five. There was Miles O'Bannon, who, with his immense strength and rhino power armor, was the muscle when needed. Then there was Hermes, the last of the Greek God Pantheon. With his bronze skin and brown hair and eyes, he served as the pilot, mechanic, and comic relief. He knew Hermes and Lord Vygon were close, and that friendship had been extended to John, something he placed a high value on.

Dizz and Cantol were the last members of Lord Vygon's death squad. They were in the same vampire house as John and specialized in assassination. He did not possess their skill with weapons or training, but he was quick on the draw and could hold his own. Both were lean, and their builds allowed them to move without effort.

Rounding out the last spot was Shandra Everoak, a tree shifter and the last of her kind. Her medium build, tan skin, green eyes, and long green hair were emblematic of the Everoak family line.

In the center of the room sat a central table that had consoles hanging off the edges at sixty-degree angles. Miles tapped at one of the consoles, causing the large screen at the front of the ship to flick on.

A shaky view of the expansive interior of a space station appeared. The view wheeled around to show a fair-skinned middle-aged man's face with sweat rolling down the sides. He had on a one-piece gray suit with a green mantle across his shoulders. "Brills here. The Evaran Protocol has been activated. Just saw Evaran, Dr. Snowden, and Emily. The Purifiers got 'em, but they're here."

The view pivoted back around to show what Brills saw as he walked toward one side of the interior shown before. Brills reached a hand up to his ear, and the view zoomed into the far side of the room.

A group of guards wearing advanced light silver armor over a gray mesh suit escorted three prisoners. A Purifier symbol stood out on the guards' upper arms and on their chests. It was a red triangle with a circle in it that had lines to each point in the triangle, all outlined in black.

Brills pointed to the first prisoner. "That's Evaran. He looks different than what I imagined." He then waved a finger between an older male and a younger female. "That's Dr. Snowden and Emily. Has to be. Station hasn't been this active since I've been here. A transport ship is coming, supposedly, but still working on getting details. Anyways, I'll be around. Contact me through the usual channels when you get this."

John let out a quick breath when he realized he had been holding it. He studied the projection. Evaran's light-gray, lightly armored, advanced-looking suit seemed out of place for someone of his status. His fair skin and dirty-blond hair reminded him of Dizz, except a bit bigger.

John scrutinized Dr. Snowden next. Dr. Snowden had on a pair of brown twill slacks with a complementary brown jacket. His brown bow tie and cotton vest stood in contrast to his white-striped shirt. It was definitely not something John had ever seen. Emily wore light jeans, a shirt, and shoes that looked like they were more for comfort than battle. John shook his head. How were these three a threat to the Purifiers?

John focused on his crew. They had been loyal to him and part of his group for almost a hundred years. John's blood boiled as he thought of all his friends the Purifiers had killed. He took deep breaths to clear his mind. Their final mission was upon them. He was aware of the crew staring at him as he contemplated what he would say.

After a moment, he raised his head. "The time has come. We've waited for this moment for a very long time. The Purifiers have finally met their match. We were entrusted with a message from Lord Vygon long ago, and through many generations . . . and here we are. We've sustained losses and setbacks . . . and here we are. The Purifiers tried to cleanse us for being what we are . . . and here we are. Evaran has arrived and will clean this corrupted timeline. All he needs is the message . . . and here we are."

The crew nodded in silence as they looked around.

"We prepare for our final mission. Although this may be our last one, I want each and every one of you to know— it's been an honor to serve with you," said John. His voice cracked. "To our countless fallen Daedrould, Outsider,

Wildborn, and other nonhuman brothers and sisters, we will avenge you." His voice rose as he jabbed a finger on the table. "No more will we hide in fear. The end of this timeline approaches. The Purification brought upon us will be removed, and with it, a new timeline created. One where humans and nonhumans alike are equals! So says Lord Vygon!"

The crew pumped their arms in the air. "Hail Lord Vygon!"

John swept his hand out. "The instrument of the Purifiers' destruction is at hand. All hail Evaran!"

"Hail Evaran!"

John paused to catch his breath as he scanned the crew. "All right then. We have a lot of work to do. We'll dock with the Purifiers' Saturn station in about an hour and a half. You've been training all your lives for this moment. We can't fail. Let's show the Purifiers what the Earth Guard is capable of."

The crew cheered.

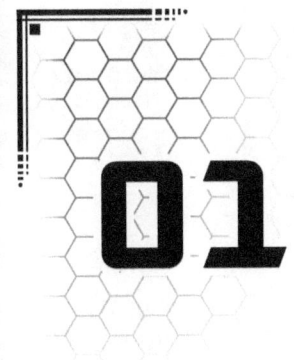

01

Dr. Albert Snowden waved his hand through the air, causing solar systems to slide across his view. He marveled at the holographic models that the planar cartography lab could generate. Standing in the middle of the room, he could use arm and hand gestures to soar through the galaxy, and beyond. He wished he had this technology back in college.

Thump! Thump! Thump! Thump!

He sighed as he ran his hand over his balding head and tufts of gray hair. After pausing the holograms, he glanced over at his early twenties niece, Emily, sitting at a desk in the corner. Of all the places to be on a ship that could travel through space and time, she chose to be there, thumping her hands away as she browsed an embedded screen in a desk. She had on earplugs that fit snugly and dodged strands of her dirty-blond hair. The nanobots that coursed through him gave him heightened senses, and one of those was hearing. Maybe her nanobots were not helping her hear his frustrated sighs.

He shook his head as he went over to her desk and tapped at it. "Emily!"

Emily looked up and pulled out an earplug.

"You're thumping your fingers again."

Emily hunched her shoulders. "Sorry."

He eyed her. After a moment, he went back to the center of the room. With a quick tap in the air, the holographic models swirled around. He had been studying a planet called Gliese 832c in a solar system about sixteen light-years away from Earth and wanted to see if there was a model with information on it. As he swiped his hands through the various solar systems, looking for Gliese 832c, he reflected on where he was. Evaran had saved them from an alien abduction and allowed them to travel with him on his ship, the Torvatta. Being able to go through space and time was just one thing they got to enjoy. He was uncertain of half the things he had learned, but there was one thing he was certain of—reality was much stranger than it let on.

Thump! Thump! Thump! Thump!

His blood boiled as he snapped his head toward Emily. With fire in his step, he hustled over to her. He slammed his hand down on Emily's desk.

Emily jumped as she took out her earplugs. "Sorry . . ."

"Isn't there someplace else you can do that?"

Emily's eyes widened.

Before Dr. Snowden could respond, Emily scrambled from her chair and ran out of the room. He sighed as he massaged his temples. His temper disappeared just as quickly as it had come. The anger flashes seemed to occur much more frequently since traveling with Evaran. There were some instances where it was warranted, but he found that even small things could set it off. Emily had become a target of it for the first time. Maybe it was the nanobots inside him. For a short while, they did carry the essence of another person, but that had been resolved. He shook his head as he pinched his hands at the holographic models. They dissipated as he exited the room.

The planar cartography lab was his favorite spot on the Torvatta. Not only could he go there to unwind, but it was a place of research. Evaran had mentioned that it had the capability to show every place in the universe, but that it was locked down to this universe, timeline, and places Evaran had been. Upon request, Evaran allowed Dr. Snowden to see additional parts of the Milky Way galaxy that coincided with Dr. Snowden's research that was done while teaching astronomy.

He walked through the empty research lab. Gadgets and devices lay around haphazardly on top of tables. He enjoyed this room a lot, although not quite as much as the planar cartography lab. His mind snapped back to the situation as he walked out of the lab and into the main area of the ship.

Looking around, he saw the front third of the disk-shaped ship was empty. He did a quick check into the two doors to his right and three doors to his left across from the entrance. The doors led to dimensional areas that did not take up any area in normal space. Dimensional mechanics, as he had come to understand it, was something he had on his list to learn more about. He went to the command area in the front of the ship and saw V, a metallic-skinned robot with lines and designs segmenting his body, in front of a U-shaped console. It still amazed him that Evaran had built V.

He stood behind V and followed V's gaze to the two front screens hanging on the transparent walls. One screen had data on it, while the other showed Evaran leaning over the blue semitransparent waist-high guardrail on the roof edge. Dr. Snowden shook his head at Evaran's hair. It never appeared to move, even in combat. Evaran's fair skin was a constant as well.

"Dr. Snowden. Is everything okay?" asked V.

Dr. Snowden jumped. "Yeah . . . was just looking for Emily." He had become used to the robotic-sounding voice of V, with its raspy digital effect, and the particular way both Evaran and V spoke.

"Analysis. She entered the living quarters three minutes ago. Her pace, heartbeat, and breathing suggest she is upset," said V.

"Yeah . . . that's on me."

"Is she in need of comforting? I am knowledgeable in several calming techniques."

Dr. Snowden chuckled. "No . . . it's something I need to take care of." He pointed a finger at the screen with Evaran. "What's he up to?"

"Analysis. Evaran is studying the rings of Saturn."

"Ahh. I'd been planning on going up there myself after the lab," said Dr. Snowden. He tilted his head at V. "I woulda thought you'd be up there."

"I am not sure if it is appropriate."

Dr. Snowden jerked his head back. "Why's that . . ."

"Evaran studied cosmic phenomena with U4, my predecessor, on the roof. It was a common occurrence."

Dr. Snowden studied V. He knew V had limited emotions but did not know that V was capable of feeling like this. "Was U4 designed like you?"

"Yes. She had a similar body and an orb mode with less functionality, but she preferred body mode, while I prefer orb mode. Her death occurred on Evaran's first visit to Earth."

Dr. Snowden's eyes widened. "Were they . . . close?"

"Yes. She traveled with Evaran for three hundred twenty-three years."

Dr. Snowden's jaw dropped as he gazed at the screen. He knew Evaran was probably older than he looked, but not three-hundred-plus-type old. "How old is Evaran exactly?"

"You must ask Evaran that question."

"Fine . . . ," said Dr. Snowden. He furrowed his eyebrows. "Do you . . . want to go up there?"

V tilted his head at Dr. Snowden. "Yes."

Dr. Snowden placed a hand on V's shoulder. "Then go on up!"

V paused as he studied Dr. Snowden. "Acknowledged."

A smile lit up Dr. Snowden's face as he watched V head to the elevator that went to the roof. His smile faded when he went to the living quarters. He took a deep breath and pressed a button on the console outside Emily's room. After a moment of no response, he pressed again. Still nothing. He pressed another button. "Emily . . . I know you can hear me. I just want to talk."

The door slid open, and he entered the room. Emily was sitting on a couch in the middle of the large living room at the end of the short hallway he was in. She sat with her knees pulled up to her chest, and her puffy eyes dominated her face. He sat in a chair perpendicular to the couch. A digitized roar made him jump up. He reached under himself and picked up Mr. Smith, a stuffed tiger toy that Dan, his deceased brother and Emily's father, had given to her as a child. He half grinned. "Why, that little rascal."

Emily chuckled.

Dr. Snowden sat back down and looked at her. "Look. Back there, in the lab. I . . . lost control. Not mad at you, just . . . edgy for some reason."

Emily looked down. "It's okay. I know when I'm not wanted around."

Dr. Snowden stiffened. "That's not it at all."

Emily raised her head with lips turned down. "Just feels like sometimes you don't want me here."

"No . . . why would you think that?"

"Mom left me when I was born. Dad left me when I went to college. Then you were going to leave me to travel with Evaran. Just feels like life is trying to make me be alone."

Dr. Snowden studied Emily. It never crossed his mind that she would feel this way. "Two of those were out of your control. As for leaving you, I wasn't going to go with Evaran if you didn't want to come. We do it together, or not at all."

"You would've resented me. I only came because you wanted to go."

Dr. Snowden sighed as he sat next to Emily. "We can leave whenever you want if you're not happy." He put his arm around her. "What's important is you're a part of my life, wherever we are or go."

Emily nodded and leaned into him.

"You're the most important thing in my life. You're a Snowden, never forget that," said Dr. Snowden in a cracked voice.

"I'm glad I'm a thing and not a person then."

They laughed and enjoyed the moment.

Dr. Snowden stood and gestured toward the door. "Want to see something interesting?"

Emily perked her head up as she dried her face with her hands.

"Apparently, Evaran traveled with U4, V's predecessor, and used to hang out on the roof, studying stuff with her. V didn't join Evaran because he didn't feel it was appropriate."

"V . . . was anxious?"

"Seemed that way. I encouraged him to go up before coming here. Care to join me?"

Emily smiled as she stood and nodded.

They exited Emily's room and headed toward the elevator. When they got there, V stood in front of it.

"V? I thought you were going up?" said Dr. Snowden.

"I am running simulations on the best approach."

Dr. Snowden shook his head. "You think too much. Come on, we're going up and you can come with us."

"Acknowledged."

They entered the elevator and exited it when it reached the top.

Evaran stood on the edge of the ship's circular roof, leaning out over the waist-high thin blue shield that ringed the edges. He turned his head to the side. "I was wondering when you three would show up."

Dr. Snowden and Emily headed off to the left side of Evaran while V went to the right.

"Things happen, you know. Find anything interesting?" asked Dr. Snowden, glancing out at the sparse objects in Saturn's rings.

"Just admiring the water ice formations."

Dr. Snowden looked around. "What ring are we in?"

"According to Earth terminology, we are in ring B," said V.

Emily shook her head. "No idea what you're talking about. It looks cool, though."

V glanced at Emily. "I agree."

Evaran tilted his head at V with narrowed eyes. "Do you like looking at things like this?"

"Yes."

"You should come up more often when I am out here."

"Acknowledged," said V, glancing at Dr. Snowden.

Dr. Snowden grinned as he saw V's lights glow a bit brighter. His grin faded when a low thumping sound emanated around them. Everything outside the ship faded to black for a brief moment, then eased back into view. It reminded him of how traveling in time looked when he first saw the Torvatta do it. "Umm . . . what the heck was that?"

"Interesting. It would appear a timeline update has occurred."

Dr. Snowden's eyes widened as Emily gripped his right arm. "A cascading timeline update. A CTU, right?"

"That is correct," said Evaran. "Do not worry. You are protected from any timeline change while on the Torvatta."

Dr. Snowden's heartbeat ramped up as he looked around. He knew that timeline updates only went forward in time, but the Torvatta's reaction was new to him. To be able to go through it, and see what update had been done, was awe inspiring to him. He hunched over and gripped the guardrail shielding as the sound faded away.

When it had passed, he heard Emily gasp as she pointed out into the rings. It had hundreds of small ships flying around the rings, shooting lasers and scooping up objects.

Evaran nodded. "Your first timeline update in a temporally shielded ship. You will get used to it. Now, are you ready to explore?"

***

They assembled in the command area. Evaran sat in his command chair, and Dr. Snowden and Emily sat in the U-shaped seating area off to his right. V put the Torvatta in stealth mode, and it flew toward the ships and scanned them.

Dr. Snowden stared at the front screens. The left screen showed the outside view, while the right side showed a close-up of each ship that was scanned at that moment, along with various statistic labels flying out around it. The moment was not lost on him. He glanced at Evaran. It intrigued him how calm Evaran was. Just another facet, Dr. Snowden guessed, of being well traveled, both in space and time. "I'm guessing humanity is a bit more advanced. Unless . . . those ships aren't human."

Evaran tapped at his chair console. "V, analyze."

V's hands flew over the console. "Analysis. Technology level is consistent with human technology from the year 5140."

"That's . . . pretty advanced. Is it still 2012?" asked Emily.

"Yes," said Evaran. "It would seem whatever change was done in the past has had far-reaching effects."

"Analysis. Space station detected outside the rings."

"Take us to it," said Evaran.

"Acknowledged."

The Torvatta veered off toward the ring edges.

Dr. Snowden enjoyed seeing the rings. He had studied the different ring swaths and the gaps and wondered why Evaran had brought them there. Not that he was complaining, but he suspected that Evaran felt at ease hovering around in the rings. Whatever this timeline update had done, he was going to find out.

The Torvatta flew out past the rings. Although Dr. Snowden could not see it on the left screen looking out, the right screen had a top-down view of the surrounding area. The Torvatta was a little blip that moved closer to a much larger blip outlined in green. After twenty minutes of silence, they arrived at the space station.

Dr. Snowden's eyes bulged. It had a cylindrical core, with equidistant torus-shaped rings encircling the length of it. The top of the cylindrical core had a larger half sphere on top of it. Antennae and smaller structures jutted out across the various surfaces. It reminded him of a large nail. As they neared it, the sheer size of the station overwhelmed Dr. Snowden. The Krotovore ship they were initially abducted on was small potatoes compared to this. If humanity had built this, then they were truly more advanced. He wondered if they got the material from a moon or an asteroid belt.

Evaran interacted with the console on his chair. "This station appears to be one of many. Long-range scans indicate there are four more. V, take us in and perform standard scans."

"Acknowledged."

The Torvatta flew around the station and scanned for the next thirty minutes. Dr. Snowden noted the various windows and segments of the station.

"Analysis. Each ring has a docking segment. Life-form analysis indicates human," said V.

"Just human? No aliens?" asked Emily.

"No alien life detected."

Emily raised her eyebrows at Dr. Snowden. "That's . . . interesting."

"I concur," said Evaran. "With technology this advanced, it would be logical for humanity to have spread out or been noticed by other species. At a bare minimum, I would have expected a Kreagan presence. V, take us out of stealth mode and then to one of the center ring's docking segments."

"Acknowledged."

The Torvatta uncloaked and headed toward a central ring. Dr. Snowden saw that the docking area V had referenced had a blue shield that seemed to cover a full segment of the ring. He wondered how larger ships docked, as they probably would not have fit. The Torvatta flew through the blue shields. To the left and right were various ships docked on landing pads that extended out. A green light lit up on the front right screen.

"Looks like they wish to communicate," said Evaran. He tapped at his chair console, and the left and right front screen disappeared, showing one full screen.

A man in a black robe with silver metallic pads on it appeared. The triangular red makeup that framed his eyes caught Dr. Snowden's attention. A shiver ran through him.

The man tapped at a console in front of him. "This is Ring Operator Twenty-Two. Identify yourself."

"My name is Evaran. I am here with my friends V, Dr. Albert Snowden, and Emily Snowden aboard my ship, the Torvatta."

"What is your intention here?"

"We seek only rest and relaxation."

The ring operator looked down at his console. His eyes widened slightly. "Oh . . . well, in that case, proceed to docking extension number 42. Enjoy your visit."

The screen flickered off.

"Docking extension coordinates received," said V.

"Take us in."

"Acknowledged," said V. He paused for a moment, then faced Evaran. "My facial analysis program indicates he was surprised."

Evaran nodded. "He was. We should be careful."

Dr. Snowden tilted his head. "He was definitely surprised. Maybe they don't get a lot of visitors. Their security seems pretty lax."

Evaran raised a finger. "Or it could mean their security is so efficient that visitors pose no threat."

"Maybe . . . guess we'll find out," said Dr. Snowden.

The Torvatta flew over to the docking extension and aligned against it.

Evaran stood and gestured toward the entrance. "Are you ready?"

A grin grew on Dr. Snowden's face as he stood. "Heck yeah. This is exciting."

Emily swatted Dr. Snowden's arm as she stood. "Let's do this!"

Dr. Snowden chuckled. Emily's exuberance to go out and learn was infectious. This was probably another field study for her. He was glad to have her here and could not imagine it any other way.

As Evaran walked toward the Torvatta entrance with Dr. Snowden and Emily, he paused to face V, who had followed them. "V, I will need you to stay here in case we need to leave."

V dipped his head. "Acknowledged."

Dr. Snowden thought he could almost hear disappointment in V's voice. If U4 traveled a lot with Evaran outside the ship, he could see how V would always feel like he was being compared against her, fair or not. "You expecting trouble?"

"No. However, this is an unknown environment run by an unknown authority. If everything checks out, V can join us."

"Kreagus was an unknown environment," said Dr. Snowden.

"Yes, but I was familiar with the Kreagans. That is not the case here."

Dr. Snowden looked at V and raised the right side of his lips.

V nodded at Dr. Snowden and headed back to the front console.

Dr. Snowden followed Evaran and Emily out of the Torvatta and through a short hallway that ended in a larger room devoid of people. A sterile smell rankled his nose, and the reflective environment caused him to squint. It was like everything had been waxed. Paneled walls and a smooth steel-like floor extended ahead of him. To his right were several other hallway exits. Ahead of him was a central archway into another large room. Long red banners with a red triangle separated by white space but outlined in black flanked the archway. The triangle had a hollow red circle in the middle with lines to each point in the triangle and white space filling the gaps. This environment was a stark departure from the colors and smells he had experienced on the Kreagan home world. The lack of anyone around disturbed him.

Emily grimaced. "This is . . . interesting."

"Interesting is one word for it," said Dr. Snowden.

Evaran nodded and waved them forward.

After clearing the arch, they found themselves in a square room. The bottom part was ringed with various storefronts, and across from them ran two large ramps on the sides of a series of elevators. The center of the room had a step-down plaza with a statue of a man posing with a hand outstretched in the middle. The attire of the man on the statue reminded Dr. Snowden of chain mail armor, except this armor looked hundreds of years more advanced. The face stood out to him. It was not one of thoughtfulness, but one of determination.

Emily gestured at the statue. "That's kinda cool. Definitely was not expecting a statue on a space station."

"Me either. Statue looks pissed," said Dr. Snowden.

Emily chuckled.

"Hopefully it is not indicative of the authority that runs this station," said Evaran. "We can check out one of these shops and maybe learn more about the station." He gestured toward their right.

They walked along the pathway, pausing to look at the various shop fronts. Dr. Snowden noticed that they all had the same configuration, a glass window with a door. Even the name above the shops was in a standardized font. If uniformity was the goal, this station had mastered it. Between each store was a banner similar to the one he saw earlier. Propaganda was not in short supply. He caught the smell of something cooking and pointed at a store. "Let's check that one out."

"Always thinking with your stomach," said Emily, swatting Dr. Snowden's arm.

Dr. Snowden shrugged with a half grin.

Inside the shop was a long counter on the right, which ended with a door. To the left of the counter was a walkway and, beyond that along the wall, a series of booths. They walked the length of the room while a man in a one-piece white suit eyed them behind the counter.

Dr. Snowden noticed another man sitting in one of the booths. The colorful clothing, stubby face, and red hair stood out against the bland setting.

The man looked up at them after taking a sip from a bowl filled with a chunky green liquid. He cocked his head. "New around here?"

Evaran faced the man. "We are. Do you mind if we join you?"

The man jerked his head back. "Not at all. Surprised you asked. Name's Sean."

Dr. Snowden stepped forward and extended a hand. "I'm Dr. Snowden."

Sean eyed Dr. Snowden's hand.

Dr. Snowden retracted his hand. He waved a finger between Evaran and Emily. "This is Evaran and my niece, Emily."

"Why'd you extend your hand like that?" asked Sean.

"Just a friendly handshake was all."

Sean harrumphed. "Yeah . . . you're definitely not from around here. Still, nice to see that rather than a salute. Come. Sit." He scooted in close to the wall.

Dr. Snowden sat next to Sean, while Evaran and Emily sat across from them.

"So . . . where you from?" asked Sean.

"Far away from here. We are travelers, and wanted to stop in and see what this place was," said Evaran.

"Don't want to say where you're from. I respect that. I'm from Shirus, 'bout ten light-years away. Run a few supply lines."

"For who?" asked Dr. Snowden.

Sean narrowed his eyes. "You . . . don't know of the Human Dominion?"

Dr. Snowden shook his head.

"You're from very far away then. This is the heart of their empire," said Sean. He cocked his head. "Hell, this is one of their stations! How'd you get this far into it without knowing that?"

Evaran raised a hand. "Our ship is unique and capable of long-distance travel. We enter in one place and exit in another, as in this case here."

Sean laughed. "I know how compressed space travel works. Even then, they have beacons you couldn't have missed. Anyways . . . at least you aren't alien."

Dr. Snowden mused on hearing "compressed space travel." He learned about it on Kreagus. The ability to pop into a condensed layer of space for long-distance travel. Sean would have no way of knowing about the Torvatta's unique ability to use portals. It was no surprise that Evaran did not elaborate on it.

Emily shifted in her seat. "What's wrong with being an alien?"

"The Purifiers," said Sean, tilting his head at Emily. "You might have noticed their symbols all over the place. Official religion of the Human Dominion. Any and all nonhumans, including aliens by definition, are exterminated by decree of the Purifier overlord."

Evaran narrowed his eyes. "Human supremacy. Interesting. They would not approve of me then."

Sean's eyes widened. "You're . . . not human?"

"No."

"I don't know how you evaded their scanners, but you need to get the hell outta here for your own safety. Not all of us buy into their purifying crap, but you need to go, like right now."

Evaran nodded. "Very well. We shall go."

"Good luck and thanks for the conversation," said Sean with a sigh. "It's been . . . interesting."

Dr. Snowden did a half wave as they exited the store. The expression on Sean's face was not one of concern when Evaran mentioned he was not human; it was one of fear. Whatever these Purifiers were doing, it seemed to keep people in line, even those who did not like them. He sighed as they headed back the way they had come. This was not the advanced humanity he was hoping to see.

02

Evaran paused as they approached the hallway that led to the Torvatta. He raised his hand. "We are not alone."

Dr. Snowden turned his head to the ramps he had seen earlier. Large men in heavy silver armor with flowing red capes stormed toward them. The red triangle symbol was emblazoned on their chests, and the weapons they carried were big and black and looked like they could deal some serious damage.

"We must go. Now," said Evaran.

They turned the corner and halted at the sight of a man in a silver robe with black lines segmenting it. A Purifier symbol was emblazoned on his chest and upper arms. Behind him was a group of men similar to the ones headed toward them from the ramp.

The man extended a hand. "Halt. You are under arrest."

Dr. Snowden turned his head to see that they were surrounded.

"For what reason?" asked Evaran.

"For being nonhuman and, more importantly, being Evaran," said the man with a finger extended. "The Evaran Protocol has been activated. You will come with me now."

"What do we do?" asked Emily in a hushed tone while looking at Evaran.

Evaran turned his head toward Emily. "We go with them." His gaze bored a hole thorughe through the man. "For now."

Dr. Snowden's heartbeat ramped up as he studied the situation. It sometimes felt to him that if Evaran were by himself, he would make different decisions. Then again, had he been alone with Seeros in their last adventure, it would not have turned out well. This was one situation where there was no way out without someone getting hurt. Hopefully Evaran had a plan, because going up against these armored monsters was not something Dr. Snowden wanted to do.

The man gestured for them to head back into the room. After an hour of being escorted through various hallways, they reached a circular room that had evenly spaced shielded doors ringing it. The room had the text Unit 4A above it. A man with heavy black armor approached them. He tapped at a console on his forearm, causing one of the shielded doors to dissipate. With a nod from the heavily armored man, the men escorting Evaran, Dr. Snowden, and Emily moved them inside the cell. The black-armored man interacted with his console, resealing the entrance, which became dark gray as a light turned on above them.

Dr. Snowden noticed a small set of benches that extruded from the wall and took a seat. Emily joined him.

Evaran scanned the cell with his ring. "Interesting. I detect emitters between the cells."

"What's that?" asked Emily.

"They could disable us in a variety of ways in here."

"Oh . . ."

The wall opposite the way they came in turned translucent. On the other side, Dr. Snowden saw a larger room with a table, a chair, and a middle-aged male dressed similarly to the man who had arrested them earlier.

The man walked up to the shielded door and peered in. He smirked and stepped back while placing his hands behind his back. "I'm Ring Commander Sheel. I'm curious . . . do you know why you're here?"

Evaran stepped forward. "We are here because I am not a human, and the Evaran Protocol has been activated."

Sheel nodded. "Yes . . . but do you know *what* the Evaran Protocol is?"

"I do not."

Sheel snorted. "Figures. Well then. Let me fill you in." He tapped at his forearm, causing a hologram of a book to appear floating to his side. "This is a book called *The Human Way*. It contains, in *great* detail, how a human should live their life, the way they should behave, and the many protocols that need to be observed. It has led to this," said Sheel, sweeping his hand in an arc, "the great Human Dominion. Yet . . . there are these . . . protocols, that I believe should not be in there."

"The Evaran Protocol."

"That is one," said Sheel with a scowl. "You got a protocol named after you, so it pollutes *The Human Way* with its very presence." Spittle flew from his mouth. "*The Human Way* was written by the overlord, and he wanted to make sure that any human that sees you or detects you follows a specific protocol. In this case, I have the honor of being the one that executes it."

"Why is there a protocol named after me?"

Sheel shook his head and walked around the table with his hands behind his back. "You are considered the highest threat and, supposedly, some powerful being." He snorted again. "Nonetheless, the overlord wishes to speak with you." He interacted with his forearm, and the book disappeared. It was replaced by a bronze-skinned head wearing a headband with a large crystal in the middle. The Purifier symbol stood around his eyes.

"I am the overlord, and from what Sheel tells me, the Evaran Protocol has been activated."

"It would appear so."

The overlord narrowed his eyes. "Yes . . . I can sense you, even as far away as you are." He cocked his head. "Interesting form . . . but a poor choice. I look forward to seeing it in person. Unfortunately for you, this will be the end of an age-old fight."

Evaran perked his head up. "Elaborate."

The overlord chuckled. "All in due time, plane traveler. I will relieve you of the burden of having that form." He looked at Sheel. "You have done well."

Sheel bowed.

"Our ship should be there in a day. I have dispatched nearby royal exterminators already. Prepare for my arrival."

"Yes, my overlord."

The overlord looked Evaran over, then smiled big. "I will make use of the Torvatta's time-travel ability and be sure that everyone knows how I got it."

Evaran shook his head. "I cannot allow that."

The overlord laughed as the hologram faded.

Sheel sighed.

"You do not agree with the overlord?"

"I think he overestimates you. If you're so powerful, how did I capture you so easily?"

"A fair point. I have noticed you did not disable us."

Sheel's nostrils flared. "The protocol is very clear on that. You're not to be harmed. If it was up to me, I would kill you and," he said, gesturing at Dr. Snowden and Emily, "whatever those . . . *abominations* are. Then there would be no more need for this protocol."

"Uhh . . . we're human," said Dr. Snowden.

"No, you're not. You have some type of technology in your body that has altered your purity. A shame, really."

Dr. Snowden's right cheek twitched. This was the first time he heard someone say they were not human. It was not something that ever crossed his mind. Sweat rolled down the side of his head as he stood up and approached the shield. "We're just as human as you, buddy."

"You're filth. Just. Pure. Filth."

Dr. Snowden's blood began to boil. He clenched his fist. "Well, thankfully that's your opinion. If your views represent what humanity has moved to, then it's a sad day."

"You judge me?" said Sheel. "You're not worthy of that. You and your dirty niece will meet the overlord tomorrow. You can discuss your inefficiencies with him."

Dr. Snowden's eyes narrowed, and his face turned red. "Don't you talk about Emily like that! You don't know me or her."

"I know you're tainted and you travel with Evaran. That's all I need to know. You're subhuman."

Dr. Snowden pounded the shield with his fist. "You're *lucky* there is a shield here. I'd be more than happy to *show* you how dirty a human can get."

"Uh-huh," said Sheel, laughing. "Just like an animal."

Dr. Snowden imagined himself breaking through the shield and grabbing Sheel. He would target the eyes first, ripping them out and stomping on them. Then he would tear out his tongue and break his arms and legs. His vision turned red as he began to hit the shield repeatedly while grunting and staring at Sheel. He jumped as Evaran laid a hand on his shoulder.

"Dr. Snowden!" said Evaran.

A pain shot through Dr. Snowden's heart as he paused. He staggered over to the wall and knelt down with a hand on his chest.

"Uncle Albert!" said Emily. She rushed over to him and helped him sit on the bench.

Evaran scanned Dr. Snowden. "You need to calm down. Your body is stressing itself. This is not normal."

"Ahh . . . can't even handle a simple disagreement. If you're representative of humans from wherever you are, then it's definitely a sad day," said Sheel with a smirk.

Dr. Snowden lunged at the shield.

Evaran caught Dr. Snowden and sat him down. "You need to relax. Sheel is not worth the effort . . . or time." He looked at Sheel. "He is just a middleman with no real power and personal issues he needs to work on."

Sheel rolled his eyes. "Whatever. I came to facilitate the overlord's hologram, and also to see what the great Evaran was like, and I leave confused. Why a protocol was designed for you, I'll never understand. You can sit in that cell and waste away your last day pondering about what the overlord is going to do to you." He tapped at a device on his belt, and the shield turned dark gray.

Evaran stroked his chin.

"Are you in pain?" asked Emily, staring at Dr. Snowden.

Dr. Snowden shook his head as his vision returned to normal. The pain had subsided and a tingling sensation shot out over him. After a moment, a chill swept across him and his breathing stabilized. "I was, but seems the nanobots have kicked in. Not sure what happened. One moment I was thinking why Sheel was doing what he was doing, the next I was dismembering him in my thoughts and everything went red."

"Your reaction was unusual. I do not know if the nanobots are malfunctioning or if there is something else going on. We will need to investigate when we get back to the Torvatta," said Evaran.

Dr. Snowden waved a hand at Evaran. "I'm fine. Don't worry about me."

"You're not fine," said Emily. "I've only seen you react like that twice."

Evaran studied Emily for a moment. "An excellent observation. The draug and Seeros. Both life-and-death situations. However, this was not a life-and-death situation."

Dr. Snowden rubbed his eyes. It felt like he had just gone several rounds with a boxer. "So . . . what now?"

"We wait. I need to think on this situation some," said Evaran as he sat opposite Dr. Snowden and Emily.

Emily scooted over and tapped her arm as she smiled at Dr. Snowden. "Why don't you take a nap."

Dr. Snowden sighed as he laid his head against Emily's arm. "Yes, ma'am." His eyes began to drift closed as he wondered how they were going to get out of this.

John looked through the front window of his cruiser as it approached the Purifier space station. Sweat trickled down the side of his face as he focused on the readouts flying around the window.

"If you want some alone time with the window, just let me know," said Hermes.

John eyed Hermes.

"Relax. We'll do fine, like we always do."

John shook his head. "Yeah . . . I know. Just had an update from Brills." He tapped at a button on the console near Hermes. The ship-wide communication system crackled. "Everyone, come to the command deck. It's almost go time." He let up on the button.

Hermes pressed the button. "And lunch time. If you're into that sort of thing."

John chuckled. "You know, if you die, I'm going to miss your humor."

"And if you die, where am I going to find someone brooding all the time?"

John snorted as he stepped down from the pilot area into the command area. Although Hermes ribbed him a lot, Hermes had proven to be a vital part of the team. His humor had defused many a situation. John's hands flew across the table console as he studied the information Brills had sent. The rest of the crew filtered in over the next five minutes and assembled around the table. A holographic projection shot up, showing a layout of the segmented ring they were hovering outside. It had eighteen levels with various shafts indicating lifts.

John surveyed his crew before speaking. "It's time. Brills has sent an update on the situation." He pointed at a red dot that appeared in the layout. "Evaran, Dr. Snowden, and Emily are here."

"I still find it hard to believe they were captured. Isn't Evaran some type of badass?" asked Miles.

"Maybe it was on purpose, hon," said Shandra, looking up at Miles while under his arm.

"I guess," said Miles.

"We don't know if Evaran had a reason or if he was just in the wrong place at the wrong time," said John. "Doesn't matter. What does matter is we are going to get him out and then head to the Gallant out past the Galvin Rim. Brills said that all of our inside contacts have left the ring segment, except for him, of course." He pointed to another red dot on the layout. "He's still in the segment command area here. We'll meet up with him, shut down the power to the cells area and docking bays, then meet up with Evaran here," he said, pointing to a third red dot. "Then we'll make our way back to our ship. Brills has opened a small window where we can slip through the ring segment shield and get to a docking bay extension."

"You mean we have to rely on Hermes?" asked Dizz.

Hermes chuckled. "If you want, I can join you on the inside part."

The crew laughed.

"I thought so," said Hermes with a smile.

John raised a hand. "There has been a complication. Brills also said the Third Royal Exterminator squad has arrived. I don't remember seeing that in the Evaran Protocol, so it must have been a decision by the ring commander."

"A full squad . . . yeah . . . that's not going to be easy," said Dizz.

"I know, but we have no choice. Once the power is down, they will know we are there. There are a few guards on the way to the command center, but nothing we can't deal with," said John.

Miles cracked his knuckles. "Exterminators or not. Bring 'em on!"

Shandra slapped Miles's chest and nodded at him.

"Okay, suit up for a protracted fight. Hermes, take us in to the prearranged docking bay."

"On it, boss!" said Hermes with a smirk.

John shook his head as he headed to his room to get suited up.

After thirty minutes, the crew had reassembled in the command area, decked out in gear. John did a final check on his crew. Miles had on his shielded heavy black armor with oversized gauntlets. He liked to charge into enemies and initiate close-quarters combat. Dizz and Cantol had on their sleek black-and-silver light armor. Their energy blade hilts rested on their backs, and their faces were covered by segmented helmets with raised areas around the eyes. Small weapons were strapped to their thighs. Shandra had on her brown stretch outfit. It was able to stay with her when she transformed.

John chuckled. All he had on was some light armor and a dizzying array of small weapons, both ranged and melee. "Hermes, where we at?"

"Almost there. I located Evaran's ship—well, where it should be. Scanners aren't detecting it, but Brills's information says it's at docking bay extension 42."

"All right then. Once we're in, head there."

"Got it."

Their ship flew through the light-blue shield and headed to a docking bay extension. Once docked, everyone except Hermes disembarked.

John noticed the Torvatta nearby with clamps on it and a bubble shield encircling it. "Hermes, once Brills has shut down the system, you will need to override that clamp and shield."

"Piece of cake," said Hermes over the group's communication channel.

John and the others walked up to a large rectangular door. John pulled a disc-shaped device with a U-shaped handle on top of it from a backpack and put it on a console. "Hermes, the overrider's in place."

After a moment, the door slid up into the wall.

"Link is established. Brills's codes actually work. I'm surprised. I've disabled the alarm system so you shouldn't have any guards tripping it. I'll unlock each door as you get to it. If you need me to swoop in and save the day, just let me know," said Hermes.

"Good work, Hermes," said John with a snort. He looked at the group. "Let's move."

They headed into an empty hallway. After several turns, they reached the corner to a hallway. Two heavily armored guards in segmented silver armor with weapons resting on their backs stood at the end.

John slapped Miles's armored chest. "Do your thing."

Miles bobbed his head. He turned the corner and charged toward the guards. The startled guards pulled their weapons and opened fire. Their laser beams lit up Miles's shielded armor. Miles crashed into the first guard, slamming him into the wall. The second guard pulled out an energy sword, which glowed blue, and approached Miles. He lunged forward at Miles's exposed back. Dizz flew in and sliced the guard's arm off. The guard screamed in agony. With a quick movement, Dizz decapitated the guard.

Miles turned around from the guard he crushed. "Hah!"

Dizz smiled. "One, one."

John, Shandra, and Cantol caught up to them.

John placed a hand on Dizz's shoulder. "Don't get cocky. There's exterminators around here somewhere."

"Door opening," said Hermes.

After the door was open, they proceeded to the next area. It was a large dining room with various Purifier personnel eating and several guards stationed around the room.

John chewed his bottom lip.

Miles looked at John. "You know what they did to our friends."

John sighed. "Yeah . . . but some of them are probably innocents."

Shandra snorted. "Innocents? They support the purifying killing machine. More importantly, they're in our way, and that's the fastest way to the command center." She put a hand on John's shoulder. "Look, I know you don't like killing civilians, so I'll put them to sleep. Remember, though, if even one of them gets loose and notifies the exterminators, we could fail this mission."

John nodded. He appreciated Shandra's ability to prick people with her poisonous vines that put them to sleep. "You're right. Mission first. Miles, draw the guards' fire. Shandra, follow Miles in and tree up in the center. Dizz, you take the left. Cantol, take the side room to the right. I'll provide cover from the back. Hermes, seal the doors when we go in. Everyone ready?"

They all nodded.

John pointed two fingers forward. *"Go!"*

Miles charged into the room. Some of the startled civilians fell out of their chairs. Others put their heads down on the table. The guards in the room lurched forward, shooting. Shandra hurtled to the center of the room and transformed into a large tree, with vines flying out from her rapidly expanding branches. Civilians passed out as her vines pricked them. Miles had knocked one guard down and was taking fire from another. Dizz ran along the wall and jumped at the guard shooting at Miles. With a quick flip and forward strike, he impaled the guard's chest with his blade.

Cantol ran to the right into a side room. He came flying back out and almost knocked John down. John helped Cantol back up. They both froze. A gold-plated and heavily armored exterminator stepped out with oversized forearms, autotracking shoulder-mounted lasers, and a visor that could unleash a wide laser. The shoulder-mounted lasers fired at John and Cantol, who dove out of the way.

"Miles!" said John.

Miles turned and screamed as he charged the exterminator. John waved to Dizz and Cantol to take the remaining guards. Miles ran headfirst into the exterminator, which held its ground. Its shoulder lasers were firing on Miles's shield, and the exterminator's visor began to glow. Miles head butted the visor, crimping it. The exterminator grabbed Miles's arm and swung him into the wall, then the ground, and finally into the wall again. John rolled behind the exterminator and pulled out two glowing daggers. He searched for a weak point, and when he found a small crease in the neck armor, he stabbed it.

The exterminator roared as Dizz, Cantol, and Shandra hurried over. Shandra reached out with her vines and grappled the exterminator's arms, holding them out. Dizz and Cantol leaped forward, and each sliced an arm off. Miles smashed the exterminator's helmet, knocking it away. With a quick pistol draw, John shot and hit the exterminator between the eyes. The exterminator crashed to the ground.

Miles shook his head. "So much for them not knowing we're here."

John looked down at the severed arms. "So they're human. I believe you just lost a bet, Miles. Hermes has already shut off the alarm systems, so we should be okay."

"Afraid not," said Hermes. "I'm seeing chatter independent of the station. Seems the exterminators use their own internal communication system. You need to get to the command center. *Now.*"

John sighed. This was only one exterminator, and it took the whole group to take it down. There were probably seven or so more on the station. Things were not looking good. He waved forward. "Let's go."

They handled the few guards on the way to the command center. Hermes informed them that the exterminator units were closing in on them. When they got to the command center, they burst into a room full of surprised Purifiers. They wore one-piece plastic-like suits and scattered to the ground. Shandra ran to the exit, turned into a tree, and pricked each one that Miles tossed at her. Ring Commander Sheel's eyes popped open as he drew his pistol.

One of the Purifiers morphed into a human male wearing a black trench coat and a bandanna mask over his mouth. He fired and hit Sheel point-blank in the face. Sheel slumped to the ground.

"Brills!" said John.

"Took you long enough," said Brills. "What an uncomfortable form. I'll have to shower for a week to get it out of my mind."

John looked around at the pile of unconscious Purifiers. "At least we spared the noncombatants."

"Yeah . . . but heard over the communication channel that you ran into an exterminator," said Brills. "Sheel was alerted by his encrypted communicator and was starting to organize a retaliation. I created some confusion from my console, but that didn't seem to help. Couldn't really do much with Sheel around anyways. The exterminators know we're here. Give me a moment to disable the lock on Evaran's ship and the cells." He sat down at a desk. His hands flew around the console. After a few moments, he nodded. "Good to go. We need to hurry and get them and ourselves outta here."

John sighed and gestured at the door across the room from them. "Let's get outta here."

03

Dr. Snowden flinched when Emily gasped. The shielding on the cells had dropped, and the lights had dimmed. He rubbed his eyes and looked around.

The anger flash from before still poked around in his head. It was the second time in a few days that his anger had slipped out of control, but this was the first time there was physical pain. What the heck was going on? Hopefully it was the nanobots and could be fixed. He knew he always had a short temper, but nothing that would cause him to fly into a blind rage. It was embarrassing for it to happen in front of Evaran, whose cool and calm demeanor he sought to emulate.

He stood and waved his hand through the door. "What's happening?"

"I do not know, but we will take advantage of the situation. We need to go," said Evaran.

They exited the cell.

"You know how to get back to the Torvatta?" asked Emily.

"Yes, I memorized the path. Although it took us an hour to get here, I suspect we can do it in forty-five minutes. Set your PSDs to stun."

Dr. Snowden and Emily complied.

Dr. Snowden had come to view his personal support device as an invaluable tool. His PSD had a slim pen-like shape and the ability to perform many functions, from augmented reality scans to the more powerful stun beam, which had proven its usefulness. His favorite aspect of it was the morphable metal that could extend and form a variety of handy tools. He was unsure of how the morphable metal was stored but suspected dimensional mechanics was involved.

As they turned into a hallway, two guards at the other end rushed around the corner.

"Stop where you are!" said one of the guards.

Evaran activated his shield and extended his utility handle into a baton. The end glowed light blue. "We do not have time for this foolishness."

The guards opened fire. Evaran angled his shield and redirected their weapon fire back at them, causing their weapons to explode. The guards crumpled to the ground.

Dr. Snowden remembered the shield could reflect beams. He saw it on the Krotovore ship when Jay, another person Evaran had saved, had his arm blown off from a stray reflected beam. The accuracy and agility required to aim the beam back at a specific angle impressed him.

They hustled through various hallways and, after thirty minutes, came upon a large, open room.

Dr. Snowden tried to make sense of what he was seeing. Purifier guards were fighting another group. The group was what caught his attention. One member had black armor and was charging around the room like a bull, knocking guards left and right. Two others were dancing around the room with glowing swords, slicing and dicing any guard unlucky enough to be in their path. A tree stood in the center of the room with vines reaching everywhere and branches hitting away guards who got too close. Another was changing forms as he fought. One moment he was a human male, the next a bird, and the next a big cat. Finally, near the corner, an individual with black light armor over black leather was dual-wielding pistols and taking shots at various guards.

"What in the world . . . ," said Dr. Snowden.

"That guy has changed shape like three times!" said Emily, pointing at the shape-shifter.

Evaran nodded. "Yes. He is an Outsider." He pointed to each individual in turn. "The person in the back and the two moving around with energy swords are Daedrould, vampire strain. The tree shifter is an Outsider, similar to the shape changer. The big guy running around is Wildborn. I believe his ability is brute strength and resiliency."

Dr. Snowden smiled. "Wish I could see energy signatures instead of just knowing they aren't human."

"Me too," said Emily.

Evaran half smiled.

Dr. Snowden had learned a lot about nonhumans and how they came to be from traveling with Evaran. The thought that exotic energy could alter a human into something so different still amazed him. He wondered if the process could be reversed. Another question to ask Evaran about later. He had learned about Daedrould energy, and how it was the source of their alteration. Wild energy created the Wildborn, who were unique one-off alterations. Those that came from other realities inside the universe were called Outsiders, like the pantheons and shifters. There were even more, with sub-divisions among the big ones. It boggled his mind that there were so many. Although he could not see the energy signature auras like Evaran could, he had begun to understand the movement and abilities enough to determine what major energy group they came from. Usually, anyways.

The group had mopped all but one guard that was barreling toward Evaran. The guard opened fire and fell when the reflected beam from Evaran's shield hit him.

The group approached Evaran. The dual-wielding pistol user stepped in front, with the others lining up behind him. The tree transformed into a woman with a tight-fitting brown suit, and the shape-shifter had turned into a human male with a black trench coat and a bandanna over his mouth.

The pistol user knelt before Evaran, causing the others in the group to follow suit. "I'm John Holington, and this is the Earth Guard."

Evaran bowed with his left hand across his stomach. "I am Evaran, and with me is Dr. Albert Snowden and his niece, Emily."

John stood. "Oh . . . we know you are." He pointed in sequence at the group. "The big guy is Miles O'Bannon. The tree shifter is Shandra Everoak. The two blade masters are Dizz and Cantol, and the shape-shifter is Brills. We're here to extract you."

Evaran nodded. "It is good to meet you all, and your timing is excellent. We were just on our way to my ship."

"The Torvatta. Right," said John. "We have freed the clamps on your ship and are responsible for shutting down the power to your cells. Once we leave here, we will need you to open a portal and let us fly through first. I can explain everything in detail once we're safe." He handed Evaran a small tablet-like device. "These are the coordinates."

Evaran scanned the device. "I have the coordinates. Outskirts of the Galvin Rim. Interesting. I have patched into your group communication channel." He glanced at Dr. Snowden and Emily. "Your PSDs are tied in as well."

Dr. Snowden nodded. He was not sure what to make of all this.

"Hermes, what's the status?" asked John.

"Exterminators are closing in on your position. Some have taken up position outside the entrance to the ships," said Hermes over the communication channel.

"The Greek god Hermes?" asked Evaran.

"Hah! Evaran . . . you old bastard. It's been over four thousand years! Where the hell you been?"

Evaran tilted his head. "It is apparent I have a lot to catch up on."

"You can say that again."

Dr. Snowden's eyes sparkled at the thought of meeting Hermes. He remembered Evaran had mentioned him in the past and said Hermes had issues. Maybe now he would find out what Evaran was referring to.

John sighed. "Those exterminators are tough to deal with. We better get going."

"I concur," said Evaran.

After twenty minutes and dealing with several guards along the way, they reached the last room. Three exterminators and a small group of guards stood fanned out around the exit to the ships.

John glanced at Evaran. "Thoughts?"

Evaran studied the exterminators. One moved toward them. "Miles and I will clear a path. Shandra, if you can provide support behind us, that should allow Dizz and Cantol to escort Dr. Snowden and Emily along the sides past them. John, you can provide long-range support, with Brills helping protect Shandra."

Miles jerked his head back. "Damn . . . you just came up with that?"

Evaran nodded. "I observed you in battle and noted your combat skills."

John nodded. "Doesn't surprise me at all. We're good to go." He slapped Miles's chest. "Do your thing."

"Always." Miles bobbed his head at Evaran. "Ready?"

"Ready."

With a scream, Miles charged ahead with Evaran at his side. Shandra and Brills followed behind them. Dizz and Cantol moved to the side of the room with Dr. Snowden and Emily and inched forward. John took up a position in the back of the room.

Miles bowled into the exterminator that had moved forward, sending it flying back. The other two rushed forward and fired on Miles. Evaran grabbed the exterminator coming from the left side of Miles and tossed it against the wall. Shandra changed into a tree behind them and, with her vines, began wrapping up the third exterminator. Brills transformed into a large bearlike creature and attacked the nearby guards. John hung back and fired at the guards, thinning them out.

Dr. Snowden and Emily kept moving along the left wall with Dizz and Cantol. They reached the corner and began moving toward the exit. Several guards broke loose from the group melee, headed toward them, and began firing. Dr. Snowden and Emily ducked into a storefront foyer area. They popped out and fired back with their PSDs, causing the guards to fall. Dizz and Cantol took advantage of the situation and rushed forward. Within a few seconds, the headless guards lay still.

Brills let out a cry as a volley of fire smashed into him. He slumped to the ground. Shandra turned her attention to a new group of four exterminators and guards that came in from where they had initially entered the room. Miles spun around and charged toward them. John was firing sporadically as he ran forward to the exit where Brills had fallen. Shandra moved toward the new threat behind Miles's charge.

Evaran zipped through the remaining guards at the exit, hitting them with his baton and knocking some against the wall. With the rest of the guards at the exit down, Dizz, Cantol, Dr. Snowden, and Emily rushed forward and through the doorway. Once through, Dizz and Cantol ran out to help fight the new group. Dr. Snowden and Emily peered out to watch.

John reached Brills and dragged him through the exit and out of sight.

Evaran scanned Brills. He tapped at his ARI. "He is alive. Stay here! V will be here shortly to administer aid."

At the back of the room, Shandra shrieked as her branches caught on fire and she got slammed from both sides by the exterminators. She shimmered for a moment, then changed back to human form and crumpled to the ground. An exterminator raised a foot to stomp her head. Miles looked back after bowling into the new group and yelled when he saw Shandra. He grabbed the exterminator about to stomp her and threw it into the air. With a quick jump over Shandra, he charged the other exterminator. He tapped his chest, causing his armor to glow.

"Oh shit . . . *Miles! No! Everyone, to the exit now!*" said John.

"What is he doing?" asked Evaran.

"He's activated his final burn. We have one minute before this place blows."

"There is no need for that. Wait here."

Evaran passed Dizz and Cantol as they rushed to the entrance. He reached Shandra and scanned her. He looked up at Miles, who had just been slammed into the wall by an exterminator. "Miles, come over here."

Miles stood up and charged through the exterminator and several guards to get to Evaran.

Evaran placed his UIC on Miles's chest panel. He tapped at his ARI, and Miles's armor stopped glowing. "Take Shandra to the exit. She is hurt, but alive."

Miles looked at the three remaining exterminators and small group of guards that were regrouping. Their weapon fire lit up Miles's shielding as he stood between them and Evaran and Shandra. He shook his head. "You can't hold them, and our mission is to extract you."

Evaran half grinned. "Trust me. I can handle this. Go."

Miles picked up Shandra and ran to the exit.

Dr. Snowden thought he saw Evaran's eyes flash a glowing fire for a moment when Evaran turned to see Miles run back to the exit. He chalked it up to maybe a random reflection or his own eyes playing tricks on him.

John directed V, who had arrived from the Torvatta, to Shandra and Brills.

V pulled out a syringe and injected Brills and Shandra with it.

"What'd you inject them with?" asked John.

"Healing nanobots. It will stabilize them."

"Okay . . . after you're done, they need to get on the ship," said John. He glanced at Miles. "Why's Evaran not coming?"

"He said to go and he would handle it," said Miles.

"What?" asked John as he turned to look out at Evaran.

Evaran rushed forward with his shield raised. He punched the first exterminator in the chest, cracking its armor. The exterminator flew backward, taking several guards with it. The other two charged, with weapons ablaze. Evaran stepped back and kneeled, reflecting fire back onto them. One exterminator burst into flames as it crashed to the ground. Several guards were caught in the reflected fire.

The remaining exterminator charged forward and reached out. Evaran grabbed it by the wrists and with a spinning motion sent it flying back at the guards. Its armor cracked when it hit the wall, and it stopped moving.

The remaining five guards dropped their weapons and pushed forward with glowing swords. Evaran dodged the first slash and turned sideways to kick the guard against the wall. He ducked as another sword swept across above him. He spun around doing a leg sweep, knocking the second guard down. He then tapped the guard's chest with his baton. The guard stopped moving.

The third guard lunged forward and struck out at Evaran's midsection. Evaran stepped back and placed his foot on the blade. With a downward motion of his leg, the blade was pulled out of the surprised guard's hand. Evaran stepped forward and tapped the guard on the head with his baton. The guard crumpled to the ground. The remaining two attacked him simultaneously, one from each side. Evaran placed his hand on the right guard's shoulder and somersaulted over him. Upon landing, he tapped the back of the guard's head with his baton, then he kicked him in the back. The guard went flying forward and crashed into the last guard. The last guard struggled to get up as Evaran approached him.

"Leave," said Evaran.

The guard nodded and got to his feet. He ran out of the room.

"Holy shit," said Miles.

"Thankfully, they weren't as strong as Seeros," said Dr. Snowden.

John snapped his head toward Dr. Snowden. "You know Seeros?"

Before Dr. Snowden could reply, Evaran ran over to the group.

"We can go. Brills and Shandra would be better served in my medical lab," said Evaran.

"No . . . no temporal shielding effect for us. Hermes said there are more on the way, and ships are beginning to close in. We need to get the hell out of here!" said John.

The Earth Guard boarded their ship while Evaran, Dr. Snowden, Emily, and V rushed into the Torvatta.

Evaran ran into the command area. He punched around his ARI. "V, take us out and open a portal to the coordinates I am relaying."

"Acknowledged," said V as he rushed to the front console.

Dr. Snowden and Emily sat in the U-shaped seating area to the right of the front console as Evaran sat in his command chair. The Torvatta pulled away from the station. After flying a bit, it held position and shot out a gold beam, opening a silver-ringed portal with a light-blue rippled surface. John's ship appeared in front of them and flew through the portal. The Torvatta followed them in.

Dr. Snowden's heartbeat was flying all over the place. These strangers had risked their lives for this rescue. What was so important that they needed to do that? It was apparent to Dr. Snowden now that Evaran could have taken the guards during their capture. Dr. Snowden figured Evaran did not because of the possible collateral damage. Sometimes he felt like he and Emily were a liability. Then again, they had saved Evaran once before. Maybe it was that balance that Evaran was okay with. Dr. Snowden shook his head as the Torvatta emerged through the portal and outside a large ship.

The Torvatta landed inside a hangar bay with John's ship parked off to the side.

Dr. Snowden looked around outside through the transparent front screen. The hangar bay was large, and several other ships were nearby. Various people ran around in brown one-piece suits with gadgets in their hands. He could tell they were all nonhumans. It made sense that if the Purifiers were exterminating all nonhumans, then the nonhumans would band together and try to survive.

"Come, let us find out what is going on," said Evaran, waving toward the Torvatta entrance.

Dr. Snowden nodded. "This new timeline has been . . . interesting to say the least."

"Yeah . . . sucks so far," said Emily.

They exited the Torvatta. Miles ran out of John's ship with Shandra in his arms followed by Dizz and Cantol carrying Brills on a stretcher of some type. They disappeared into a large hallway. John and Hermes approached Evaran.

Dr. Snowden noted that Hermes looked a lot different than what he had imagined. A part of him expected to see some type of ancient Greek clothing and armor. Instead, Hermes wore a lightly armored gold-and-white suit over his thin build. It made sense given the time period they were in.

"Evaran . . . you crafty dog!" said Hermes with a wide smile and both hands flashed out to the side. When he was near Evaran, he extended his arm.

Evaran exchanged a forearm grab and shake with Hermes. "You are still alive. Impressive."

"Well . . . can't kill what they can't catch."

"Fair enough," said Evaran. He turned toward John. "Let Miles and the others know that no medical intervention is needed for Brills and Shandra. The healing nanobots will stabilize their condition. If anything, they just need a place to lie down and recover."

John nodded and relayed Evaran's message.

Hermes extended a hand toward Dr. Snowden. "Dr. Snowden, glad to meet you. I'm sure Evaran has mentioned me to you a lot."

Dr. Snowden shook Hermes's hand. "We . . . have heard of you."

"All good, I hope," said Hermes. He held out a hand toward Emily, palm up.

Emily glanced at Evaran. She raised her eyebrows as she put her hand in Hermes's hand.

Hermes bent forward and kissed Emily's hand. "You would make Aphrodite jealous."

Evaran eyed Hermes. "Hermes . . ."

Emily's face turned a shade of red as she pulled her hand back.

Hermes pointed a finger at Evaran. "Right!" He grinned and winked his right eye. "Old habits die hard."

"We have heard a lot about you and Emily," said John.

Dr. Snowden shook John's hand as did Emily when John offered it.

"We have a lot to discuss. Let's go the command center so I can get you up to speed," said John.

Evaran gestured forward. "Lead on."

They exited the docking bay and entered a large hallway.

As they walked, John pointed around. "This is the Gallant, the Earth Guard's mobile command base. We had to position it way out here because . . . well, the Purifiers are everywhere else."

They turned a corner onto a slightly angled ramp that went on for a bit.

"What is the Earth Guard exactly?" asked Emily.

Hermes slid over to Emily and smiled. "Well . . . originally we defended Earth from all threats." He crooked a thumb at Evaran. "He wasn't always around, so someone had to do it."

John nodded. "Yes, what Hermes says is true. However, as time went on and the Purifiers gained dominance over Earth, we had to flee. Our mission changed per Lord Vygon."

"Lord Vygon . . . an ancient vampire," said Evaran. "I have heard of him."

"An ancient one? How's that different from a regular one?" asked Emily.

John chuckled. "They are a different vampire strain and tend to be a lot older, stronger, and faster, for one." He grinned at Emily. "You have nothing to fear from us. No vampire would ever bite you."

Hermes raised a finger. "Now those Greek gods on the other hand . . ."

Emily chuckled.

"Why would a vampire never bite Emily?" asked Dr. Snowden with wrinkled eyebrows.

They hit the top of the ramp and turned into another hallway.

"She's protected, as you are," said John.

"I guess that goes without saying," said Emily, tossing a quick grin at Evaran.

John glanced sidelong at Hermes. "That's not what I meant. You have nanobots." Before a puzzled Dr. Snowden could respond, John waved them into a room. "We're here."

Dr. Snowden wondered why nanobots would prevent a vampire from biting them. Maybe John knew something even Evaran did not. He had seen Brills and Shandra get an injection of nanobots, so he did not think that they were toxic to nonhumans. The ones in him and Emily were different than the healing nanobots. Maybe they were lethal to anyone else. He surveyed the room as they entered it. The room was rectangular for the most part, except the end, which was a half circle. The rounded part of the room had a large screen covering the wall, with a podium-like structure to the side. In the rectangular part of the room were three long tables placed in a U formation, with the open area pointing toward the rounded part of the room.

John indicated for Evaran, Dr. Snowden, and Emily to sit at the leftmost table. Hermes sat on the edge of the table opposite them. John went up to the podium and tapped at its slanted surface. After a moment, the large screen lit up blue. "Give me one moment . . ."

Hermes smiled. "He has to configure what can and can't be said."

"Why?" asked Dr. Snowden.

"Oh, you know . . . which Evaran shows up . . . what companions are present . . . has Evaran met Lord Vygon . . ."

"I see," said Evaran. "This briefing is intended to avoid mentioning anything in particular about my personal future."

Hermes sucked his lips in and raised his eyebrows as he nodded.

Dr. Snowden looked at Emily, who shrugged. In their previous adventure, they had come across someone who had met a future Evaran in the past and would not say anything about that meeting.

"Before we begin, I just wanted to say how impressed I was back at the station," said John. "It took a group of us to fight one exterminator, and you handled a group by yourself."

"That's Evaran. Always beating one group down or another," said Hermes with a smile.

Evaran narrowed his eyes. "I avoid violence if at all possible."

Hermes laughed. "I know . . . but you're like a violence magnet!"

Evaran looked down.

Dr. Snowden studied Hermes and Evaran's interaction. It was true that violence always seemed to find Evaran. Maybe that was the price paid for standing up against injustice. Given the types of people Evaran ran across, it made sense to Dr. Snowden that violence would be inevitable, even if it was just self-defense.

"Okay, I think we're ready," said John, clearing his throat. He tapped at the podium console, and the screen changed to a horizontal timeline. He pointed to the first dot on the far left. "This is 2635 BC. Starting then and roughly one hundred years forward, nonhumans disappeared. Talking pantheon Outsiders . . . ancient vampires . . . Wildborn . . . and the like."

"What is known of the disappearances?" asked Evaran.

John gestured toward Hermes.

"Ahh . . . yeah . . . was a pretty rough time. There was no trace of someone once they were gone. Literally, none. Some guys in black clothing always seemed to be around when it occurred, so we think they are related, but we had no hard proof."

"Did your pantheon survive this?" asked Evaran.

"We did . . . but almost everyone left back through our portal and sealed it off. Obviously, some of us decided to stay."

"I am sorry to hear that," said Evaran. He nodded at John. "Go on."

The screen changed to a global map with large red circles appearing across it.

"The red circles represent areas where Lord Vygon could not sense any nonhuman presence," said John. "When he presented this to the Helians, they didn't believe him. These Purifiers then announced themselves by destroying Atlantis, and with that, any resistance the Helians might have done was gone. Most pantheons left Earth around this time, leaving most of us other nonhumans to fend for ourselves."

"Did you say Atlantis? The mythical city in the sea?" asked Dr. Snowden.

Hermes snorted. "Not mythical at all. It was the home base of the Helians. They didn't share technology and hoarded it. Didn't do 'em much good in the end."

"Yeah," said John. The screen changed back to the timeline. "By 1100 BC, the Purifiers had, for the most part, conquered Earth. Every nonhuman at this point was off the planet somewhere in space, hiding on the planet, or back in the original pocket universe they came from." He pointed at Evaran. "Lord Vygon believed that you would come and that you would not allow this to occur."

"I am curious. Why did he believe this?"

"He was temporally aware and said he knew the future that would come was not the one unfolding before him."

"He had seen the future then."

"Yeah . . . I can't say how, though."

Emily chuckled. "Let me guess, Evaran's rules."

John bobbed his head. "Yeah . . . You've run across them before, I take it?"

"Not too long ago actually. How widespread are the Purifiers now?" asked Emily.

John nodded and pointed at AD 100 on the timeline. "Well, by here, they had conquered the solar system." He pointed to AD 500. "By here, they had defeated the Seceltor Empire. The thing that really marked their purpose came out then. They exterminated every alien they found. Genocide."

"Wow . . . these are some deranged people. Surely the Kreagan Star Empire stood up to them," said Dr. Snowden.

John shook his head as he pointed to AD 1500. "This was when the Kreagan Star Empire ceded almost eighty percent of their territory after the Battle of Kreagus. The emperor had been killed and the Kreagans were fleeing en masse. To be fair, they fought hard, but they couldn't keep pace with the Purifier technology. It seemed to jump much faster than the Kreagans could respond, and they never found where it came from."

Emily looked at Evaran. "So our adventure with the Fredorians . . ."

Evaran nodded. "Never happened in this new timeline."

"Oh . . . ," said Emily, glancing at Dr. Snowden.

"Is anyone providing resistance to them other than yourselves?" asked Evaran.

John pointed at Dr. Snowden. "You mentioned Seeros earlier. He heads up a small group of civilizations that use floating cities to harass and defend their territory. He's actually won a few battles. The weird thing is, Seeros fights not to liberate, but because he was offended at the Purifiers' Evaran Protocol."

Dr. Snowden shook his head. "He's crazy in any timeline, it seems."

Hermes chuckled. "Maybe so, but he singlehandedly destroyed a platoon of exterminators *without* a weapon. There is a rumor that he squared off with the overlord himself, and made the overlord retreat. I think the Purifiers fear him. They even have a Seeros protocol."

Emily looked at Evaran. "What about Max, or the great selector? Wouldn't they get involved?"

Evaran shook his head. "Most likely not. They may be aware of it, but would not interfere. Otherwise, this would have been over long ago."

John tilted his head. "Max?"

"A powerful being we met a while back. He would be under guard still, though," said Evaran.

"Well, I think it's clear what needs to happen then," said Dr. Snowden.

"Yes. We will head to 2635 BC."

John raised a finger. "You can start by looking for Atlantis. They should know where Lord Vygon is."

"He doesn't know where he was back then?" asked Dr. Snowden.

"When he changed the mission of the Earth Guard to deliver this information, it had been over three hundred years by then," said John.

"Point taken," said Dr. Snowden.

Hermes smiled. "I do have a question before you go." He glanced at John, then at Evaran. "It would settle a debate."

"Go ahead."

"If you correct the timeline, we won't exist anymore, at least in this state," said Hermes. "Traveling in your ship is known to have a temporary temporal shielding effect. So the question is . . . assuming you're successful and change the past and me and John have this shielded effect, would we experience the rest of our lives in this timeline, or would we pop into the old timeline due to our temporal shielding?"

Evaran smiled. "It depends. The temporal shielding effect has a lifespan of several days. It is independent of any universal timeline and is tied to the Torvatta's timing. If a timeline change occurs within that window, you pop into the new timeline at the point you got the temporal shielding. If it has dissipated, you live out your life in the old timeline. For example, if you both had the effect now, and we successfully changed the past in one day relative to the Torvatta, you would pop into the new timeline. If it took us five days, you would still reside in this timeline and disappear with it."

Hermes jumped up. "Hah! We're both right."

John smirked. "At least we now know."

"What's the Earth Guard gonna do now?" asked Emily.

John studied Emily and gave Hermes a sidelong glance. "The Gallant is a colony ship. We're leaving to another part of this galaxy. I guess in the end, it won't matter since I'm guessing Evaran will change the timeline. If we're to experience the rest of our lives, though, better to do it in peace than in a war we can't win."

Evaran nodded. "I agree with your assessment and wish you the best of luck." He stood and looked at Emily. "It appears your wish to see the past has been granted."

04

After spending the next day on the Gallant, they assembled in the Torvatta's command area the following morning. Evaran sat in his command chair while V fidgeted with the command console. Dr. Snowden and Emily took their usual seats.

Dr. Snowden reflected on his time on the Gallant. He had enjoyed his conversations with Hermes. They were enthralled by Hermes's stories of how pantheons worked, where they fit into the nonhuman power structure, how they got to Earth, and the various politics involved. Dr. Snowden chuckled at how excited Emily had been, not that it was a surprise to him. Being a history major, she would have naturally gobbled all that up. Of course, Hermes more than enjoyed talking to Emily, with a few raised eyebrows from time to time from Dr. Snowden.

They had visited the medical center and checked on Brills and Shandra. Both were doing fine, as expected, with a recovery time of a few days. Shandra filled them in on the Everoak lineage and tree-shifter history. Miles, Dizz, and Cantol had a bevy of questions for Evaran. Miles in particular wanted to know exactly how strong Evaran was, which led to an awkward pushing contest. Evaran won with ease. Dizz and Cantol exchanged fighting techniques with Evaran.

Dr. Snowden also enjoyed his conversations with John. It was apparent John was a great leader. He kept the Earth Guard organized, and Dr. Snowden noted that John seemed relieved that the Gallant could finally leave. Dr. Snowden spent quite a bit of time digging into the vampire hierarchy, history, and politics. What surprised him was how well-known Evaran was to the ancient vampires. Even more surprising was how many types of vampires there were, each with their own organizational structure. John had mentioned that he, Dizz, and Cantol were not ancient vampires but chose to be turned by Lord Vygon. As such, they served under him in House Vygon. They were all that was left of it.

Dr. Snowden studied the front right screen, which showed the Gallant growing smaller. He wished they could come, but Evaran had said that they belonged to this timeline. He glanced at Evaran. "So . . . to 2635 BC then?"

Evaran nodded.

Dr. Snowden walked up to the guardrail around the front of the ship. Emily joined him. He always loved watching the stars disappear and reappear during time travel.

The stars outside the Torvatta shimmered briefly before fading to pure black. After a moment, they eased back into view with a slight shimmer effect.

"Analysis. We have arrived at June 3, 2635 BC, at nine a.m."

Emily looked at V. "That's a pretty specific date, and I don't think it was called June back then."

V tilted his head at Emily. "The universal translator converts universal time into a time reference you would understand."

"Oh . . . ," said Emily.

Evaran glanced at her. "It is the same time translation that takes place on your PSD. You can configure it to show multiple time references. However, they are based off a universal time system independent of any interpretation."

"Gotcha," said Emily.

"V, take us to Earth and extend the utility rods," said Evaran.

"Acknowledged," said V. The front right screen showed a shot of the sides of the Torvatta. Two black rods extended out with an orange tip. "Utility rods extended beyond shielding."

A gold beam shot out from the Torvatta, opening a portal. The Torvatta flew through it and exited above Earth.

"Scan for communications," said Evaran.

"Acknowledged."

V's hands flew across the front console. "Communications beacon detected. Scanning for matching protocol." The front right screen showed a rapid dissemination of code before a segment highlighted. "Protocol found. Relaying."

Both the right and left screen faded, and a bronze-skinned male wearing a white robe-like outfit with a light-blue belt appeared on the screen. A golden mantle rested on his shoulders with a silver bar on the right side and a blue circle on the left side.

"Is that a Helian?" whispered Emily.

Evaran nodded. "Yes, before they had personal holograph emitters. In the future, they look different. V, open communications."

"Acknowledged."

The Helian interacted with the glass desk he sat behind. "Alien ship, identify yourself."

"I am Evaran on my ship, the Torvatta. With me are the humans Dr. Albert Snowden and his niece, Emily."

"Origin?"

"Travelers beyond the Galvin Rim."

"Interesting answer. Purpose?" asked the Helian.

"We are looking for someone."

"Lost and found," said the Helian with a smirk. He tapped in rapid succession at his desk. "I'm relaying to you the rules and regulations for this planet. You're expected to obey it at all times. Failure to do so will result in a quick and exact response from the Helian authority. Is that understood?"

Evaran nodded. "Perfectly."

"Landing coordinates have been relayed. You will be escorted in and need to register once you are down."

The screen faded.

Dr. Snowden looked out the left front window. "Well, that was interesting . . ."

Evaran half smiled. "This beacon and greeting is not present in the future."

"The Helians sorta looked like the Purifiers," said Emily.

"They do a bit. V, take us in."

"Acknowledged."

The Torvatta flew toward a spot in the Atlantic Ocean, forty miles west of the southern region of modern-day Portugal. Two small ships flew alongside the Torvatta.

Dr. Snowden noted that although they looked advanced, they were not nearly as cutting-edge as what he had seen on Kreagus.

As the Torvatta approached the ocean surface, a domed city shimmered into view with a bubble-like shield around it. The city sat on an eight-pointed star base. In the middle was a large structure that rose to the clouds. Around it were various smaller buildings. On the underside were underwater structures that clung to the floating city. A square portion of the shielding faded away, and the two ships escorting them flew off. The Torvatta flew through the opening, and after a moment, it landed on a pad on one of the arms of the star.

Dr. Snowden noted that the point of the star arm had enough landing pads to fit a dozen or so Torvattas. Since the Torvatta landed facing toward the inner part of the city, he got a good view. The city seemed low-tech compared to Kreagus, but still much more high-tech than what was on Earth at the time, or even in his time. He briefly wondered if they would be visited by a docking authority.

They exited the Torvatta. Evaran took point while Dr. Snowden, Emily, and V in body mode trailed behind him. A Helian dressed similarly to the one they spoke to on the screen approached them.

The only difference that Dr. Snowden could see was that on the gold mantle, there were two silver bars on the right side.

The Helian bent his arms so that his hands were touching in front of his chest. The left hand was palm up, and the right hand was a fist. "Welcome to Atlantis. You'll need to register yourselves and your ship. Follow me."

They followed the Helian along the wide path that led away from the landing pad. After a moment, the Helian stopped before a metallic canopy-like structure with side walls. It stood about thirty feet tall and extended forward roughly ten feet.

Two Helians with silver light armor stood at attention in front of the structure. They had a single silver bar on their right arms and a blue circle on their upper left arms. What stood out to Dr. Snowden was the sleek black weapon in their hands. It was medium sized and looked like it packed a punch.

The Helian that was escorting them tapped a button on his silver forearm guard. He waved for them to go through the structure.

They walked through the structure, and halfway through, the walls lit up red.

The Helian scrambled toward them. He interacted with a screen that had appeared above his right forearm band while looking at Evaran. "We can't detect your internals, although you have mass."

Evaran nodded. "That is to be expected. We are not from this planet."

"I don't think so. What are you?" asked the Helian.

"From your perspective, an Outsider."

The Helian looked down at his screen, then looked at Dr. Snowden and Emily. "It appears you two are infected with some disease."

Evaran raised a hand. "It is not a disease. They are Wild-born. It is inherent in their makeup."

Dr. Snowden grinned. It was odd to see Evaran use deception, but when he did, it was convincing. Dr. Snowden wondered if Evaran had used it on him and Emily before.

The Helian snorted. "The only normal one is the robot. Go figure." He exited the structure ahead of them and waved them forward. Once they were through, he said, "You're registered, as is your ship. An agent is on his way to help you."

"Thank you," said Evaran.

"Don't thank me yet. These missing person cases seem to be occurring a lot lately."

"How many so far?"

"Around thirteen this month. Usually get one or two a year."

Evaran narrowed his eyes. "That is odd. Thank you for your help."

The Helian nodded and exited back toward the landing pad.

"Seems like whatever is going on has already started," said Dr. Snowden.

Evaran looked around. "It would appear that way."

Five minutes later, another Helian arrived. He was dressed similarly to the one that registered them, except he had two silver bars on the right side of his mantle and a red square on the left side. The Helian performed a salute while surveying them. "I'm Special Agent Asher. If you'll follow me to my office, we can file your claim."

Dr. Snowden nodded and did a Helian salute in return.

Asher smiled. "It's not expected for you to emulate our cultural greeting. We understand that there are a variety of cultures that have different greeting rituals."

"Just trying to fit in," said Dr. Snowden with a half grin.

"It's appreciated," said Asher. He nodded and waved at them to follow him.

As they walked, Dr. Snowden hustled up alongside Asher. "So . . . these bars and symbols on your mantles . . . I'm guessing some type of rank system?"

Asher grinned. "You got it. Left side symbol represents the branch of the Helian authority that you work for, right side is rank. In my case, the red square represents the investigative branch, and the two silver bars means I'm a special agent. One silver bar would be a general agent. My specialty is investigating missing persons cases."

"Huh . . . how many branches are there?"

"More than we need," said Asher, chuckling.

They reached an interior courtyard where Dr. Snowden saw Helians engaged in discussion. After stepping onto a ramp that moved upward, he studied the Helians. There were various symbols and bars and even outfit differences. If the Helians were this advanced this far back in human history, it was no wonder to him that they represented Earth when the Kreagan Star Empire came knocking. The version of Helians he knew from the future had glowing eyes and wings. Then again, Evaran had mentioned personal hologram emitters, making them look like angels. He suspected that was not by coincidence.

After several minutes, they disembarked from the ramp and entered Asher's office a short distance away.

Asher gestured for them to sit as he took his seat.

After they sat, Evaran raised a finger. "Before we begin, we have not lost anyone. We are actually looking for someone."

Asher paused, then eased back into his chair. "Well . . . that's different. Who're you looking for?"

"Lord Vygon."

"The Daedrould?"

"Yes."

Asher tapped at his desk, causing a screen to rise up in front of him. After a few quick motions, he twisted his fingers on the screen, causing it to orient toward them. He pointed at a glowing circle. "He's here. I'm afraid if you want to get a hold of him, you will have to activate our communication beacon there."

Emily studied the screen. "Looks like it's in Illinois. Near St. Louis."

Asher cocked his head and wrinkled his eyebrows.

Emily cleared her throat. "With all this technology, can't you just contact him?"

Asher narrowed his eyes. "Hardly. The Daedrould don't like to be contacted directly. They prefer you go to their territory, activate the beacon we set up, and then they send someone to get you."

Dr. Snowden smirked. "They don't like visitors."

"Now you're beginning to understand the Daedrould," said Asher. He faced Evaran. "I'm curious, though. I've heard whispers of your name. Involved in previous events, yet no one seems to really know who it is or what the involvement was. You wouldn't happen to be that person, would you?"

"We just arrived on Earth, so it could not be me," said Evaran.

Asher nodded. "Yeah . . . that's what I figured. Probably someone else with a similar name. Anyways, good luck meeting Lord Vygon, but I wouldn't expect a warm greeting. He is a Daedrould after all."

Dr. Snowden fidgeted in his seat. "What do you mean by that?"

"Well . . . I guess you wouldn't know," said Asher. "There is a pecking order of nonhumans on this planet. Daedrould are at the bottom, we're at the top. Daedrould kill their own kind and harass humanity. We organize our own and try to protect humanity. If all the Daedroulds were gone, Earth would be better off."

Dr. Snowden thought about John. His face turned a light shade of red. The memories of what he learned traveling with Evaran about the Helians' involvement in off-world human slavery galloped through his mind. "You sure about that protecting part?"

"Of course."

Dr. Snowden stood up and pounded the desk. His breathing went haphazard. "I'd suggest you look into the human slavery you're involved in!"

Asher jerked his head back. "Excuse me?"

"Dr. Snowden!" said Evaran. He stood and placed a hand on his shoulder.

Dr. Snowden's heartbeat rampaged through him. He turned to look at Evaran and was startled out of his rage by Evaran's intense gaze. After an awkward moment, he licked his lips and nodded. He flung his arm into the air in a dismissive gesture. "I'm okay."

Evaran bowed at Asher. "We appreciate your help and will be on our way."

"Okay . . . ," said Asher with wide eyes. "If you . . . uh . . . need any more help, let me know."

Evaran nodded as they exited the office.

Emily squeezed Dr. Snowden's arm. "Uncle Albert?"

Dr. Snowden turned his head toward her. "I'm fine. Just . . . lost my cool is all." He furrowed his eyebrows as he looked forward. It was more than just losing his temper. Anger control was always an issue in his life, and as of late, he seemed to escalate from normal to blind rage in just a few seconds. Something was off. At first he thought it might have been the nanobots, but he could feel them trying to calm him down. It must be something else. Maybe it was just the stress of traveling with Evaran. Seemed every place they went, there was always danger. He shook his head.

It took an hour for them to get to the Torvatta and fly over to the spot Agent Asher had showed them.

Dr. Snowden sat on a slab in the medical lab. "Anything?"

Evaran perused a console next to the slab. "I am not seeing anything. I do recall seeing some notes on your anger from the virtual simulation. However, this change appears to be recent."

"Uncle Albert's always been short-tempered," said Emily as she squeezed Dr. Snowden's arm.

Dr. Snowden sighed. "Yeah . . . but I've always been able to keep it under wraps. I'm not sure what's causing me to fly into a rage. I didn't have this problem when we helped the Fredorians."

Evaran cocked his head. "Well . . . you had another emotion that overrode any anger you might have had, and even then, it did flare through at times."

"Yeah . . . can't say I miss that whole fear thing."

Evaran rubbed his chin as he studied Dr. Snowden. "Starting tomorrow, we will begin a new program. Every morning, you and I will have a session. It will take time, but I believe you can control it."

Dr. Snowden nodded. He half smiled at Emily. "At least you won't have as many opportunities to call me a jerk face."

Emily swatted his arm as she smiled at him. "I wouldn't bet on it!"

They shared a laugh.

V walked into the room. "We have landed."

"Excellent," said Evaran. "You two can wait here while I investigate."

Dr. Snowden shook his head. "I'd like to go. Really could use the fresh air."

Emily nodded. "Me too."

Dr. Snowden studied Emily. While he wanted to go, he wanted her to stay, in case things got out of hand. There was no way she would be by herself, though, even if it was just on the Torvatta. It was not her nature, and he suspected that as much as he needed to control his anger, she would one day need to learn to be comfortable being by herself. He slid off the slab.

"Analysis. I could use some fresh air as well."

Emily and Dr. Snowden chuckled.

Evaran half smiled. "Fine. Before we go, follow me to the research lab. I have made some adjustments to your PSDs' design and need to sync them with the Torvatta."

They assembled in the research lab.

Evaran stood next to a table that had a rubberlike mat on half of it and a glass-like top on the other. He gestured at the side with the rubber mat. "Place your PSDs there."

Dr. Snowden and Emily complied.

Evaran tapped at the glass, and a projection of the PSDs appeared. He extended his hand toward it, causing a menu to appear off to the side. With a quick motion of his hands, he selected sync, which caused the PSDs' projection to change to a slightly bulkier model. After waving his hand toward the rubber mat, the PSDs morphed to match the projection. Evaran handed the PSDs back to them.

Emily looked her PSD over. "Three buttons now?"

"Yes," said Evaran. "The first and second are customizable. The third projects a miniature screen above the PSD that lets you switch between what the buttons will do. You can also access the main interface from there as well. On the side is a small switch that toggles if the PSD expands or shows a projection."

Emily opened and closed her PSD in both modes.

"Why the upgrade?" asked Dr. Snowden.

Evaran nodded. "After the events of our last adventure, I realized that in a survival situation, you would need something more robust than what the PSD offered. To that end, I have added a survival modification as well as some training videos I did long ago. You will notice the end is a bit wider.

That is to support a wider array of options for the morphable metal."

"That's pretty cool," said Emily. "What type of survival options we talking about?"

Evaran half grinned. "I figured you would be interested in that. In addition to information, you can now extend a container that will purify water. There is also a food pellet dispenser option, but I would caution you on using them. Each pellet contains your caloric requirements for one day, and it is packed with all the vitamins you need. Your nanobots know how to distribute it. It would be detrimental on anyone else. There is about a nine-month supply there."

"The PSD is using dimensional mechanics for the dispenser, right?" asked Dr. Snowden.

"That is correct," said Evaran. "Okay, are we ready?"

Dr. Snowden and Emily nodded and pocketed the PSDs. They exited the Torvatta and entered a forest clearing.

"V, scout mode."

"Acknowledged. Scout mode engaged," said V. He took off flying through the trees.

"According to Agent Asher, the beacon is masked as a tree nearby," said Evaran.

Dr. Snowden looked around. "Well, at least we aren't too far away." The strong smell of the forest pervaded his nostrils. Sunlight filtered down through the trees, creating rays of light. Although he did not hear any animals, the unmistakable sound of buzzing insects was ever present. He was sure Emily would love that.

They trudged through the forest, making sure to walk around dense clusters of trees. V flew back and projected a hologram. It showed two Native Americans hunting off in the distance. "Analysis. Two humanoids detected."

Evaran studied the projection. "I do not think either is Lord Vygon."

Emily smiled. "Well, this is the archaic period. They are probably hunter-gatherers out . . . hunting and gathering."

"Look at you," said Dr. Snowden. "Miss History over here."

Emily swatted Dr. Snowden's arm. "Maybe you should have read some of the books I suggested for you."

Dr. Snowden grinned.

"V, distraction hologram," said Evaran.

"Acknowledged," said V. He shot off through the forest.

They continued their journey, pausing every now and then to verify they were on the right course. Dr. Snowden had pulled out his PSD and enabled the navigation system. He pointed forward as they walked, and the PSD would show a holographic arrow with the distance above it ahead of him. It was like a compass and global positioning system in one.

V arrived back ten minutes later. "Analysis. The human-oids have fled."

"Excellent," said Evaran.

Dr. Snowden tilted his head. "What hologram did you use?"

"A grizzly bear."

"Well, that would definitely do it."

"I increased it to four times its normal size and doubled its movement speed."

Emily's eyes popped open. "Uhh . . . yeah . . . that'd do it."

V's lights glowed a bit brighter.

Evaran gestured at a tree in the distance. "Come, we are close."

They arrived at a large, slightly glowing tree that stood out among the surrounding forest.

Evaran scanned it with his ring, causing portions of the hologram to fade. A four-foot cylinder sat on top of a base behind the hologram. He approached it and reached through the hologram.

A rustling sound shot around them.

Dr. Snowden rubbed the goose bumps on his arm as a slight breeze wafted past them. Evaran snapped his head to follow the trajectory of a medium-sized man falling from the tree. The dark-skinned man had on black pants and a black vest. The vest was lightly padded and segmented into rubberlike sections. A black cape fluttered behind him with a silver line indented around the edges. On his forearms were bronze metallic structures that wrapped around. A ridge ran the length of them. His profile stood in contrast to the light from the hologram. Straight silver hair flowed to the sides, and his silver eyes glistened. The man turned his head slightly as he surveyed them. "Evaran?"

Evaran nodded. "Yes. You must be Lord Vygon."

Lord Vygon's eyes misted. He shook his head. "You're impossible. You know that?" He rushed forward and hugged a startled Evaran.

Dr. Snowden glanced at Emily, who shrugged.

Lord Vygon laughed as he stepped back. "Time travel is truly bizarre." He extended a hand toward Dr. Snowden. "An honor to see you again, as always."

Dr. Snowden wrinkled his eyebrows and shook Lord Vygon's hand.

Lord Vygon bowed his head slightly as he extended a hand toward Emily. "You look well."

"Thanks," said Emily with a smile. She shook Lord Vygon's hand.

Lord Vygon jerked his head back. He narrowed his eyes and raised a finger. "Okay . . . something's off here."

"Meeting others out of sequence at this point in my personal timeline is not uncommon, especially for an area where I spend some time, such as Earth. It is inevitable I will meet others who have met a future version of me, Dr. Snowden, or Emily," said Evaran.

"Right . . . so . . . this is your first time meeting me then, I'm gathering."

Dr. Snowden found this aspect of time travel fascinating. It highlighted the difference between a personal timeline and universal timeline. In the universal timeline, sometime in the past, Lord Vygon met Evaran, and by extension him and Emily, for the first time. That would be how Lord Vygon knows them now in the present. However, for Evaran, in his personal timeline, that event in the past has not occurred yet, so he would not know Lord Vygon. Dr. Snowden remembered Evaran had said that the future already exists. That must apply to both personal and universal timelines, regardless of scope.

"Yes," said Evaran. "This is our first meeting."

Lord Vygon nodded. "Well then . . . not sure what brought you out here, but my base is nearby."

"We could talk on the Torvatta," said Evaran.

Lord Vygon shook his head. "No temporal shielding for me."

"Very well."

Lord Vygon waved forward. "Follow me."

They followed Lord Vygon as he wound through the forest. After several minutes, they came upon a large rocky structure with a cave opening. Evaran launched his illumination orbs as they neared it.

"You won't need those," said Lord Vygon. "The cave is lit inside."

Evaran snapped his head around. "We are not alone."

Lord Vygon flung his arms to his sides as he stood beside Evaran. Blunted blades extended above his forearms and wrapped around to the front of his fists. The bases of the blades were anchored to the forearm guards' ridges. "I hear them too."

Evaran gestured for Dr. Snowden and Emily to move to the cave entrance as bald, black-clothed male humanoids swarmed the area. They wore padded boots and a covering over the lower half of their faces. A small circular crystal was embedded in their foreheads. Red triangles surrounded their eyes. They wielded metal staffs with a glowing crystal embedded on one end, while curved daggers hung off their belts. A barrage of beams shot out. Lord Vygon ran behind Evaran as the beams hit Evaran's shield.

"They are shooting mass teleport beams," said Evaran, studying his ARI. He extended his utility handle into a baton and aimed at several of the humanoids. *Boom!* White concentric circles shot out, sending several of the humanoids flying. Those not hit moved behind the trees.

"That won't work well here. Too many obstructions," said Lord Vygon. "You can't be teleported, so draw their fire. They also shoot bolts, those will be the ones to block. I'll hit the perimeter. I could use V's help with distraction. Just like old times."

Evaran tilted his head. He sidestepped one of the humanoids that had charged forward and batted him away. "Are you sure?"

Lord Vygon ducked as a beam shot over his head. "Of course. Don't worry, I won't kill. My blades are blunted."

Evaran narrowed his eyes and nodded. "V, assist Lord Vygon."

"Acknowledged," said V. He flew high into the air, dodging beams as Lord Vygon shot out into the forest.

Evaran hunkered down, letting the beams hit his shield, and switched to his ranged stun beam. He took potshots, but the amount of bolts trying to hit him caused him to focus on moving his shield around. As Lord Vygon and V went around the perimeter, the amount of bolts began to decrease.

Dr. Snowden's breathing went haphazard as he watched the fight. Lord Vygon was a blur, and the bodies being tossed into the air were the only way for Dr. Snowden to track him. V flew around casting multiple copies of Lord Vygon, which seemed to confuse the attackers. Dr. Snowden faced Emily and gestured to move farther into the cave.

"Uncle Albert?" asked Emily as she grabbed Dr. Snowden's arm.

Dr. Snowden spun around as one of the humanoids dropped to the ground in front of them. Dr. Snowden barreled forward, yanking Emily to the ground in the process. His eyes raged as he bowled the man over. Dr. Snowden scowled as his fists went into a fury of strikes. He pummeled the man until he was barely moving.

"Uncle Albert!" said Emily as two others dropped to the ground.

Dr. Snowden jumped up and tackled one of the humanoids. The other took a step back and shot a beam at Emily. She cried out as she vanished in a bright flash of light.

"*Emily!*" said Dr. Snowden as he wrestled the staff away from the one he knocked down. He swung at the second humanoid, causing him to fly out of the cave entrance and over Evaran. He felt a sharp pain in his side as the humanoid he took the staff from shot him with a bolt. He wheeled around and cracked the man over the head with the staff. The man faltered for a moment, then stopped moving. With a toss of the staff, he dropped to the ground on all fours. He crawled over to where Emily had vanished and frantically searched the ground. *"Emily!"*

Evaran, with shield raised, walked backward to where Dr. Snowden was. When he got there, he pulled Dr. Snowden back into the cave and out of sight.

"Where . . . where is she?" said Dr. Snowden as his voice cracked.

"I . . . do not know," said Evaran with wrinkled eyebrows. "We will scan the area when the rest of the attackers are gone." He proceeded to peep out, shooting his stun beam. After a few minutes, a silence washed over the area.

Lord Vygon and V joined Evaran and Dr. Snowden. "They're leaving. That was a small group. We were lucky." He scanned the surroundings. With a tilted head, he said, "Oh . . . this is not good . . ."

"Where is she!" said Dr. Snowden. He burst forward to where Emily had vanished and kicked the dirt and leaves around.

"We will find her. You need to stay calm," said Evaran.

Dr. Snowden shook his head violently. "Calm? Emily's g—" He put a hand on his chest as a jolt of pain shot through him, causing him to grunt and fall to the ground. His breathing slowed, and his vision dimmed as he saw Evaran and Lord Vygon rush toward him. Everything went black.

05

Dr. Snowden inhaled deeply as he opened his eyes. It took a moment for them to adjust, and when they did, he scanned the room he was in. The rocky floor and walls indicated to him that he was in a room somewhere in the cave. The wooden bed he was on had a thick blanket of furs as a mattress.

A torch flickered on the wall, causing shadows in the room to jump.

He removed the thin cloth blanket over him and swung his legs over the side. Emily jumped into his mind. She was gone. The pit in his stomach deepened as he stood and stretched. He could hear voices farther in the cave. Running a hand over his chest, he remembered the pain he had felt earlier. It seemed to be gone. He shook his head. Another mystery. Great, just what he needed. He took a deep breath and exited the room.

Evaran and Lord Vygon sat around a pit fire in a large room. Like the room Dr. Snowden was just in, it had a rocky floor and walls. Various openings led off to other areas.

"You are up. How are you feeling?" asked Evaran, gesturing for Dr. Snowden to join him and Lord Vygon on a series of crude wooden benches around the pit fire.

Dr. Snowden ambled up to one of the benches and sat across from Lord Vygon and Evaran. "Pain's gone . . . what happened?"

"You flew into a blind rage and your nanobots shut your body down to protect you," said Evaran. "They were also trying to deal with the poison from the bolts, and your anger was exacerbating the situation."

Dr. Snowden chewed on Evaran's words. He thought his reaction was normal, given the circumstances. "Well . . . I had just seen Emily disappear . . ."

Lord Vygon raised a finger. "I can shed some light on that. We've examined one of the sentinel's staffs. Evaran was right . . . again. It's a teleportation weapon. Fire . . . and whatever it hits gets sent away."

"Where?" asked Dr. Snowden with narrowed eyes.

Lord Vygon bobbed his head. "We did a test using one of Evaran's quantum beacons, and shot it with the weapon. It terminated after arrival a few minutes later, so we suspect it was destroyed. Apparently, they are sending people to what you would know as Egypt."

"Egypt? What the heck is in Egypt?" asked Dr. Snowden.

"I do not know," said Evaran. "We will find out, though. I do not suspect Emily is harmed. If they had meant to kill, they would not bother with teleportation."

Dr. Snowden exhaled from his nose and closed his eyes for moment. He opened them and looked at Lord Vygon. "You called them sentinels?"

"Yes," said Lord Vygon. "These humans are the scouts of an unknown organization. They're intelligent and trained for reconnaissance. I've heard reports from other nonhumans that they've been targeted by these sentinels. They seem to ignore humans, and for the most part, humans avoid them. One of my human friends actually talked to one and gathered some information for me a while back. Didn't catch the organization's name, but I know that they fight for human purity."

"Sounds like the Purifiers," said Dr. Snowden. Ring Commander Sheel flashed in his mind. "This is one human they better not try to talk to." His blood began to boil.

Lord Vygon tilted his head. "Purifiers?"

"A human supremacist group led by an overlord," said Evaran. "Their goal is nothing less than the dominance of humanity, and the purification of everything nonhuman."

"That would validate what I know of them," said Lord Vygon. "The fact you are here means you must have met them in the future and come back to this point. Am I right?"

Evaran tilted his head and eyed Lord Vygon. "Yes . . . I suspect these sentinels are just the vanguard, removing what they can while remaining hidden in the shadows."

"Well, if these are the vanguard, I'd hate to see what comes next."

"We need to find them. Make them wish they never set foot on Earth!" said Dr. Snowden as he stood with fire raging in his eyes.

Evaran extended a hand toward Dr. Snowden. "Relax."

Dr. Snowden snorted and shook his head. "I just don't need this right now."

"We will find Emily and figure out what is going on with your anger."

"How about this time you tell me when you find something out instead of waiting."

Evaran paused as he studied Dr. Snowden. "You have my word. Now that you are up, we were going to question one of the sentinels."

"All right then," said Dr. Snowden. His eyes softened. "You caught one?"

"Yes. After we got you inside, we went back and caught them trying to take their fallen away. We let them go, except for one. Lord Vygon . . . convinced him to come with us."

Dr. Snowden cocked his head.

"You shall see."

"Good. Maybe I can convince this sentinel to bring back Emily."

Evaran eyed Dr. Snowden. "Perhaps I should do the questioning."

Dr. Snowden sighed.

They stood and exited the large room and walked through numerous hallways lit by torches anchored on the walls. After fifteen minutes, they arrived at a room with a makeshift wooden slab.

On the slab rested a strapped-down unconscious sentinel. The black clothing was gone, leaving a minimally clothed body. He wore sandals on his feet and had a leather loincloth. Leather straps crisscrossed his chest, and a segmented metal guard was around his neck. His clothing and weapons lay on the ground.

V hovered nearby. "Dr. Snowden. We will find Emily."

Dr. Snowden swallowed hard and nodded.

"It would seem these sentinels have a small crystal implanted in their head," said Evaran. "I cannot scan it or use my UIC on it, which is unusual. I do not know what its purpose is, other than it has tendrils that connect to the brain."

"Okay . . . that doesn't sound good."

Evaran raised a finger. "It is not. Another thing that is odd is that I could not activate the staff. Lord Vygon had to instruct the sentinel to fire it at the beacon for us. I suspect the crystals have some type of bond I am unaware of."

"Instruct?"

Lord Vygon smirked. "My hypnotic gaze. Ready to see it in action?"

Dr. Snowden shrugged. "Sure."

Lord Vygon extended the man's arm, and then bit into his wrist.

Dr. Snowden raised his eyebrows.

After a moment, the sentinel's eyes opened. He looked at Lord Vygon. "Filthy nonhuman. What are you doing?" He scanned Dr. Snowden, Evaran, and V. "You're all going to die."

Dr. Snowden scowled. "Yeah . . . keep talking . . ."

Lord Vygon put both hands on the side of the sentinel's head, then gazed into his eyes. "You are under my command now. You will answer every question posed to you with as much information as you know. Do you understand?"

The sentinel's face went blank. "Yes, my master, I understand."

Dr. Snowden studied the sentinel. That hypnotic gaze was quite a powerful ability. He wondered if all vampires had it or if it was just an ancient vampire thing.

Lord Vygon stood back and gestured at Evaran. "Have at it."

Evaran approached the slab and stood next to the sentinel. "Where are you sending the nonhumans you are targeting?"

The sentinel cocked his head. "Prison."

Dr. Snowden swallowed hard. "What do you mean by that?"

The sentinel looked at Dr. Snowden. "Nonhuman filth is sent to prison."

"Emily's not filth! Where'd you send her?" said Dr. Snowden as his face turned red.

"Prison."

Dr. Snowden's eyes raged as he stepped toward the sentinel.

Evaran moved between Dr. Snowden and the sentinel. He placed a hand on Dr. Snowden's shoulder. "Relax. Let me and Lord Vygon do the questioning."

Dr. Snowden eyes smoldered. He leaned against one of the walls and crossed his arms.

Lord Vygon narrowed his eyes. "We know where you are sending nonhumans. Is that where the prison is?"

The sentinel pivoted his head toward Lord Vygon. "No."

"How many sentinels are on Earth?"

"One hundred twelve."

Lord Vygon's eyes widened. "It's worse than I thought."

"I concur," said Evaran. He faced the sentinel again. "What is the goal after all nonhumans have been eliminated?"

"Assimilation."

Dr. Snowden smirked. "Well, that's not happening."

Evaran looked at Dr. Snowden.

Dr. Snowden looked away.

"How many have been sent to prison so far?" asked Lord Vygon.

The sentinel's head wobbled for a moment. "Twenty-one."

Lord Vygon glanced at Evaran.

The sentinel shook violently.

Evaran scanned the sentinel. "The activity around the crystal tendrils has increased significantly."

"I'm guessing that crystal is trying to fight off the effects of my gaze. We should probably make him unconscious again."

Evaran nodded as he pulled out his utility handle and extended it into a baton. He tapped the sentinel with the blue end of the baton, causing the sentinel to shudder for a moment, then go limp.

Dr. Snowden sighed. "So . . . Egypt?"

Evaran nodded. "Yes. We can head there now."

"I'll need to get a few things before we go," said Lord Vygon.

"You wish to come with us?"

Lord Vygon smirked. "Of course. Someone has to watch out for you." He looked at V and Dr. Snowden. "Nothing against either of you."

Dr. Snowden shrugged and glanced at V, whose lights pulsed for a moment.

"Very well," said Evaran. "You mentioned before that you did not want any temporal shielding."

"Yeah . . . but now I know we're fixing something that happened in the future. From my perspective anyways. If we were going to the past, that would be a problem. I wouldn't want to be shielded if you fixed something in the past and then I met my double. Besides, my base is compromised now. I can't stay here."

"You know a great deal about time travel."

Lord Vygon smiled. "I had a good teacher."

"I see," said Evaran as he studied Lord Vygon. "We can leave then when you are ready. V, bring the Torvatta here."

"Acknowledged."

Dr. Snowden sighed as he watched V fly off. He replayed in his head the scene where Emily was teleported. If he had controlled his anger, maybe he could have prevented the sentinel from firing at her, or at least went with her. Instead, he charged off like a mad bull. He swallowed hard as his eyes watered. He would find Emily, and it did not matter how many Purifiers he had to go through.

An hour later as the Torvatta approached Egypt, Dr. Snowden studied Lord Vygon sitting on the left side of the command area. He had a lot of questions he wanted to ask based on what he learned from John, but the unsettled twists in his stomach distracted him. All he could think about was where Emily was and if she was okay.

The Torvatta flew over the desert. Structures began to outline in green on the left front screen. Dr. Snowden watched the lights in the distance begin to grow. He knew Emily would have loved this. He glanced at Evaran and wished he could contain his emotions like he did.

"Analysis. The location the beacon flagged is ahead," said V.

"Keep us in stealth mode. Standard scans," said Evaran.

"Acknowledged."

The right front screen lit up, showing a smooth triangular shape with labels around it.

"A shielded pyramid," said Lord Vygon. "A bit out of place for this time period."

Evaran scrutinized Lord Vygon for a moment, then focused on the front right screen. "You are correct. It is not yet the age of pyramids. Its presence here now may have had some historical influence." He looked at his ARI. "V, there is not much data being retrieved."

"Analysis. Shield is preventing penetration. Only visual is available."

"Hmm," said Evaran. "Then that is not a normal shield. We will need to monitor it and see if anything enters or leaves it."

"So we have no way of knowing if Emily is down there?" asked Dr. Snowden.

"Not for the moment. However, the sentinels must be entering and leaving it somehow," said Evaran. He faced Dr. Snowden. "Get some rest. We will run a continuous scan through the night."

Dr. Snowden sighed and nodded. "All right." He stood and headed toward the living quarters. As he passed Evaran, he felt a hand on his shoulder.

"You have my word that I will find Emily."

Dr. Snowden gulped as his eyes misted. "I know."

"In the morning, I would like to begin a training regime for your nanobots and anger issue."

Dr. Snowden nodded and headed off to the living quarters. He was not sure what Evaran had in mind, but at this point, he was open to ideas. Something had to be done. He cursed not being able to control it on his own. Was he that weak-minded?

Growing up, it had shown itself in the form of fights he had gotten into with bullies at school. His friends gave in to the bullying, but he would get angry, then get beaten down when he fought back. That is, until his older brother, Dan, threatened the bullies. He missed Dan. Dan was always the steady rock he could go to. Dr. Snowden knew it was rougher for Emily. On Dan's deathbed, he told Dr. Snowden to watch over Emily. Dr. Snowden sighed. What a great job he was doing. When he got to his living quarters, he went through the bedtime motions in a daze, then went to bed.

Ten hours later, he awoke and lay in bed, staring at the ceiling. His stomach churned as he felt the heat from his body swirl around him. He half expected Emily to call him on the PSD and let him know she was having breakfast. With a deep swallow, he pushed himself out of bed and got cleaned up.

He went to the conference room and got a cup of coffee. Looking at the empty table brought back a memory of when Emily was eight. Dan had gone on a business trip and asked Dr. Snowden to house-sit for a few days. Dr. Snowden agreed. While working at the dinner table late that night, he heard Emily scream and shout his name. When he entered her room, she was wide eyed and held her covers tight. She said she thought she saw someone outside her window. He checked and saw nothing. She then asked to sleep on the couch in the living room next to where he was working. He allowed it, and after she snuggled into the couch, he hugged her and told her he would always be there to protect her. As quickly as the memory had come, it left.

Dr. Snowden wiped his eyes and sighed as he headed to the command area. Evaran was in his command chair, V at the front console, and Lord Vygon sitting in the left seating area. The front right screen was awash with various bars and graphs and complex mathematics swirling around. Dr. Snowden took a seat on the right and took a sip of his coffee.

"You are awake. Did you sleep well?" asked Evaran.

Dr. Snowden shook his head. "Slept soundly, but feel a little nauseated."

Evaran stood and nodded. "You have been under pressure. When you finish your coffee, we can head to the holo room for your first training session."

"Sure," said Dr. Snowden. He glanced at Lord Vygon. "Did you sleep at all?"

Lord Vygon smiled. "I'm an ancient vampire. When I sleep, I sleep for years at a time, sometimes more."

Dr. Snowden jerked his head back. "Must be nice."

"It also means I'm vulnerable for an extended period."

Dr. Snowden nodded. He was coming to understand that life was precarious. One slipup and bad things could happen. He finished his coffee and followed Evaran to the holo room.

Evaran called up a program that showed Dr. Snowden's vital signs as vertical bar graphs hovering in the air behind Evaran.

The only seating was the chair Dr. Snowden sat in.

"I have tied your internal body systems to these graphs, thanks to your nanobots," said Evaran. "First, I want you to breathe deeply. Make sure each breath is coming from your stomach area, and not your chest."

Dr. Snowden pictured a tornado of air rising from his gut and then being expelled. After a moment, a wave of relaxation swept over him.

"Now, in your head, for each breath, say the word *relax* in your mind."

Dr. Snowden complied.

"Imagine a place that is serene to you. Describe it."

Dr. Snowden recalled the first time he had looked up and seen the stars as a kid. "It was in my parents' backyard. They had a telescope and I'd spend hours looking up at the stars."

The room changed to a backyard with a telescope.

Dr. Snowden's eyes widened as he looked around. "Umm . . . it looked a lot like this . . ."

"Your nanobots are sending information to assist in the recreation."

"Okay . . . hopefully that's the only thing they're sending . . ."

Evaran half smiled. "Do not worry. Okay, now breathe, say the words, and focus on the scene and the feeling it gives you."

Dr. Snowden spent five minutes breathing, saying the word *relax*, and looking around. He felt his heartbeat slow, and a wave of relaxation mixed with a tingling sensation washed over him. It was the first time in a long while that he had felt truly relaxed. The graphs reflected his mood.

"Good, you adapt quickly. I am impressed."

"Wow," said Dr. Snowden. "I actually feel . . . normal."

"Every morning and night, you should do this until you reach a state of relaxation. Tomorrow we will go over some exercises that will also help. Later on, we will do cognitive restructuring. You can control your outbursts, but it will take time."

Dr. Snowden swallowed hard and nodded. "I . . . appreciate your help with this."

"I know you do not like to ask for help, but I am always available if you need me," said Evaran. He gestured toward the exit. "Come, let us head to the command center."

"Before we go, I did feel a tingling sensation over my body when it was relaxing. Nanobots?"

Evaran rubbed his chin. "It could be. You cannot communicate with them directly, but they do respond to your body's cues. I do not know what form that takes on, but a tingling sensation may be a sign of that."

Dr. Snowden raised his eyebrows.

"Come."

They headed back to the command area and took their respective seats.

Evaran faced Dr. Snowden. "Based on the scans we ran over the night, we will need help in gaining access to the pyramid."

"Is it that heavily guarded?"

"Yes. There is a small rectangular entranceway that opens at specific times," said Evaran. "We observed several sentinels coming and going. It is too small for the Torvatta to go through. However, V went in when it was open and came back out when it opened again. He was able to scan quite a bit of the inside. There are several structures hidden from view by the shield. There are also a lot of guards, both inside and outside."

Dr. Snowden slid to the edge of his seat. "Any sign of Emily?"

Evaran looked down. "None."

Dr. Snowden clenched his jaw. His face turned a slight shade of red as his focus shifted to thoughts of dismantling the Purifier base.

"Breathe," said Evaran.

After several minutes of breathing, Dr. Snowden's focus returned. "So . . . where do we get help then?"

"We should check with the Helians," said Lord Vygon. "They have advanced technology, troops, and as the so-called protectors of the planet, they should help."

Dr. Snowden furrowed his eyebrows. "That could take forever for them to act, and they don't like Daedrould apparently."

"Yeah . . . they don't care for us. That's okay, though. They aren't as powerful as they think they are. Nonetheless, it's worth it to see what they can do."

"Great."

"V, take us to Atlantis," said Evaran.

"Acknowledged."

After twenty minutes of travel, the Torvatta arrived at At-lantis. Using the credentials from their last visit, they were granted a landing pad. Once it touched down, everyone, including V in orb mode, disembarked and headed toward the Helian who had registered them before. Evaran carried the teleportation staff.

"Back so soon?" asked the Helian.

Evaran gestured at Lord Vygon. "We found who we were looking for, but need to talk to someone with authority. We have evidence of illegal activity."

The Helian eyed Lord Vygon. He gestured for them to walk through the walkway scanner. After going through it, the Helian tapped at his forearm screen. "Lord Vygon . . . surprised to see you here again."

"Well . . . only here to help my friends," said Lord Vygon. "I'll clean the *stench* of this place off me later."

The Helian scowled. "And we will sanitize everything after you leave." He looked at the weapon. "What's that?"

"Part of the evidence," said Evaran.

The Helian gestured for Evaran to hand it to him. "I'll hold it until an agent arrives. He will be here shortly."

Evaran handed the weapon over. The Helian moved over to a wall console a bit away.

Lord Vygon snorted. "He knew who I was. Just wanted to hassle me." He shook his head.

"You've been here before?" asked Dr. Snowden.

"Yeah. As an ancient vampire, I run my own house," said Lord Vygon. "It's empty at the moment, but I still hold some political power in my area, and the Helians recognize it."

Dr. Snowden narrowed his eyes. "So the communication beacon near your base was really only for the Helians, and not just any Outsider wanting to visit."

"You got it," said Lord Vygon. "It also signals to others that the Helians are not to be killed on sight and that they are there to communicate."

"I was not aware relations were that bad," said Evaran.

"It's a mess. We get along with the Outsiders near us, but the ones posing as gods and protectors have issues."

After a few minutes, a Helian dressed similarly to Agent Asher arrived. His mantle had the same symbols on it. He held the transporter weapon in his right hand and brought his left hand to it in the Helian salute. "I'm Special Agent Joktan. I hear you have evidence of illegal activity and this weapon is part of it. Is this correct?"

Evaran returned Joktan's salute. "Yes, is there someplace we can discuss it?"

Joktan turned around and walked with a forward-waving motion. "Follow me."

They followed Joktan and reached the ramp to Agent Asher's office. Dr. Snowden's throat constricted as he remembered going up it with Emily. He paused to unwind his throat.

"Dr. Snowden?" asked Lord Vygon.

Dr. Snowden looked up and saw that Joktan and Evaran had already gone down a different path. "Coming." He walked with Lord Vygon and turned his head toward him. "So . . . you know a future Evaran?"

"Yep," said Lord Vygon.

Dr. Snowden paused for a moment. "Are me and Emily with him?"

Lord Vygon drew his head back. "I can't tell you that."

"But you can tell me that you know a future Evaran?"

"Yes, part of Evaran's rules."

"Damn the rules! Are we with him or not?" asked Dr. Snowden. His face began to turn red.

"I'm sorry, I just can't. Would you tell me my future if you knew it?"

Dr. Snowden pondered Lord Vygon's question. His mind knew he probably would not, but his heart told him otherwise. "Depends on the situation."

"If you broke Evaran's rules, you would not travel with him. Would it be worth it?"

"If it gets Emily back, then yes!" said Dr. Snowden.

Lord Vygon looked down and sighed. "All I can tell you is you'll be fine. No details."

"I'm not asking about me . . . I'm asking about Emily."

"I know . . . but that's all I can say."

Dr. Snowden rolled his eyes as he shook his head. He was not getting anywhere and Lord Vygon was too loyal to Evaran to break a rule. It was not fair. Everyone played by the book when it came to Evaran's rules. Maybe there were consequences he was not seeing, but it was difficult to think of anything other than finding Emily.

After a while, they arrived at Joktan's office. It was larger than Agent Asher's and was divided into two rooms. The first one had a conference table in it. The second was a smaller room with a desk and chair in it. Joktan waved them into the first room. He went to the head of the conference table and took a seat. Evaran sat to his right and Lord Vygon and Dr. Snowden to his left.

Joktan laid the weapon on the table. "So . . . is this weapon your only evidence?"

"No," said Evaran. He gestured toward the middle of the table. "V, display the sentinel."

V displayed a holographic video showing the meeting with the sentinel that they had interrogated earlier.

Joktan put his hand on his chin as he watched. When the holographic video was done, he faced Evaran. "So the weapon is a teleporter."

"Yes. It teleports whatever it hits to a pyramid in Egypt."

"Egypt?"

Evaran paused for a moment. He then tilted his head. "You would know it as the lands of Pharaoh Djoser. The pyramid is just outside Memphis. We checked it out, but it appears to be shielded. V, display the pyramid."

V projected the pyramid.

"What an unusual structure. However, that would be Ra's domain," said Joktan. "I would suggest you talk to him except—"

"Let me guess, Ra is missing," said Lord Vygon.

Joktan let out a measured breath. "Yes . . . it was reported, but that doesn't mean it was due to this . . . teleporting weapon. Ra is known to take off for periods of time, and we have had reports filed on him."

Lord Vygon smirked. "You just heard what the Purifiers are going to do. You have seen the weapons they are using to enact their plan. You have seen where they are sending people and where their base is. You *know* Ra is missing. This doesn't worry you?"

"I can't verify any of this. All I have seen is a video that may or may not be true. A weapon which might teleport to a structure that has not been reported as being an issue. Nonetheless, we will look into it."

"You have also had a recent increase in missing people," said Evaran.

"Well . . . almost all Daedrould and, of course, Ra. Doesn't mean what you're showing me is the cause."

Lord Vygon shook his head. "Typical. I bet if it were the pantheons reporting this, you'd give it top priority."

"I said we'll investigate it, but we are stretched thin at the moment."

Dr. Snowden slammed his hand on the table. "I can't believe this. My niece is missing because of these Purifiers, and your response when provided evidence is that you're stretched a bit thin?"

Joktan jerked back in his chair. "To be honest, this evidence is all circumstantial. We would need to talk to the pantheon, since Ra is missing, in that area and ask about the structure. We need to run tests on the weapon. And the sentinel you speak of, where is it? It takes time to do all these things."

Dr. Snowden scowled as he shook his head. "In the future, these Purifiers kill all nonhumans. You want evidence? How about I shoot you with the teleporter and then see what you say!"

"Dr. Snowden!" said Evaran.

"Just sick of these worthless Helians. This trip was a waste of time. Emily is out there somewhere and I'm standing here listening to this guy rationalize why he isn't going to help. We don't have time for this!"

"Breathe," said Evaran.

"What?"

"Breathe."

Dr. Snowden paused as he stared at Evaran. He looked away as he slowed his breathing down. After a few moments, his face returned to a normal shade. "Fine."

Evaran faced a startled Joktan. "Thank you for your time. We will be going."

"Look . . . I'm sorry. You have my word it will be looked into, just not maybe right away," said Joktan.

Lord Vygon smirked. "Well, at least you're aware of the situation now. Good luck if the Purifiers come here."

Evaran gestured toward the door. "Let us go. We have some planning to do."

06

Inside the Purifiers' pyramid in Egypt, Emily appeared in front of two crystal rods that were about fifteen feet apart with a gold rhombus-shaped base. Small silver rings were attached at equal intervals on the rods. She whipped around as a group of bronze-skinned men approached her, with curved swords, staffs, and crossbows drawn. They wore gold light armor that covered half their bodies. Black masks with eye, mouth, and nose holes covered their faces.

Emily stiffened as her heartbeat raced. These men were serious.

The room she was in was large, with featureless stone walls and a device standing at the back of the room next to an entrance. The device had a cylindrical base, with a slanted surface coming off it halfway down. A metal rod extended up from the base and ended in an upside-down dome-shaped structure. Several white-robed Purifiers stood in front of it.

"Face the portal," said one of the men.

Emily's breathing went erratic as she spun around to face the crystal rods.

The rods lit up, and a light solid golden surface appeared between them.

Emily felt the tip of a staff nudge in her back. "Go through."

"I don't want to," said Emily with a wavering voice. She squinted when a sharp pain shot through her leg, causing her to buckle to the ground.

"Get up and go through the rift door, dog!"

"No . . . ," said Emily with a cracked voice. "Please . . ." She screamed as the men grabbed her arms and legs and carried her toward the rift door.

Once they were within arms' distance, they tossed her through.

She flew out into a similar room as the one she had just left. As she lay sprawled on the ground, two men grabbed her and held her down. Another man grabbed her arm and extended it out. Two tanned men in golden robes with the Purifier symbol in the chest area rushed out. Their bald heads glistened under the room's light. They had elaborate markings on their faces, especially around the eyes, and one of them carried a syringe.

"Hurry! We only have thirty seconds," said one of the gold-robed men.

The man carrying the syringe jabbed Emily in the arm.

"Stop it!" said Emily.

The other gold-robed man slapped her. "Shut up, filth!"

After extracting some of Emily's blood, the man held the syringe up and eyed it. "Got it. These little wonders are going to make us." He waved in a dismissive gesture. "Dispose of this trash."

The three men held Emily up. The rift door surface changed from gold to red. They carried her forward as she kicked out.

"No!"

A sense of weightlessness washed over her as she flew through the portal and down a red tunnel. After a moment, she crash-landed onto a stone floor.

A pain shot through her body for a moment, causing her to wince. Her leg pulsed, and bruised spots on her sides ached where the men had kneed her. While squinting and trying to catch her breath, she took a look around.

The floor sat on top of a stepped pyramid sitting outdoors. Four metal pillars rose from the corners of the platform, ending in a circular roof. Near the top of the pillars, a small segment blinked. They emitted a blaring horn sound.

A rush of adrenaline shot through her. She hunkered down and waited out the horn sound. After it stopped, she continued to look around. Her nose rankled at the sweet smell of exotic flowers intermingled with the decayed smell of plants and animals. Looking up, she figured that whatever that thing was she came through, the ending must have spawned on the bottom side of the roof. She crawled over to one of the pillars and used it to stand up. Her breath staggered as she looked out.

Around the stepped pyramid was a small open area, separated from a lush jungle by a scattered white stone strip. A podium stood out at the base of one of the sides.

The ambient sounds of animals she did not recognize filled the air. One in particular caught her ear. It was a loud gurgling shriek that seemed to be coming closer.

She swept her gaze across the other sides. After a moment, she pulled out her PSD and tried to contact Dr. Snowden and Evaran to no avail. Her lips drew in as her eyes misted.

The pain in her arm throbbed where she had been stuck with the syringe. She rubbed the area, causing a tingling sensation to intensify. Probably the nanobots. She caught her breath and used the augmented reality view on her PSD to scan her surroundings.

A cliff loomed off in the distance, and a river had been detected nearby. Outside that, it was jungle everywhere.

Her stomach churned as a sense of dread welled up inside her. Maybe if she stayed put, Evaran and Dr. Snowden would be along soon. She gulped and then climbed to the nearest step, which was about three feet down. At least she could go see what the podium was. She knew her pain would subside, and the tingling sensations she was feeling seemed to minimize it.

After a few minutes of sitting and sliding down the steps, she reached the podium. It was metallic, like the pillars, and the top surface was caked with dried dirt. She cracked the crust and swept it away, revealing a smooth metal surface. She jumped back and shrieked when a beam shot out and scanned her. The surface then lit up and went semitransparent, showing a map. She approached the podium while surveying her immediate surroundings. After verifying there was nothing around, she scrutinized it.

The map showed a large landmass ringed by islands, with multiple yellow dots on it. Some dots were larger than the others. At the top of the landmass was a large blue dot.

A blinking yellow dot on the southern part caught her eyes. She figured that was her current location, assuming this map was accurate. With a press, several green dots appeared north of where she was.

The size of the dots seemed to follow a progression. The dot she was at was small. The green ones were a bit larger, and the blue one was massive relative to the others.

She switched to navigation mode on her PSD and held it up. After a few moments, she was able to determine the direction of the northern blue dot using the cliffs and the river as markers. The podium was on the south side of the pyramid. She was not planning on having to go anywhere, but at least now she had an idea of where she was.

A chattering sound punctuated by periodic shrieks raised the hairs on her arm. She glanced around and focused on the jungle. It was imperceptible at first, but a dark mass, like a carpet being rolled out, moved toward the white stone strip barrier below. She cocked her head as she examined it with the PSD.

She froze as she realized the white stone strip was bones, as if they had been swept off the pyramid and got caught on the jungle transition area. A quick look past it and her eyes widened.

The dark mass was a group of individual turtle-like shells, roughly a foot in length, ambling toward the pyramid. One of the turtle shells stopped. It reared up, showing a six-legged body underneath it with a somewhat humanoid face near the front. It let out a gurgled shriek and pointed toward her.

She gagged at the thought of one-foot bugs that resembled humanoids with shells. Her breathing sped up as the creatures reached the bones. She had to move. Were these creatures responsible for the bones? She was not going to wait to find out. Facing north, she eyed the cliff in the distance. She remembered seeing a river on the way there when she was surveying the land earlier. Maybe these things could not swim.

She climbed down to the ground and headed around the corner to the right to head north. At least the creatures were coming from the south, so she would have a head start. As she approached the bones to the north, she slid to a stop.

Another mass of the creatures was ahead of her.

Looking to her right, she realized they had surrounded the entire area. Maybe they could not climb. She hustled up several steps.

As the first wave hit the first stone, they paused to allow the second wave to stack on top of them.

Her mind went wild as she realized they were forming a living ramp. Snapping her head left and right, she saw some had already made it up the first step. She set her PSD to a repulsion blast. *"Get away!"*

The creatures moved to the second step.

She scrambled up to the third step.

Some of the creatures on the step below her from the south were beginning to come around the corner.

She aimed at the wave on the second step and fired her repulsing beam.

The creatures went tumbling, but their empty space was quickly filled by others.

She exhaled quickly. *"Leave me alone!"* She fired in a downward-sweeping motion, clearing a temporary wide path through the creatures. Adrenaline, accompanied by a tingling sensation, shot through her. It was as if time itself slowed down when she jumped three steps to the ground. She blasted a path through the creatures and took off running. With a quick leap over the bones, she burst into the jungle. She could hear the creatures gurgling and shrieking as they changed course. The sound of the river ahead made her speed up.

She crashed through branches, vines, and underbrush in her rush. Startled animals fled on her approach. Large insects that would normally have made her jump out of her skin were all around, but she did not care, and they did not either, it would seem.

After reaching the river, she stopped to catch her breath. The sounds of the creatures breaking through the jungle were unmistakable. After a quick scan of the twenty-foot-wide, fast-moving brown river, she tucked the PSD into her pants pocket, then jumped in and swam over to the other side. She hoped the color of the water was due to disturbed silt.

The creatures approached the other side of the river. They paused and gurgle shrieked. Two tried to enter the water and were swept away. The others backed away. Some were snapped up by the large insects she had seen earlier.

"Yeah! How 'bout that!" she shouted while bobbing her head.

The creatures dispersed into the jungle.

Looking around, she noticed the cliffs were not too far off. She expected the Torvatta would be around soon, but if she was going to stay the night, shelter would be needed. After calming down, she pulled out her PSD and selected the purifying water container. It formed out of the morphable matter aspect of the PSD. She took a scoop of the river water and then pressed a button on the handle. The brown water cleared. She gulped it down and repeated this several times until her thirst was slaked.

She let out a deep breath as she scanned toward the cliffs. The PSD showed them to be about four miles away. The jungle was less dense on this side of the river. She could not go back to the pyramid, and she knew that animals would come to drink at the river, so staying there was out of the question. If the Torvatta came, it would be able to find her, or so she hoped. With a look back over her shoulder, she decided to head to the cliff and took off.

Her adrenaline wore off over the roughly two hours it took to reach the base of the cliff. Looking up, she noticed unusual openings on the rock wall sitting on a ledge. It reminded her of housing she had seen in her Native American studies. The climb looked rough, but it was either that or stay the night on the ground. At least that high up, she would not need to worry about something sneaking up on her. That was her thought, anyway. She did not know when it got dark, but she figured she had some time to get up there. Better to wait there.

Her eyes softened as she thought of her situation. She missed Dr. Snowden, Evaran, and V. Where were they? She sighed and began the arduous climb. Her journey to the ledge was not as bad as she thought it was going to be. A few flying animals had come close, but a shot from the PSD sent them packing. When she got to the ledge, she wrinkled her eyebrows as she saw small doors carved out of the stone. She pulled herself up and approached the first one with the PSD aimed forward. Looking in, she saw what appeared to be a small living space. Whatever had lived there was long gone. Maybe due to those creatures.

She stepped into the enclosure and swept it with a light from the PSD. Nothing was in there as far as she could tell. She went to a corner in the back and slumped down. With knees pulled up to her chest and a frown on her face, tears began to flow. Her quick, successive breaths did not help the situation. She stared out the door with a numbness in her head.

She was alone.

The night seemed to get dark around 6:00 p.m., according to the PSD clock. Emily had spent the rest of the day checking out her surrounding area on the ledge. Using her

PSD, she was able to determine that the rooms were over a thousand years old.

A sharp pain shot through her foot the next morning, waking her out of her sleep.

A small owl-like bird pecked at her foot.

Her eyes popped open as she waved it away with her hands and kicked out. "Shoo!"

The bird flew out of the enclosure.

She yawned and then looked around. A small beetle-looking bug was on her shoulder, making her jump up. She stepped forward while checking the rest of her body. This enclosure would need some cover for the nights, assuming Dr. Snowden, Evaran, and V had not already arrived. Her heart sank as loneliness crept in. She had been alone before, but always around people to some degree. To truly be alone made her palms sweat.

She stepped out of the enclosure and perched herself on the ledge to scan the jungle she had come through before. In all the excitement of the previous day, hunger had taken a backseat to more immediate concerns. She had shelter now, and the river could provide water. Her stomach grumbled as she thought of having breakfast. Dr. Snowden was probably having his morning coffee. Hopefully it was while they were trying to find her.

She pulled out her PSD and checked the survival section. Looking at it jogged her mind about the new food pellet feature Evaran had talked about. With a press of a button, a food pellet came out of the PSD and fell to the ground. She picked it up and dusted it off. It was brown and about the size of a quarter. She had a nine-month supply, but hoped she would not need more than a day or so.

With a shake of her head, she chewed the food pellet. It was tasteless, like chewing cardboard, but she knew it would give her the vitamin and caloric intake she would need. She briefly smiled as a thought popped into her mind of what she would say to Evaran about the pellet's taste. The smile wound down as she remembered where she was.

Her bowels gurgled. She had already decided to go to the river to get water. May as well make use of it as a toilet. If she had to go, better to do it somewhere other than where she was going to stay. Maybe there was a place to do it nearby. Wherever she went, it needed to be soon. At least she would not need to worry about menstrual flow due to the nanobots breaking it down and reabsorbing it into the body. Evaran had mentioned that the process could be reversed, but would require some time to research. Even without them, the stress would have probably made her miss a few.

She climbed down the cliff face and headed toward the jungle. It was muggy, but it was not the temperature that brought her spirit down. Loneliness was ever encroaching into her thoughts. She gulped as she trudged through the sparse landscape.

It took her about an hour and a half to reach the river. She shaved off thirty minutes by going a different route that she scoped when perched on the ledge earlier. One of the interesting things she discovered was that the jungle was filled with poisonous trees. The PSD had warned her of that when she scanned them on her way through. It would explain why there were so few animals. Even insects were rare other than an annoying insect that reminded her of a fly. She was sure that she had touched some of the trees on the way through, but did not feel or see anything that would indicate she had a rash. Maybe the nanobots had protected her. She looked across the river as she took off her pants. There was no need to go over there. Ever.

The brown river was as she remembered it. Fast flowing and decently wide. It had a strong odor, which was something she did not notice her first pass through.

She drank several times using the purifying container and then stepped into the river. The strong current pushed firmly against her as she relieved herself. She spent the next few hours sitting next to a set of rocks where her pants were. With the two suns beating down, it did not take long for her to dry off.

She headed back to the enclosure and sat outside, dangling her legs off the side. The light breeze calmed her, but her morale was tumbling. With nothing to do but wait, she pulled out the PSD and browsed through the survival section.

The videos section caught her eye. They covered everything from basic tips to fighting techniques. She smiled as she saw Evaran going through them and showing examples in the holo room. How did he have the time to do all these? Or did he do them for someone else previously?

Most of the day went by as she studied the videos on the PSD. Evaran had even added one on the recent food and purifying container features. She had a brief moment of joy when first hearing Evaran's somewhat emotionless voice. If she was going to be alone while she waited, these videos could occupy her time.

Later that night, around 9:00 p.m., she hunkered down in the enclosure. With two rocks holding the PSD back against the wall and pointing toward the open doorway and window, she activated the shield. It initially shot out a small square shield. One of the videos explained how to extend the shield and shape it. She was not sure she fully understood some of what was being shown, but she was able to extend the shield to the front wall, and expand it to touch the floor and almost the ceiling. A small slit near the top allowed air in.

She snuggled into the corner, satisfied with her setup. Looking through the shield out into the night, she wondered what Dr. Snowden, Evaran, and V were up to. A lump formed in her throat as she cried herself to sleep.

Two weeks later, she had a routine down. Trips to the river were done in the morning and at dusk. She spent half the day exploring her immediate area and the other half learning from the videos.

The loneliness ate at her but did not make itself really felt until she was secured for the night. Several times she had panic attacks, thinking maybe the Torvatta could not come here and this was it. Maybe they were unable to come because they were dead. She fought these thoughts, but as each day passed, the sinking feeling that something was wrong grew stronger.

Another week later and even the routine was failing to keep the loneliness at bay. She tried to find anything to keep her mind off the situation, but hopelessness was beginning to set in.

On the last day of the week, the blaring horn sound that had announced her arrival earlier rang out. She was sitting by the rocks near the river at the time and almost jumped out of her skin. After putting on her clothes in record time, she hustled to the stepped pyramid, only to see a young man being devoured by the shelled creatures she had run into when she first arrived. Although she could not help the man, it was a brief light of hope that maybe she would not have to be alone if she could help the next one. When that would be, though, she did not know.

Although she did not want to go back to the stepped pyramid, she did over the previous weeks. The creatures she had run into earlier were in large mounds around a tree not too far away. It seemed the blaring horn brought them in, like a dinner bell. They did not bother her during her trips, as she was careful to be as quiet as possible. If they had, she knew she could outrun them if given a head start.

She spent her time there studying the podium. The blue dot on the map intrigued her. It was like a beacon. When she touched it, it showed a picture of a humanoid race with dinner-plate-shaped heads and black eyes on the underside, smiling, eating, and drinking. Whatever the place was, it had to be better than the cliffs. The green dots between the yellow dot, representing the stepped pyramid, and the blue dot appeared to be facilities of some type. The function of them was not obvious to her.

She had taken a picture of the map with her PSD and was able to calculate distances by establishing how far away her enclosure was. How accurate the numbers were was another question to solve, but even if they gave a rough approximation, she had an idea of how far away the blue dot was. It was approximately 150 miles away. The nearest green dot was ten miles north of her enclosure.

After another week, the decision to head to the green dot had become her focus. Sleeping was an issue for her. The loneliness that assaulted her increased to the point that it physically made her sick. She needed to do something to jolt her out of the state of despair she was circling into. The thought that maybe the blue dot would have some answers on where she was enticed her. Maybe there would be a way out as well.

After a morning dip, she rinsed her clothes in the running water and relaxed as they dried. She stayed on the banks a bit longer than she normally did, and when her clothes were dry, she headed back toward the enclosure.

Looking up at the place that she had called her safe spot for almost a month, she debated leaving again. Leaving felt like she was giving up hope on a rescue, and that thought clung to her mind. She shook her head and took off.

After several hours of traversing, the cliffs ended at a large body of water. She scaled the cliff, ripping her pants and shirt. The cliff top was not large, and after thirty minutes, she reached the northern edge.

Looking down, she could see a massive, flat forest. Far off in the distance, the forest appeared to get hilly before running into a mountain. She imagined the green dots popping up with signs pointing her toward the blue dot.

With a grimace, she scaled down the cliff and headed toward the forest edge. She ran her hand along the fractured dirt on the ground, noting that it had an unusual smell that reminded her of vinegar. It could have been the sporadic clumps of grass nearby producing it, but she was not sure.

With determination in her eyes, she set off. When she was several hundred feet from the forest, she heard the sound of something thudding her way. When she turned toward the sound, she froze.

A massive, overmuscled humanoid charged toward her. It had mottled brown skin, a ram-horned head, digitigrade legs, and sharp claws on its hands and feet.

She took off running but could hear it gaining on her. The cliffs were not too far away. She hoped it could not climb. When she got to the cliff, she began to scramble her way up it. She paused to look down when she was twenty or so feet off the ground. Her eyes widened as the creature launched into the air toward her.

"No!" said Emily.

She hung with one arm as she tried to aim her PSD at the incoming creature. The impact of the creature washed over her like a tidal wave, causing her to drop her PSD. On the periphery of her vision, time slowed down as she saw the cliff wall approach her face. She struggled to breathe. The foul smell of something she could not identify engulfed her. A tingling sensation shot through her face as it hit the rocks.

Her eyes closed.

07

Dr. Snowden followed Evaran and the others back to the Torvatta after leaving Joktan's office. He scowled as his hopes evaporated in that maybe the Helians would step in and help. They acted like they did not care. If anything was going to be done, it was up to him, Evaran, V, and Lord Vygon. He sighed and shook his head.

They had walked most of the way back to the landing pad when Evaran tilted his head.

"I hear it too," said Lord Vygon, narrowing his eyes.

Dr. Snowden crooked his head and heard clanging sounds and men shouting in the distance.

Evaran flashed two fingers forward. "V, go."

"Acknowledged."

Evaran pulled off a remote viewing orb from his belt and tossed it in front of him.

The orb shot up a projection of the city as V flew over it. When he got to the landing pads, it showed a battle between a swarm of sentinels and Helians taking place. The bubble shield was gone, and several landing pads had been captured by sentinels.

"You've gotta be kidding me . . . ," said Dr. Snowden. He noticed that the sentinels were teleporting in on top of a circular pattern at the end of the landing pads. There were multiple patterns established, and the sentinels were coming in fast.

Evaran studied the projection. "This attack appears to be well coordinated. Notice their movement. They must be able to communicate somehow without speaking. I suspect the crystals are involved."

Lord Vygon shook his arms forward, causing his forearm blades to pop out.

Evaran ushered Dr. Snowden to a nearby office. "You need to wait here."

"Why? I can help."

Evaran stared at Dr. Snowden.

Fine . . . ," said Dr. Snowden with a sigh. "You think I might lose control and do something crazy."

"I just want you to be safe," said Evaran.

Dr. Snowden drooped his head as he stepped into the office.

Evaran waved at the office door. The remote viewing orb floated into the office with Dr. Snowden. Evaran tapped at his ARI, causing the hologram projection to change to the view from Evaran's chest.

It reminded Dr. Snowden of when they were escaping the docking bay on the Krotovore ship when they first met Evaran. It allowed him and Emily to see what was going on without being in harm's way. He took a seat in a nearby chair and threw an arm into the air. "Go."

Evaran placed his UIC on the office door console and locked the door.

Dr. Snowden watched the hologram projection as it showed Evaran and Lord Vygon head off toward the landing pad. Sentinels were everywhere. The Helians responded with a mass of guards. Laser fire erupted from the Helians, and the sentinels unleashed a barrage of bolts. The sentinels were also using their daggers in melee range and swords he had not seen on them before. It seemed they did not want to teleport, they were here to kill.

He admired the way Evaran and Lord Vygon seemed to work together intuitively in combat. Evaran would lead and provide cover while Lord Vygon cleaned up behind him. They fought as a team, and it was effective. Dr. Snowden did not see V anywhere. Maybe he was flying above stealthed. Dr. Snowden wondered why V was not in robot mode out fighting.

Lord Vygon intrigued Dr. Snowden in that he never verified Emily's presence in the future, but he suspected she was there. He recalled how Lord Vygon jerked his head back when they first met, as if in surprise that Emily had smiled. Dr. Snowden's heart sank. What would make Emily stop smiling? He could not bear the thought of her being unhappy. Lord Vygon probably had answers, but they were not available to Dr. Snowden. Still, the thought that Lord Vygon might know of a future Emily comforted him.

Over the course of the next few hours, sentinel after sentinel continued to drop, but more appeared to replace them. With support from Evaran and Lord Vygon, the Helian guard made headway, but for every small victory, there was tremendous loss. A thought occurred to Dr. Snowden that if Evaran were not here, this fight would have been over much quicker, and not in the Helians' favor. The Helians were not going to win this fight, even with Evaran and the technological advantage.

His attention was drawn to the medium-sized transparent window. Outside it stood a sentinel that stared in.

Dr. Snowden's face turned red as his eyebrows angled down. He raised his head a bit and stared down the sentinel. When the sentinel moved, Dr. Snowden stood up and pulled out his PSD. He set the repulsion blast as his first button and focused on the door.

The sentinel disappeared from view for a moment. Muffled sounds emerged from the door as the sentinel tried to get in.

Thump!

Then there was silence.

Dr. Snowden clenched his jaw with his thumb hovering over the repulsion blast button on his PSD. Sweat rolled down the side of his face.

The door unlocked, and Evaran stepped through.

Dr. Snowden let out a deep breath.

"Come. We must go. Now!" said Evaran, gesturing for Dr. Snowden to leave.

Dr. Snowden hustled out the door. His eyes popped open at the swarming mass of sentinels not too far off in the distance. "So . . . uhh . . . what's the plan?"

Evaran directed Dr. Snowden toward the Torvatta, which sat in an open plaza. "We are leaving. The city is lost."

Dr. Snowden ran toward the Torvatta, where he saw Lord Vygon and V, in body mode, fighting off sentinels.

Once everyone was on board, the Torvatta lifted off. They assembled in the command area.

"V, take us up and stealth," said Evaran.

"Acknowledged."

Dr. Snowden wrinkled his eyebrows. "Is it that bad?"

"Yes. V estimates there are over one thousand sentinels attacking the city, with more coming in. We do not have the means to defeat them all."

"You and Lord Vygon seemed to have no problem with them back at his base."

"That was just a handful. We need help, and fast," said Lord Vygon.

"So uhh . . . I thought there was like . . . one hundred and twelve or something."

"That's what the sentinel we captured thought," said Lord Vygon. "Apparently . . . he was wrong. Misinformation. Not a bad tactic."

"I thought they had to answer truthfully under your hypnotic gaze thing."

"He probably did. I meant he was fed misinformation on purpose. Maybe that is the Purifier way."

Dr. Snowden snorted. "Go figure. Are there any nonhumans that could help?"

"No . . . sadly," said Lord Vygon. He paused and extended a finger. "Actually . . ." He shook his head. "No . . . I thought maybe . . ."

Dr. Snowden circled a hand in front of him.

"Maybe another ancient vampire house and the Ollikrin, but convincing them to help would take some time. They like to take their time on big decisions, especially ones that might involve the death of their group members."

Dr. Snowden squared his shoulders. "We're time travelers. Why can't we go back in time, talk to them, let them take their time deciding, and then pick them up at this point?" He glanced at Evaran. "Like we did before with the lost Arkaron crystal. Get something we need from the past to use in the present."

Evaran narrowed his eyes as he studied Dr. Snowden. "An intriguing proposal. However, since they would know of the attack, they could change the timeline."

Lord Vygon shook his head. "Talking to just the leaders could minimize any timeline interference. I trust both of them."

Evaran eyed Lord Vygon. "You could run into your previous self, or have your previous self gain knowledge that might affect the current state of the timeline."

"Well . . . I wouldn't run into myself if it was far back enough."

"Elaborate."

"I awoke two years ago. Five years of sleep prior to that. If we went back three years, I couldn't run into myself because I would still be sleeping. My other self, that is."

"Do you think you can convince these groups to help?" asked Evaran. "We would need quite a few."

Lord Vygon nodded. "They each control a sizable group. It's worth a shot. I won't guarantee anything, though."

"It is decided then. V, take us back three years and keep us in low-Earth orbit."

"Acknowledged."

The Torvatta ascended to low-Earth orbit.

Lord Vygon's eyes lit up as he watched the outside disappear, then reappear. "I never get tired of that."

Evaran eyed Lord Vygon. "So you *have* time traveled in the Torvatta."

"Quite a few times."

"I see," said Evaran. "We are now back three years in time. Where should we head first?"

The Torvatta streaked over a forest in the northwestern part of North America. Dr. Snowden watched as vast forests rolled out under them. From space, it had only taken about a half hour to get there. He was more at ease now after rationalizing that Emily was not dead. Maybe she was and he had misinterpreted Lord Vygon's initial reaction to seeing Emily, but his gut told him otherwise.

"Whom are we seeking?" asked Evaran.

"The Ollikrin Nation. Mixed group of nonhumans. They're led by Delia Everoak, an ancient tree shifter and one of the oldest nonhumans I know of. She's not one to rush into anything, or someone you want to be on bad terms with," said Lord Vygon.

Dr. Snowden remembered Shandra Everoak mentioning Delia before as the first Everoak, and now he would get to meet her. He glanced at Evaran.

Evaran narrowed his eyes. "Interesting. How will you convince her to help?"

Lord Vygon shook his head. "I'll be honest and explain the situation. I know you don't like showing the future to others . . . but it would really help if you showed some visuals. Maybe of the sentinel, and from V's scan of the city being attacked."

Evaran rubbed his chin for a moment. "In this case, that may be okay. We will need to talk to her privately. If we are successful, then from the point in time we left Atlantis, they would already have assembled somewhere and just need picked up."

Dr. Snowden wrinkled his eyebrows. "So why don't we go forward in time and just pick them up?"

Evaran shook his head. "The timeline needs to be updated. This part still needs to occur in order to set that up, and there is no guarantee they will help. If we went there now, there would be no one there since this part has not happened."

"I thought the future already existed, though."

"It does, but we must respect the sequence of events. This event is tied to them either being there or not. If this event does not occur, then the timeline will not update with them there if they decide to help."

Dr. Snowden shook his head with raised eyebrows.

Lord Vygon laughed. "Ahh . . . the brain-twisting aspects of time-travel. Can't say I missed it."

"We are approaching the designated coordinates," said V.

"Excellent. Set us down and disengage stealth," said Evaran.

"Acknowledged."

Evaran faced Lord Vygon. "I assume you know how to get in contact with them."

Dr. Snowden watched Lord Vygon fidget in his seat. The small facial movements seemed to fight a grimace from appearing.

"The Ollikrin will know we are there," said Lord Vygon.

"Very well."

The Torvatta landed in a grassy field next to a forest. They exited the Torvatta and stood outside the shield.

After five minutes of waiting, Dr. Snowden put his hand on his neck. The smell of the forest was pleasant, but the unusual silence made his nerves tighten. The forest seemed larger than what he remembered from pictures. "So . . . are we supposed to be looking for something?"

Lord Vygon raised a finger. "Just wait."

After another ten minutes, two massive bearlike humanoids walked out of the forest. Their fur was brown, and they stood around ten feet tall. A light armor made of wood chunks covered parts of their bodies. Their hands and feet had large claws, and along with fearsome short snouts, they presented an image that made Dr. Snowden shudder. He remembered Evaran mentioning werebears before, and assuming that was what these were, he could see why any alien trying to abduct them would have had problems.

Evaran motioned forward at V in orb mode. "V, scout mode."

"Acknowledged. Scout mode engaged," said V as he shimmered, then flew off into the distance toward the werebears.

"They're just investigating," said Lord Vygon. "As an ancient vampire, they would be able to detect me easily."

"I hope they're friendly," said Dr. Snowden with raised eyebrows.

"The Ollikrin are not usually aggressive, but provoke them, and you will know their strength. They typically surround themselves with like-minded individuals, so it's not uncommon to see a wide variety of nonhumans, and even humans, among their numbers."

"I see," said Evaran as he perused his ARI. "V says there are others in the forest studying us. We should proceed forward."

After arriving in front of the werebears, Lord Vygon raised his head. "I am the ancient vampire Lord Vygon. I come seeking the counsel of Delia Everoak."

The first werebear walked up to Lord Vygon and sniffed around. In a deep growling voice, it said, "Who're the others?"

Lord Vygon gestured toward Evaran. "This is Evaran, a friend of mine, and to his left is Dr. Albert Snowden, another friend. They possess information that will be needed during counsel."

The first werebear glanced back at the other one standing near the forest. The second werebear walked up and sniffed around.

The first werebear focused on Evaran. "What are you?"

"I am a traveler," said Evaran, pointing up.

The werebears stepped back and roared.

Dr. Snowden's eyes popped open. "Uhh . . . what's happening?"

Lord Vygon raised a hand. "Wait! He may not be from this planet, but he is not associated with the black-clothed humans you've probably been seeing. That's why we're here actually. Please, we just want to talk to Delia."

The werebears stopped roaring and stepped back and to the side. They knelt facing each other as a large tree slid toward them out of the forest. Standing more than thirty feet tall, it towered over them. Vines swirled around the branches. A face etched on the main trunk had yellow eyes, and the mouth was just an opening.

Dr. Snowden gulped as he stood behind Evaran.

The tree paused as it scanned them. After another moment, it shifted down into an older woman with light-brown skin and green eyes. She had green hair that flowed down her back. Pieces of wood rose on her upper arms and legs, and a sleeveless robe made of patches of foliage hung off her shoulders. Vines swirled around her body like snakes hunting a meal.

Dr. Snowden averted his eyes as the woman approached them, with both werebears to her sides. Others had emerged from the forest as well. It was like the forest had come alive. Various small tree shifters appeared along with other animal shifters. The owl ones made his skin crawl.

Lord Vygon knelt, causing Evaran and Dr. Snowden to kneel.

"Excuse my personal bodyguard. These are dire times, and aliens aren't exactly welcomed here with open arms," said the woman. "I am Delia Everoak, matriarch and leader of the

Ollikrin Nation, protector of these lands. Why do you wish counsel, ancient vampire?"

Lord Vygon rose with the others and then stepped forward. "There is a threat that I believe impacts all non-humans. You may have already seen the scouts of these new enemies. They take the form of men in black clothes and have a crystal embedded in their heads."

"We have seen them," said Delia. "They shoot at us with beams of light, and those they hit disappear. However, they do not survive for long in this forest. We have killed every one of them that has entered."

"Yes . . . we've had someone close to us disappear as well," said Lord Vygon, glancing at Dr. Snowden. He faced Delia. "I know you don't care for the Helians, but their city was attacked by these men. They won't survive unless I can bring others to help defend it. If they go down, we're all in danger."

"We can defend ourselves should that come to pass. The Helians only seek to control. Perhaps this is their reckoning."

Lord Vygon sighed and glanced at Evaran.

Evaran narrowed his eyes. "Before I bring up my points, may I request that we speak privately?"

Delia studied Evaran, then raised her arm off to the side at a ninety-degree angle. The assembled group behind her faded back into the forest, along with the werebears. After they had departed, she focused on Evaran. "Your wish has been granted . . . time traveler."

Evaran glanced at Dr. Snowden then Lord Vygon before returning his gaze on Delia. "It would seem I am no stranger to you."

"You're not. As one of the oldest nonhumans on this planet, your journeys through time have not gone unnoticed, and I suspect what you're about to tell me involves it to some degree."

"You are very perceptive," said Evaran with a nod. He cleared his throat. "We are from three years in the future. However," he said, gesturing at Dr. Snowden, "Dr. Snowden and I came from roughly four thousand years in the future prior to that."

Dr. Snowden expected Delia to be surprised, but instead, she just smiled. He thought it was interesting that Delia knew of Evaran. Given that Lord Vygon did as well, he wondered how many other powerful nonhumans knew of Evaran's adventures in Earth's past.

"And you felt it necessary to come back here, to enlist our aid to stop these men?" asked Delia.

"Yes. The Human Dominion, also known as the Purifiers, is here now, in the past, removing threats prior to consolidating power. Once they are in power, they will use superior technology to hunt and kill you. In the future of this current timeline, I rescued the last of your kind, your granddaughter actually. She fought these Purifiers in a losing battle," said Evaran.

Delia raised her head a bit and eyed Evaran. "The last . . ."

Evaran nodded. "She was brave and fought well. I have a video of her if you wish to see it. It would not affect the timeline since if this is corrected, she would never have existed, at least in that incarnation."

Delia nodded.

"V, show the recording from my chest during the last fight with the Purifiers on the Saturn station."

V shimmered into view and flew in front of Evaran. "Acknowledged."

Delia took a step back.

Evaran extended a hand. "I apologize. No deception was intended. V is my friend and can show you."

Delia studied V for a moment, then nodded and gestured for Evaran to continue.

V shot down a projection showing Shandra in tree form fighting the Purifiers. It showed her getting hit and then reverting to a human form. Then it displayed Evaran ordering Miles to carry her away.

"Did she . . ."

"No. I healed her back to health. The one carrying her is a Wildborn, and also her husband. She kept the Everoak name, though."

Delia looked down for a moment as her eyes misted, then back up at Evaran. "How do you know these men here now are Purifiers?"

"We captured one in an earlier encounter. This is from three years in the future at Lord Vygon's base. V, display our meeting."

"Acknowledged," said V.

A projection shot out showing the discussion in Lord Vygon's base with the sentinel.

Delia frowned as she watched it. When it was over, she clenched her teeth. "So these sentinels . . . are sending our kind to a prison."

Evaran nodded. "Yes. This is the next day on Atlantis. V, show Atlantis."

"Acknowledged," said V.

The projection showed Atlantis being swarmed by the sentinels from their earlier encounter.

Delia's eyes widened as she watched over the next few moments. "So many . . ."

"Their numbers are formidable, and even though their technology is low-tech compared to the Helians, their ranged weaponry is quite powerful. We are asking for your aid to help even the odds. There may be some casualties, but the stakes are high. All we would ask is that you assemble a group here, in three years from this exact day, to help defend Atlantis. Once Atlantis is secured, we would then assault the Purifiers' main base."

Delia cocked her head. "That's a big request. I will need to confer with our internal council."

Lord Vygon nodded. "We figured as much. That's why we came into the past, instead of from where we were in time."

"You were wise to do so," said Delia.

"Wasn't my idea," said Lord Vygon. He pointed at Dr. Snowden. "It was his."

Delia scanned Dr. Snowden, who looked down. "A human . . . with machines in him." She stood in front of Dr. Snowden and caressed his face with a vine that snaked out from her body. "You're in great pain."

Dr. Snowden swallowed hard as his eyes watered. "They took my niece."

Delia smiled. "You care for her a great deal, I can feel that." She tilted her head. "She was human, though."

Dr. Snowden nodded. He was not sure how she could see or feel it, but a sense of calmness washed over him in Delia's presence. Her acceptance of the evidence presented did not surprise him. She seemed to know things beyond the visual.

Evaran put a hand on Dr. Snowden's shoulder. "They probably sensed the machines in Emily and classified her as a nonhuman."

One of Delia's vines lightly squeezed Dr. Snowden's arm. "I'm sorry to hear that."

Dr. Snowden exhaled as he half smiled at Delia.

Delia stepped back and eyed Evaran. "I will bring it up to the council. You can check back here in three years' time to know our answer. We may have some concessions if we agree to help, though."

Evaran nodded. "That is fair. I would suggest you tell your internal council that if they help, a new global council will be formed, and the Ollikrin Nation will be one of its founders."

Delia half smiled. "A powerful concession. I will mention it."

"Thank you for your counsel," said Lord Vygon with a bow.

Dr. Snowden wiped his eyes and bowed. After Evaran bowed as well, they headed back to the Torvatta.

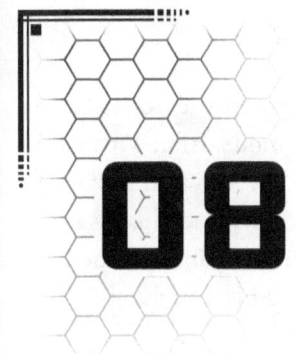

08

Several hours later, the Torvatta touched down on a beach. The front right screen showed a view from above of a large body of water in southeastern Russia.

"So . . . where are we and who're we contacting?" asked Dr. Snowden as he studied the map. The thought that time was slipping by every moment was not lost on him. He understood why they were gathering help, but thinking of Emily and what she must be going through made him sweat.

"In your time, this is known as Lake Baikal, the largest freshwater lake in the world. As to whom we seek, I defer to Lord Vygon," said Evaran.

Lord Vygon nodded. "We're looking for Lord Noskov, one of four ancient vampires in the world, including me."

"I know him," said Evaran, tilting his head. "He was quite helpful."

Lord Vygon snorted. "Well . . . then you must have met him in the future. He's a bit . . . rough. This will not be easy. Let me do the talking."

"Very well. Shall we proceed?"

Lord Vygon nodded, and they all exited the Torvatta. Evaran motioned for V to go into scout mode. After V took off, Lord Vygon gestured for Evaran and Dr. Snowden to stay where they were as he stepped forward and closed his eyes. He placed both hands on the sides of his head in an arched position, with the fingertips at the top and his thumbs at the base of his jaw.

Dr. Snowden looked around. He was not sure what Lord Vygon was doing but figured it must be some type of communication. A light breeze massaged Dr. Snowden's skin, and the smell of the lake washed over him. He could see a gently sloped grass hill off to the right with sporadic groupings of trees on it. The beach did not extend far inland before meeting up with a forest. Forests and nonhumans seemed to go together, but it made sense to him if they were hiding out. If this were not such a pressing situation, it would be a place he could relax in.

His attention focused on the four blurs of motion that appeared before him. These were definitely vampires. He had come to understand their movement, and although he could not tell exactly the type of nonhuman, the movement of various types was becoming familiar. Vampires seemed to move in a blur, and when standing still, it was like their movements were stuttered. The first vampire in front of the other three moved faster and had on some type of bone armor, with fur filling in the gaps. A fur cape fell behind him. He had pale skin, black eyes with no white in them, and short black hair. The others wore similar outfits but were less pronounced.

Lord Vygon lowered his hands, opened his eyes, and nodded at the lead vampire. "Lord Noskov."

Lord Noskov dipped his head. "Lord Vygon."

"I come to you with my friends Evaran and Dr. Albert Snowden," said Lord Vygon. "We have some things to discuss . . . in private."

Lord Noskov walked up to Evaran and looked him over. He then did the same to Dr. Snowden. "They look human . . . but they aren't."

"Umm . . . I'm human," said Dr. Snowden with raised eyebrows.

Lord Noskov snapped his head toward Dr. Snowden. "You can understand the ancient vampire language . . . impressive. You look human, but don't smell like it. You smell toxic, like metal." He walked back to his group and faced Lord Vygon. "I thought you were sleeping?"

"I am," said Lord Vygon. "It's . . . a bit complicated."

Lord Noskov studied Lord Vygon, then snorted. He waved his hand in the air, and the other three vampires took off back to the forest. "You have my attention."

Lord Vygon nodded. "Let me start by asking if you've seen any men in black clothes with a crystal embedded in their heads."

Lord Noskov smirked. "Seen them . . . yes . . . and killed them with ease. They come into our forest with staffs that shoot beams of light. Sometimes they use poisoned bolts." He waved a hand in the air. "Haven't seen one in a while, though. I think they learned not to mess with House Noskov."

"Did you talk to any of them before killing them?"

Lord Noskov chuckled.

"Yeah . . . I figured not. We captured one at my base and recorded our conversation with it," said Lord Vygon. He glanced at Evaran.

Evaran nodded. "V, display the meeting."

V shimmered into view. "Acknowledged."

Lord Noskov recoiled and hissed. He pointed at V. "What is that thing?"

"I am a variable utility artificial intelligence orb. My shortened name is V."

"What?"

"V is my friend," said Lord Vygon. "Yes, he's a machine, but it's—"

"Complicated . . ."

Lord Vygon nodded. "Right. There's nothing to fear from him. Go ahead, V."

"Acknowledged," said V. He projected the meeting with the sentinel at Lord Vygon's base.

Lord Noskov studied the projection.

Dr. Snowden wondered why so many nonhumans seemed to be comfortable with advanced technology when explained. The Helians must have acclimated most of them to it was his thought. The holographic projection did not seem to bother Lord Noskov, but the presence of V startled him, so maybe there were some limitations on what they knew to be possible. It was a topic he looked forward to discussing with Lord Vygon at some point, and a welcome distraction from the constant panic he felt at the edges of his mind when thinking of Emily.

"So they're attacking nonhumans," said Lord Noskov. "Why does this concern me? They've been easy to handle so far."

"Atlantis has been attacked and is about to fall," said Lord Vygon. "We need help in defending it. Delia Everoak of the Ollikrin Nation is considering lending her aid to the effort. It's a chance for nonhumans that aren't Helians to become part of the global community."

"The Ollikrin? Last time I encountered them, they tried to kill me . . ."

Lord Vygon bobbed his head. "Well . . . you do have a bounty on your head for . . . what you did."

"It was justifiable," said Lord Noskov with narrowed eyes. "Besides, even if I agreed, it would take time to get there."

Lord Vygon bobbed his head. "It wouldn't. This is where it gets complicated. We are from three years in the future."

"What?"

"Right now, there are two of me," said Lord Vygon. "One is sleeping at my base, the other is me, here, right now, except I'm from the future."

"Time travel is not possible," said Lord Noskov.

"You'll have to take my word for it," said Lord Vygon. "I know you'd rather kill Helians than help them, but if you agree to help . . . I'll stand with you in having the bounty from the Helians retracted."

Evaran tilted his head. "If it helps, I will as well."

Lord Noskov snapped his head toward Evaran. "I don't know what weight you carry. It's none with me."

"For now. That will change."

Lord Noskov narrowed his eyes. "I'll consider it." He looked at Lord Vygon. "For now, brother, join me for an early dinner. It's been too long since I've seen another ancient."

Lord Vygon glanced at Evaran and Dr. Snowden, who nodded. "Lead on."

They followed Lord Noskov into the forest. Dr. Snowden rubbed the goose bumps on his arm as the clouded sky caused the forest to take on a more sinister look. The smells of the damp woodlands washed over him. He could see a fire in the distance, with various blurs moving around it. Dr. Snowden had imagined Lord Noskov's base would be a cave similar to Lord Vygon's, but maybe with a bounty out on Lord Noskov, it was best to be mobile.

After ten more minutes of trudging through the forest, they arrived at Lord Noskov's base. A pit fire raged with various wooden tables and chairs around it. Dr. Snowden noticed that most of the vampires had on similar outfits to the three they had met on the beach. One in particular stood out to him. It was a bald-headed man with just his lower half covered. He towered over the others and sat in silence scrutinizing Dr. Snowden, Evaran, and Lord Vygon. The hair on the back of Dr. Snowden's neck stood up. He was surrounded by killers.

Lord Noskov gestured for them to take seats next to him at a large table. After sitting, Lord Noskov clapped his hands. The big vampire Dr. Snowden had seen before disappeared for a moment, then came back out leading a naked man with his hands tied. The vampire pushed the man down in front of the fire. Lord Noskov nodded, and the vampire pulled out a sharpened blade.

Evaran stood up. "I invoke the house challenge."

A silence spread across the camp.

"For what?" asked Lord Noskov.

"I cannot let you kill that man in my presence," said Evaran, pointing to the man in front of the fire.

Lord Noskov and the other vampires burst into laughter. "And you want to . . . invoke the house challenge . . . for that? Tell me . . . what do *you* know about the challenge?"

"I can issue a challenge to a house. The house allows for the request to be granted if the house lord, or his champion, can be defeated in hand-to-hand combat," said Evaran.

Lord Noskov glanced at Lord Vygon. "Did you tell him of this?"

"No, I didn't."

"Where'd you hear this?" asked Lord Noskov, staring at Evaran.

"From someone far in the future," said Evaran.

Lord Noskov jerked his head back. He studied Evaran for a moment, then leaned forward with his gaze focused on Evaran's eyes. With a tilt of his head, and in a deep voice, he said, "You don't want to fight me . . ."

Evaran half grinned. "Your hypnotic gaze, while effective on most, will not work on me."

Lord Noskov rubbed his chin as he studied Evaran. "That's . . . interesting . . . Well then. Since you seem to know of the rule, then you know only an ancient can issue it to another ancient."

Lord Vygon half smiled. "Consider it from me, on Evaran's behalf."

Lord Noskov paused as he scrutinized Lord Vygon. "Very well. You shall have your house challenge. I will assume you know of the no-weapons rule."

Evaran nodded and then handed his utility handle to Dr. Snowden.

Lord Noskov gestured to the right, and the vampires on the right moved back. With a motion to the left, the left side stood back. He extended his hand toward the fire. "I will deal with this personally. I've never lost a fight. Your death will be quick."

Evaran narrowed his eyes as he went to the open area in front of the fire.

Lord Vygon shook his head.

"Worried?" asked Lord Noskov with a smile, revealing two sharp fangs.

"Not about Evaran . . ."

Lord Noskov laughed.

The man who had been brought out to be sliced up was moved to the side.

Dr. Snowden swallowed hard. He knew Evaran was tough, but Lord Noskov looked menacing. Some of the fights Evaran had been in were with tough individuals, but Evaran had the advantage of his gadgets and preparation to even the odds, or a group around him. He was not as sure as Lord Vygon was.

Lord Noskov circled Evaran, who turned to face him. Lord Noskov reached out with his right arm to grab Evaran. Evaran grabbed Lord Noskov's wrist and yanked down hard. Lord Noskov flew to the ground. He shook his head as he stood. With a growl, he slashed out with his now-clawed hands. Evaran caught Lord Noskov's arm. He pulled him forward while jumping over him. When Evaran was halfway down, he kicked Lord Noskov in the back. Lord Noskov sprawled to the earth.

Lord Noskov got back up and grunted. He charged, but then stopped when Evaran jumped over him. Lord Noskov reached up. He grabbed Evaran's ankles and slammed him to the ground. Evaran winced. Lord Noskov jumped on Evaran and in a flurry of blows shredded Evaran's chest. Evaran reacted by grabbing Lord Noskov's right wrist, then his left wrist. With a concentrated effort, Evaran moved Lord Noskov's hands up, then rolled over.

Evaran, now on top, spread Lord Noskov's arms to the side and held him down. "Submit."

"Never!" said Lord Noskov.

Evaran released his grip on Lord Noskov's wrists and rolled forward. Lord Noskov scrambled to get up, and Evaran took up an opposite position. Evaran flattened his hands as Lord Noskov approached in a blur of motion, moving erratically from side to side. When Lord Noskov reached him, Evaran struck the inside of Lord Noskov's right forearm. *Snap!* With a motion to the left, Evaran hit Lord Noskov's inside left forearm. *Snap!* In a flash, Evaran kicked Lord

Noskov's right knee. *Snap!* With another kick, Evaran struck Lord Noskov's left knee. *Snap!*

Lord Noskov fell to the ground and cried out in pain.

Evaran knelt beside Lord Noskov's head. "Submit."

"Never!" said Lord Noskov in a strained voice.

Evaran shook his head. "I cannot accept that. I have need of your service later. You will heal." He stood up and panned the hushed group. "By right of the victor, I claim this fight over and allow the house lord to live." While pointing to the naked man who was to be dinner, he said, "That man will come with us."

Lord Noskov rolled to his side and, with the help of some of his group, sat up. He spit blood while squinting. "Fine . . . you've ruined dinner anyways."

Evaran waved his hand off to the side for the naked man to come over to him. "If you agree to help us, then in three years from this day, gather your men where we first met and prepare for a fight."

Lord Noskov paused as he studied Evaran. He glanced at Lord Vygon and Dr. Snowden, then turned his head toward Evaran. "I'll think about it."

"It's all we ask," said Evaran. He gestured at Dr. Snowden. "My utility handle, please."

Dr. Snowden tossed it over to Evaran.

Evaran caught it midair and extended his utility handle into a baton. The naked man crumpled to the ground as Evaran's baton, with a glowing blue end, touched him. Evaran slung the man over his shoulder and gestured back to the Torvatta. "We are done here."

After dropping off the unconscious naked man at a nearby village, the Torvatta jumped three years into the future to five thirty in the morning on the day they initially left. Evaran sat in his command chair, Lord Vygon in the left seating area, Dr. Snowden in the right seating area, and V on the front console.

"V, stealth mode, then take us down to where we met Delia. We need to be careful to not be detected by ourselves," said Evaran.

"Acknowledged."

Dr. Snowden thought it was interesting that they came back two and a half hours before they had left to go into the past. Their previous selves would be at Lord Vygon's base. His other self would be waking up in thirty minutes in a cave room. Since they were going to be in different areas, maybe it would not be too much of an issue. Based on what Evaran said, the Torvatta in stealth mode must have made it invisible even to itself.

The Torvatta stealthed and headed to the Pacific Northwest, where they initially met the Ollikrin. As the Torvatta descended, the sensors picked up a mass of people near the landing area. The Torvatta touched down, and they exited it.

Dr. Snowden jerked his head back as he scanned the assembled crowd behind Delia. He guessed there was about a hundred or so. There were various packs of werebears, werewolves, owl shifters, tree shifters, and other shifter types he did not recognize. They wore various types of bone and stone armor in a patchwork manner. This was a tough-looking group. Several Native Americans were in the group as well. He wondered if they were Wildborn. Several of the assembled were huge versions of animals instead of a shifted humanoid form. His heartbeat raced a bit upon seeing the large crows.

Delia walked up to them.

Evaran bowed. "It is good to see you. It appears you have made your decision."

Delia nodded. "You have our support. After this is over, the balance of power will for once be an actual balance." She glanced at the Torvatta. "How are we all going to fit in there?"

Evaran half smiled. "You will see. Everyone will need to be in humanoid form. V will show you where to go." He glanced at Dr. Snowden. "Would you mind helping?"

Dr. Snowden nodded. "Sure." He smiled for the first time in long while. Something about Delia made him at ease, as if her mere presence demanded calm. He hoped to spend more time getting to know her.

Delia circled her hand in the air, and the crowd around her transformed into humanoid forms. She followed V and Dr. Snowden into the Torvatta. Her group lined up behind her and followed her in. Evaran had transformed the holo room into a larger version of the conference room. There were multiple tables with replicators scattered about at the end of the tables. In the back of the room were various doors. Dr. Snowden assumed those were bathrooms. It did not take long for the Ollikrin to board.

Once they were ready to depart, Delia took a seat next to Lord Vygon in the command area. She glanced at Evaran. "Your ship is quite impressive. That room should not exist, yet it does. I have seen alien ships before, but this is new. I'm unfamiliar with this technology."

Dr. Snowden half grinned. "Dimensional mechanics, and yeah . . . it takes a bit to get used to."

Delia looked at Dr. Snowden. "It would be very useful for many situations."

Dr. Snowden nodded.

Delia faced Evaran. "So, to Atlantis now?"

Evaran shook his head. "We have another group to pick up."

"Who?"

Lord Vygon cast a sidelong glance at Delia. "House Noskov."

Delia narrowed her eyes.

Lord Vygon extended a hand. "There are only four ancient vampires in the world, as you know. What you may not know is that the first two are asleep, and their houses are, for the most part, just their bodyguards. I am a solo house, and Lord Noskov's house is the only one with a formidable group."

Dr. Snowden studied Lord Vygon. He thought it was interesting that he had already met Lord Vygon's house in the future, except they called themselves the Earth Guard. Maybe this was the event that would lead to their formation.

"You know what he did to that village . . . The bounty is one thing I agree with the Helians on," said Delia.

"Yes, I'm aware of that. What you might not be aware of is that the village killed his four-hundred-year-old wife. Lord Noskov only killed those who did the actual deed," said Lord Vygon. He gestured outward. "Nonetheless, I ask that you put that to the side for this. We are hoping that you might give him a reprieve after this event."

"I was not aware of this information."

Lord Vygon shook his head. "The Helians . . . left that part out when they issued the bounty. Of course, they only had footage of the resulting action by Lord Noskov. It makes you wonder how they happened to be in the area. To them, it was an opportunity to thin the power of the Daedrould."

Delia studied Lord Vygon for a moment. "You have proven yourself in the past to be trustworthy. We have watched you from afar. Based on this new testimony, we will suspend any justice."

Evaran nodded. "You have my word that if they are coming to help, they will help. The Lord Noskov I know is honorable, despite what his past might be."

Delia nodded. "Let's hope so."

After an hour, they approached the landing site where they met Lord Noskov. The beach was packed with several hundred or so bone-clad vampires.

A chill went through Dr. Snowden as he surveyed them. Although he knew they were there to help, he could not help thinking about how many people they must have killed between them.

The Torvatta landed, and they exited it.

Lord Noskov raised his head a bit. "Delia Everoak."

"Lord Noskov. We meet again," said Delia.

"On better terms this time, I hope," said Lord Noskov, flashing a fanged smile.

Delia nodded. "For now. Evaran and Lord Vygon have vouched for you, and I have suspended any retribution. How you act will determine the next steps."

Lord Noskov glanced at Evaran and Lord Vygon, then back at Delia. He dipped his head.

Lord Vygon stepped forward. "I'm glad you came. What made you decide to help?"

"You vouched for him," said Lord Noskov. He looked at Evaran. "That and I've never lost a fight. You're pretty tough."

"Relative to an ancient vampire, perhaps."

"I suspect you went easy on me. Why?" asked Lord Noskov.

Evaran half smiled. "I am honoring a request."

Lord Noskov narrowed his eyes.

Evaran nodded. "V will guide you to where you need to go. Afterward, please join us in the command area."

Lord Noskov nodded and then waved for his group to board the Torvatta. Dr. Snowden helped V guide them to the living quarters. It made sense to keep them separated from the Ollikrin. After they were all boarded, Lord Noskov joined them in the command area and sat next to Dr. Snowden.

"Nice ship," said Lord Noskov. "It's more advanced than anything I've seen from the Helians."

"The Torvatta is unique. You will never see another like it," said Evaran. "V, engage stealth mode and take us to Atlantis."

"Acknowledged."

The Torvatta flew into space, and after jumping forward an hour, descended to Atlantis. As it approached, the front right screen picked up the chaos of the sentinels swarming on the landing pads.

"In five minutes, our previous selves will be leaving the city to go back in time," said Evaran. "Two minutes after that, they will be back in time. V, at that point, contact Helian command."

"Acknowledged."

Dr. Snowden's attention focused on the front screen. Five minutes later, it showed another Torvatta flying out of the city. He shook his head. It was weird to think that he just saw the Torvatta with a past version of him in it. The concept of what is now intrigued him. At least they could get the city cleared, then hit the pyramid. Then they would be one step closer to finding Emily.

After two more minutes, V interacted with the front console.

An elder Helian dressed similarly to the other robed Helians appeared. The difference was that his robe was gold and his mantle was black. A symbol of a hollow gold circle with a line through it was on the left side of the mantle, and the right side had ten silver bars. He had gray hair and bronze skin. "Who is this?"

"I am Evaran, and I have with me Lord Noskov of House Noskov, Delia Everoak of the Ollikrin Nation, Lord Vygon of House Vygon, and my friends V and Dr. Albert Snowden. We are here to offer assistance."

"I'm Cyrus, first elder of the Helians. We welcome any support."

Evaran nodded. "I am sending you coordinates where we will land. Lord Noskov and Delia have with them their respective groups. If you can send all available Helian guards to that location, they can come with me and Lord Vygon."

Cyrus eyed Evaran. "How can I trust you?"

"The alternative is we do not help and your city is lost."

Cyrus paused as he sighed. "Send your coordinates."

"Excellent. When the city is safe, we will meet in person."

Cyrus nodded, and the screen went blank.

"V, send the coordinates."

"Acknowledged."

"Delia, Lord Noskov, the Torvatta will land in a place with only a handful of sentinels. Prepare your groups for combat."

They nodded and headed to their respective rooms.

The Torvatta landed in an open square area of the city. Evaran and Lord Vygon stood at the end of the Torvatta's ramp as V and Dr. Snowden helped Delia and Lord Noskov unload their groups. Dr. Snowden saw some snarling and jawing going on between the groups, but they were shut down immediately by Delia and Lord Noskov. Dr. Snowden pulled out his PSD as he watched the nonhumans begin to move forward.

Evaran extended a hand, palm facing forward. "I will need you to stay on the Torvatta."

"Again?" said Dr. Snowden.

"I need you on the Torvatta alongside V to help coordinate this."

Dr. Snowden sighed. "Fine . . . what do you need me to do?"

"The Torvatta will sit above the city doing a continuous scan," said Evaran. "It will detect the sentinels and nonhumans. Delia and Lord Noskov have communicator devices, and we have a shared channel. The city overlay will be divided into grid cells. You just need to call out the cells that have sentinel activity and direct where everyone needs to go."

"I'm not a tactician . . ."

"I know," said Evaran, lightly squeezing Dr. Snowden's shoulder. "But you are more capable than you realize."

Lord Vygon slapped Dr. Snowden's arm. "Trust me, there are only a few people I would trust to do this. You're one of them."

Dr. Snowden raised his hands with palms out and shook them. "All right, all right. I'll give it my best shot."

"Excellent," said Evaran.

Dr. Snowden watched as the last of the nonhumans left the Torvatta. Lord Noskov and Delia had taken off with their groups, and Evaran and Lord Vygon had left with a sizable Helian group that met them at the landing spot. He went back to the command area and stood next to V at the front console. The front screen was halved, the right side showing the city with a grid over it and the left side showing a real-time view of the city. The grid had colored dots to represent a sentinel or nonhuman. V showed him the basics of how to interact with the console. He was glad to have V there to help him figure out how to interact with it.

For the next seven hours, Dr. Snowden coordinated the movements of the various groups. The ebb and flow of the battle was nonstop. He found it fascinating to watch as each cell was secured. It was almost like playing a video game. The grid highlighted once all cells were secured.

Looking at the number of dots left, it seemed there were some losses. He had moved Evaran's group to the center of the city, where the sentinels had massed up. Lord Noskov's group was sent to the landing pads to take out the teleporting patterns since their speed gave them an advantage against the sentinels' ranged weaponry. Delia's group swept through the areas of the city with more obstructions. Dr. Snowden moved them there because with their size and speed, they would make more effective use of cover. He figured if they could fight on a battlefield like a forest, fighting in a city would not be too much different.

Managing the groups was easier than he thought it would be. Although he could communicate with Lord Noskov and Delia, he was not sure how they were able to communicate to their respective groups. Maybe something he could talk to them about later.

The next step was to meet with Cyrus and the Helian council. Dr. Snowden's mind was not on the meeting. It was on Emily. Although he had been focused on helping secure the city, he could not help but wonder if Emily was holding up. He grinned as he thought of the loss the sentinels were just handed. It did not make him feel that much better, but at least he contributed to punishing them. He was coming for Emily. She just had to survive, wherever she was.

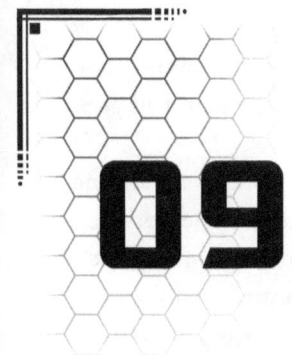

Emily coughed as her eyes tried to open. Her right eye did not budge, but her left eye was able to squeeze open a bit. Pain raced throughout her body, making her clench her jaw.

She took a moment to focus on breathing, but even that hurt. Small stones slid around her as she struggled to sit up. She moved her right arm to her face but abandoned that after the pain told her to. Using her left arm, she was able to feel her right eye. It was puffed up, and tingling surrounded it. From her understanding of the nanobots, she knew they were trying to repair whatever damage was there.

The tingling sensations were stronger than she could recall. It was almost like she could feel them at a lower level. As bad of a shape as she was in, the nanobots must have been working overtime.

She reached down to her pants pocket. Her eyebrows wrinkled as she realized she was naked.

It took her roughly ten minutes of small movements to sit up. Her breathing had stabilized, and the pain had given her a headache.

Looking around, she saw she was in a stand-alone cone-shaped cell made of metal bars. Several other empty cells were around her. It was like pillars of metal from different structures had been ripped out and then stuck at a slant into the ground. There was a hole in the floor a few steps away. She could tell what the purpose of the hole was based on the nauseating smell that emanated from it. Looking through the bars, she found herself inside a dimly lit cave. Torches around the perimeter lit up the interior. Another smell caught her nose just as she looked at a table near the cells.

It was the smell of rotting flesh.

She dry heaved and looked away.

The table had various human bones and parts slopped into buckets on and around it. A rack of various knives hung over the table, along with a crude rack containing bowls of something. In the center of the room was a pit fire with a pot hanging over it. Several rocks serving as chairs circled it.

The pot caught her eye. Whatever lived here was not a senseless monster. Her breath staggered as the image of the creature that attacked her ran through her mind. She swept her eyes across the entirety of the cave but did not see it. Was this its home? Regardless of what it was, she was in no condition to move.

She saw her clothes on another table. It looked like every piece had been cut off instead of pulled off.

She took stock of her body and noticed bruising was everywhere on her right side. That must be what was causing all the pain. The memory of being slammed into the cliff wall roared back into her mind. She had turned instinctively to the left, making her right side take the impact. Probably some broken bones, although after testing her movement, she did not think so.

Using one of the cell bars, she was able to stand after several more minutes. It took her a moment to orient herself. She rolled her head to the side gently, then to the other side. It felt good to stretch. She repeated this with her arms and legs.

Squeezing the bars confirmed to her that they were metal. The top had a ring where all the bars tied to it. The bars appeared to extend deep into the ground.

She knew this was engineered. After pulling and pushing on one of the bars, she sighed.

The bar did not budge.

After grabbing two bars, she tried to pull them apart, but stopped as pain took her breath away. Despair washed over her as she sat down and began to cry. The PSD had become her constant companion, and now even it had left her. She remembered it dropping out of her hand during the attack. Listening to Evaran's voice always calmed her down. In the cell, though, there was nothing, not even her clothes. She sighed as she lay down on her good side and closed her eyes.

Several hours later, her eyes popped open at the sound of something coming in from the other side of the cave. Out of the entrance appeared the creature she had seen earlier. Her heartbeat ramped up, and her breath went shallow as she studied the creature. It had a middle-aged female human slung over its shoulder but carried her like she weighed nothing.

The creature walked over to her cell and peered in. White, curled, bony horns shaped like a ram's sat on either side of its head. Its skin was semihairless, and its hands ended in large claws on each finger. Tiny black eyes with pointed ears on either side sat above a mouth with large, sharp teeth. The creature snorted, then carried the woman over to a horizontal metal spike that jutted from the wall.

Emily's eyes widened as she saw that the woman was alive and barely breathing.

The woman's eyes moved a bit in reaction to being impaled on the spike.

A shiver went through Emily as she swallowed hard. It was evident this creature was a killer. Her attention focused on a scraping sound.

The creature had pulled up a chair next to her cell.

She crawled over to the opposite side.

After several minutes of the creature staring at her, it spoke in a deep, gravelly voice. "Do you understand me?"

She tried to talk, but it was as if her throat was not moving. It took her a few moments before she could respond. "Yes . . ."

The creature smiled, revealing its sharp teeth in perfect detail. "I'm Kazaal. Who are you?"

"Emily."

"Someone who I can talk with . . . finally," said Kazaal. He let out a roar that made her flinch. "So . . . Emily . . . how can you understand me?"

"I . . . I . . . dunno."

Kazaal laughed. "You don't even know. How interesting." He leaned forward, rapping his claws against each other. "You've probably guessed that this cave is mine. And humans are my prey."

She nodded.

"You've earned some time . . . from being a meal. It has been a long . . . long . . . time since I've talked. We shall see if you are worthy of being spared . . . for now."

She exhaled sharply through her nose.

"Now . . . I have some meal preparations to do," said Kazaal. "There's a hole for your body functions, if you haven't seen it yet. I will give you food and water every morning for the day. Use it sparingly. It's all you get. Do you understand?"

She nodded her head again.

"Good," said Kazaal. He walked over to the table she had seen earlier. After perusing the knives, he pulled off two of them. One was wide like a butcher's knife, the other was slim and reminded her of a small saw.

She looked away as Kazaal went over to the woman on the spike and began slicing. After thirty minutes, she glanced over at the remains.

The woman's legs were missing, and entrails were inching themselves out to the floor.

Emily turned away and scurried over to the hole in her cell and puked.

Kazaal smiled at her as he divided up the cuts into various containers made of bone and skin. "Don't like what you see?"

She shook her head while grimacing.

"Be thankful you can speak to me. Otherwise, this would've been you."

After wiping away the vomit on her lips, she said, "Why do you hunt us?"

Kazaal paused as he laid down his knife. He walked up to her cell. "Have you seen what's outside of here? This is a prison planet. Only the strong survive. If you're weak, you're prey. It's that simple."

"You . . . you could help them. Look after each other."

Kazaal laughed. "That sounds like a lot of work. Why do all that when I can take what I want, when I want."

She shuddered as the slopping sound of organs hitting the ground momentarily disrupted her attention. She focused back on Kazaal. "Did you . . . come through a portal thing?"

"Yes . . . the overlord's eyes the humans called it," said Kazaal. "They rounded up everything that wasn't human, then tossed them through it, except for those of my kind. They just killed us outright. I escaped through, and here I am." He smiled.

"You don't have to kill others."

Kazaal snapped his head toward her. "Oh? I think it's perfect. Humans banish and kill my race. Now . . . they're on the other end."

"But what about those like me, who had nothing to do with that?"

Kazaal shrugged. "All humans are the same to me. Taste the same anyways."

Her eyes dulled. "So you're just going to keep me around until you're bored, then eat me."

"That's the plan. If I were you—"

A metal pillar, similar to the one she had seen on the stepped pyramid, lit up at a far corner of the cave.

Kazaal put away his knife and headed toward the entrance. "Don't go anywhere. Looks like today is my lucky day." He exited the cave.

She glanced at the upper half of the woman on the spike. The woman's blank expression made Emily's eyes water. She never thought she would miss the enclosure that she had stayed at her first month. Getting out of the cave was her first priority. She lay on her back as tears ran down her cheeks.

In this situation, being alone was not a bad thing.

Emily spent the next week studying Kazaal's patterns. Every time the metal pillar lit up, he would disappear for about a day, then come back with a dead, or barely alive, human. He would then slice them up and store parts away in his bone containers. Parts he did not like were tossed down a hole in another part of the cave. Personal items and clothing were stripped and tossed into a side room in the cave. He did not spend much time in the cave, leaving her alone most of the time. When he did come into the cave, he usually moved bodies, cleaned up his prep area, or wanted to talk. Although time was hard to gauge, it seemed like he left around nighttime.

Their discussions covered many topics, and over the course of the week, she had learned a great deal about Kazaal's race. They were known as the Dool Tak'ra. The thing that threw her was that the planet Kazaal described was unlike any Earth she knew of. The Purifiers had established themselves on Kazaal's planet, then purified it of any nonhumans. When tossed through the rift door, any exotic energy or matter was stripped, leaving a weakened being on the other side. She must have retained her abilities with the nanobots since they were not exotic by nature.

Being alone was not as difficult as she thought it would be. It meant Kazaal was not around. She could be left alone with her thoughts, and memories of her past kept her going. She had dreams of the facility where she had been prior to coming here. In it, she could control a swarm of nanobots and with minimal effort killed all those who sent her here. They were vivid and lucid, as if she were actually there. Then she would wake up to the silence and death around her.

Her pain had dissipated for the most part, and she spent much of her free time practicing the close-quarter combat moves she had learned from the training videos. It kept her mind occupied.

The water Kazaal gave her tasted strange, but after a while, she got used to it. For food, she had fruits and boiled vegetables that Kazaal would make. He had given her a piece of smoked human flesh, but she did not touch it. The hole Kazaal tossed the body parts down seemed to be some type of geothermal vent, keeping the cave warm. What scared her was she was settling in, getting used to the routine, and this was not a place where she wanted to do that.

On the night of last day of the week, Kazaal brought back a young, thin, fair-skinned male human who was still alive. Kazaal carried him over to a cell similar to Emily's and tossed him in.

The young man curled up into a ball while sneaking glances at Emily.

She could tell he was having the same reaction she did when she first awoke.

"I brought you some company . . . for a short while," said Kazaal. He eyed Emily. "Tell him to take his clothes off and then toss them out, or I will."

Emily sighed and leaned against the cell bars. "My name's Emily. The creature that abducted you is called Kazaal. He has asked that you take your clothes off and toss them out of the cell, or he will."

The young man turned toward Emily with wide eyes. "What's going on? What is this place?"

"Calm down . . . what's your name?"

"Ezekial."

"Okay . . . Ezekial . . . just do as Kazaal says. Otherwise . . ."

Ezekial's head trembled as tears streamed down his face.

"Just do it. We can talk afterward."

Ezekial nodded and stripped down. He tossed his clothes out of the cell.

Emily noticed the patch of the telltale red triangle with a circle in the middle emblazoned on the right arm of Ezekial's shirt. Although the situation was tough, she was happy to have someone to talk to other than Kazaal.

"Very good . . . hmm . . . ," said Kazaal. "You may be more useful than I thought." Kazaal roared at Ezekial, causing him to curl into a ball. Kazaal then exited the cave.

Emily wondered where Kazaal went. Maybe he had another cave he lived in. She focused on Ezekial. "Hang in there."

Ezekial peeked his head out and gazed around before looking at Emily. "What is that thing?"

"It's a Dool Tak'ra. I know more about him than I care to," said Emily. She pointed at the shirt he tossed out of the cell. "I see that you're a Purifier."

Ezekial shook his head. "Was . . . I got caught helping a friend, so they tossed me through."

"That seems like an odd reason . . ."

"My friend was a Wildborn," said Ezekial as he stretched out his legs. "I didn't even know he was. Still, I tried to warn him they were coming." He gulped. "We both were sent through, but I appeared here alone, then ran into . . . Kazaal. How long have you been here?"

"About a week."

"Why does he make us strip?"

"I dunno. Maybe he had a bad encounter with someone who had something hidden in their clothes."

Ezekial whimpered as he focused on the human remains. "So . . . this Kazaal . . . eats us."

"Yeah," said Emily, nodding. Although she would have preferred more light in the cave, this was one instance where she was glad it was dim to hide her nakedness.

"So what are we supposed to do then?"

"I dunno. Guess we wait until he's tired of us. Until then, do something to keep your mind occupied."

Ezekial sighed.

Emily could almost feel Ezekial's frustration and terror, but she had gotten over her jitters. She tilted her head. "So . . . this portal thing. Kazaal called it the overlord's eye. What does that mean?"

"They're rift doors. They weren't created by us. They were . . . from a civilization that died out long ago. The overlord just figured out how to use them. He was able to decipher the language and figured out the destination code for this prison planet."

"It's appropriately named."

"Yeah . . ."

Emily heard Ezekial's breath shudder. She felt bad for him, but the thought that she would get out or that Evaran, Dr. Snowden, and V would appear kept crossing her mind. Ezekial had none of that. "Well . . . hang in there. Get some rest."

Ezekial walked up to the nearest cell bars and, with wide eyes, looked at Emily. "How are you so calm?"

"Been here a while."

"Have you found anything that might get us out of here?"

"Not yet. If there is a way out of here, we'll figure it out."

Ezekial sighed and slumped down.

Over the next week, Emily learned a lot about the Purifiers. They were run by a powerful overlord who seemed to have special gifts. It was his decree that all nonhumans be wiped out. It seemed to her that the overlord was nonhuman, but Ezekial insisted the overlord was a god in human form. The overlord had found these rift doors and began expanding his human supremacy empire wherever they went. The prison planet's ability to capture exotic matter and energy from individuals passing through it gave the overlord unusual levels of power. He was feared by all Purifiers.

Ezekial had adjusted to the situation, and even smiled a few times.

Emily had talked him through various training exercises to keep his mind focused. Her body had healed up, and she could feel the tingling sensations more often now. She had tested the metal bars again and found that with some focus, she could bend them slightly.

On the first day of her third week there, after Kazaal had left for the night, she gestured for Ezekial to come over. "I have a plan. I think I can bend these bars. If I can, and I get out, I'll get yours. There is a room nearby with some clothing we can get and a table with some knives to defend ourselves. Then we make a break for it. Are you up for it?"

Ezekial nodded. "I'd rather die trying than become food for this monster."

"Okay," said Emily. She walked up to the bars facing Ezekial's cell and put her hands on two of them. The tingling in her arms went wild as she began to pull the bars apart. They separated easily, like they were made of thin wood.

Ezekial's eyes widened. "Are you . . . a nonhuman?"

Emily shook her head as she walked over to Ezekial's cell. "No, just human . . . with an edge." She opened Ezekial's cell, and they went to the clothing room.

After donning some robes and footwear, they grabbed some of the knives from the table. They crept to the cave entrance and peered out. Emily had expected to see some type of rocky hills, but it was grassland all around them, with a tree here and there in the distance. She felt a tug in her mind toward a direction. The feeling was slight, but any direction was good. She waved for Ezekial to follow her, and they exited the cave.

As they ran across the grassland, she took in the fresh air. Being down in the cave had made her accustomed to the smell of death and rotting flesh. She looked back and saw a speck in the distance. Although she could not fully see what it was, the unmistakable movement made her heartbeat go into overdrive. "Ezekial! Run!"

Ezekial looked back. "Oh, Overlord!"

They ran for several minutes but were losing ground to Kazaal. The edge of a forest loomed in the distance.

Emily pointed at the trees. "In there!" She continued running, and when she looked back, her heart sank. Ezekial was on the ground, his head pulverized into pieces, and Kazaal was charging toward her. As she got to the trees, she felt Kazaal right behind her. She wheeled around and extended the butcher's blade she had taken from the cave.

"Ahh . . . so you thought to escape me . . . how interesting."

"I'm not going back!"

"I think you are," said Kazaal. He charged Emily.

Emily thought time slowed down as she stepped out of the way and sliced at Kazaal's side. He howled as he pivoted and backhanded Emily. She flew across the field. Kazaal rushed over to her as her eyes fluttered. She struggled to get her breath. As her vision dimmed, she heard Kazaal say, "I'm not done with you yet."

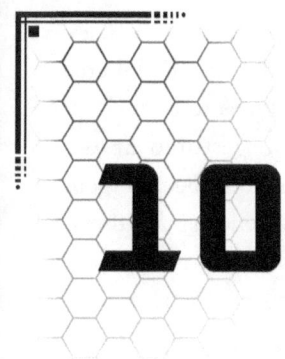

10

Dr. Snowden surveyed the assembled group in the Helians' chamber.

Cyrus, the elder Helian they had talked to initially, sat at a circular table surrounded by pathways up to raised, slanted seating areas, where Dr. Snowden sat alongside V. Evaran and Lord Vygon sat in front of them. To Evaran's left was Lord Noskov, and some of his men sat in the seating area behind him. Delia sat to the right of Evaran and Lord Vygon, and behind her sat her group. Opposite all of them was another Helian council member named Ira. Behind them sat several others of their race.

Dr. Snowden figured the other Helians in the seating area were council members as well.

"Thank you for coming to our aid," said Cyrus. "I'm not sure we would've made it without your help."

Evaran nodded. "I am sorry for the devastation wrought by the sentinels. We came as quickly as we could."

"I'm . . . ," said Cyrus, looking at the other Helians. "We're . . . a little confused on how you knew to come."

"Understandable," said Evaran. He gestured at Dr. Snowden and Lord Vygon. "We had just left Special Agent Joktan's office. Our intent was to show evidence of this threat in the hopes that you might be able to help."

"Well, I'm afraid we won't be of much use to anyone for the immediate future."

"Of course." Evaran gestured at Lord Noskov and Delia. "However . . . they did not provide help without certain concessions should the city be saved."

Ira snorted. "Why am I not surprised they wouldn't do it to help another nonhuman."

Lord Noskov smirked. "I helped you even after you placed a bounty on me . . ."

"You broke the rules," said Ira.

Evaran extended a hand, palm down. "I think it is fair for the Helians to make concessions. Your city was spared by the efforts of both Lord Noskov and Delia. They did not have to help you, but they did. The Purifiers are not a threat that one group alone can handle. It requires cooperation. Yes, there are some details that need worked out, but at a high level, there are several immediate points that need to be addressed in the coming days."

Ira exhaled from his mouth.

Evaran raised a finger. "One. The bounty on Lord Noskov is to be dropped. He risked his life along with those of his men. There were heavy casualties."

Ira shook his head. "Not so sure about that . . ."

Evaran cast a sidelong glance at Lord Noskov. "I know his character to be good, even if he does not know it himself. Lord Vygon will vouch for that as well. Also, from what I understand, the bounty was placed without all the information being considered."

Cyrus extended a hand toward Ira, palm down. He raised his head. "Acceptable. Your second point?"

Evaran raised two fingers. "Two. A new assembly will be formed. It will contain representatives of all nonhuman groups. Policies, protocols, and proceedings will need to be defined." He glanced at Delia. "A new senior council will be the initial drafters. It should comprise Delia, Lord Vygon, Cyrus, and Lord Noskov." He looked at Cyrus. "If you wish for other Helians to help, that would be acceptable. The goal of this senior council is to forge what will be the operating framework going forward for a unified front against all threats to Earth."

Cyrus swallowed hard. "That's . . . quite ambitious. We already protect Earth from most alien threats. These . . . Purifiers are different, though." He glanced at Delia.

Delia nodded. "Lord Noskov and I are committed to this, as is Lord Vygon."

Dr. Snowden noticed that Delia garnered an unspoken respect from even the Helians. He saw why Lord Vygon chose her. If anyone would be able to keep things calm while discussing controversial topics and policies, it would be her.

"Very well," said Cyrus with a sigh. "Next?"

Evaran raised three fingers. "Three. The Purifiers have a base near Memphis. We suspect it is their main one here on Earth. We have enough information to assault it. Delia and Lord Noskov have volunteered a portion of their force. The Helians, as part of the newly formed assembly from point two, should send aid as well."

"We just had our city ransacked!" said Ira.

"Yes, but I suspect there are those within your military that would like a bit of revenge."

Cyrus chuckled. "You speak like a diplomat. It's a language I know, and it is appreciated. We can spare an elite unit. They aren't large, around twenty or so, but I assure you, they are battle-worthy."

"Excellent," said Evaran. "That is all I have to say for now. We leave for the Purifiers' base in the morning at six. I will stay here to help coordinate the groups until we have to leave."

Cyrus nodded.

The seated members came forward to talk with their respective leadership. Dr. Snowden and V approached Evaran and Lord Vygon.

"That went well," said Dr. Snowden.

"It did. However, nothing will be done until the Purifier threat is eliminated."

Dr. Snowden half smiled. "Yeah . . . I figured." He gestured toward the door. "I'm gonna wait at the Torvatta. Could really use some food and maybe get some rest."

"I'll go with you," said Lord Vygon, glancing at Evaran, "unless you need me here right now. I can come back after getting some food."

Evaran tilted his head. "No . . . that will be fine. V and I can handle things here until you get back."

Dr. Snowden exited the building with Lord Vygon at his side. Dr. Snowden found the meeting fascinating. He knew little of the Helians in the time period he was from, other than their human slavery issues. Maybe with such a diverse council and parts of this new organization, the left hand did not know what the right hand did. And it all started just an hour ago, right in front of him. It could also be gone in the future that he knew. Although elation would be his normal reaction, it was tempered as thoughts of Emily flashed in his mind. He knew these steps needed to be done to get to her, it just seemed so painfully slow to him.

As he walked through the streets, the stench of death hung in the air. Helians and other nonhumans were clearing the streets of the dead. Although he had been able to see a real-time view of the battle as it progressed, most of his visual perspective had been on the Torvatta's right screen, which had a map and grid system. Seeing it up close like this made him catch his breath. Emily appeared in his mind again. What would she think of all this, he wondered.

As Lord Vygon walked alongside Dr. Snowden, he tilted his head at him. "Emily's on your mind."

"That . . . and all this," said Dr. Snowden, gesturing around him. "At least we're one step closer now."

"Definitely."

Dr. Snowden cocked his head at Lord Vygon. "I know you won't talk about Emily's future . . . but . . . does this anger thing I have ever go away?"

Lord Vygon looked away as they continued walking. After a moment, he said, "You're much stronger than you know. Your anger's in your head. When you realize that, things will change. I'm curious, however. I've never known you to have this. When did it start?"

"I've had it all my life," said Dr. Snowden with a chuckle. He gestured outward. "Of course, traveling with Evaran seems to have the tendency of putting me on edge. I guess that's expected."

"Ahh . . . was it the reason you moved from Florida to Ohio when Emily was in college?"

Dr. Snowden snapped his head toward Lord Vygon. "You . . . know of that?"

Lord Vygon half smiled.

Dr. Snowden ran a hand over his cheek. It was not something he spoke of, or wanted to remember. The day he had lost control on a fellow professor and was subsequently let go was forever etched in his mind. Finding work was hard, and he took the first offer he got from a major college willing to give him a second chance. Leaving Dan and Emily was one of the hardest things he had to do. He had no one to blame but himself, though. Being a burden and asking for help was not in his nature, and he was not going to ask his brother to bail him out on that one. It was not the first time his anger got him in trouble, but it was definitely the most memorable.

"Don't worry, your secret is safe with me," said Lord Vygon.

Dr. Snowden sighed. "I'm . . . trying to figure out how you know about that." He narrowed his eyes. "Did Evaran tell you?"

Lord Vygon shook his head.

Dr. Snowden harrumphed. Lord Vygon was an enigma to him, just like Evaran was. It was evident, however, that Lord Vygon would probably turn out to be a close friend. Dr. Snowden had not told Evaran about the cause of his move back to Ohio. Yet here was Lord Vygon with that insight. Dr. Snowden chuckled. "No wonder you and Evaran are friends. You're both mysterious as hell."

They shared a laugh as they arrived at the Torvatta. Once inside, they headed to the conference room.

Dr. Snowden got a burger and some fries from the food replicator and sat at the table. He watched Lord Vygon order a drink, then take a seat opposite him. The drink was bloodred and looked like it had chunks floating in it. He pointed at the drink. "So . . . is there blood in there . . ."

Lord Vygon nodded. "Of course. I always take advantage of the Torvatta's ability to make my special drink."

"Surprised the replicator knows how to make it," said Dr. Snowden.

Lord Vygon smiled. "From your perspective, it doesn't yet."

Dr. Snowden stopped mid bite as he tilted his head. "Come again?"

"Interesting . . . I see Evaran hasn't explained that aspect of the Torvatta to you," said Lord Vygon. "Or maybe . . . Evaran doesn't know yet."

Dr. Snowden eyed Lord Vygon. "And I suspect you're not going to tell me, are you?"

Lord Vygon stroked his chin as he studied Dr. Snowden. "Well . . . let's just say the Torvatta is contextually time stream aware at some levels. I suspect Evaran probably knows this and has not told you. Something for you two to talk about."

Dr. Snowden took a bite of his burger as his mind chewed on what Lord Vygon had just said. It sounded like the Torvatta knew who had visited it, including those from the futures of him and Evaran, and showed or allowed certain functionality based on that. The concept was intriguing and was probably something that would keep him up thinking at night.

After some light discussion, Dr. Snowden retired for the evening. He performed his breathing exercises and then went to bed. V tapping his arm caused him to wake up. Looking at his PSD, he saw it was 6:00 a.m. He must have been more exhausted than he thought. After performing his morning routine, he went to the command area. Lord Noskov and Delia sat in the left seating area. On the right were Lord Vygon and a Helian in heavy armor. He reminded him of a paladin.

Dr. Snowden took a seat next to Lord Vygon and extended a hand toward the Helian. "I'm Dr. Albert Snowden."

The Helian took off his helmet, revealing fair skin, golden hair, blue eyes, and a well-trimmed beard. He shook Dr. Snowden's hand. "I'm Captain Laban of the Fourth Helian Guard. Your skill as a tactician was appreciated, and you command great respect in the eyes of my fellow Helians."

Dr. Snowden jerked his head back. A chill ran up his spine as he recalled being called "the great Dr. Snowden" in a previous adventure. Was this where he got that name? He nodded at Captain Laban and then sat back and watched as the Torvatta took off toward Egypt.

After a short while, the Torvatta hovered just out of range of the Purifier base.

Captain Laban faced Dr. Snowden. "Looking forward to hearing your plan on this one."

"Umm . . . I'll defer to Evaran," said Dr. Snowden.

Evaran nodded. "I will fly the Torvatta up to the entrance-way and push a part of it inside, effectively sealing the entrance. It will be able to hold the shield open while it is blocking. That will allow everyone to exit the ship and go into the area between the shield and the pyramid. The sentinels' arrival and departure appear to be random, but there is a sentinel nearby that is returning."

"So who we killing?" asked Lord Noskov with a smirk.

Delia eyed Lord Noskov.

Evaran interacted with his chair console. The front right screen showed a layout of the interior of the pyramid shield. Four buildings were shown a bit away from each point at the base of the pyramid. Evaran pointed at the buildings. "These are bunkers with a slit to allow ranged fire. The shield prevents those on the outside from seeing them, but you will see them once we are inside the shield. The bunkers have an underground component which I suspect are barracks."

"Underground . . . I like it," said Lord Noskov.

Evaran raised an eyebrow at Lord Noskov, then swiped his hand in the air. The layout moved to the left front screen, and an image of a new type of Purifier appeared on the front right screen. The Purifier had a black mask with eye, nose, and mouth holes. Unlike the sentinels, they were not robed and instead wore a suit of light metal armor over the chest, arms, and legs. They carried large shields with curved swords. A crossbow-like weapon was slung over their backs. "These are the guards. Based on V's scan, they are physically stronger than the sentinels."

Delia shook her head. "This will be a tough fight. How many are we expecting?"

"There were about eighty or so life signs detected. However, from what we have seen at Atlantis, we should not underestimate them."

Captain Laban shook a fist in front of him. "They will taste Helian steel."

Evaran nodded and faced Captain Laban. "The shields you carry are capable of blocking their ranged weaponry. Your guard will need to be the front line when approaching the bunkers. Delia and Lord Noskov's group will follow and attack once the bunkers are reached. The bunkers must be secured first. Once that is done, there is a ramp at the base of the pyramid that leads underground. That will be our next target once the perimeter is secured."

"We will do our part," said Captain Laban, standing. He glanced at Lord Noskov and Delia. "You can trust in our ability. We will hit them like a hammer."

Delia stood and nodded. "We are ready."

"Finally," said Lord Noskov as he rose from his seat.

Evaran gestured toward the Torvatta entrance. "Get your groups ready. You all have communicators, and Dr. Snowden will be watching from above with the view that V will provide, along with real-time information, like he did in the city. The ultimate goal is to pierce into the underground base. We can then shut off the shield and determine where the nonhumans who were sent there are or went."

Dr. Snowden sighed. He wanted to get out there and unleash his aggression on the Purifiers, but helping coordinate seemed to be more important. Whatever was needed to get Emily back, he would do it.

Captain Laban, Lord Noskov, and Delia all nodded and then headed to their groups.

Evaran faced Lord Vygon. "We will handle any guards that come out of the pyramid."

"Ready as always," said Lord Vygon.

Evaran faced Dr. Snowden. "V will provide an aerial view like the Torvatta did in the city."

With a nod, Dr. Snowden said, "I don't think I will need to do much here, the plan you have sounds solid."

"Perhaps. However, in combat, things can change quickly. Having you able to detect and inform will be a big help."

"Sounds good."

After a short while, the screen showed the entranceway shielding dissipate as a sentinel approached it.

"V, take us in," said Evaran.

The Torvatta surged forward. It slammed into the sentinel, knocking him through the entranceway. A portion of the Torvatta was stuck inside the shielding, preventing it from closing. A horn blared out.

Evaran motioned toward the screen. "V, go."

"Acknowledged," said V as he strode toward the back of the ship.

After a moment, his stealthed orb appeared on the front left screen as a green outline. It did not take long for V to reach the top of the pyramid near the shield generator. When he got there, the front right screen changed to an overhead view with a grid. The colored dots popped up, showing the Purifiers.

The left screen showed arrows and bolts trying to breach the Torvatta's shielding, but they had no impact.

With a nod at Lord Vygon, Evaran said, "It is time for us to go."

Lord Vygon followed Evaran to the back of the ship.

Dr. Snowden watched as everyone disembarked and joined the battle. He did not have V's physical presence to help, but he understood the front console interface enough now to work it. The guards were a lot tougher than they looked. The Helians went into two groups initially, one for each of the front two bunkers, followed by a supporting group from both Lord Noskov and Delia. Evaran and Lord Vygon took the area outside the ramp in front of the pyramid, fighting those that came from the base and those who strayed away from the bunkers. Everything seemed to be going well.

Once the first and second bunkers were secured, the mixed groups moved to the third and fourth bunkers.

Dr. Snowden noticed that there was Purifier movement underground between the bunkers. They were moving a group from the rear bunkers to the front bunkers in order to flank. He reorganized the groups so that Lord Noskov's group rushed back to the front bunkers while the Helians and Delia's group pressed on to the rear bunkers. He figured that Lord Noskov's group would do better handling the smaller Purifier group headed to the front bunkers. He kept the Ollikrin with the Helian guard as the main assault group. The

Ollikrin had raw power, and Dr. Snowden noted that if one of them got into an enclosed space, they would dominate.

It took an hour, but the plan worked. All the guards were either dead or dying or had fled underground. The bunkers had been secured.

Dr. Snowden sighed as he slumped down in Evaran's chair. Coordinating these battles was grueling. He welcomed the focus needed as it distracted him from Emily, but the thought of now finding out where she went danced in his mind.

Evaran appeared on the front right screen. "Excellent job. There were heavy casualties, but you kept it to a minimum. We are going to proceed into the underground structure."

Dr. Snowden stood up. "I'm coming."

Evaran studied Dr. Snowden. "Very well. Meet us at the underground ramp door."

Dr. Snowden nodded and hustled out of the Torvatta. As he ran toward the meeting spot, he scanned the surroundings. Dead or dying guards lay around. Surrounding them were wounded and dead Ollikrin, Helians, and vampires. The fight took its toll. His nose recoiled as the smell of death caressed it. Maybe it was a good thing he stayed in the Torvatta. On his way there, he noticed two posts with the Purifier banner in front of the ramp. On the pyramid itself was a larger banner. It reminded him of the Purifier Saturn space station. These Purifiers wanted to make sure their presence was felt. He reached the ramp and proceeded down it to the large rectangular door at the end.

Evaran stood by a massive stone door with Delia, Lord Noskov, Lord Vygon, Captain Laban, and V in orb mode around him.

Dr. Snowden noted the somber looks on everyone when he joined them.

"We took more casualties than expected," said Captain Laban.

Evaran nodded. "Yes, and it will not be forgotten. You, Lord Noskov, and Delia can attend to your fallen. V will help you load them into the Torvatta and provide any medical assistance. Lord Vygon, Dr. Snowden, and I will breach the interior. There were only three life signs left."

"There may be more if they are shielded," said Delia.

"Perhaps, but we can handle whatever is inside."

Lord Noskov looked at Delia. "I will direct my men to aid you. I think I should stay and help Evaran just in case."

Delia paused as she studied Lord Noskov. She nodded and headed off with Captain Laban.

"I'll be back. Just need to tell my remaining group to help. Don't go in without me."

Evaran nodded. "Go."

Dr. Snowden watched Lord Noskov take off up the ramp. He could not fathom how they were taking the losses in their groups. While Emily was maybe alive, the nonhuman casualties were not. Captain Laban looked like he had struggled to keep it together. How many of his guard had he trained or known personally? Delia was calm as always. Even death did not faze her. Lord Noskov was somewhat cold about it, but maybe that is how vampires deal with death.

Lord Noskov returned ten minutes later. He pointed at the door. "Thought you would have had that open by now."

"We were waiting on you," said Evaran. "However, now that you are here, we may proceed with your help."

Lord Noskov smirked as he shook his head.

Evaran, Lord Vygon, and Lord Noskov placed their hands on the stone door. After some effort, they were able to slide it to the side, exposing a large stone hallway. Dr. Snowden noted that the stone was polished and there were no doors or windows visible. Torches lined the walls at equal intervals. After walking the length of the hallway, they encountered a ramp at the end. Two closed doorways stood in front of and to the sides of the ramp. The doorways had a stone slab similar to the one at the entrance, but appropriately sized.

Lord Noskov tilted his head. "I smell humans."

"Same," said Lord Vygon, extending his arm blades.

Evaran approached the door on the right, and after help from Lord Vygon and Lord Noskov, slid the stone door to the right. He entered the room with his shield raised. The others followed him.

Dr. Snowden thought the room looked like an administrative office. There were various stone tables scattered around. The Purifier banners he had seen outside draped the room. Only two torches were lit, revealing wooden cabinets with scrolls and writing devices lined against the walls.

A bolt was fired at them. Evaran blocked it with his shield as Lord Noskov charged around Evaran. Lord Noskov grabbed a guard and threw him into the wall. The guard slumped to the ground. Lord Noskov snapped his head toward a trembling human woman and man standing in the back behind one of the stone desks. Both had bronze skin, but the man, at around six feet tall, stood about a half foot taller than the woman.

Evaran tossed two illumination orbs into the air, then scanned the Purifiers. The Purifier symbols stood out on their otherwise clean white robes.

"Please . . . don't hurt us," said the man.

Evaran extended a hand. "We will not harm you."

Lord Noskov paused as he jerked his head back. "We won't?"

Evaran shook his head. "No, we will not." He approached the humans who fell back against the wall. "Who are you?"

"J-J-John," said the man.

"Leah," said the woman, looking down.

"Are there any other shielded areas with more people?" asked Evaran.

"Just us now," said Leah. She pointed at the unconscious guard. "And our personal guard."

"Where does the ramp outside this room lead to?"

"The rift room."

Evaran rubbed his chin. "What type of rift is in the room?"

John and Leah looked at each other.

Evaran gestured at Lord Noskov. "Perhaps I was in error and Lord Noskov's assessment was correct."

John stepped forward. "We . . . just manage the arrivals and departures here. We're administrators, not fighters."

Evaran tilted his head. "Arrival and departure . . . from where?"

John gulped. "Several places. Depends on what the destination is set to."

Evaran walked over to John and Leah and sifted through the scrolls on the desk. He extended his hand, and a projection of Emily shot up from his ring. "Did she come through here?"

John nodded. "Yeah . . . I remember her."

Dr. Snowden's blood boiled as his eyes lit up. Tingling sensations intensified across his body. He faced John and Leah. "So my niece went through one of these rifts?"

John gulped.

"What was the destination?"

John shrugged. "She went to Azoculus, then to a prison planet from there, I'm guessing. I don't know where the prison planet is, but it's where we send nonhumans."

Dr. Snowden scowled as he pointed a finger at John. "She *is* human. *You* made a mistake."

"She had . . . unusual characteristics. Definitely not human. Not pure anyways."

Dr. Snowden surged forward. He grabbed John and slammed him up against the wall. "Don't you *ever* talk about my niece like that, you hear me?"

"Dr. Snowden!" said Evaran, placing a hand on Dr. Snowden's shoulder.

"He doesn't even care that he sent Emily to wherever she is!"

"Breathe."

Dr. Snowden paused as the fire in his eyes burned a hole in John's startled face. He stepped away and then shoved John back into the wall. "I like Lord Noskov's option."

Evaran guided Dr. Snowden behind him. He wheeled around to face John and Leah. "You will take us to this rift room. I would suggest no deception."

John and Leah nodded vigorously.

Evaran pointed at the unconscious guard. "Lord Noskov, can you take him to the Torvatta?"

Lord Noskov swayed his head as he stared at John and Leah. "Yeah . . . you sure you don't want me to take these two as well?"

"We need them alive."

"Bah! Fine," said Lord Noskov.

Dr. Snowden watched as Lord Noskov exited the room. Lord Vygon was next, followed by John, Leah, and then Evaran. He followed suit. The tingling sensations were still there. He knew to breathe, lest he black out again. At least now there was a definite chance that Emily was still alive. The question was now where.

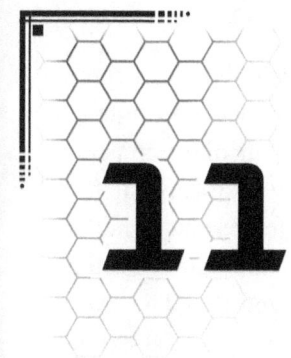

11

Emily shuddered as she cracked her eyes open. A pain shot through her chest as she took a breath. The familiar smell of Kazaal's cave filled her nostrils. She coughed as she lifted her head to look around. The metal poles of her cage greeted her, and the widened bars had a new pole between them. She sat up and checked her body in the dim light. The robe she had found was gone, and she was naked again.

A strong odor made her turn her head to the spike on the wall. Ezekial hung there with his legs missing. She clenched her jaw as her hands gripped the rocky floor. The thought of Dr. Snowden, Evaran, and V coming to rescue her seemed remote at this point. So much time had passed, and although she did not know the exact time, it felt like several months since she had arrived. It was times like this she really missed her PSD.

Her thoughts drifted to her PSD. She was sure now that the urging she felt when she was outside was the PSD. Evaran had mentioned that Dr. Snowden and she were bonded to their PSDs. Maybe Evaran meant the nanobots had some type of communication, which ended up being an urge to move in a direction. She was not sure, but one thing was clear: she had to leave this cave. Looking around at the shadows dancing from embers of the pit fire reminded her of how alone she was, something she never thought she could handle. She sighed as she slid back down and closed her eyes.

Several hours later, she awoke to a squatting Kazaal staring at her and tapping on the metal poles of her cage. "You run pretty fast . . ."

Emily sat up.

"Your friend was unusually strong. I wonder if the overlord's eye is losing its strength."

Emily grimaced.

"Ahh . . . I sense you disapprove of me killing your friend. I would have kept him alive, but it is obvious he broke out of his cage and then opened yours. The fool actually tried to fight me to give you some time."

Emily studied Kazaal. It seemed he did not believe she was capable of widening the bars. She wondered if he smelled the nanobots on her and just ignored it. He no longer elicited fear from her. He was now an obstacle to be overcome. She paused at her change in thinking. The possibility of death no longer bothered her. If anything, it seemed to empower her. She was not going to let him be her death. He did not deserve that right.

Kazaal struck one of the metal poles with a claw. "Speak! Do not ignore me or your usefulness ends."

Emily's eyes narrowed as she balled one of her fists. "What do you want me to say . . ."

Kazaal's gaze bore a hole through Emily. "You're only alive as long as you provide some entertainment. Remember that."

"I'm glad my misery is entertaining to you."

"Do not test me!"

Emily snorted. "Or what? You'll kill me? You would've already done it if you didn't find some value in me being here."

"You're angry. I get it. I'll go get you another companion. A female this time. Someone weak."

"So you can kill them after a week?"

Kazaal roared.

The pillar in the back of the cave lit up.

"Looks like you may get one sooner than later," said Kazaal as he stood. "Don't go anywhere."

Emily's face turned red. "Like I have a choice."

Kazaal stared at Emily for a moment and, after growling at her, exited the cave.

Emily knew that it took about a day for Kazaal to go out and bring someone back. A plan formulated in her head. The last time she had left with Ezekial, it was just when Kazaal had left for the night. Apparently Kazaal was close enough to catch their scent. Going after someone coming through the rift door would give her more time. She calculated that if it took half a day to get to where Kazaal went, he would be out of range to catch up to her if she got a good start and was able to get her PSD.

She scanned the environment. The knives at the nearby butchering table were gone. The room with clothing and supplies was still there. She could use that again. The fire pit had the remains of Ezekial's legs near it, but no cooking utensil that would help her. When she left, it would just be some basic clothing, any footwear she could find, and her determination to get her PSD.

She waited for around five hours before testing the bars opposite from the ones she had broken out of earlier. A tingling sensation enveloped her as she lightly pulled. The poles seemed weaker from the last time she tried, as they parted with ease. After slipping through the bars, she headed to the clothing room. She found another robe and a belt as well as some fur-clad footwear on the edges of the pile. It only took her a moment to slip them on. Pawing through the pile, she found a cloth backpack and some leather pouches that would fit on her belt. After slinging the backpack over her shoulders and tightening the pouches, she exited the cave.

The fresh air was intoxicating as it washed over her nose. She paused for a moment to take several deep gulps, as if it would somehow cleanse her system of the foul-smelling air in Kazaal's cave. After scanning the surrounding area and seeing no sign of Kazaal, she took off. The directional urging she felt before had returned. The pain in her chest had subsided, but she did not know if it was the nanobots suppressing it or if it had fully healed from her first trip to Kazaal's cave. Either way, she was not going back to that cave alive.

After arriving at the forest edge where she had been captured earlier, she paused to look back. There was no sign of Kazaal. She frowned as she looked at where Ezekial had been killed. He had given his life to give her time to escape. She did not know him very well, but his act of courage inspired her. Escaping Kazaal would be her way of honoring Ezekial.

She ran through the forest. Startled animals took flight, and some of the larger animals studied her, but did not pursue. She wondered if it was because they smelled death from the cave on her. It did not take her long to reach the cliff edge from there. The urging was stronger, and it was almost as if she could see the PSD in the rocks at the cliff base. Her breath quickened as she rushed forward. She let out a deep breath as she scanned the rocks.

The PSD lay where it had fallen.

Her hands were like lightning bolts as she grabbed and opened it. It took her a moment to get reacquainted with the interface. The communications screen showed there had been no contact. Her heart sank as she swallowed hard. Looking at the time, she had spent roughly two and a half weeks in Kazaal's cave. The first month almost seemed like a vacation compared to that. She fumbled around the interface and pulled up the food option. A flavorless food pellet emptied into her hand. She devoured it, savoring the flavorless taste of it. Getting water from the river near where she had spent her first month here was her next priority. She set the stun beam as active and then put the PSD in one of the leather pouches on her belt.

Looking up, she estimated the climb would be rough, but the alternative was Kazaal. With that in mind, she began her ascent. During her climb, several animals swooped at her but backed off with a warning shot. She was not going to be anything's meal. The climb was rougher than she thought it was going to be. Rocks that looked solid sometimes fell out. Being in Kazaal's cave had sapped her strength, despite the nanobots' tingling sensation giving her a boost.

After she got to the top, she lay down for a moment to look at the sky. It was a serene blue with clouds. Something she would expect if she were in the backyard back home. She enjoyed the feeling of dirt under her, instead of the rough cave floor she had been on. Her thoughts drifted to what Dr. Snowden was doing, and if he was okay. Knowing him, he was probably trying to find her with everything he had, which made the fact that he had not come yet puzzling. Was this place somewhere even the Torvatta could not go?

The distinct roar of Kazaal echoed through the forest below. She jumped to her feet and ran toward the other side of the cliff. He must have come back early, or maybe he did not go where she thought he was going. She quickened her pace as she continued her charge to the other side. After arriving on the other side and assessing the downward climb, she began her descent. Going down was much easier for her. She did not know how far away he was, but given how fast he could run, she was going to put some distance between them. Maybe he would give up on hunting her; although if she ever wanted to move past that area, she would have to deal with him. She hit the ground running.

After twenty minutes, she reached the jungle near her former enclosure. While avoiding the poisonous trees, she made her way to the river. It seemed odd to her to be on familiar territory and be relieved. This was not her home, but compared to where she had been the first month here, it felt like it. After arriving, she took a moment to use the purifying container to drink some water. Her eyes closed as she savored the cool water rushing down her throat. There was no comparison to the water in Kazaal's cave.

Her attention focused on the cliffs she had run from. A brown blob stood on the edge of the cliff. Her heartbeat increased, and her breathing was staggered as she realized it was Kazaal. If she could see him, then he could see her. The familiar cloak of defiance wrapped her as she decided that he was no longer going to be a threat to her. She was done being his captive. It was apparent to her now that he had to be stopped or she would never be able to fully rest.

With a clenched jaw, she crossed the river and headed toward the stepped pyramid. She had a vague idea of what she needed to do, but would figure out the rest when she got there. Fifteen minutes passed, and the pyramid was in sight. The closeness of Kazaal's startled roar made her move faster.

He must have hit the poisonous trees. She wondered if he was immune to them or if they would have any impact. When she got to the stepped pyramid, she rushed around it to the south side. After stepping over the bone border she had seen earlier, she pushed forward into the jungle.

She thought she could feel the pounding of Kazaal's feet when they hit the ground. She scanned the jungle ahead as she ran and found what she was looking for. Several large mounds circled a tree and towered over the jungle floor. The creatures she had encountered in her first few moments in this world were scurrying about. The pattern of the mounds intrigued her. Maybe it was a symbiotic thing, but it was what she had been looking for.

She could sense that Kazaal was closing in fast. Her burst forward to the tree elicited an immediate response from the creatures. Wasting no time, she scurried up the tree, shoving off the creatures that were in her way. When she had reached the first major branch, she pulled out her PSD and made sure the first button was set to a repulsing blast and the second to a stun beam.

Her eyes flared when Kazaal appeared at the outer ring of the mounds.

"So . . . it was you who bent the bars . . . I'll need a stronger cage," said Kazaal.

"I don't think so," said Emily. "You're a monster."

Kazaal laughed as he strode toward the tree.

When he was near the base of it, Emily fired a stun beam at him.

Kazaal flinched in pain as he stepped back. "That little beam is harmless."

"We'll see," said Emily. She fired the repulsing blast at several of the mounds, causing them to explode. An angry swarm of the creatures burst from the ground toward Kazaal. She fired a continuous stun beam at him, and he fell to his knees. The creatures swarmed over him and began biting.

Kazaal looked up at Emily. "You're not a killer. I'm sorry. Help me!"

Emily shook her head slowly as she stood on the branch. Her compassion wanted to help, but her fury said otherwise.

"Please!" said Kazaal between roars.

"No."

Kazaal twitched one final time.

She trembled as she watched Kazaal die. The creatures were effective and could apparently handle even the tough hide of Kazaal. If they had not, the outcome would have been very different. She watched as his legs, arms, and head were severed and carried off.

This was her first kill, albeit indirectly, but still something she would need to deal with.

Alone.

After spending the night in the familiar enclosure she had discovered on her initial arrival, Emily set out to the river. Her sleep had been solid, something that had been missing when she was in Kazaal's cave. With him gone, she felt at peace for the first time in a long while. She quenched her thirst and enjoyed cleaning herself in the river. The robe got a good washing and was laid out to rest on a nearby rock.

As she lay naked against a tree, she grabbed her PSD from the leather pouch she was carrying it in. She opened it up and checked to see if there had been any contact. There probably was not, but she had not given up hope that Dr.

Snowden, Evaran, and V would appear in the Torvatta. Her head drooped as the PSD showed no activity or communications. She missed them, especially having breakfast with them in the conference room. Her eyes fluttered as she nodded off with positive thoughts of them.

Several hours later, she woke up and got dressed. She had decided to go back to Kazaal's cave and do a thorough search of the place. Maybe there were more items she could find. It would also be a mental victory for her. The green dot that she had wanted to go to was close by, so she would not have to go too far out of her way. After downing her food pellet and taking in her morning drink, she headed back toward Kazaal's cave.

It took her a while to get there. Although she was healing, there was still some pain in her chest. She figured there was probably some residual damage from when Kazaal hit her, but the nanobots should handle it. The climb up the cliffs and then down them were done at leisure this time, instead of in a hurry. A lump formed in her throat as she approached the forest. She thought of Ezekial again, who just wanted to live. At least he had been avenged.

When she arrived at the outskirts of Kazaal's cave, she paused. It had only been yesterday that she was his captive. She scowled and wrinkled her nose as the overpowering scent from the cave wafted past her. Looking around, she saw nothing that would bother her. She entered the cave and then pulled out her PSD and activated the illumination beam. The cave had additional rooms she had not seen before, probably due to the dim lighting.

The first room had containers made of bone supports with cloth wrapped around them. They had various items in them. One of the containers had feathers. She guessed from the birds Kazaal had killed or maybe a humanoid with feathers. Others had bones, unusual-looking rocks, and sand-like powders. It reminded her of a large spice rack, except the smell rising off them was anything but pleasant. The second room had equipment-based supplies. She walked around the various piles of objects, poking her light around them. There were a few things here she could use.

She headed back to the main room and then to the clothing room. The robe had worked well in a pinch, but she needed something closer to the skin that would not impede her movement. After rummaging through the pile, she found some leather pants and a cloth shirt. She put them to the side and continued browsing. After a bit, she found a fur head covering that had a soft interior and tough exterior. It was a bit large for her, but there was a leather strip on the back that allowed it to fit snugly on her head. She gathered up the items and headed back to the main room. The pants would need trimmed a bit, but she could do that before she left.

Drawing her lips to the side, she gazed at the second room. There had to be something of value she could use to help her survive better. With determination in her eyes, she entered the second room and took a good look at the various piles. One of the piles caught her eye. It looked like bone armor pieces held together by leather straps. She wondered who Kazaal killed to get them. There were four leg pieces, four arm pieces, and a chest plate that also had a back part to it. She tried on the various armor parts and noted that with a bit of tweaking, they could fit her. The leg armor covered the lower and upper leg, and consisted of a series of vertical bones strung together. It reminded her a bit of the cage Kazaal had put her in. The arm armor was similar. They would need some modification, as whomever Kazaal had killed to get them had large legs and arms, so the part where the ends met were overextended on her.

After another look around, she found a neck guard that consisted of sculpted wooden half rings held together by leather straps. She could definitely use that. After several minutes more of filtering through the other piles, she gathered up the bone pieces and neck guard and headed back to the main room.

It did not take her long to trim the pants. She liked the loose feeling of them on her legs. They would not impede her movement and tucked nicely into the fur boots she already had. After putting on her cloth shirt, she tightened the arm bone armor by removing the end pieces until they wrapped firmly around her upper and lower arms. She repeated this for the leg ones. The chest plate was big, so she cut it in half using a tool from the PSD. It now only covered her chest and half her back, but it was better than nothing.

She walked around the main room to get a feel for the clothing. Her movement was fluid, and having a second layer could be the deciding factor in a bad situation. She scoured the main room and found a fur rug. After halving it, she rolled it up. Along with using the backpack as a pillow, she would have something portable to sleep on. She packed it up and slipped on her adjusted fur head covering. The knives that Kazaal had moved were nowhere to be found. They were the one thing she had hoped was left around somewhere. She still had her PSD, but if she needed to use the stun or repulsion blast, she would not be able to with the morphable matter object out. With a last look around, she exited the cave.

She was greeted by a light breeze that carried the smell of grass. It was something she now savored. It was dark out, and the night sky was clear with a bright moon shining down. She could not see any stars, which sent a chill through her. After consulting her PSD, she headed off toward the green dot. Her path would take her through the grasslands to a forest. Given how close it would be, she figured it would take several hours to get there.

Halfway through the grasslands, she caught a strong animal scent. Her heartbeat raced, and she pulled out her PSD. The scent drew closer as she continued to walk. She noticed that her nanobots were tingling, almost as if they knew something was going on. Scanning toward the scent highlighted several shapes in the distance. She focused her gaze on them and made out some canine-like creatures. Her breath quickened as they headed toward her. When they got close, she could see that they resembled wolves, except they had scales instead of fur and had several horns on their bodies. With a snap of the PSD, she switched it back into pen mode. Her eyes had adjusted in the moonlight, and she stood her ground while singling out the leader of the pack. He was easy to pick out by his size and the way the others acted around him.

She fired a repulsion blast at the ground in front of him. The leader growled as he halted his advance, causing the others to stop. She fired again, this time right over the head of him. The leader spun around and took off. She figured he could feel the power of the blast, and she was happy she did not have to hurt it. Her eyes narrowed as another thought crept into her mind. If it had attacked, she would have killed it. Being seen as weak was dangerous in this environment, and she was tired of being attacked. If she could scare away attackers, that would be her first choice. Otherwise, they would fall victim to the brutal laws of survival.

There were no more distractions as she reached the edge of the forest. It was oddly formed with sparsely populated trees that reached the sky. The porous canopy allowed the moonlight to form rays that gave it an almost magical feel, but she knew this place was anything but that. The hairs on her neck shot up as she sensed another presence nearby. She sniffed the air and scanned her surroundings with the PSD. Although the PSD turned up nothing, the strong scent of something lingered. She paused and strained to see if she could hear it, but to no avail. With her PSD out and her eyes scanning all around, she crept forward.

There were insects buzzing around, some quite large, but nothing that would threaten her, or so she thought anyways. Small rodent-like creatures scurried about but ran away when she approached them. The presence of something behind her did not fade. She spun around at one point and thought she caught a glimpse of a face, but it was not a face she recognized. It was pale and drawn out, with an oversized mouth, black eyes, and wild black hair that shot off in every direction. The body the face was attached to was slender and tall, probably around ten or eleven feet tall. When she focused, it seemed to disappear. She knew that if she did not have the nanobots, she would not have even seen whatever it was, or sensed it. Maybe that was what it was expecting, and she caught it by surprise. Either way, she quickened her pace.

The trip through the forest should have taken an hour, but going slowly and scanning continuously added another half hour. When she came upon the spot where the green dot was, her eyes widened. A structure resembling a miniature stepped pyramid, similar to the one she came through on, was in front of her. Large pylons stood at each corner, with glowing tops. She observed it from the forest edge, unsure of what to do. The sound of rapid footsteps behind her caused her to spin around. Although she could not see it, she knew whatever it was would be on her in a few seconds. She ran forward toward the mini pyramid. She spun around with her PSD aimed forward and saw nothing. Whatever it was, it seemed to keep its distance from the pyramid. She jumped and pivoted when a beam from one of the pylons scanned her. The sound of scraping stone caught her attention. The pyramid slid back, revealing a ramp leading underground.

With a final look around, she entered the ramp way.

12

Evaran and the others followed John and Leah down to the rift room.

Dr. Snowden noted that the ramp took several turns, with rooms at each bend. He wondered where the guards or personnel that manned them were. Once they arrived, he took a moment to look it over. To their immediate right was a device that had a cylindrical base, with a slanted surface coming off it halfway down. A metal rod extended up from the base and ended in an upside-down dome-shaped structure.

His eyes narrowed as he noticed the two crystal rods that were about fifteen feet apart with a gold rhombus-shaped base. They stood at the back of the room and had evenly spaced silver rings on them. The featureless walls were in stark contrast to the device and crystals.

Evaran looked around the room. "Where is everyone?"

"They left," said Leah.

"To . . ."

"To Azoculus. Per our protocol, all personnel are to leave if the base comes under attack, except for the guards."

Lord Vygon shook his head. "So the guards just sacrifice themselves to stall for time."

"Yeah . . . ," said Leah. "Except they locked us in our room. I guess we're expendable."

"Interesting." Evaran walked over to the device and placed his UIC on it. It tried to connect, but the blue light never stabilized. "This is unusual. This object has . . . different matter in it, similar to the sentinel staff." He looked at John. "How does this work?"

John shrugged as he looked at Leah.

"I suspect you are withholding information."

John sighed. "May as well tell them. Not like we're getting out of here, and even if we did, we'd be killed for suspicion anyways. I have to ask, though, what're you going to do with us?"

Evaran tilted his head. "You will go to Atlantis, and the Helians will deal with you there. If you continue to help us, I will speak to that on your behalf."

John looked at Leah, who nodded. "In that case, we don't really know how it works. We're administrators, not rift operators, but we are trained in the basics on how to use the rift controller."

Lord Vygon smirked. "Not a bad strategy if you think about it. Give advanced tech to low-tech people, and if they're ever captured, they truly wouldn't know how it worked. However . . . you do know how to operate it."

John nodded. "To some degree. We only know of one destination."

Evaran gestured toward the console. "Azoculus, as you mentioned. Please show me what you would do to open the rift door."

John and Leah walked up to the rift controller and began to show Evaran how it worked. While Evaran listened to them, Dr. Snowden and Lord Vygon broke from the group and walked over to the crystal rods.

Dr. Snowden noticed a circular pattern with raised edges on the floor in front of the crystals. It reminded him of a rubber doormat that had been carved into an elaborate design, then tossed on the ground. He tapped Lord Vygon's arm and pointed to it. "Check that out. I remember seeing them in Atlantis."

Lord Vygon studied the pad, then looked around. "I bet that's where the sentinels' staff weapon sent people." He pointed at the bottom of one of the walls where a crushed beacon lay. "Evaran's beacon stopped transmitting a few moments after it was teleported. I'm guessing they decided they didn't like it."

Dr. Snowden looked at the crushed beacon, then at the pad. "If she appeared there, she wouldn't willingly go through that rift."

Lord Vygon looked down. "Yeah . . . I'm pretty sure it wasn't consensual."

Dr. Snowden scowled. He thought of Emily appearing, confused and terrified, and then being forced through. His face turned red as he clenched his jaw. He turned his head when he felt Lord Vygon's hand on his shoulder.

"Come, let us join the others."

Dr. Snowden exhaled a slow breath from his nose as they both walked back to Evaran. He focused on his breathing and repeated the word *relax* in his mind.

Evaran raised his head when he saw Dr. Snowden and Lord Vygon return. "The teleport system has been shut down. I am guessing that was part of the base attack protocol. I am intrigued by this rift technology. It is powered using something called a rift stone. I have never heard of that before, but suspect it is related to rifts in general, as is all this technology."

Lord Vygon stepped forward. "It allows a controlled rift to form when bombarded with a specific type of energy."

Everyone stared at Lord Vygon.

"You have seen this technology before?" asked Evaran.

Lord Vygon put his hand on the back of his neck. "Yeah . . . but I can't tell you from where. If John and Leah can operate the rift controller, they should be able to open a rift door, and we can toss a quantum beacon through."

"Why can't we just go through the rift door?" asked Dr. Snowden.

"The Purifiers know this base is compromised," said Evaran. "The other base is probably secured by now. A quantum beacon will at least tell us where it leads, even if they destroy it."

"We can take on whatever's over there!"

"Not likely," said John. "They probably have it shielded by now. Anything that goes through from this side would get splatted."

Dr. Snowden snorted. "Well . . . won't that happen with the beacon?"

Evaran nodded. "Yes. However, like the beacon we sent to get this location, it would transmit the location before being . . . splatted."

Dr. Snowden sighed.

Lord Vygon looked at Evaran. "I can go get the beacon, assuming you left it in the usual place in the research lab. If not, V can help."

Evaran studied Lord Vygon for a moment. "Go."

Lord Vygon nodded and then exited the room in a blur of motion.

"Hmm," said Evaran. "So once they go through the rift door, they go to this Azoculus planet, and from there, to the prison planet. Does the other facility have just one rift door?"

"Yeah," said Leah.

"Then the rift door can take on multiple destinations. Can we get to the prison planet from here?"

Leah bobbed her head. "You could . . . if you knew the destination code. The rift operator here would not have known that, and me and John only know Azoculus. Knowing a destination's code is taken very seriously."

"Could the rift door be opened from the other side?" asked Evaran.

Leah nodded. "Yeah . . . there will probably be more coming through later to try to reclaim the base, unless this rift door is shut down or shielded."

"I see," said Evaran. "Once we find out where Azoculus is, then you two can shut it down."

Dr. Snowden shook his head. "How did these Purifiers get over here in the first place?"

"That'd be the main rift stone," said John. "It has the ability to open doors to other places, without needing an active rift door on the other end. It's on the capital planet, but it never repeats an exact destination, although it can get one close by sometimes. It's kind of random from what I heard."

"That needs shut down, or Earth might get another wave of this ridiculous purification," said Dr. Snowden.

"I concur," said Evaran. "We will after we find Emily."

"Sounds good to me."

Evaran walked over to the crystal rods with everyone following him. Dr. Snowden pointed out the pad. Evaran rubbed his chin and then tapped the pad with his foot. He scanned it with his ring. "Interesting. With the teleport down, we should probably shield the rift door. Leah, can you do that until Lord Vygon gets back?"

Leah nodded.

Everyone followed Leah to the rift controller. She placed her hand on the bottom part of the upside-down dome and pressed a panel. The panel emitted a glow as it sank in. A projection shot up showing a scattering of dots with lines linking them. She tapped a finger at a dot, causing the projection to zoom in, and a rectangular box appeared under it. When she tapped at the box, a grid of tiles with unusual designs embedded on them appeared where her finger was.

Dr. Snowden studied the tiles. "I can't translate them . . ."

"If the universal translator cannot translate, that would indicate that this technology is from somewhere outside this universe."

"Universal translator?" asked John.

Evaran shook his hand. "Not important." He gestured at Leah. "Go ahead."

Leah selected one of the tiles. The grid disappeared, and the tile now showed underneath the dot. She repeated this sixteen times, which caused the box to blink. The crystal rods shimmered for a moment before a light-blue semitransparent shield surrounded them. "Done."

"Excellent," said Evaran.

John slumped down against the wall and sighed. "This is the first planet I've seen that's fought back. I've heard of others, but never seen it done."

"What planet did you come from?" asked Dr. Snowden.

John eyed Dr. Snowden. "Leah and I are from Forath. Oddly enough, it looks a lot like this planet."

"A parallel timeline maybe?" asked Dr. Snowden as he looked at Evaran.

"Possibly," said Evaran. "These rift stones could be linked, so if they were split up across timelines, exciting them with exotic energy would seem to open a door between them." He faced John. "I assume that this prison planet, however, is something else."

John nodded. "Yeah . . . don't really know much about that. Or what a . . . parallel timeline is."

"You may know of it as an innerverse, same concept."

John shook his head. "Yeah . . . don't know about that either. We just know there's a special destination. Makes the rift door have a red surface. From what I've heard, it strips nonhumans of their abilities."

Evaran tilted his head. "Elaborate."

"Well . . . not sure if *strips* is the right word, but people who pass through it have whatever makes them nonhuman taken out."

Dr. Snowden wrinkled his eyebrows. "Emily had nanobots, so it probably would not have done anything to her, other than send her to wherever, right?"

John shrugged. "I . . . don't know what nanobots are. I've only seen pictures of the prison planet rift door before."

"I see," said Evaran. "This rift technology is far beyond the Purifier knowledge level."

"They aren't Purifier technology. The overlord discovered them and adapted them for our use. He seems to be the only one that truly understands them. And maybe the high priests."

Lord Vygon entered the room, carrying a sphere the size of a basketball. "Took me a while to find. Wasn't where I was used to seeing it. The research lab had a different configuration." He shook his head with a smile. "Nonetheless, here's the quantum beacon."

John tilted his head. "Once you find Azoculus, how are you going to get to it?"

"We are going to fly to it in my ship."

John jerked his head back. "In your ship . . . as in through the air?"

Evaran picked up the quantum beacon from Lord Vygon. "Not quite. Leah, can you remove the shield and set the portal for Azoculus."

Leah took a breath and then interacted with the rift controller. After a moment, the shielding disappeared, and a solid golden surface appeared between the crystal rods.

Evaran tossed out an orb from his belt. It projected an image of V in the Torvatta. "V, have you set up the tracer?"

"The tracer has been activated."

"Excellent," said Evaran. He walked over to the rift door with everyone in tow and then rolled the beacon through it.

"Transferring visual," said V.

The projection changed to a diagram of multiple cylinders. A line zigzagged horizontally across the cylinders before coming to a rest. The line then disappeared.

"Analysis. Timeline 4501 is the destination."

Evaran rubbed his chin. "Interesting. V, we are headed back. Are there any other Purifiers alive?"

"There are six. Two are in the medical lab, and the other four are under guard by the Ollikrin."

"Very well. Once we are aboard, take us to Atlantis."

"Acknowledged."

"Leah, please shut down the rift door."

Leah interacted with the rift controller, and after a moment, the golden surface disappeared. "Done."

Evaran gestured toward the room exit. "We are done here. There are some things to discuss back at Atlantis, then we are off to timeline 4501."

As they filed out of the room, Dr. Snowden smiled. He now knew where Emily had gone. Hopefully, the prison planet was not as rough as he was imagining, but knowing Emily, she would not only survive, but come out stronger. The question burning in his mind was how this would impact her long-term. He shook his head. First things first. Find her, then he would deal with that.

John and Leah sat to the right of Evaran in the council room. Delia, Lord Noskov, and Lord Vygon had taken their seats to the left of Evaran, along with Captain Laban.

Dr. Snowden also had a seat next to Leah at the table. He had not expected to be sitting there. Looking around the circular table, he noticed it was almost filled. Helian elders Cyrus and Ira rounded out the table.

Evaran raised a finger. "The Purifier base has been captured. There were heavy casualties, but the Purifiers will no longer be a threat to this planet for the time being."

"That's good news," said Cyrus.

"Yes," said Evaran. "However, I have some points to go over before I leave."

"You're leaving?" asked Cyrus.

Dr. Snowden noted the concern in Cyrus's voice. Evaran had been the unofficial leader which is something that seemed to happen whenever he was present. Maybe it was Evaran's confidence, which he exuded, or the way he backed up his talk with actions. Either way, Dr. Snowden suspected that Cyrus was not looking forward to having to deal with Daedroulds and others on equal terms.

"I am," said Evaran. "Dr. Snowden's niece, Emily, is still missing. We know where she went from here, and we are going after her. I am not asking for anyone to come, as there is important work to be done here."

Lord Vygon slapped Lord Noskov on the back. "I'll let Lord Noskov speak for the vampire houses while I'm out with Evaran."

Lord Noskov jerked his head back. "What? I'm no politician."

"Then don't be one," said Lord Vygon. "You know the issues as well as anyone. Be yourself. Once I come back, assuming I do, I can rejoin the effort." He faced Delia. "Any concerns?"

Delia eyed Lord Noskov, then shook her head. "None. He has shown himself to be a leader, and I accept him as such."

Lord Noskov raised his eyebrows.

Dr. Snowden chuckled. He had come to like Lord Vygon, and even had a begrudging respect for Lord Noskov. Having Lord Vygon along made him feel better. Not just for himself, but for Evaran as well. Dr. Snowden now knew that Lord Vygon and Evaran would become great friends, and that he and Lord Vygon would be as well at some point. Lord Vygon was easy to get along with, was knowledgeable, and, if it came down to it, was a force to be reckoned with in a fight. He shook his head. Lord Vygon would be the perfect traveling companion for Evaran. Maybe he was at some point in Evaran's future.

Evaran cleared his throat. "First point, there are sentinels still out and about. Each sentinel has an implant, and it can be detected. I will transfer that information before leaving."

"How many are we talking about?" asked Cyrus.

"Unknown. The sentinel we spoke to said there were one hundred twelve, but the attack on Atlantis had thousands.

The cleanup effort will take some time, but with a unified council, it should be a top priority."

Captain Laban raised a finger. "I will guarantee it will be handled."

Lord Noskov flashed a fanged smile. "For the first time, I find myself agreeing with a Helian."

"The sentinels' teleporting weapons won't have any impact now. However, they still carry weapons and can be dangerous."

Captain Laban glanced at Lord Noskov. "I think we can handle it."

Lord Noskov smirked and nodded.

Dr. Snowden thought it was interesting that two people who formerly would have been enemies were here now agreeing to work together. He knew that bonds forged in battle could be strong, and maybe Evaran's insistence that the Helians be involved in the base fight was to bring that about. It seemed to be working.

"Point two," said Evaran as he gestured to his side. "This is John and Leah. They are Purifiers who cannot go back since the rift door is no longer active. They were administrative staff, and I do not want them punished."

Ira narrowed his eyes. "Purifiers . . . and you want to just let them go?"

"Yes. They were able to operate the rift door to help us."

Ira snorted. "Sorry . . . if you think Purifiers are going to be treated with any respect here after what they did . . . you're crazy."

"We aren't really Purifiers by choice," said John. "The Purifiers took over me and Leah's world, and you either joined or died. We decided to live."

"And that excuses your involvement?" asked Ira.

Delia raised her hand. "They can stay with us." She looked at John and Leah. "My domain is . . . not technology based like here. It's mostly forest and grasslands. You can choose to stay here or make a new life in my domain. Obviously, Purifier ideology won't be tolerated."

"Well, I was a farmer before all of this," said John. "While I'd like to go back to my home world, it would be suicide and . . . they killed my family." He looked at Leah. "Maybe we could have a farm?"

Leah smiled and nodded. "Considering the alternatives, I'm okay with that."

Ira slammed his hand on the table. "They. Need. To. Be. Punished."

"Then let's vote," said Delia, shooting an icy gaze at Ira. "All council members who agree to allow John and Leah to come with me, raise your hand."

Lord Noskov, Lord Vygon, Cyrus, and Delia raised their hands.

Delia nodded. "It is settled then. They will come with me."

"This is ridiculous," said Ira. He crossed his arms and sat back in his chair.

"What about the other Purifiers?" asked Lord Noskov. "They were guards, trained to fight. I don't think they would want to settle down."

"They are welcome to come with me if they wish," said Delia. "I suspect imprisonment here is not high on their list."

Ira shook his head. "*Someone* has to pay for this. If not these two, then the other ones should."

Evaran eyed Ira. "That decision needs to be agreed upon by this council. You need to remember . . . if Delia and Lord Noskov did not come to your aid, they would be making this decision . . . with *no* Helians around. You should be thankful this council even exists."

"I agree with Evaran," said Captain Laban. "I will abide by this council's ruling."

Evaran nodded. "That brings me to my third point. I want Captain Laban on the council. He has proven himself to be honorable and of sound mind."

"He's just a captain," said Ira with wrinkled eyebrows.

"Perhaps, but he is trained in leadership, and has a battle bond with Delia and Lord Noskov, something neither you nor Cyrus have. That balance will be needed."

"No problem here," said Lord Noskov.

"Likewise," said Delia.

"Same," said Lord Vygon.

"Then it is settled. Captain Laban, do you accept?"

Captain Laban did a Helian salute. "I will do my best."

"I know you will. That is all I ask," said Evaran. "Point four. As you all may or may not know, I am a time traveler. As such, in future meetings, I am not to be made aware of any event I may have participated in, unless I mention it. A protocol will need to be established to deal with that."

Dr. Snowden smirked. "The Evaran Protocol."

Evaran nodded. "Yes. As I will be around this planet for some time, there is the possibility that I may interact with this council. Just ensure that if you meet me, do not volunteer information unless directly asked. If it appears I do not know of the event, assume I have not experienced it yet." He eyed Lord Noskov. "It will get harder in time to remember that, but I wanted to at least put it in place."

"Why're you looking at me?" asked Lord Noskov.

Lord Vygon chuckled.

"Also, as part of this protocol, my involvement in any event should be scrubbed from the records," said Evaran.

Cyrus jerked his head back. "Okay . . . I understand the first part, but why the second part?"

"As a general rule of time travel, you should not know what your personal future holds, and if it is recorded, it could be used against me."

Cyrus glanced at Ira, who shrugged.

Evaran half smiled at Cyrus. "Point five. Communication will be critical. As such, I will update your communication technology. I do not typically interfere with technology in a given time period. However, since I will be here for a long time, I will make this one exception."

"Our technology can already do that," said Cyrus.

"Not securely," said Evaran. "Nonetheless, I would suggest that Atlantis house one representative of each faction for a general assembly. The communication upgrade will allow the representatives to communicate back to their faction in a secure manner. Each communication channel will be specifically encrypted for that faction."

"You think we'd spy, don't you?" asked Ira.

"Of course. I have monitored your communications and have seen your spying apparatus at work. Also . . . it is not something that goes away apparently in the future."

Ira snorted. "More of this time-travel ridiculousness."

Lord Vygon smirked. "I just realized, he doesn't know how Delia and Lord Noskov knew to come. We time traveled back three years to get them to consider it, then picked them up on the day the sentinels attacked. You may not believe in it, but the results are clear."

Cyrus extended a hand. "It's not that we don't believe it isn't possible, it's just that we have never seen it and our research shows it to be impossible."

"I will leave that up to Delia, Lord Noskov, or Lord Vygon to elaborate on should they choose to do so. The less people know about it, the better," said Evaran. "My final point deals with slavery."

Cyrus cocked his head.

"Alien slavers have been raiding this planet for a while. I know the Helians have been fighting them. As a cornerstone of this council's new policies, I want to ensure that it is kept as a high priority. With the new communication technology, hopefully that will be easier to accomplish."

Dr. Snowden smirked. He knew that in 1534, the Helians would sign a treaty with the Kreagan Star Empire on this subject. That was almost 4,169 years from now. He wondered what happened during that time, since from what he knew from traveling with Evaran, it was the Helians and them alone calling the shots. Given how volatile and ambitious this new council was going to be, he suspected there was a breakdown somewhere in that time and the Helians went at it alone. Evaran would know this as well, but maybe at least while this council is active, things would be better.

Cyrus nodded. "We will make it one of our priorities."

The council members all nodded.

"Very good. I will take my leave then."

"You're coming back, though, right?" asked Lord Noskov.

"Yes. I will have to if Lord Vygon is coming with me," said Evaran as he stood. "I will also check in to see how things are going. Is there anything anyone needs from me before I go?"

John and Leah shook their heads and stood. They crossed their hands against their chests and bowed.

"Thanks for being kind. We . . . are not used to that," said John with misted eyes.

Leah nodded.

Evaran half smiled. "If I stop by your farm, I expect a vegetable soup."

"You got it."

Captain Laban stood and saluted Evaran. "Good journey. Fight well."

Evaran saluted back.

Lord Noskov rose and shook Evaran's hand. "Well . . . this'll be interesting."

"You can do this."

Lord Noskov smirked.

Delia rose and bowed. "Travel safe, and may nature guide you. It was an honor to finally meet you."

Evaran bowed. "The honor is mine." He did a Helian salute to Cyrus and Ira. "Good luck, and I shall see you all again soon, assuming things go well." He gestured for Lord Vygon and Dr. Snowden to exit the room. "Let us go find Emily."

13

Emily pulled out her PSD and turned on the illumination aspect of it. She jerked her head back as embedded light strips lit up on the sides of the ramp. Running her hand along the walls verified it was made of some type of metal. It reminded her of a space station, and the high-tech nature of it stood out to her.

The dust particles in the air made her sneeze when she took a few whiffs. Her head cocked and her breathing intensified at the sound of the pyramid sliding back over her after she was halfway down the ramp. The impulse to run back out swept over her, but she figured if the area had been designed to be a death trap, there would have been more effective ways do that.

Her breathing normalized as she continued down the ramp to a doorway. She peeked her head in and looked around a circular room with four doorways, two on her left and two on the other side. Her attention was drawn to the ceiling. It was made of a black glass-like material and reminded her of the black strips she and Dr. Snowden had seen when Evaran rescued them from an alien ship. They had been used for holographic technology. Maybe these served the same purpose.

As she approached the center of the room, a beam shot down from the ceiling in front of her. She jumped back and whipped her PSD forward as a hologram of a thin three-foot-tall beige humanoid with a dinner-plate-shaped head appeared in front of her. The wide black eyes were on the underside of the head, and a small mouth was just south of it. It wore a blue jumpsuit with silver lines and black boots. The top of the head looked armored with bumps, and the skin on the rest of the body was smooth. The being was similar to the one she had seen at the podium before. A second beam shot down and enveloped her, causing her to shudder. It disappeared as quickly as it came.

"Translation matrix has been initiated. Welcome to Coraanan research facility number thirty-four. I am the virtual interface, Kal."

Emily stared at Kal with her mouth agape. After a few moments of studying it, she said, "Umm. Hello?"

"Hello."

"What are you?"

"I am the virtual interface Kal."

Emily shook her head. "No . . . I meant . . . what species are you?"

"I am modeled after a male Coraanan."

"Okay . . . what is researched here?"

"The Coraanan researched specimens sent through the rift doors."

Emily circled her hand. "Specimens?"

"Convicted offenders of Coraanan law."

Emily grimaced. This research facility was a glorified watchtower. She walked over to the first doorway on the left. "Where does this go?"

"This door leads to the living quarters. It is composed of two levels, with fifty individual rooms each. Each room consists of a sleeping pod, a hygiene pod, an eating pod, and an entertainment pod."

"Sounds interesting . . . ," said Emily. She glanced at Kal, who stood staring at her. Although Kal was not real, she was glad to have something to talk to that did not want to murder or eat her. It was a nice change of pace. She walked up to the second door on the left. "Where does this one go?"

"This door leads to the specimen surveillance lab, which the Coraanan used to monitor incoming offenders. It consists of twenty workstations, each networked into the central database."

Emily was beginning to get a feel for Kal. He seemed to have short descriptions of everything, but it seemed that in order to dig for more information, the right question would have to be asked. "What else is in this central database?"

"The central database contains records on each specimen. Audio, visual, and text is stored and identified by a specimen ID. Research, facility maintenance, and personal employee information is also stored."

"And how many specimens are we talking about?"

"There are currently eighteen thousand nine hundred thirty-six specimen IDs."

Emily's eyes widened. It was obvious this was a large-scale operation. If this was a prison planet as it seemed to be, then the Coraanan were either prolific in sending people through or they had been at it a long time. "How old is this research facility?"

"This research facility is seven hundred eighty-nine years old."

Emily paused as she digested what she had just heard. A quick check on her math revealed that to be about twenty-four specimens a year, or two a month. She had been on the planet just a few weeks away from two months, so there would have been two to three others. The one she had seen devoured where she had come in crossed her mind. Then there was Ezekial, and the other one that Kazaal had gone after when she escaped. Her mind focused on the Coraanan. "Are . . . there any Coraanan here now?"

"There are currently no Coraanan at this research facility."

"When was the last time one was here?"

"The last Coraanan was here three hundred eight years ago."

"Where did they go?"

"Unknown."

Emily sighed. "Did they leave a note or log or something?"

"The central database contains many logs."

Emily wrinkled her eyebrows. "Any on why they left?"

"There are three hundred logs with the word *left*."

Emily snorted as she walked over to the other side of the room. The difference between V, an artificial intelligence, and Kal, a virtual intelligence, was much clearer to her now. She had a vague understanding of it before, but the conversation she was having now was illustrating it quite well. One thing that was a pleasant surprise was that the place smelled clean. "What powers this place?"

"This research facility is powered by both geothermal and nuclear power."

Emily bobbed her head as she pointed at the first door on the right. "Where does this lead to?"

"This door leads to the specimen storage rooms. Specimens were brought in for study if they reached a certain distance from the portals. Native denizens of this planet were also kept here."

"Certain distance?"

"If a specimen was able to survive and move away within a range threshold, they were brought in for study. Neurological and physical analysis was obtained."

"And . . . how was that done?"

"The specimens were dissected and studied."

Emily harrumphed. Not only were these Coraanan heartless, they were also unethical. She shook her head. What was it about highly advanced civilizations and their perversion of ethics? Maybe it was her view that was perverse to them. She pointed to the next door. "And where does this one go?"

"This door leads to the transportation system. Each research facility on a landmass contains a hub that is connected to other hubs at other research facilities. The hub at this facility is currently inactive due to breaches."

"What do you mean by that?"

"The transportation system tunnels are not functional. The tunnels' exterior walls have been exposed to the surrounding environment. Multiple blockages were reported."

"What caused it?"

"Unknown."

Emily studied the doorway for a moment. She planned to check it out, but given what she had seen outside, it would be no surprise that something would have gotten into the subterranean tunnels. The fact that there were no Coraanan around and that their transportation system was busted probably meant something bad happened, something she would need to research. For now, checking out the living quarters and getting some rest, food, and water were on her mind. The thought of that creature outside gave her pause as she faced Kal. "Is this facility secure? I saw some pillars outside."

"This facility is secured by guardian pillars. The two entrances to the facility are currently shut down."

Emily let out a measured breath. "And there is nothing alive here?"

"You are the only being with the status of alive."

Emily nodded. "Well then . . . take me to a room in the living quarters."

Kal bowed and floated off toward the first door on the left. Emily followed him into a split-level entrance. Kal went up the right side and into an elongated room with evenly spaced doors lined up on the walls. The first door on the right slid open at their approach.

Entering the room caused Emily's eyes to pop open. It was relatively luxurious from what she had been getting used to. The central room had a workstation and a couch, along with a large screen on the wall. Small tables were dotted up against the wall and between entrances to the other pod areas. She turned back to the door they had just walked through and looked for a console. She found it on the wall to her right. "How do you lock this?"

Kal raised a hand toward the console and a performed a walk-through of how to lock the door.

Emily repeated the steps to lock the door and then looked for the hygiene pod. Walking to her right, she peered in and saw a lowered platform with grill holes around the base. A console screen stood out on the wall. She was not sure exactly how it worked, but she would figure it out. Turning toward Kal, she said, "Okay . . . I think I'm good now."

Kal looked at Emily.

"You can go away now."

"If you require my assistance, you can activate me from a console or say my name out loud followed by the word *activate*. To shut me down, say my name followed by the word *deactivate*." Kal stared at Emily.

Emily sighed. "Fine. Kal, deactivate."

Kal shimmered, then disappeared.

Emily stripped down and stepped onto the lowered platform. She interacted with the console. It took her a bit to figure out the interface, but she was able to set the temperature of the water and intensity of it. She jumped when the water first came down since it did not come from a nozzle, but instead from holes in the ceiling. As the hot water caressed her body, she let out a measured breath.

The last time she had a hot shower escaped her, but the weeks of grime seemed to wash away. Looking around, she saw an indented area with several nozzles and a mesh glove. She tapped at one of the nozzles, and it spurted out a gooey blue substance. She sniffed it as best she could in the shower and determined it was some type of cleaner. Rubbing a bit of it on the ends of her hair caused it to foam up. Tapping at another nozzle caused a gel-like substance with miniature objects in it to spew forth. She scrubbed a bit on her forearm and half smiled at the feel. After putting on the mesh glove, which seemed to expand to the size of her hand, she cleaned herself thoroughly. Even though she had washed herself twice over, she spent some additional time just standing. It felt too good to move.

After a while, she tapped at the console and turned off the water. She cocked her head at the drying options. Playing around with it showed that there were controls on air flow. She selected a warm air and its intensity and stood while the sides of the enclosure slid down to reveal slits every foot or so. Warm air blasted out. She felt her eyes droop. If she ever got back to the Torvatta, this would be something she would recommend as an upgrade.

She grimaced as she thought of Dr. Snowden, Evaran, and V. They seemed so far away to her. At this point, she was sure something was wrong. There was no way they would not have come, unless there was some reason they were unable to. She would have to survive out here, alone. No help was coming. Her heart sank as tears rolled down her cheeks. She still had hope that she might be wrong, but as each day and trial passed, it was becoming more and more remote.

After drying off, she headed to the bedroom with her clothes and equipment in her arms and found a cocoon-shaped bed. She checked her PSD and saw it would be roughly 11:00 p.m. back on Earth. Tossing her clothing and equipment at the side of the bed, she crawled inside and slipped under the covers.

Exhaustion took over, and her eyes closed.

Emily awoke the next day and lay in bed for a bit. She stared out at the clothes and equipment she had been using. They were still tossed on the ground next to the bed. The memory of how tired she was last night jumped into her mind briefly, then exited as she swung her legs off the side of the bed.

She stretched and yawned and checked her chest for pain. The nanobots had been at work. She grabbed her PSD off the ground and checked the time. It showed eleven in the morning. A twelve-hour rest was unusual for her, but maybe the nanobots needed the time. At least there was no pain.

She noticed a closet in the room and investigated it. It had several pieces of an outfit embedded in a block that took up half the closet. The other half was a space with a button on the wall. The flooring of it had a rubber mat of some sort. Her eyebrows wrinkled as she studied the blue jumpsuit. To the right of it was a smaller white garment that reminded her of a one-piece swimming suit. Under that was a thin silver wristband. She cocked her head as she noticed unusual-looking socks next to the combat-like boots on the ground. Everything seemed a bit small for her.

"Kal. Activate."

Kal shimmered into view. "Good morning. How may I be of service?"

Emily gestured at the clothing display. "What is this?"

"It is a clothing adjuster that adjusts the sizing of the clothes based on your body."

"How do I tell it my size?"

"Step into the clothing adapter pad and press the button."

Emily raised her eyebrows as she stepped onto the pad. She pressed the button and jumped a bit when a thin line of light scanned her from top to bottom. Once it was done, she stepped out and noticed that the outfit embedded into the block was larger. She grabbed the smaller white suit and slipped it on. It felt like underwear and was soft on the skin. She slipped on the blue jumpsuit, socks, and boots. With a few quick turns and movements, she adjusted to it. It seemed to flow much better than what she had on before. She sat on the edge of her bed and put on her bone pieces. That was not something she suspected this place would provide.

The wristband slipped effortlessly onto her wrist. It was not fully closed but had a small gap that pulled apart enough to fit her wrist through. She eyed it. "Kal, what is this wrist-band for?"

"It contains the translation matrix needed for translation and also records my interaction with you."

"Oh," she said. "Guess that would be handy for other facilities."

Kal stared at her.

She shook her head with a small smile. "Kal. Deactivate."

Kal shimmered out of view.

She headed to the hygiene room and washed up. She pulled her hair back into a ponytail and used a leather strip to tie it off. Putting on her fur head covering completed her outfit. Throughout the rest of the day, she kept Kal activated. Kal would follow her around in silence, and she was getting used to his presence. Although not a living being, it felt like another person.

Over the next month, this would be her morning routine. Her afternoon routine involved her going to the specimen surveillance room and researching. She spent a few hours a day meditating and trying to focus on her nanobots. Other hours were spent on practicing her training and learning more about the PSD.

She had no desire to leave the facility during this time, other than scouting out the transportation hub. Looking at the visual feeds from outside from time to time showed no signs of the presence. She had wondered if it was waiting for her to leave. If it tried to attack her, it would learn she was not easy prey, just like Kazaal did.

If there was going to be any information on this planet, she suspected it would be in the specimen surveillance lab. That would be better than trying to figure out what keywords to use with Kal. He had mentioned that even though the Coraanan were gone, the rift doors still sent automated information. While browsing the latest entries, she found hers, along with Ezekial's. The one statistic that stood out to her was potential strength levels. For Ezekial, he had one point four. She was not sure what scale was being used but assumed one was an average. Hers was four. She knew that she had additional strength at times but did not think it was four times a normal human's, assuming Ezekial was a normal human.

Studying the transportation system showed that there were multiple research facilities across the landmass. The tunnels connecting the facilities were also damaged. There was not a lot of detail on why, just that some areas of it were considered unsafe.

The communication system between the facilities was down. Maybe that was why the last group of Coraanan left. She asked Kal how the rift doors could send automated information when the communication system was down, and he said that they were different networks. There were several, and the automated one had better redundancy according to Kal.

The blue dot information had caught her eye. It was the exit point for the planet and was called Central Command. There was a rift door that allowed for travel back. It did not specify where, though. She had smiled as she read it. Maybe there was hope. All she had to do was get there. She tracked the various facilities she could use on the way. The trip was about 140 miles, with a facility every 40 miles or so. The next one she would need to get to went through a mountain range. Or she could take the tunnels.

While her daily research took several hours, another few were spent focusing on her nanobots. She had learned that if she focused on them, she could get the tingling sensation all over her body. When her focus had been amplified, everything slowed down a bit. It was an adjustment to get used to the timing as she trained at staff fighting and other techniques from her PSD.

The specimen storage room was one place she did not go much. There was nothing of value in there except rooms with glass-like windows and bones everywhere. It was apparent that the Coraanan left behind whatever was in there to die. It seemed to her that the Coraanan evacuated in a rush.

At the end of a month, she was ready. She was dismayed that there were no weapons, but she did find a much more solid backpack and filled it with metal containers of the cleaning goo and other hygiene gels. She also packed some hard candies she had found patterns for on the food replicators. One item she treasured was a flat, circular light beacon that she could wear around her neck. It was the size of a small dinner plate and shot a wide beam forward. She figured it would be helpful if she needed to use her PSD in a darkened situation. Although unsure of the power source, she hoped it would last to the next facility.

The thought that maybe the presence would have found a way into the tunnels had crept into her mind. She felt she was ready to take it on if she had to. Her stun and repulsion beams should be more than a match for it. She hoped it would not come to close-quarters combat, but if it did, her nanobots and fighting training would help out.

With a good night's rest behind her, she stood at the entrance to the transportation system door. "Kal. Activate."

Kal shimmered into view. "Good afternoon. How may I be of service?"

Emily smiled. "I'm leaving. I just wanted to say thank you."

"Visual log recorded."

"Kal. Deactivate."

Kal faded away.

Emily snorted and headed down the winding ramp after going through the doorway. She had scouted the transportation hub under the facility during her month stay. It reminded her of a train station in that it had travel compartments on some type of rail in the middle, with wide platforms along each side. High above on each side were lighting strips. The tunnel was a straight shot to the next facility, and forty miles long. With a final look around, she began her journey.

The first few miles went without incident. She had not seen any breaches in the metal walls. There was little noise outside her footsteps and breathing. The dimming of the lights as she progressed seemed ominous to her. It reminded her of scary movies. If she had been on a couch watching herself, she would have yelled at herself to go back to the safety of the first research facility. She used the PSD to track her progress and checked it occasionally. She was not expecting to reach the second facility for at least three days.

By the fifth mile, the tunnel had become dimly lit. Her breathing staggered a bit as she turned on her light beacon. The shadows played tricks on her mind for the next several miles. It was still eerily quiet. She did not want to sleep in total darkness but kept an eye out for a place to bed down for the night. One thing she noticed was that every fifth mile, there was a small room off to the side that acted as a passage to a smaller tunnel. She suspected it was an access room for maintenance. It had doors that could be manually locked from the inside. The room was small, but large enough she could lie down. The window facing the tunnel was a bit unnerving to her, but it would have to do. She took a quick break.

At the tenth mile, she took another rest. Her legs were a bit sore, and her feet were starting to hurt. She locked herself into the side room. Turning off the light beacon caused goose bumps to appear on her arm. It was much darker and took a while for her eyes to adjust. She laid her backpack on the ground and pulled out the fur rug she had taken from Kazaal's. She doubled it over as she lay down and rested her head on the backpack. With a quick check of her PSD, she noted it was about twelve in the afternoon. She figured she would stay for the night at the next stop, but for now, she just needed to rest her legs. After two hours of relaxing peacefully, she packed up and continued forward.

She got to the fifteen-mile marker and settled into the side room. Her legs were pulsing, and her feet were pounding. Before locking the doors, she used the rail line area to relieve herself. Being half naked in the now almost pitch-black tunnel was something that did not scare her. Kazaal's cave had removed that fear. After locking up, she watched training videos until she fell asleep several hours later.

She awoke mid sleep to the sound of the door handle shaking. Her heart froze and her breathing staggered as she reached for her PSD. Focusing on her nanobots caused tingling sensations to resonate throughout her body. She lay as still as possible with her eyes fixated on the window. Although it was pitch-black, she had the feeling something was watching her through the window. Her face turned red. Whoever or whatever it was on the other side of the door was making a mistake in thinking she would be easy prey. After a few minutes, the door handle shaking stopped. She jumped as she thought she saw a shape move past the window.

She repositioned so that her feet were against the door. If something did come through, at least it would physically wake her. It took a bit for her to relax. Exhaustion had set in, and she closed her eyes as she thought about Dr. Snowden, Evaran, and V.

The next morning, she surveyed her surroundings upon waking up. She was still in the same position, and her bowels demanded her attention. Relieving herself outside the room would expose her, so she did her business in a corner and used the paper she had stowed away from the facility to clean herself. After checking everything, she made sure her PSD had both the stun and repulsion set. With a tap of her light beacon, digestion of some of the facility food she had stored, and a quick sip of water she had brought, she was prepared to leave.

She paused as she peered at the window. Her heart raced as the greasy imprint of two hands and a drawn-out face became visible.

14

Dr. Snowden looked out at space through the left front screen of the Torvatta. His nerves were pulsating at the thought of finally finding Emily. It seemed like ages to get to this point, and he understood the steps were necessary. They had left Atlantis only minutes ago and were preparing to jump to the parallel timeline that the Purifiers sent Emily to.

"V, status," said Evaran.

"Analysis. Dimensional location acquired. Portal configuration is complete."

Evaran nodded.

Dr. Snowden glanced at Lord Vygon. "Just like old times?"

Lord Vygon shook his head. "Never done a parallel timeline jump before. This is new to me."

Dr. Snowden caught Evaran giving Lord Vygon a sidelong glance. It would seem then that most of Lord Vygon's travels with Evaran took place in the same timeline. The Azoculus planet they were going to would be a parallel Earth. Since they did not time travel, it would be in the same time period.

A thought brushed his mind that he wished Emily could see it, and then he realized she had seen it, albeit through force.

His attention focused on the silver beam that shot out from the front of the Torvatta. Usually it was a golden beam. The portal that formed was not the silver border and light-blue surface he had come to expect. The border was blue, and the interior surface of the portal was red. He wondered how many different types of portals there were.

The Torvatta flew through the portal and exited above Azoculus. The right front screen lit up with an image of the planet. Dr. Snowden noted that it looked just like Earth. A red dot pulsated around where New York would be.

"The quantum beacon is no longer active, so I suspect the rift door was either shielded as John mentioned earlier or it was destroyed upon arrival by other means," said Evaran.

Dr. Snowden sighed. "And I bet Emily is not down there either."

"Probably not if she went through to the prison planet, but we will check. V, attempt to contact Emily."

"Acknowledged."

V's hands flew over the console. A static image of Emily appeared on the front right screen with a border that pulsated. Dr. Snowden's heart raced as he held his breath. After a moment, the screen went black.

V faced Evaran. "No PSD signal was found."

Dr. Snowden sighed.

"V, put us in stealth mode and scan the surrounding area when we get there."

"Acknowledged."

The Torvatta descended through the atmosphere toward the pulsating red dot. As it got closer, Dr. Snowden began to see the outline of familiar places. The North American continent looked a little different in that the land bridge to

South America was much larger. This planet was not exactly like Earth. The Appalachian Mountains came into view as the Torvatta got closer. When it had descended to a mile above the ground, he noticed that where there should be cities, it was just the natural environment. "Where is everything . . ."

"Preliminary scans show no civilization," said Evaran. He raised a finger. "Perhaps in this timeline, humanity never evolved."

Lord Vygon cocked his head. "Wonder what did evolve then . . ."

"I do not know."

"Structure detected," said V.

Dr. Snowden studied the visual on the left screen. It appeared to be a small, low-tech, triangular fort with a stone wall surrounding it. He counted three buildings around a larger one. It was the corpses impaled on spikes that caught his attention.

"What in the world happened here . . . ," said Dr. Snowden. It did not look good, and the fact Emily might have been tossed into this made his stomach churn.

Evaran studied the left and right front screens. "V, analysis."

V interacted with the front console. After a moment, he said, "No life-forms detected outside the buildings. Structural damage is present on all buildings."

"I see. Land us inside the walls just past the entrance door."

"Acknowledged."

The Torvatta descended to just inside the walls behind a sealed door and landed.

Dr. Snowden's eyes popped open as he got a better view of the impaled corpses from the ground. Most of the bodies wore similar clothing to the guards from the Purifier base, while others had on similar outfits to John and Leah. He rubbed the goose bumps on his arms.

Evaran stood and gestured toward the Torvatta entrance. "This could be dangerous. I was expecting some resistance, but it appears something has already taken care of that part. Dr. Snowden, you may want to put on a survival suit." He glanced at Lord Vygon. "There are additional suits should you want one."

Lord Vygon tapped his chest as he stood. "This light armor is special. It's all I need."

"Very well."

Dr. Snowden hustled into the research lab and slipped into the oversized survival suit. Once he zipped it up, it shrank down to be formfitting. He liked using the suit. Its usefulness had been made clear when helping the Fredorians achieve their destiny. He tested the right repulsor blast on his right hand and the shield on the left forearm. With a brief tap at a small device on his chest, he verified that the suit interface appeared as a hologram in front of him. He pressed the left button on his neck guard, causing the familiar transparent helmet to shoot over his head. With a few tweaks on the suit interface, the heads-up display, or HUD as he had to come to know it, appeared inside the helmet. He adjusted the internal temperature and then joined Evaran and Lord Vygon outside the ship.

Evaran and Lord Vygon stood next to a corpse. V flew around in orb mode, scanning the surrounding area.

Evaran scanned the corpse. "Interesting. This spike formed from the ground, yet it appears as a smooth continuation of the ground, like it was always here. That is unusual."

Lord Vygon rubbed his chin. "A matter mage? I don't sense one."

Evaran shook his head. "I do not sense one either."

"So . . . you're saying these spikes were always here, and these people just impaled themselves?" asked Dr. Snowden.

"It would seem that way, but I do not suspect that is what happened."

"Uhh . . . you think this area . . . is alive?"

"No. I believe something morphed the matter under the person, then formed a spike. This was recent. There must be another party here we are unaware of. And a powerful one at that, although I do not sense anything."

Dr. Snowden sighed. "That's just what we need."

Lord Vygon chuckled as he slapped Dr. Snowden on the back. "Whoever or whatever it is, we can handle it. We are a powerful group as well."

Dr. Snowden admired Lord Vygon's easygoing nature. Even when surrounded by death, he had a positive outlook.

Evaran gestured toward the main entrance of the central building. "Come."

Dr. Snowden surveyed the surrounding area as they walked. The facial expressions on the corpses indicated surprise. He could not imagine trying to run and having a huge spike form under him. If it was not a matter mage, then it must be something on par. He was glad to have on his survival suit, the smell of the rotting corpses would have been powerful. He activated his repulsor on his right hand and the left forearm shield.

"Expecting trouble, are we?" asked Lord Vygon.

"Doesn't hurt to be prepared. I'm almost hoping Emily isn't here."

Lord Vygon smirked. "With you there."

When they reached the door, Evaran indicated for Lord Vygon to help him move the massive split stone doors.

Dr. Snowden noticed that the doors must be opened and closed internally. This would be so much easier if they had a console that Evaran could override, but even then, the technology at the Purifier base had stumped even the UIC. He joined the effort and worked on helping push the right part of the door into the building.

It took ten minutes, but they were able to open it enough to slip into the building. They entered a large, open room with stone tunnels and ramps leading off in different directions.

"V, scout mode," said Evaran, gesturing forward.

"Acknowledged. Scout mode engaged," said V. He shimmered out of view as he flew off.

The one aspect of the HUD that Dr. Snowden enjoyed was the real-time visual display from V. Without the helmet, he would have no idea, but with it, he could see what V saw, along with his scanning results. He knew Evaran could see it in his ARI without a helmet. The images V was showing made Dr. Snowden's palms sweat. Dead bodies everywhere, and a misty cloud seemed to hang in the dimly lit corridors. "Seems more of the same from outside."

Evaran nodded. "Yes, and the technology level here is consistent with what we saw at the Purifier base. I suspect it is low-tech and rift based as well."

They searched the main room and did not find anything of interest.

Dr. Snowden jerked his head back as V scanned a shielded door deeper in the structure. "You seeing this, Evaran? That looks way more advanced than anything up here."

Evaran studied his ARI. "It would appear there are two levels of technology here. It may be possible my UIC can interact with that. We should proceed cautiously. V, hold position."

"Acknowledged," said V.

They proceeded through one of the ramps leading off to the side. V had mapped out the area, which turned out to be a maze of tunnels, ramps, and small rooms. It did not surprise Dr. Snowden that they were headed underground. It seemed the Purifiers liked that type of design. Evaran had tossed out his illumination orbs to light the way since the torches on the wall were burned out.

After twenty minutes of traversing, they met up with V. The light from the shielded door merged with the orb's illuminations and lit up the surrounding area.

Evaran scanned the shielded door with his ring. A small line appeared off to the side to a console. He placed his UIC on it, and after it stabilized, the shield shut down. He tilted his head.

"I sense it too," said Lord Vygon.

Dr. Snowden raised his eyebrows. "Sense . . . what exactly?"

"Movement consistent with a humanoid. It is a bit away, though," said Evaran. He waved for Dr. Snowden and Lord Vygon to follow him into the small room.

A side room contained several advanced workstations and an impaled corpse. This one had a metal spike through it.

Evaran scanned the corpse and then placed his UIC on the still-powered screens embedded into the steel desk. "This technology is not rift based. Intriguing. I will need some time to analyze this." He swiped his hand across his ARI, causing the door to close and lock. "You two relax while I go through this, then we will investigate the movement detected earlier."

Dr. Snowden slumped against the wall next to Lord Vygon. They were getting closer, or so he thought. He was not sure what Evaran would find, but the thought of Emily being impaled on a spike flickered through his mind. He grimaced as he drooped his head.

⎯⎯⎯⎯⎯⎯⎯⎯⎯⎯

After thirty minutes, Evaran turned to face Dr. Snowden and Lord Vygon. "It would appear this technology is from a civilization that went extinct. They were the originators of the rift technology. The Purifiers did not understand it, but were able to use it. I suspect that is due to its ability to bind with living matter, like we saw in the sentinels."

"That would explain the technology differences, but not these impaled corpses," said Lord Vygon.

"I concur," said Evaran. "However, there is a significant portion of the facility I could not interact with or get information on. It seems some parts of this technology has rift components. The UIC cannot work on those hybrid pieces."

"Means it's not from this universe, right?" asked Dr. Snowden.

Evaran nodded. "I am unsure of how it got here, but given that the rift doors can cross timelines, I am going to guess their origin was from a pocket universe ejected from another universe."

Dr. Snowden shook his head. "Wait . . . so this pocket universe was in another universe, got kicked out, landed in this universe, somehow got discovered by the Purifiers, and they adapted what they found for their use. That about right?"

Lord Vygon smirked. "Yeah . . . that sounds kinda crazy to me too."

"Perhaps," said Evaran, raising a finger. "The part I am unsure of is how the Purifiers gained access to a pocket universe. I suspect this Purifier overlord has something to do with that, and the list of other beings who might be able to do it is quite extensive."

"Great," said Dr. Snowden. "Did you find anything on Emily?"

"Just that she arrived here. The visual feed on the rift room is missing for her arrival, yet others are not."

Dr. Snowden snorted. There always had to be something. His blood began to simmer.

"This is a large facility. We should see what else we can find," said Evaran. He exited the room with Dr. Snowden and Lord Vygon in tow.

They navigated the myriad of metallic hallways and rooms. Dr. Snowden's breathing went uneven as each room came up empty. He knew Emily was not here, but the thought that maybe V's scans were wrong and Emily would be waiting in one of the rooms pervaded his thoughts. The sound of footsteps ahead made him perk his head up.

Evaran gestured forward to V, who shimmered and flew ahead.

Dr. Snowden watched through V as he approached a bend in the corridor they were in. As V flew around the corner, Dr. Snowden's heart pumped furiously.

Emily's head peeked out of one of the doors, and then disappeared into a side room.

Dr. Snowden tore off running toward V.

"Dr. Snowden, wait!" said Evaran.

Dr. Snowden felt a tingling sensation flow over him. Time seemed to slow down as he burst around the corner. He ran up to the room he saw Emily duck into and activated his hand light. Shining it into the room showed Emily cowering in a corner. She still had on her jeans, comfortable shoes, and

T-shirt from when she disappeared. "Emily!" He pressed the button on his neck guard, causing his helmet to drop.

"Unc . . . Uncle Albert?" asked Emily as she looked up with wide eyes. She jumped and ran out of the room, hugging Dr. Snowden tightly.

"I thought you were gone," said Dr. Snowden as tears rolled down his cheeks. He squinted and trembled as he held on to Emily. She would never be out of his sight again. He felt Emily shake as she cried into his chest.

"Dr. Snowden . . . ," said Evaran as he stood a few feet away with Lord Vygon.

Dr. Snowden turned his head toward Evaran. "We found her! I can't believe it!" It took a moment for his smile to wind down as he saw Lord Vygon had extended his arm blades and Evaran had his baton and shield out. "What's . . . going on . . ."

"Please step away from her."

Emily looked at Evaran and ran toward him.

"Do not come any closer," said Evaran as the end of his baton intensified its glow.

Emily's eyebrows wrinkled as she grimaced. "Evaran?"

"What are you?"

"I'm Emily!"

"Emily was organic."

Dr. Snowden jerked his head back. He circled around Emily and stood at Lord Vygon's side.

"It's me. What are you talking about?"

Evaran tossed out an orb. It shot up an image of Emily, with various labels off to the side.

Dr. Snowden swallowed hard as he stared at the projection. Emily was ninety percent metal. His eyes bulged as veins popped out on his neck. "What did you do with Emily!"

"Uncle Albert?" said Emily as she staggered toward Dr. Snowden, tears flowing freely onto her face.

"Get *away* from me! Whatever you are!" said Dr. Snowden with balled fists. "Where's Emily!"

Emily frowned as she turned and ran down the hallway.

Lord Vygon put a hand on Dr. Snowden's shoulder, then went flying as Dr. Snowden lashed out.

Dr. Snowden glared at Evaran. "What did they do to Emily!" After a moment, he walked a bit back the way they had come and slumped against the wall. He clenched his jaw as his throat constricted.

Evaran approached Dr. Snowden and faced him on the opposite side of the corridor. He slid down and sat cross-legged. Staring at Dr. Snowden, he said, "Dr. Snowden. Look at me."

Dr. Snowden looked down and flung a hand in the air.

"Look at me. In my eyes. Now."

Dr. Snowden bored a hole through Evaran with his eyes. His breathing went haphazard, and a rising warmth was beginning to swarm his body.

"Breathe."

"Not in the mood for that right now."

"Unacceptable. Breathe."

Dr. Snowden sighed and focused on breathing. His mind was a jumble of thoughts flickering through his mind like lightning bolts, and he knew Evaran would not let him be.

"I am not going to suggest you say the word *relax* in your head," said Evaran. "That does not seem to work with you. I want to try something else. You are a scientist. You use logic in your day-to-day job. Ask yourself this one question. How does losing control help the situation?"

Dr. Snowden's nostrils flared as his breathing came under control. "It doesn't."

"Correct. Now, do you feel a tingling sensation anywhere on your body?"

Dr. Snowden nodded.

"Good. Imagine a wave of relaxation sweeping over the tingling sensations. Focus on the wave increasing until it is sweeping across your whole body. While this is occurring, rationalize your current state to yourself. Does it make sense to be in the state you are in?"

Dr. Snowden concentrated on the waves coursing through his left arm. The tingling sensation began to amplify. He focused on his right arm, and where there had been no tingling, it matched his left arm. After a few moments of moving the wave over every part of his body, he felt he could do a full wave from top to bottom. While this was occurring, he tried to rationalize losing control, but every answer was illogical to him. After a moment, he hopped up and gave Evaran a quizzical look. "The tingling. It's . . . it's everywhere."

Evaran scanned Dr. Snowden with his ring, then looked at Lord Vygon.

Dr. Snowden looked at Lord Vygon. The usual odd movements that he had come to associate with Daedroulds, and vampires in particular, were gone. It was like Lord Vygon had normal movement. Dr. Snowden cocked his head. "What in the world . . ."

"Your senses are heightened," said Evaran. "I suspect your focus is as well. Are you still angry?"

Dr. Snowden wrinkled his eyebrows as he looked at his hands. "No, and there was no reason to be. Whatever it is we saw sounded and looked like Emily, but was not her. The Emily we know is still out there somewhere, and we will continue looking for her."

Lord Vygon smirked. "And we'll find her, assuming you don't knock me around again."

Dr. Snowden extended a hand toward Lord Vygon. "Oh . . . sorry about that. I . . . I wasn't thinking right. I am now, though." He looked at Evaran. "I can't believe that worked."

Evaran nodded. "Oddly enough, I cannot either. It seems you have gained some ability to call upon your nanobots. Take solace in the knowledge that if you can do it, then Emily probably can too. It would give her an edge."

Dr. Snowden let out a deep breath. "So what do we do about this other Emily?"

"That's simple," said Lord Vygon with a smile. "We find her and figure out what she is."

Evaran nodded. He put a hand on Dr. Snowden's shoulder and squeezed, then headed off down the hallway.

Lord Vygon gave Dr. Snowden a quick look, then followed Evaran.

Dr. Snowden followed Evaran while looking at his hands. He could feel the nanobots. The strength, speed, focus, and clarity he felt was intoxicating. There was probably a downside to being amped like this, but it took him from a blind rage to calm in an instant. He was not sure how long it would last, but it would be something he would practice when he had time.

His thoughts turned to the Emily he had seen. It was an exact replica of her, even down to the smell of her perfume. Was it a robot with her consciousness? Could it be that her consciousness was downloaded somehow into this new body? He shook his head as various thoughts and ideas of her origin bounced around in his head. Several times Lord Vygon had to tap his arm to get him to focus on where he was walking. One thing that bothered him was that if that was some clone or duplicate of Emily with her consciousness and thoughts, his and Evaran's rebuff would have had a devastating impact on her. The guilt of that weighed on his mind. Emily was still his niece, in whatever form she was in.

Finding this new Emily and figuring out her origin was his new goal.

15

Emily continued her journey to the second research facility with sore muscles. The position she had slept in had been uncomfortable, even if it gave her peace of mind. The first breach came at about the eighteenth mile. The side had caved in, and a massive hole leading away from the tunnel became visible. An odd light danced inside the hole, giving the breach an unusual appearance against the darkness. The hairs on her neck rose. Skittering sounds echoed around the breach, punctuated by loud shrieks. They reminded her somewhat of the creatures near the pyramid.

She moved to the platform opposite the breach and tapped her light beacon off. As she crossed past the rail line, she sensed the presence that she had been feeling all along nearby. It seemed to be getting closer but at a slow pace. She wondered if it was responsible for shaking the door handle the previous night. The wall was her guide as she crept forward, and after a few moments, she had crossed past the breach. She snapped her head forward at the sound of something shuffling along the ground.

At a tap of her light beacon, several slug-like creatures the size of a small cat appeared. Their legless, ringed, plump white bodies had a black beaded head with antennae hanging off of it. Massive mandibles and a short tube above them rounded out the face. Her heart raced as she hit her light beacon and froze. Maybe they could not see. One thing she was certain of was the foul odor they seemed to emanate. She took exaggerated steps back to the side of the tunnel where the breach was.

When she was past the breach area, she let out a deep breath. The light from the breach she had passed did not filter down this far. She looked back and tapped her light beacon on and then off. In the brief moment it was on, she saw that the creatures had changed course and were slithering over to her. They must either have good smell or hearing, but she doubted the latter. Maybe they sensed vibrations. She took off running down the tunnel and jumped when she heard the shrieks intensify. It also coincided with the feeling that the presence was trying to keep pace with her. Maybe it got the slug-like creatures' attention. It certainly had hers.

She turned on her light beacon and surveyed the environment. The noises from the creature were falling off as she distanced herself from the breach. She wondered if the breach was active when the Coraanan were around, or sometime after their departure. The breach would have been fixed, she figured, if they were still around.

The side room at the twenty-mile mark came and went. She had taken a break in it with a locked door. Hopefully she would not have to revisit the rooms anytime soon. When she approached the twenty-five-mile mark, she took another rest. Her legs were throbbing from their previous soreness, and walking long distances was not something she did on a regular basis.

She moved her mouth around as she contemplated going to the next side room. It would put her within five miles, but if that presence decided to make itself felt, she might need her energy. Her face grew hot at the concept that something was stalking her. It was not enough that she was in an abandoned tunnel with unsafe areas in pitch-black conditions. There had to be something determined to follow her. She shook her head. This presence would know her wrath if it made a move.

She settled on the safer approach and decided to rest before continuing on. The next push would be to the second research station's hub. It would be ten miles, and she would be tired and sore, but the thought of reaching it kept her focused. Although the trip so far had the presence and the breach, she felt better about it than if she had to go through the mountains. She could only imagine what creatures and terrain issues she would have had to deal with. She closed her eyes.

After several hours, a loud sound woke her up from her nap. She had been lying in a crumpled position with her feet at the door. She reached for her PSD and sat up against the back wall. Looking around, she could not see anything. Her nanobots began to tingle, making her more alert. She tilted her head, as she thought she was able to see a bit in the complete darkness. The nanobots gave her heightened senses, but to see in pitch-black surprised her.

Thwack!

This time, she saw that it was something being tossed at the window. Whatever it was, there was a creature out there that wanted in. She swallowed hard as she stood up. Her heartbeat took off as she surveyed the window. After thirty minutes of standing rigid, she began to relax. Whatever it had been, it seemed to have stopped. A brief thought ran through her mind that her resting pattern being disrupted may have been a goal. This would indicate some type of intelligence. Or maybe it just really wanted to get to her.

The rest of the day was filled with her tossing and turning after she had lain back down. Every slight noise made her jump. Her nerves were frazzled, but the second research facility with its creature comforts being not too far off consoled her.

She woke from her nap around 8:00 p.m. according to her PSD. The darkness in the tunnel was not helping her circadian rhythm. She sat up slumped against the wall. Her stomach was churning, and she had a headache. She missed Dr. Snowden, Evaran, and V and would give anything to be with them now. A tear ran down her cheek as she thought of never seeing them again.

She went through her morning routine at night, noting how odd it seemed. Her legs were looser, and her feet did not throb. The nanobots did not seem to need much rest to repair her body. She paused as she was about to leave. When she turned on her light beacon, it showed something smeared on the outside window. She grimaced as she exited the room. The smell from the window indicated it was feces spread out on it. It seemed the feces had been smeared by a set of hands. After a quick scan of her surroundings, she moved on.

As she approached the thirty-fifth mile, the lights on the sides of the tunnel began to shed light. It was still dim, but compared to the total darkness, it was a welcome change. She shut off her light beacon and quickened her pace. The thought of a hot shower and decent food danced in her mind. The presence had kept its distance but remained just out of visual range. Several times she peered back but never saw anything. It was there, though.

Her legs had gotten used to the walking, so they were not as sore as they were when she first started. As she continued on to the second research facility's hub, the lighting became much brighter, and she enjoyed not having to squint. She stopped to relieve herself just a mile out from the hub. It was tedious to have to face toward where she had come from. She was in an awkward and vulnerable stance, bent over with one hand extended holding the PSD in case of an attack. After she cleaned up, she pressed on with the Torvatta in her mind. A half grin crept onto her face as she thought that if Evaran were here, he would send V to scout the tunnel. Having V around would make things so much easier. No wonder Evaran created him.

The sight of the transportation hub of the second research facility made her smile. She reflected on how odd it was to raise her lips. It seemed more natural to keep her lips flat. When she reached the door leading up to the facility, she noticed the console to the right of it showing the word *Lockdown*. Kicking and pushing against the door had no effect.

Butterflies fluttered in her stomach. The thought that she might not be able to access the facility crossed her mind. She had assumed it would be available.

"Interface. Activate," she said, looking around.

Nothing happened.

"Kal. Activate." She jumped back when Kal appeared.

"Translation matrix has been initiated. Welcome to Coraanan research facility number sixteen. I am the virtual interface, Kal."

"I know who you are. Why's this facility in lockdown?"

"It was set when the Coraanan left."

"Well . . . unlock it."

"To change lockdown status, you must initiate it from a system inside the facility."

She sighed. They must have kept one person inside just for this purpose. Unless they all left. She leaned back against the wall and snapped her head at Kal.

Through Kal's semitransparent form, she saw the creature she had seen in the forest running toward her. This was the presence she had felt. The creature was humanoid, and its almost white face looked like someone had grabbed the chin and forehead and stretched them apart. The clothing on the humanoid was tattered, and its fingers were long, slender claws. Intense black eyes stared at her with hunger. The large mouth displayed razor-sharp teeth between its always-smiling lips. The strong smell of feces permeated the air.

Her heartbeat rampaged as her eyes popped open. The humanoid burst through Kal and slammed her into the wall. It stepped back and swiped. She blocked it with her arm, then cried out as the claws raked over the exposed area between the arm bone plates. The tingling sensation ramped up and coursed over her body. She kicked out and connected with the creature. It went flying back. Her head tilted as she watched it tumble away due to her kick. It seemed like everything had slowed down, but she could still move at normal speed. She shook her head and pulled out her PSD.

She fired a repulsion beam as the creature stood back up.

The creature held its ground as the repulsion blast washed over it.

She swallowed hard as she fired the stun beam at it.

The creature raised its arm and roared, then flipped to the side.

Although she knew it moved fast, it seemed to be moving at normal speed to her. The blasts had minimal effect on it, and this creature meant to kill. She extended the PSD into a staff and adopted a defensive posture.

The creature jumped around as it charged her.

As it got close, she sidestepped it. With a swing of the staff at its legs, it went tumbling forward and crashed face-first into the wall. Her blood boiled. She struck out at the backs of its legs. *Snap!*

The creature roared and pivoted around in an unnatural manner. It swiped at her.

She hit the wrist of the creature. *Snap!*

It roared again and slid to the side a few steps away. It extended its hand and, after a moment, had full motion with its wrist. The leg had already healed, by the way it was moving.

Her face turned red. This thing would follow her until it killed her. And it did not go down easily. Something that large with the ability to move around the way it did bothered her. She exhaled sharply. Enough was enough. She was tired of this, physically and mentally.

"Come on!" said Emily as she held her staff in front of her.

The creature roared. It jumped from side to side as it angled toward her.

Her nanobots pulsed. The creature came closer. Her breath quickened. The creature dove at her. She jumped up and spun around, delivering a hit with all her strength to the back of the head. The creature fell to the floor and twitched.

Emily hustled up to it. *"Why couldn't you just leave me alone!"* Tears cascaded down her face.

The creature tried to turn around.

"Why!" said Emily.

It was the creature or her. She rushed forward and struck the creature's head repeatedly, crying between strikes.

The creature stopped moving.

She slumped against the wall as her breathing staggered. Tears ran off her cheeks. She just wanted to live. Why did everything want to kill her?

She stayed there for a bit as she focused on the next step. It seemed unusual to her that she was so focused. A creature was dead due to her directly killing it, yet she did not feel remorse like she thought she would. Kazaal was an indirect death, but this was her first kill. She thought that maybe she would go crazy, but her heightened state suggested otherwise.

With a calm determination, she stood up and walked over to the door leading up to the rest of the facility. Standing back, she delivered a kick that caved in a part of it. Several kicks later and the door was bent in enough that she could climb through. While grimacing, she took a last look at the dead creature, then climbed through the door.

Emily awoke the next morning after a long rest. She really liked the beds. They did not have the neural effect that beds on the Torvatta had, but they were soft, and the shape of the bed was inviting. The pillows were soft as well. It made her feel like the bed was holding her.

She looked at the ground as her legs swung over the side. Before she had gone to sleep, she locked the inner door to the transportation system. No way could she rest if that creature somehow regenerated and cheated death. She did not feel bad for killing it. It had tried to kill her, and she simply refused to be its victim. Her morning list of things to do included checking to see that the creature was still dead.

As she went through her morning routine, she thought about Dr. Snowden, Evaran, and V. What would they think of all this? What would Evaran have done to that creature when his stun baton failed? She concluded he would have done the same as her, unless he had other tools or gadgets she was unaware of. Maybe he would have run, but given Evaran's strength displayed after one round, the creature would have probably fled. It would have known this was not someone to mess with, but with her, it decided to. It had no way of knowing she had nanobots that would give her strength.

Her mind drifted toward the nanobots as she headed to the specimen surveillance lab. They had pulsated with a ferocity she had only felt for brief periods before. During the fight, they were steady, and she could move faster and focus much easier, and she felt stronger. She wondered if she could call upon them as needed or if they were only triggered by life-and-death situations. Her head bobbed as she contemplated staying for a bit to focus on trying to reach that state in a safe environment.

When she arrived at the specimen surveillance lab, she sat at a workstation and began to peruse the system. It seemed the communications system was down, like at the first facility. "Kal. Activate."

Kal shimmered into view. "Good morning. How may I be of service?"

"When did the Coraanan leave this facility?"

"The Coraanan left this facility three hundred eight years ago."

Emily rubbed her chin. "The same time as the other facility. I don't suppose you know why they left."

"The Coraanan left due to an assault on Central Command. Before communications broke down, a general alert was issued to all researchers to leave their facilities and head there."

Emily jerked her head back. The first facility must not have gotten that message but ventured out due to the communication system being down and breaches in the tunnels. "What attacked Central Command?"

"The assailants were unknown."

Emily studied Kal for a moment as she decided to look up the message. It took her a bit of navigating through the various menu options, but she found the alert. It was a planet-wide evacuation order. All researchers were to proceed to Central Command for extraction. Her heart sank at the thought that Central Command might have been destroyed. If the rift door had been shut down there, what did that mean for her? She swallowed hard as her eyes misted. Living the rest of her life at one of these facilities alone was not something she had given much thought to.

With a sigh, she opened the overland map. She had gone forty miles so far, and with the ten to the first facility, that meant only one hundred miles to go. Going through tunnels again was not something she was interested in. The fresh air and daylight did wonders for her mood, whereas the pitch-black darkness of the tunnels kept her on edge. In addition to that, there were not many options on places to go if the tunnels had an obstruction she could not pass, only back the way she had come.

She tilted her head as she noticed that the next facility did not have a tunnel leading to it. Instead, it went east. The tunnels and facilities seemed to ring a chasm, with a total distance of about four hundred miles. The tunnels were out, not that she minded. She zoomed into the chasm. It looked large and very deep and was four miles across. No wonder they did not try to build a tunnel through this. There was a path over the chasm. Her eyes lit up. Maybe it was a bridge.

She pointed at the path. "What's this?"

"It is the air route over the chasm. There are two facilities on each side that provide transportation."

"What type of transportation?"

"An automated air pod system transports passengers across the chasm."

She tilted her head. "Can the air pod be overridden to fly elsewhere?"

"Overriding the air pods' destination is strictly forbidden."

She sighed. If the air pods were hackable, Kal was not going to be much help. Although Central Command had been attacked long ago, a sense of urgency pervaded her. Even if it had been attacked, it might still be the best place to be on this planet. There may even be other people there.

She stood up and stretched. "Kal. Deactivate."

Kal shimmered out of view.

The rest of the afternoon was spent in the main area of the living quarters. She focused on trying to connect with her nanobots. Straining and wishing for them to activate did not seem to help. A glimmer of hope spiked through her when she relaxed and imagined the tingling sensation in her left forearm. She ran her hand over it and then focused on imagining it on her upper left arm.

After a few minutes of targeting other body parts, a gentle wave pulsed over her body. It was not quite at the level it had been with the creature around, but it had a definite impact. She could sense things with more accuracy. Her hearing and eyesight were improved. She stood up and went through several combat moves she had learned from studying Evaran's videos. Everything flowed with ease.

Another few minutes went by, and the tingling subsided. Her breathing got heavier as she took a seat on the ground. It seemed there was a tax to be paid for activating them like this. She imagined it more as a burst ability than something that would always be on, but wondered if she could raise her base level with them. It was a new challenge for her, something her competitive side appreciated.

She spent the rest of the day training, but did take several breaks. The first one was for dinner. Eating at the facility was a luxury compared to the pellets. The second one was to verify that the creature that had attacked her in the transportation hub was still dead. She figured it was, but the thought of it regenerating and breaking into the facility skirted the edge of her thoughts.

After a full day of activity, the cocoon-shaped bed in her living quarters welcomed her with open arms.

The next morning, she woke up in a sweat. She had dreamed about being in a building with metal walls and floors. It was empty, but after running around for a few days, the sound of others approaching filtered through the air. To her delight, it had been Dr. Snowden, Evaran, Lord Vygon, and V. The excitement was short-lived, as Evaran said he did not know who she was. Dr. Snowden had snapped and yelled at her. Lost and confused, she had run before waking up. The way Evaran had said what he did was something she could see him saying. She shuddered as she got up and got a drink of water and then proceeded with what would be her daily routine.

Several weeks later, she was ready to go. Her nanobots could activate on command to several levels higher than where they were. After much conditioning, the tax it had caused before was gone. She did not come close to the life-and-death levels she felt with the nanobots, but figured over time, she would get there.

Her training had progressed as well. She discovered that in a heightened state, moves became instinctual and learning was rapid. Staff fighting and unarmed combat were the focus, although she spent time practicing sword fighting and moves with the stun and repulsion beams as well. If she ever saw Evaran again, she would have to thank him. She frowned as she once again thought of Dr. Snowden, Evaran, and V. With a heavy sigh, she did a quick check that she was restocked and then headed out from the facility.

The air pod facility was a few miles to the north, and there were no issues getting there. The fresh air and sunlight made the trip almost enjoyable. After arriving at the facility, she noted it was a large warehouse-like building. Pillars stood just outside each of the building's corners. A beam scanned her, and the door slid open. When she walked in, the lights turned on and machines whirred to life.

The building was one large room with multiple small cubed metallic ships. Kal had said the system was automated, so with a deep breath, she approached one of the ships. It had a window on the front and a door on the side. The back of it had a blue ring, and various antennae-like structures rested on the top.

She ran her hand along the roof before opening the door. The seats were small. It was obviously built for Coraanan, but with her small form, she was able to slip in. It was a tight fit, but as there were no controls, it would do. Once the door was closed, the ship trembled, then lifted off. An opening at the far side of the building opened up, and the ship flew out of it.

As the ship flew over the chasm, she peered out the front window. The chasm was deeper looking at it from above. No wonder the Coraanan did not build a tunnel here. She swallowed hard around the halfway point when the ship trembled. The thought crossed her mind that maybe the ship would have issues being so old, but given that the Coraanan were obviously advanced, maybe not.

When the ship reached the other side, she saw a similar warehouse-like building. It had an air pod entrance that struggled to open. Her heartbeat increased as she saw it approaching the semiclosed doors. When it was twenty feet out, she opened the air pod door and jumped out.

The ship crashed into the building, but with little damage. It tried several more times to go in, but eventually settled on the ground.

She shook her head as she realized she must have jumped fifteen feet. Her fall had been graceful, and she landed without any injury. The nanobots had kicked in, and she was sure her focus on landing on her two feet helped things. She shuddered to think what that would have been like without the nanobots helping.

A white silky web encased the bottom half of the building. She had not seen it or the busted pillars when coming in. This building had been claimed by something, and she had no desire to find out what owned it. The shrieking and skittering noises coming from inside helped confirm that decision for her.

She scanned the pathway ahead. Seven miles were done, four of them over the chasm. Another thirty-two to go until the next facility. The overland map had shown the next segment of her trip to be a forest, but there was a path through it. The thought that she had not seen any type of land transportation crossed her mind. A dirt bike would have been great for these.

She shook her head with a sigh and headed out on the path into the forest.

16

Dr. Snowden examined the hallways they walked through with great intensity. The nanobots were still pulsing inside him, and every detail he could see was amplified. From the miniature cracks in the walls to the impaled corpses, it was all available in high detail. The downside was the pronounced smell of rotting corpses. He could raise his helmet, but he wanted to sense everything in this state. Each step was effortless, and he felt like he could run a marathon.

Evaran and Lord Vygon walked ahead of Dr. Snowden as they wound around various corridors. V had been flying around, and since Dr. Snowden had his helmet down, he did not know where V was.

After five minutes, they came to a large room. Inside it was a mix of rift technology similar to the rift door and the advanced portion of the pyramid they were in. Workstations lined the walls with a command table in the middle of the room.

Dr. Snowden's eyes narrowed as he studied the impaled corpses. "They were caught by surprise."

Evaran faced Dr. Snowden, then scanned the corpses. After a moment, he said, "I would agree. Whatever created these spikes moved quickly. I do not suspect it was a creature at this point."

Lord Vygon sniffed the air. "Yeah . . . not smelling anything in here except death."

Evaran placed his UIC on a console, and after a moment, it connected. He perused his ARI and then faced Lord Vygon and Dr. Snowden. "Perhaps I can find something here. There is more access and information available here than the first stop. However, it will be difficult to obtain and will take some time. You two can find Emily while I work on this."

Dr. Snowden glanced at Lord Vygon, who nodded.

They exited the room together.

Dr. Snowden could feel the nanobots beginning to wind down. He shook his hand in front of him at the odd sensation. "Starting to come back down."

Lord Vygon half smiled. "That's normal."

Dr. Snowden smirked. "I forget, you've seen a future me. I guess I learn to control them at some point."

"Of course. You're a scientist."

"Yeah . . . I guess," said Dr. Snowden. He cocked his head as they continued down the corridor. "I guess the Emily you know learns to control them too . . ."

Lord Vygon chuckled. "I forgot how persistent you can be."

"Oh, c'mon . . . you obviously know who it is we're looking for and whether it's Emily or not."

Lord Vygon shook his head. He paused and raised a hand. "I detect movement ahead, in the room to the right."

Dr. Snowden focused his senses. He noticed it too, and not just the sounds of movement, but the smell. He homed in on the door and thought he could almost see the air fluctuating. With a wave of his hand forward, he stepped in front of the door.

Emily was curled up on a bed in the corner of the room. There was not much in the room in terms of furniture, but there was a smaller door farther inside the room.

"Emily?"

Emily looked up with a wet face and puffy eyes.

Dr. Snowden exhaled from his nose. "Look . . . I'm sorry what I said back there. I was just . . . confused. I was expecting . . ."

"Not me," said Emily as she sat up on the bed. She looked down.

Dr. Snowden sighed. "We can figure all this out. Why don't you come with us, and we can talk to Evaran about it."

"You hate me because I'm not her," said Emily. "What am I?"

Dr. Snowden entered the room and knelt in front of Emily. He grabbed her hands as his eyes misted. "I won't lie to you. I don't know what you are, but you act, sound, and smell like Emily to me. You may be her in another form, I don't know. Until then, you have the benefit of the doubt."

Emily looked up and sniffled.

Dr. Snowden opened his arms, and Emily leaned forward and hugged him. He ran his hand up and down her back. "It's okay. We'll figure this out and get through it."

Emily trembled as she cried. After a few minutes, she pulled back. With a half smile, she rose, wiped her eyes, and gestured at the exit. "I'm ready then."

Dr. Snowden looked at Lord Vygon, who nodded, and they proceeded back to the room where Evaran was.

Evaran sat at one of the workstations, studying the embedded screen on the wall perpendicular to the desk. He turned his head as Dr. Snowden, Emily, and Lord Vygon entered. With a quick swivel of his chair, he stood and faced Emily. "I am glad you came."

Emily drooped her head while looking at Evaran.

Evaran scanned Dr. Snowden and Lord Vygon, then proceeded toward Emily. He extended his arms. "No hug?"

Emily lifted her head and, with a big smile, bear-hugged Evaran. She squinted as she sniffled.

Evaran hugged Emily and rubbed her back.

Emily stepped away and sighed. "This is so confusing."

Evaran nodded and gestured for everyone to take a seat. After everyone sat, he raised a finger. "I have found some interesting information."

Dr. Snowden sat on the edge of his chair as he rested his arm on one of the desks. Whenever Evaran raised a finger, it usually meant something big was about to drop.

"I am going to go through what I found in chronological order in terms of events," said Evaran. "The first event was the arrival of Emily here from Lord Vygon's base. There is no visual feed of her arrival or departure, but there are logs that show she was here."

Dr. Snowden let loose a controlled breath.

"Second event. They took a nanobot sample from her and then tossed her through the prison planet rift door. It is powered down, most likely due to the rift controller being disintegrated."

"Well . . . how are we going to know where this prison planet is?" asked Dr. Snowden as his nerves pulsed.

"We will get to that," said Evaran. He tossed out an orb. "Third event. The nanobot sample was brought to a research lab deeper in this base, and they tried to fuse it with rift technology. They were trying to weaponize it, but the end result was a nanobot swarm that fanned out, killing every living thing it found." With a swipe through his ARI, a projection shot up from the orb. It displayed different locations, but each scene was the same. The ground pulsed like a wave toward the Purifiers, and when it hit them, a spike shot up.

"Is the ground . . . rippling?" asked Dr. Snowden.

"Yes," said Evaran. "It is actually the nanobot swarm traveling through the ground. They formed a spike on any living creature they encountered."

"Well . . . that explains the surprised looks," said Lord Vygon.

Evaran nodded. "It moved relatively quickly." He swiped at his ARI. "Fourth event. Once the nanobot swarm cleared the facility, this occurred."

The projection showed a room with a slab. The ground around it came alive and crept up the slab. It then formed an exact replica of Emily lying on top.

Emily gasped with wide eyes.

"They formed you," said Evaran, looking at Emily. "However, before they did, they scoured the base in search of rift technology and devoured it, all except the crystals on the rift door. Unfortunately, the rift controller was a victim of its hunger."

Emily narrowed her eyes. "I've only been here a day or so. I think."

Evaran shook his head. "Not quite. You were on the slab from the moment you were created until we arrived. Approximately three days."

"What? How . . . how is that possible? They pricked me with a syringe, I blacked out, and woke up on that slab, and now you're telling me I'm actually a murderous nanobot swarm that's been asleep for several days?" said Emily. Her breathing intensified.

Evaran extended a hand out. "Relax. You may be the end result of the nanobot swarm, but you are not it."

"I don't understand," said Emily, swallowing hard.

Evaran looked down for a moment.

Dr. Snowden could see that Evaran was wrestling with a decision. He remembered seeing it on the Krotovore ship when Evaran had first explained what was going on when they were awakened out of the virtual simulation. This must be something important given how long he was looking down.

Evaran raised his head and let out a measured breath. "I . . . did not want to explain this, but it is needed." He swept his head across everyone. "I trust you all and this information is pertinent to Emily. What I say here is not to be repeated unless necessary. Is that understood?"

Everyone nodded.

"Good," said Evaran. He paced back and forth in front of the station he had been working at. "This parallel timeline we are in, as you know, is part of the universe. The universe is part of a multiverse, which is part of a plane. Each universe in the plane has a shell around it." Evaran put his hands out as if holding an imaginary ball. "Each shell is composed of layers, with each layer having a specific role. The layer we are interested in is the life layer. Before I continue, I am curious." He faced Lord Vygon. "Have I ever mentioned this to you before?"

Lord Vygon shook his head. "No . . . you haven't."

"Interesting."

Dr. Snowden narrowed his eyes. This explanation must be something Evaran kept very close to his chest if Lord Vygon did not know about it, especially given how close he thought they were.

Evaran nodded. "Continuing then. This life layer forms a link to inside the universe. When the link is established, you refer to it as consciousness. This life layer link, or three-L as I call it, is something I can see if I look for it. I do not understand what triggers the link, but it is something I aim to learn more about," said Evaran. He pointed at Emily. "Although she is a nanobot swarm, she has a three-L. Most machines and artificial intelligences do not."

"So . . . this three-L thing makes me . . . alive?" asked Emily.

Evaran raised a finger. "Well . . . it is a bit more complicated. I know quite a few three-L patterns. They appear to me as part of the energy signature that surrounds all life. Yours is almost identical to the Emily who went through the rift door."

"That might explain the dreams then."

Dr. Snowden tilted his head. "You can dream?"

"Yeah . . . but it was scary. I was in a jungle running from some small creatures. Then I got captured by something that . . . was . . . I don't know how to explain it. It was bad, and kept me naked in a cage. I felt like . . . I'd been there for weeks."

Evaran looked down for a moment, then back up. "Dreams are part of another layer. The three-L crosses through it. Think of the dream layer as more of a morphable matter layer that takes cues from a three-L on what to form. It can also be used to communicate, and since it is independent of time, it can be used for some interesting aspects for those who . . . have a gift for it. I suspect your dreams in this case were used to see what the other Emily was experiencing. Maybe not."

Dr. Snowden's eyes popped open as he looked at Evaran. "That's just great." He sighed. "If the rift controller is busted, how do we find Emily then? I mean . . . my Emily . . . well . . . you know what I mean!"

Emily looked down.

Evaran put a hand on Emily's shoulder. "For all intents and purposes, this is Emily, just duplicated in a new body. She may not have the same physical history as the original Emily, but her energy signature is almost identical." He looked at Emily. "To avoid confusion, we will call you Nanobot Emily and the original Organic Emily. Fair enough?"

Nanobot Emily nodded.

"Good. As to finding where that rift door leads, I suspect we will find out more in the rift room. Nanobot Emily's brain, unlike the majority of her body, is composed of nanobots with rift technology. I suspect that is why she has a three-L. I believe, with some focus, that may be of use down there."

"I'll do whatever I can to help," said Nanobot Emily with a half smile. She flinched when Dr. Snowden put his arm around her. With a wipe of the tear that had fallen onto her cheek, she smiled.

"Two nieces . . . now the Purifiers are *really* in trouble," said Dr. Snowden with a chuckle.

Nanobot Emily swatted his arm as she stood up. "Let's do this!"

Dr. Snowden studied the ground as he walked behind Evaran and Lord Vygon. Nanobot Emily had latched onto his arm like Organic Emily always did. The sensation of there being two Emilys was a new one for him. On one hand, he was happy that Nanobot Emily was an actual duplicate. It was Emily, even if the body did not have the history of Organic Emily. He knew he would not be able to tell the difference if they were side by side. On the other hand, he was worried about Organic Emily. Nonetheless, it was reassuring to have either Emily on his arm.

Nanobot Emily looked up at Dr. Snowden and smiled. "Thinking about the situation, aren't cha?"

"Yeah . . . what do you think Dan would've thought of all this?"

Nanobot Emily chuckled. "He woulda said, Well . . . hell."

They laughed as Evaran glanced back at them.

After twenty minutes, they arrived at the rift room. Dr. Snowden noted that it was similar to the first rift room he had seen at the Purifier base on Earth. This one was missing the rift controller. He shuddered to think of Organic Emily appearing and getting pricked, then shoved through the prison planet rift door.

Evaran walked up to the crystal rods and scanned them with his ring. "As we do not have access to the rift controller, we will need to use another method of access." He faced Nanobot Emily and pointed to the right crystal rod. "Please place your hands around that."

Nanobot Emily complied.

"Now . . . focus. See if you can sense any rift technology components."

Nanobot Emily furrowed her eyebrows as she dipped her head and closed her eyes. After a moment, she popped them open. "Whoa . . . I can sense it! It's like . . . cheese in a pretzel."

Lord Vygon raised his eyebrows and looked at Dr. Snowden.

Dr. Snowden smirked. "Yeah . . . someone's hungry."

Evaran pointed at the crystal rod while looking at Nanobot Emily. "Okay, hunger notwithstanding, can you concentrate on reaching out to it?"

Nanobot Emily half smiled. Her hands glowed a bit, causing everyone to stand back. "I can't. Can only sense it. But . . ."

Evaran tilted his head. "What did you find?"

"They're all connected," said Nanobot Emily. "The rift doors, that is. There is another on this planet."

"Can you get its location?"

"I think so. Trying."

After a minute of concentrating, Nanobot Emily dropped her hands to her sides. "I . . . think I have it. Kinda vague. Not sure how to show you."

"Put your palm out."

Nanobot Emily complied.

Evaran placed his UIC on her hand. It glowed a mix of blue and red for a moment, then stabilized.

Dr. Snowden remembered that the UIC could connect in a limited fashion to organic manner. It had been given this ability by a matter mage on their last adventure when helping the Fredorians. He had also learned that the UIC was originally gifted to Evaran by the matter mages for helping them. The mixed colors intrigued him since he expected it to only be blue.

"I can feel it trying to connect," said Emily. "How do I transfer?"

"Just focus on the information. Imagine it shooting from your brain to your hand. The UIC should be able to pick it up."

Nanobot Emily chuckled. "This is so weird."

Evaran perused his ARI, then tossed out an orb. It shot a projection showing the planet they were on, with two red dots. He pointed to one of the dots. "We are here, and the other appears to be the same."

Dr. Snowden noted that the first dot was blinking. He figured that indicated where they were. The second one looked to be in Peru.

"Yeah," said Nanobot Emily. She tapped the crystal rod. "Wish I could just turn the darn thing on, but it needs a rift stone and controller . . . and I ate it."

"It is okay," said Evaran with a chuckle. "We can head to the one in South America. It stands to reason that if this base has a mirror in our timeline, then the one in South America would as well."

"Of course," said Dr. Snowden. "However, the first base in our timeline was in Egypt. This second one might be somewhere else."

"It is possible. Come," said Evaran. "We will verify its location in this timeline and then use that as a base to find it in our timeline." He waved forward as he exited the room.

They weaved their way back up to the Torvatta and, once inside, sat down.

Dr. Snowden noticed that Nanobot Emily took her usual seat next to him. It felt natural to have her near him. His jaw tightened a bit as he thought of Organic Emily. The one he gave airplane rides to when she was a kid. If Nanobot Emily's dreams were a glimpse into what Organic Emily was experiencing, then it would be a nightmare for her. Stranded alone, fighting who knows what. He exhaled from his nose as he looked down.

Nanobot Emily placed her hand on his shoulder. "We'll find her."

Dr. Snowden looked at Nanobot Emily and half grinned. He reached over and squeezed her hand.

"V, take us to the South American base," said Evaran.

"Acknowledged."

The Torvatta ascended and began to fly toward the next destination.

Lord Vygon tilted his head. "How are we planning on breaching it?"

"V is going to breach it," said Evaran.

V turned around. "I am?"

Dr. Snowden and Nanobot Emily chuckled.

"Yes," said Evaran. "Once we verify its location, you will go in with scout mode. The goal is to observe all rift controller interactions. While you are doing that, we will head back to our timeline and verify if there is another base there."

"Acknowledged."

"We will not leave this timeline until V is in position."

Lord Vygon tilted his head. "We could make it easy. I could try to run past them all, grab the operator, and knock out anyone who gets in my way."

"You could, but if the alert is raised, the operator could leave. He could also set it into shutdown. At that point, we would not have the prison planet destination code."

Lord Vygon shook his head. "Yeah . . . I'm fast, but probably not fast enough to prevent him from getting that shutdown process off."

Nanobot Emily cocked her head. "Maybe I could interface with the rift controller."

Evaran shook his head. "Possible, but it may not have audit or history logs of destinations. I suspect the reason operators are the only ones who know destinations is to ensure that only a few know how to operate the rift doors and where they go. I do not think the overlord wants informed minions who know how to get to every point in his empire. We can keep that as a last resort option."

Nanobot Emily nodded.

Evaran faced Lord Vygon. "Let us take a break. We should be at the South American base in about an hour. V, notify us when we arrive."

"Acknowledged."

Dr. Snowden sighed. "Well, I'm going to get something to eat then."

"I will join you," said Evaran.

They assembled in the conference room and picked up food and drink from the sustenance replicators. Evaran sat at the head of the table, while Dr. Snowden and Nanobot Emily sat to his left and Lord Vygon to his right.

Dr. Snowden took a bite of his burger and closed his eyes. "I sometimes forget to eat, and after taking a bite of this, wonder how that is possible."

Nanobot Emily giggled. She took a sip of her orange juice, then spit it out. She shook her head. "Okay . . . that definitely does not taste like I remember it."

Evaran half smiled. "I believe you would probably like what V drinks. It is a mineral drink, but has the consistency of oil."

Nanobot Emily shuddered. "Yeah . . . I'll just sit that one out."

"Very well," said Evaran. He cocked his head at Lord Vygon. "I do not recognize that drink. Did the Torvatta make it?"

"Yep. I call it the Lord Vygon special."

Evaran perused his ARI. "There is no drink with that pattern name in the replicator database."

Lord Vygon glanced at Dr. Snowden. "It's there, you just can't see it."

Evaran cocked his head for a moment, then narrowed his eyes. "Contextual time stream data. Interesting. I was not aware the Torvatta had that ability."

"It has a lot more data than you might know," said Lord Vygon. "It's hard to believe as long as you've been around, that you never knew that. I guess, though, you never really stuck around in one spot for too long to find out."

"You are full of surprises," said Evaran.

"That I am. That I am."

"Tell me. Have you seen the future?"

Lord Vygon took a sip of his drink. "Not the one that brought you here, but another one. I'm aware of what awaits humanity, and by extension, us nonhumans. Of course, it could all change. Your presence here reminds me of that."

Evaran perched his chin on his left hand as he eyed Lord Vygon. "I have the feeling we will cross paths many times."

"That we do," said Lord Vygon with a smile.

They finished their food, and after an hour of light discussion, V poked his head into the room. "We have arrived."

Evaran stood. "It is time to navigate V to the portal room then. Come." He waved for everyone to follow him.

They assembled in the command area as V went into the research lab. He came back out in orb mode and hovered near the front console. "I am ready."

Dr. Snowden looked out the left screen. It showed the same base as the other one, except this one did not have spikes. He could see the guards outlined in green walking around the perimeter and the towers. He noted that the Torvatta was just inside the main gate and slightly above the main building entrance.

"V, scout mode," said Evaran as he interacted with his chair console. The front right screen switched to a visual of what V saw.

"Acknowledged. Scout mode engaged," said V. He shimmered for a moment and then disappeared.

Dr. Snowden studied the right screen as it showed V exit the Torvatta and fly toward the main doors.

When V scanned the door, it showed the stone composition as well as handprints and other organic residue on the doors. He flew off toward one of the towers and, after a moment, had passed through the top open part where two guards stood.

Dr. Snowden grinned as he watched V's scans of the guards. It outlined them with multiple labels indicating everything from body temperature to breathing as a sound graph. He appreciated the glimpses into how V viewed things.

It did not take long for V to descend from the tower via an internal ramp to the inside of the side building. He twisted and turned through the tunnels, flying above the guards, until he located a shielded door similar to the one in the first base. After scanning it, V flew back toward a room where two guards were resting. He projected a hologram of Evaran running past the room and imitated the sound of hurried footsteps. Flying back to the shield, he disabled the hologram but kept the sounds up until the guards reached the shielded door.

"I know I saw something," said one of the guards.

The other guard accessed the door console, dissipating the shield. "Check inside. I'll check out here."

The first guard nodded and passed through the doorway, with V in tow. The door shielded back up once they were through.

Dr. Snowden gestured at the right screen. "That was pretty good."

Evaran nodded. "V is quite resourceful."

"How would U4 have handled that?"

Evaran snapped his head toward Dr. Snowden. "I have never mentioned U4 to you before."

Dr. Snowden's eyes popped open. "Ohh . . . uhh . . ." He gestured at the right screen. "V mentioned her to me earlier . . . umm . . . before the timeline change when you were up on the roof."

"I see," said Evaran with narrowed eyes. He clenched his jaw for a moment. "U4 was not equipped with stealth. She could not have done this."

Dr. Snowden glanced at Lord Vygon, whose eyebrows were raised, then focused back on the right screen. Evaran did not show emotion well, but Dr. Snowden knew the small movements and facial gestures that acted as proxies. He concluded that this was still a sensitive subject.

V had reached the portal room and hovered in the corner of the room above the podium. The angle showed the Purifier operator standing at the rift controller as well as a good view of the rift room. "Destination reached."

Evaran tapped at his chair console. "Very good. Hold position and record all that you can. We will be back in a bit."

"Acknowledged."

The front right screen switched to an outside view as the Torvatta ascended.

"Back to our timeline," said Evaran.

17

Emily walked for several miles through the forest without incident. It was dense, with large trees surrounded by smaller ones that looked like they were competing for space. She shook her head at the thought that the trees would be sentient, although she had seen stranger things.

The smell of the wood caressed her nose. It reminded her of camping with her dad and Dr. Snowden. Her eyes softened as she recalled her favorite part about camping, the stories around the campfire. With a sigh, she trudged on.

It was about thirty miles until the next facility. She could make it with one overnight stop, maybe two if there was trouble. Places to rest with defensive capability were on her mind. She knew how hard it was find anything like that out here.

Five miles later, she took a break near a large tree. The forest had gotten darker, mainly due to the trees around the path extending overhead. Normally she would have found this ominous, but with recent events, it did not register with her. She sat against a tree on the side and pulled out her PSD. After chewing on a piece of dried meat, she took a small sip from her water container. She let her legs rest and stared up. It was peaceful, and the ambient noise of the forest almost lulled her to sleep.

She jumped when a pang shot through her leg. Reaching down, she pulled out what looked like a sharp pine needle. Her PSD vibrated on her leg. Could it be? A jolt of excitement coursed through her. She pulled her PSD out and opened it. The outline around the communications icon pulsated. Her breath went haphazard as she pressed it.

"Emily!" said Dr. Snowden.

Emily paused for a moment as she studied it. "Unc . . . Uncle Albert?"

"We're on our way! Stay where you are!" said Dr. Snowden.

The PSD went blank.

Emily shuddered as tears ran down her face. It was finally over. She slumped back down against the tree. No more trying to survive in this hellhole. She smiled as she thought of figuring out what she would do back on the ship.

After a few minutes, the Torvatta landed on the path. Dr. Snowden burst out of it with Evaran and V in tow.

Emily jumped up, ran over to Dr. Snowden, and hugged him tightly. She trembled as Evaran reached them and put his arms around her.

"It's good to see you," said Evaran.

Emily narrowed her eyes. Her nanobots were at full throttle when they should not have been. Her focus became pinpoint. Something was off. She stepped back and studied Evaran. "You sound different."

"What're you talking about?" asked Evaran.

Emily's eyes narrowed. "You never talk like that."

"I've always talked like this."

"No . . . you haven't," said Emily. She looked around. "This isn't real."

"You've been here a long time, but you're free now. No more Kazaal, shadowy presences, or weird creatures," said Dr. Snowden.

Emily frowned as she shook her head. She slumped to the ground.

"Emily?" asked Dr. Snowden.

"I never told you of those things. I haven't even seen you yet. This isn't real."

"Of course it's real," said Evaran. "Ezekial is on board the Torvatta. We were able to save him."

"Ezekial's dead!" said Emily as she stood and balled her fists. Her nanobots pulsed wildly. A sharp pain on the side of her stomach made her eyes pop. Another pang traveled up from her leg. Blood spots appeared on her clothing as the environment began to shake violently.

Dr. Snowden ran over and put his hands on Emily's shoulders. "Emily! Stay with us!"

"Get away from me!"

The environment shuddered, then stopped. The Torvatta, Evaran, and Dr. Snowden were gone.

Emily looked down and saw blood soaking her shirt. A small spear stuck out of her leg.

Two humanoids standing three feet tall with dark skin stood before her. They were covered in some type of white dried substance that looked like caked mud. Dome-shaped helmets that also seemed to be made out of mud covered their heads. One had a spear and was approaching her. The other was behind the first and reaching for the spear in her leg.

She pulled the spear out and shouted in pain, startling the two humanoids. With a quick glance, she tossed the spear at the nearest humanoid. It busted through its helmet and into its head as it went down.

The second one yelled and pulled out a large knife. It charged her. When it got close, she knocked its arm down and hit it on top of the head, shattering the helmet. She could feel bones breaking from her hit.

The humanoid walked around for a moment in a stupor, then collapsed.

Her breathing went all over the place as her vision flickered on and off. She cursed herself for not bringing any medicine. Hopefully the nanobots would be able to cure this much damage. The smell of blood permeated the air. The decision to head back the way she came was an easy one. If she was going to pass out, better there than here.

With her hands applying pressure to her stomach and upper leg area, she limped back toward the air pod facility. Maybe she could use the air pod itself to rest in. Although it crashed, it was still intact, and more importantly, it had a door she could lock. It took her three pain-filled hours to cover the seven miles. She figured her injuries must not have been too critical; otherwise she would have passed out much earlier. When she reached it, the familiar skittering sounds broke the silence, but she did not care.

She found the air pod and climbed in. The door slid shut. Her eyes widened as it lifted, spun around 180 degrees, and began to fly over the chasm. Even better, she thought. At least the other air pod warehouse was secure. When it arrived, she crawled out and crashed to the ground.

Her eyes closed.

Four hours later, she awoke. She lifted her head and got up on all fours. Vomit flowed from her lips. Her body shook. The nanobots were trying to help her, but whatever was in her system was not going down without a fight. She decided to head back to the third facility. There was a medical station there and hopefully something to help. She stood while using the air pod as a brace. Her breathing was shallow, and nausea rocked her body, but the drive to get to the facility overpowered that.

It was dark when she hobbled out of the warehouse. The bright moonlight was her companion as she trudged back to the facility. It was only three miles away and a predator-free path with grasslands all around. Several times along the path, she thought she was going to pass out. Her eyes fluttered as the facility came within reach.

A brief thought of the creature she killed in the tunnels ran through her mind. If she had let it live and it caught her in this condition, she would have been easy prey. She smirked despite her pain. The lesson learned there was to end the threat or it could be a problem later. The pillars scanned her, and the mini pyramid slid back. She used the wall of the ramp as support as she entered. The pyramid above her closed.

"Kal! Activate!"

Kal shimmered into view. "Good evening. How may I be of service?"

"Something's wrong with me."

A beam scanned her as she entered the main room and headed to the medical area in the living quarters.

"You have the mimecan trail parasite inside you."

"What is that?"

"The mimecan trail parasite is an organism that lives symbiotically on the mimecan trees. It ingests the seeds of the tree, then infects a living host. The death of the host signals the parasite to expel the seeds. The decomposing body then serves as nutrients for the seeds."

She grunted in pain. "How do I kill it?"

"Antiparasitic medicine specific to the mimecan trail parasite is available in the medical station. You will also need antivenom."

"What?"

"The mimecan trail parasite uses venom to paralyze its host."

She reached the medical room. "Well . . . I'm not paralyzed."

"That is not possible."

"I'd say otherwise! Where is the antiparasitic?"

Kal walked over to a cabinet. "It is here."

She limped over to the cabinet and tapped it. It slid to the side, revealing a host of metallic containers, syringes, and plastic pouches. *"Which one!"*

Kal pointed to a container. "This is the mimecan anti-parasitic." Kal pointed to a plastic pouch. "These pills are the antivenom."

She grabbed both and leaned against the wall. She pressed the top of the container, which popped out a pill. "How many of each?"

"Two of each, given your body size."

She popped the container again and then swallowed both pills. The antivenom pouch opened with ease as she gobbled two pills. She slipped off her clothing and assessed her damage. "Is there anything I can cover these wounds with?"

"You have internal bleeding," said Kal. He walked over to another cabinet. "Pads, sealants, and recovery gel are here."

She sighed as she used the counters to walk over. Opening the cabinet revealed a bevy of various-sized white pads, trans-lucent blue pads, and a container that reminded her of a whipped cream can. "What do I need to do?"

"Apply the gel to the wound, then seal it."

With a quick motion, she grabbed the can and applied the gel as it oozed out across her puncture wound on her stomach and leg. The pads had a sticky substance on their edges, and when applied, they seemed to form a fit that still allowed breathing via the small holes scattered around it. She eyed a bed in the corner and walked over to it. Once she was settled in, she looked at Kal. "Lock the door."

Kal waved his hand to the side, and the door to the room slid shut.

"Don't go anywhere, and alert me if anything comes near me."

"You are the only living being in—"

"I don't care! Just do it!"

"As you wish."

She gripped her PSD as her breathing slowed and her eyelids got heavy. After a moment, she was asleep. Dreams of the incident danced in her mind as she tossed and turned through the night. Each time she awoke, she checked the room and asked Kal if she was the only one there. The thought that she was only alive due to her nanobots did not escape her. If they had not interfered in the hallucinations she had been seeing, it would have been all over.

When she awoke the next morning, she clenched her jaw. She did feel a bit better, but there was pain all over. A headache pounded away inside her head. "Kal, is the parasite gone?"

A beam scanned her.

"The parasite has been cleansed, and its poison removed."

She sighed. "How are my other wounds?"

"The internal bleeding has stopped. No vital organs were punctured. The gel has formed a protective cover over your wounds."

"Feel like shit."

Kal stared at her.

She shook her head. The smell of feces and urine rankled her nose. Looking down, she saw that her bodily functions did not care if she had been asleep. "Ugh . . . I need a shower. Is there something that can waterproof the pads?"

"The blue pads can be applied over your current pads."

"Fine . . . I'll come back and clean this bed later then."

"The bed is self-cleaning. Once you leave, it will automatically clean itself after one hour."

She nodded at Kal and slid her legs to the side. Pain shot through her as she climbed off the bed. Limping over to the cabinet, she was able to get the translucent blue pads and apply them over her wounds. She reached her living quarters and went directly to the hygiene pod. Sitting in the shower area as the water massaged her sent waves of relaxation through her. After cleaning up, she went to her bed and lay down.

She closed her eyes and fell asleep.

Emily opened her eyes and stared at the ceiling. She reached down and touched her pad. The pain had been minimized. Touching her leg wound verified that. The nausea had gone as well as her headache. Tingling sensations were still active around the wounded areas, but for the first time since the incident, she felt normal. She looked around for her PSD and found it had rolled out of her hand and to her side.

Opening it up, she half expected to see a message waiting for her, but she now knew that was a hallucination. It had been so real to her. Her head lowered as she remembered the sensation of hugging Dr. Snowden, then Evaran hugging both of them. The realization that she was just a week shy of being on the prison planet for three months danced on the edges of her mind. If the Torvatta had not come by now, something was very wrong. She hung her head as she thought again of having to spend the rest of her extended life on this nightmarish planet.

After checking her injuries, she cleaned up. The gel that had been on under the pads looked like it had sealed the wounds. However, the pain underneath them suggested she was not at full health. At least she could take off the pads she had wrapped. When she was in the shower, she paid extra attention to making sure she did not aggravate the new skin that had formed overnight. She suspected the nanobots had a hand in helping to speed it along.

After showering, she stood in front of the clothing adjuster closet. "Kal. Activate."

Kal shimmered into view. "Good morning. How may I be of service?"

She gestured at the empty block that had embedded clothes in it before. "I need a new outfit. My old one is torn and blood soaked, and I don't know what else might be on it."

"What type?"

"You mean there are other types of outfits?"

"There are seven outfits available."

She sighed. "And you . . . didn't mention this before because . . ."

Kal stared at her.

She shook her head. If V had been here, he would have told her of the various suits, probably to the last detail. She had gotten used to Kal, but found it easier to look it up in the Coraanan systems sometimes. "Well . . . which one has the best defensive capability?"

Kal waved a hand. "The field guard suit."

A gray mesh-like suit with rubberlike pads on every segment of the body appeared in the clothing block. It was a one-piece suit and looked much bulkier than the one she had previously. The neck area had a circular metal band separating the body from the wet-suit-like head covering. To the sides in smaller embedded blocks was a small forearm guard, a set of rubberlike boots, and a belt with various pouches on it.

Emily looked at Kal. "What defensive capabilities does it have?"

Kal pointed at the mesh. "The underlying mesh is highly resistant to physical force while allowing freedom of movement. It is also waterproof." He tapped the upper leg rubber pad. "The defensive pads can mitigate large amounts of physical and energy damage." He gestured at the boots. "These can absorb falling damage."

"You mean like if I jumped off a cliff?"

"It can sustain up to around fifty feet."

She eyed the forearm guard. "What about that?"

"It is the interface. It allows for interaction with the suit and general information."

She sighed. "What interaction and what general information?"

"The interface allows the suit to extend a helmet and camouflage. It also displays general information such as the time and has an onboard database for identifying objects."

"This woulda been nice to have back in the first facility," she said. "But I guess I asked the wrong questions. Lesson learned the hard way."

Kal stared at her.

"Kal. Deactivate."

Kal shimmered out of view.

She stood on the clothing adjuster pad and hit the button. Once the suit and other items had been adjusted, she slipped into them. The suit had a zipper-like device in the back, and she noticed that it went all the way around to the front of the crotch. She smirked at the thought that it would be easy to unzip if she needed to relieve herself. The boots slipped on with ease, and the forearm guard snapped into place. She had half a mind to cut her hair as she tucked it into the suit. Moving around, the suit seemed just as light as the other one. She wondered why they did not just wear this all the time.

The forearm guard had several buttons on it, but the big green button seemed obvious to her. When she pressed it, a vertical screen shot up with various options available. She pressed the helmet option. Out of the metal neck guard shot a series of overlapping steel bands. A glass-like shield shot down over her face, and a HUD appeared on the edges of the inside. She pressed the helmet button again, and the helmet slid back. Her senses had been obscured when it was up, but maybe there was a situation where having it out could be advantageous.

The field guide feature would highlight an object positioned in front of the screen and provide additional information about it. She could see the usefulness of the suit if out and about in the field. It reminded her of the PSD's augmented reality feature. The camouflage option intrigued her. When she activated it, she could still see herself. Going in front of a mirror told another story. Although it was not perfect, her form was somewhat still visible in the light distortions, but it would be hard to see at a distance. She leaned flat against the wall and noticed that her suit took on the appearance of the wall.

Outside the general information like time and the overland map feature, the power bar stood out to her. It looked like it could operate for a week or so at a time continuously. If she did not use the systems much, maybe she could stretch that out. She figured there was probably a recharge station somewhere in the facility.

She placed her PSD in one of the side pouches and headed up to the specimen surveillance lab. Several hours passed as she perused the field guide, a section she had skimmed over before. Looking at the section that covered the area between this facility and the next one, she saw the tree and parasite that had infected her. She snorted. If she had known this beforehand, the life-and-death drama could have been avoided. Another lesson learned. Take the time to be prepared.

She eased back into the chair. It irked her that letting her guard down, even for a moment, almost led to her death. That was a brutal lesson to learn, but one she would hold close and make instinctive. She had to if she wanted to survive. Some things would be hard to prepare for, like Kazaal. Even the advanced suit she wore would not have helped much. It might have slowed Kazaal down, but she concluded that the end result would probably have been the same.

She spent the next two weeks healing up and researching. Going out would only be feasible if she could respond to a situation without being hampered. The healing went by fast, but she knew that if she had to do it without the facility's help, it would have been much longer. The creatures that she had run into were not listed in the field guide. She suspected they must have appeared after the Coraanan left, although if not through the rift doors, then from somewhere else. The field guide was probably out of date, but it did have some pertinent information. She still had her PSD to help out.

Getting her sleep cycle in sync had been hard, but with the help of some sleeping medicine, she was back on track.

On the last day of the final week, she did a final check. She had found a backpack that was a bit bulkier than the one she had before. The suit had some load-bearing qualities to help offset that. She made sure to test out her training with the suit on and found it flowed naturally.

The waterproof sleeping bag was her second-favorite find. It had a similar material to the suit mesh, but without the rubber pads. There was a button to seal it, and it had micro holes to allow air in. The part she liked about it most was that it was small when folded up and lightweight. She planned to use it in the upcoming journey. With a restock of water and food, she headed out.

The trip to the air pod facility three miles north stirred memories of going the other way. She grimaced as the memory of the pain shot through her mind. This time around, no tree or creature would get the jump on her.

She slipped into a different air pod when she reached the warehouse. The smell and the bloodstains on the floor served another pain-filled memory. The air pod lifted off and, after thirty minutes, arrived at the other side. She jumped out before it rammed into the semiclosed doors. The shock absorption of the boots from hitting the ground made her appreciate them. She surveyed the path ahead as skittering noises filled the air. Standing still, she focused on everything around her, from the sounds of the creatures in the warehouse to the light breeze blowing around her. Her heightened senses seemed to be more aware of her surroundings.

When she arrived near the spot where she had been attacked, she paused to survey it. She noted that there was not much left of the creatures to look at, mostly stains and bits of the white dried substance. The wooden spears were still there.

She picked one up and studied it. It had simple designs on the body of it, and the end piece looked like some type of sharpened stone. The memory of being stabbed by it jolted through her mind as she rubbed her leg where it had been punctured.

Looking up at the tree, she could now see the needles. They were scattered in dense groups on the branches. Even if an animal did not try to feed on the scattered nuts on the ground, they could still be pricked by the needles falling on them or scattered about.

After completing eight miles of the thirty-three left to go, she decided to take a break. Using her PSD, she found a tree she could climb without being used as fertilizer. After reaching the top, she surveyed the forest around her.

Smoke rising in the east caught her attention. Using the PSD, she zoomed in. A village with dull gray buildings that reminded her of clay appeared. It was about two miles away. Probably where those humanoids came from that attacked her earlier.

Looking north, she noticed a valley with a large tree about three miles away. She checked the overland map and decided she would go around it. Something about the tree seemed unusual to her. Maybe it was the size, or the way the branches and foliage looked.

She shimmied down the tree and had a late lunch. In one day, she had covered seventeen miles, four of them by the air pod. Her legs were not as sore as she had figured they would be, but she did not want to overtax them. She went west off the path and into the forest, looking for a place to bed down. A large tree lying on the ground presented an opportunity. Using the morphable metal to make a shovel from her PSD, she dug a small crevice against it. Several bugs scattered away at her activity. She paused to look at them run. Before all this began, she would have run screaming. Now they were just a nuisance.

After walking a bit away to relieve herself, she headed back to her new enclosure and unpacked her sleeping bag. The thought of watching training videos crossed her mind, but dissipated as she remembered the last time she let her guard down in a hostile environment. One thing she did differently this time was scout out a parasite-free tree that she could scramble up if need be. She slid the sleeping bag into the crevice. After crawling in, she sealed it while still wearing all her gear and closed her eyes.

Emily's eyes popped open as a squealing noise rang out nearby. She swallowed hard and checked her PSD. It was 9:00 p.m., meaning she was out for five and a half hours. Fatigue seemed to be hard for her to judge. Sleeping was almost on command. She did not know if it was because she was just tired all the time and not aware of it or if her body just responded on demand. These trips screwed with her sleeping cycle.

She held her breath as she focused on the squealing sound. From the intensity of it, she guessed it was about half a mile away. After unsealing the sleeping bag, she pushed it to the side and scanned in the direction of the sound. Whatever was going on was getting closer. She jumped up, grabbed her sleeping bag, folded it up, and slipped it into her backpack. The tree she had scouted earlier was nearby, and after climbing it, she accessed the forearm interface. The light from the screen was bright, so she tapped the helmet option, then closed the interface as quickly as possible.

When the helmet slid over her head and snapped into place, she scanned below and around the tree. The outlining ability of the helmet was in full effect as it showed a boar-like creature running in the distance. The red outline showed this creature was in a hurry. She glanced a bit behind the animal and saw five shapes chasing after it. Focusing on them made her stomach tie up in knots. It was the humanoids she had seen earlier. Apparently, they were also nocturnal hunters.

She held as still as she could when the creature passed with the humanoids in hot pursuit. When the humanoids ran by where she had slept, one of them paused. She cursed herself for not activating the camouflage ability, but doing it now would definitely draw their attention.

The humanoid sniffed her sleeping area, then looked around. Its eyes traveled up the tree, and it scrutinized the branch she was on. Its eyes popped open as it screamed out.

She slid down the tree and shot her stun beam out. The humanoid crumpled. The rustling of the other humanoids approached. She gritted her teeth. Running away was getting old, and she was tired of being a victim. Respect had to be earned out here. She knew if she was going to be crossing their territory, they needed to stay away from her, or it would be a perpetual chase.

After opening her interface and camouflaging herself, she slipped behind the tree and aimed at the stunned humanoid. It did not take long for the others to surround their fallen member. She aimed just left of the group and then swept her stun beam to the right, knocking out three of them. The last one she hit with a repulsion blast, which knocked it into the fallen tree. She disabled her camouflage and extended her

PSD into a staff and approached the startled and trembling humanoid.

It raised its hands and turned its head to the side. She cocked her head at it and extended the staff forward. The humanoid whimpered.

"Stay away from me," she said.

The humanoid looked up at her with parted lips.

She was not sure if it understood her, but it seemed surprised. With one final stare at the humanoid, she walked north. She did not want to kill the humanoids, and had some regret for killing the previous ones, but this environment did not favor mercy. Letting the environment define her was something she fought. She showed mercy because that is who she was at heart. Maybe in this setting, being human was an anomaly.

Putting distance between her and where the incident occurred was her top priority. Moving through the forest at night was not as bad as she thought. She angled her walking so it coincided with the path northwest from where she started. The ambient noise of the forest was soothing. It reminded her again of camping with Dr. Snowden and her dad. She sighed and then swallowed hard. Although she did not want to give up hope of being rescued, the thought that this would be her new home was becoming more and more real to her.

After going another five miles, she paused to take a break. She was halfway to the next facility, about twenty miles away, and making good time. Her legs had adjusted to the walking, and going an additional mile or two more than her daily average was no longer out of the question. One more break around the ten-mile mark and she could make it there by the next day.

She scanned the trees for a safe spot and, after finding one, slumped down against it. The power indicator bar on her HUD showed she had quite a bit of power left. The Coraanan field guards must have been formidable, even though they were half her size. She had seen images of them with weapons, but Kal had stated that no weapons were able to be created or stored in the facility, except for visiting field guards. Central Command had been their base, and the tunnel system maintenance one of their tasks, along with escorting researchers out into the field.

She could not imagine anyone wanting to come here, but if they had a way to get back out, it would not be as foreboding to them as it was to her. Hopefully the rift door was still operational, because if it was not, that would be it. Just her and this world. Her new home.

She pulled out her PSD and studied the overland map. The third facility was a straight shot from where she was. With renewed vigor, she rose and continued forward. It got colder the farther north she journeyed. Even though the suit kept her warm, she could feel it in her hands. It also seem to coincide with less and less animal life, something she was not going to complain about. The terrain around her had become rocky. The path went up and around hills, and there was even a river where she was able to refill her water container.

It took her four hours to reach the point just ten miles shy of the third facility. She decided to break for the day. It was still dark at 4:00 a.m., and her feet were starting to throb. The rougher path had taken its toll. It had been another seventeen-mile trip for her, and the thought of reaching the next facility gave her purpose.

A nagging doubt about having to use the tunnel to get to Central Command crept into her mind. There was a moun-tain range ahead, similar to the one between the second and third facility. Although the path seemed to go through it, she was not sure if she wanted to try that.

After taking care of her basic needs, she set up her sleeping bag, crawled in, and then nodded off with thoughts of reaching the next facility.

After a solid eight-hour rest, she awoke to the sound of wind whistling by. She checked her PSD, which showed it was noon. With a shake of her head, she unsealed the sleeping bag. A burst of cool air slapped her in the face. She jerked her head back as she resealed the sleeping bag. It was helmet time. The one thing she would look for upon reaching the next facility was gloves. The thought she would need them did not occur to her in the warmer climate she had seen so far. Even more puzzling to her was why it was not a part of the suit to begin with.

She braced herself as she exited the sleeping bag. Her hands let her know it was not going to be a comfortable ten-mile hike. After folding and packing her sleeping bag, she had a small bite and drink, then headed back onto the path.

As she progressed toward the new facility, she noted that the trees had colorful leaves. The animals she did see were small relative to her. She chuckled when she saw a squir-rel-like creature running around a tree. It reminded her a bit of the information broker that she had met on a previous adventure with Evaran.

Her eyes softened as she thought of the training videos. Although they were only videos of Evaran, they continued to be her lifeline of hope. She knew that Evaran was not one to give up, and even if it took him a long time, he would still come, even if she was not alive. Dr. Snowden would be right there with him. Even if they did come late, they could always just travel back to when she arrived and pick her up, she hoped anyways. She smiled for a brief moment. All of this could be wiped out, like it never happened. Regardless, she was living it whether they came or not. It reminded her of the question Hermes and John had asked Evaran. Even if the timeline changed, from their perspective, they would live out the rest of their lives. She focused on the path ahead.

Ten miles went by quickly as she mused on the next big part of her journey. She wished the paths between the facilities had been more like this than the ones filled with wild creatures. The cool air had not been kind to her hands, and she resorted to tucking them in her armpits to stay warm. Her mind cleared of those thoughts when she saw the familiar stepped pyramid surrounded by crystal pillars. She rushed up to the pyramid and exhaled from her nose as the familiar scans enveloped her and the pyramid slid back.

She ran her hands along the metallic walls before exiting the ramp into the main entry room. "Kal. Activate."

Kal shimmered into view. "Good morning. Welcome to Coraanan research facility number ten. How may I be of service?"

"Any living beings other than myself here?"

"There are no other living beings here."

She sighed and looked down. Maybe it was too much to hope that somewhere on this planet was a sentient being that was not a murderer. "Let me guess, the communications and transportation system are down too, right?"

"The communication system is not functioning. The transportation system is functional."

Her eyes perked up. "Functional . . . you mean . . . it can be used?"

"Yes."

She circled a hand. "And . . . where can it go?"

"The only destination available is Central Command."

She let out a deep breath, then headed to the transportation hub. When she got there, she saw three box-shaped transportation units. They reminded her of air pods, but fitted to work on the rail in the transportation system. Peeking into the first one, she saw the similar featureless interior, with the exception of a small console jutting out before the front window. Her eyes misted as she smiled. Finally, something was going her way.

After restocking supplies, deactivating Kal, and making sure to pick up gloves, she entered the first unit. The console lit up with an overland map. Most of the green dots were dimmed, but the blue dot was lit. She pressed the blue dot, and after the door sealed shut, it began to move.

The space was cramped, just like the air pod. Watching the platform go by as the unit shot down the rail made her appreciate not having to walk fifty miles. The side rooms brought back memories of tangling with the creature that stalked her between the first and second facilities. At least she would not have to sleep or take breaks down here.

As the unit neared Central Command, the tunnel ascended and came to a stop at a massive circular transportation hub. Her eyes widened as she looked around and saw at least forty units ringing it. Her unit rotated ninety degrees, and the door lifted. She hopped out onto the circular platform and surveyed the environment. The smell of feces wafted past her nose. She tightened up as she pulled out her PSD.

"Kal. Activate."

Kal shimmered into view. "Good evening. Welcome to Central Command. How may I be of service?"

"Is there anything alive here other than myself?"

"Yes."

18

Dr. Snowden pondered what Organic Emily must be up to. It had been roughly three days since she had been teleported, but it felt like a lifetime just trying to figure out where she was. Three days was not too long, and he was sure she could survive for that time. She had her PSD, and knowing her, he was certain she would not go down easily, if at all.

The parallel timeline intrigued him. Azoculus was Earth, just different. He was glad to be back in what he termed the original timeline. The information on the right screen showed that they had only been gone an hour from the timeline's perspective, even though they had been in the parallel timeline much longer. He concluded that the Torvatta's ability to jump to any point in space and time must not be restricted by what timeline they were in or going to. He imagined it as an unclosed triangle. Leave at one point in the timeline, arrive at another point in the parallel timeline, spend a long time there, then come back to the original timeline just one hour after the initial departure.

"We are here," said Evaran.

Dr. Snowden studied the left screen. It showed a pyramid deep in a jungle, similar to the one in Egypt. The right screen indicated the shielding was down. Two life-forms appeared as red dots in front of the pyramid. "Why do I sense a trap . . ."

"It is possible," said Evaran as he tilted his head. He tapped at his chair console, and the Torvatta descended toward the pyramid. "I am going in. I suspect they are not here to fight."

"Maybe not, but I'm coming with you," said Lord Vygon.

"I can handle two Purifiers if it comes to that."

"Okay, you do that, but I'm still coming," said Lord Vygon.

"Me too," said Dr. Snowden.

"And me!" said Nanobot Emily.

Evaran looked down for a moment, then sighed. "You all are very persistent. It is your choice to come, but even with two, it might be dangerous." He faced Dr. Snowden and Nanobot Emily. "You two should put on survival suits."

Dr. Snowden rose and gestured back toward the research lab. After he and Nanobot Emily were suited up, they met Evaran and Lord Vygon at the exit ramp of the Torvatta.

Evaran looked Dr. Snowden and Nanobot Emily over, then waved for them to follow. He exited the Torvatta and headed toward the two Purifiers.

Dr. Snowden noticed the Purifiers looked different than the ones he had seen before. They wore more advanced-looking suits, but kept the Egyptian-like theme.

A small platform sat on the ground between the two Purifiers. It had two poles on the sides used for carrying it. On top of the platform was a mounted crystal with a golden base that supported it.

After reaching the Purifiers, Evaran tossed out a translation orb.

"The overlord wishes to speak with you," said the left Purifier.

"Very well," said Evaran. He gestured at them to proceed.

The right Purifier adjusted the base, causing a beam to shoot up from the crystal. The bust of a bronze-skinned middle-aged man appeared. The two Purifiers knelt on the ground facing the projection.

The overlord reared his head back as he surveyed Evaran and the others. After a moment, he spoke in a deep voice. "Who are you?"

Evaran stepped forward. "I am Evaran, and with me are my friends."

The overlord smirked. "An Evaran . . . it makes sense now. My base on Azoculus was . . . ravaged. The other base on this planet is shut down. And now . . . I find out an Evaran is involved."

"There is only one Evaran, and it is me."

The overlord chuckled. "It appears I know you better than yourself then." He looked around, then focused on Dr. Snowden and Nanobot Emily. "These humans . . . this world . . . do you protect them?"

"I do. I will not let timeline invaders change this timeline."

"Timeline incursions are not rare. You know this as an Evaran. Yet . . . on this specific world, in this universe, on this one plane, an Evaran decides to defend against it."

"I cannot be everywhere at once."

The overlord smiled. "Oh, I know. You're not the first Evaran I've come across, nor will you be the last." He gestured at Dr. Snowden and Nanobot Emily. "I seek the same as you. To protect humanity. The difference is I elevate them wherever I find them."

"I do not think conversion-or-die tactics can be considered elevation of the human race."

The overlord laughed. "A minor issue when first inducting a new timeline version of humanity. Once it is complete, the human race is united and I lead them to their full potential."

Lord Vygon smirked. "You also kill nonhumans and strip what makes us nonhuman."

The overlord narrowed his eyes at Lord Vygon. "Of course . . . you aren't human anymore. Why would I want *that* to pollute the purity of the human race?"

"That is not why you kill nonhumans," said Evaran. "I know that you siphon their exotic energy. There are many uses for that energy, but I do not suspect you do it for the human race."

"Enough!" said the overlord.

The two Purifiers sank their heads lower.

"I have come to make you a proposal."

Evaran cocked his head. "I am listening."

"I will leave this timeline to you. In exchange, you promise to not interfere in any timeline I'm in."

Dr. Snowden scowled. "Your . . . Purifiers sent my niece to a prison planet!" His blood began to boil as tingling sensations swept across him. When they reached the point where his breathing was staggered, the heightened state he had felt earlier kicked in. A calmness washed across him. He could hear the Purifiers breathing and noticed their subtle movements.

The overlord shrugged. "A small price to pay for the safety of your timeline."

Evaran shook his head. "I cannot turn my back on the genocide that you will rain down across the timelines."

Dr. Snowden's eyes popped open as he noticed the right Purifier fiddling with a device in his hand. It was hard to detect, but from his angle, the minute movements stood out. He thought he could almost see the interactions between the device and the crystal. "It's a trap! Get away from the crystal!"

Evaran snapped his head toward Dr. Snowden, then spun around and took off toward the Torvatta with Lord Vygon in tow. Dr. Snowden had spun around and grabbed Nanobot Emily's arm and followed Evaran.

"Your pathetic morality!" said the overlord, crowing in the distance. "I come here, offering you a way out, and you *spit* in my face."

The crystal began to glow.

The overlord continued to boast. "You have made your choice. I leave you with a parting gift."

They hustled toward the Torvatta, and when they were within a few feet, an explosion erupted behind them. Evaran pushed Dr. Snowden through the shield, causing Dr. Snowden to sprawl on the ground. Lord Vygon tackled Nanobot Emily, pushing them both through the shield. Evaran spun around and raised his shield as the explosion hit him. The force of it pushed him through the shield. A wave of energy coursed over the Torvatta's shielding. After a moment, it dissipated.

Dr. Snowden's eyes scanned the devastated landscape. It seemed like everything around the Torvatta and in front of the pyramid had been reduced to ashes, including the two Purifiers. The pyramid had been partially vaporized. His breathing staggered as he looked around. He ran over to Nanobot Emily, who had stood with the help of Lord Vygon.

"That guy has a problem," said Nanobot Emily.

Lord Vygon dusted dirt off his armor. "That he does."

Evaran scanned everyone. "Everyone appears to be okay." He faced Dr. Snowden. "You detected it before I did. I am impressed."

Dr. Snowden smirked. "Well . . . to be honest, I actually felt like I was about to lose control. Then I did that wave thing, and everything was . . . noticeable."

Evaran put his hand on Dr. Snowden's shoulder. "You have come a long way. I am thankful once again."

Dr. Snowden nodded.

Evaran stepped out of the shield.

"What are you doing?"

Evaran turned his head to the side. "I need to shut down the portal. It appears this base has been abandoned already, so I am not expecting any resistance. It will not take long."

Dr. Snowden watched Evaran head off to the pyramid. He could tell something about the discussion with the overlord bothered Evaran. He looked at Lord Vygon. "The overlord spoke like there were other Evarans. You ever hear of anything like that?"

Lord Vygon looked down for a moment, then back up. "Yes . . . but not in that context. I don't think Evaran has heard it in that manner either."

"I can see how that would be unsettling," said Nanobot Emily.

"Yeah . . . assuming the overlord was speaking the truth," said Lord Vygon. "He's a genocidal maniac after all."

Dr. Snowden chuckled. "Good point." He gestured toward the Torvatta entrance. "Guess we wait inside then."

They assembled in the command area, and after thirty minutes, Evaran returned.

"The rift door is shut down," said Evaran. "When this is over, we will need to destroy both of them."

"No problems with that. I'll make sure it happens," said Lord Vygon.

Evaran nodded. "Good. Now, back to pick up V. If the overlord sent these two Purifiers through there, then hopefully V recorded the destination codes to the capital world."

Dr. Snowden tilted his head. "You think they came from the planet with the main rift stone?"

Evaran raised a finger. "I do. However, we will find out when V shows us what he recorded."

"Sounds good to me."

Evaran tapped at his chair console, and the Torvatta lifted off. It flew into space, and after opening a portal to the parallel timeline, it jumped through.

It took about another thirty minutes for the Torvatta to arrive at the South American base in the parallel timeline.

Dr. Snowden raised his eyebrows when he saw there was only part of the base similar to the first one on the ground. The rest of it had been vaporized. "What in the world . . ."

V appeared on the front right screen. "Reporting in. My location has been sent."

Evaran nodded. "We are on our way to pick you up."

"Acknowledged."

The screen went blank.

"Whew, at least V is okay. This overlord guy likes to blow things up," said Nanobot Emily.

"It would seem so," said Evaran as he ran his fingers over the chair console. "Let us head to the conference room."

After a minute or so, the Torvatta hovered near the coordinates V had sent and picked him up.

After switching to body mode, V went to the conference room, where everyone had assembled. After greeting everyone, he took a seat.

"It is good to have you back," said Evaran.

V tilted his head. "Acknowledged." He interacted with the table console, causing the recording he had taken to begin playing. "There are several interactions with the portal that I recorded. Displaying the first one."

Dr. Snowden watched with rapture as it showed the first destination codes light up before the rift door was active. The rift operator interacted with the rift controller, and a solid red surface appeared between the crystal rods. The two Purifiers who had died earlier walked through.

"Interesting," said Evaran. "I did not know the rift controllers would show the incoming location. If so, that may be the main rift stone destination code."

The next interaction showed an older man falling out of the rift door. The rift door deactivated, and after a moment, the rift operator tapped at the rift controller, causing a red surface to appear. Several guards grabbed the man and pushed him through.

Dr. Snowden scooted to the edge of his seat. "The prison planet."

Evaran nodded. "It would appear so. However, we cannot try any of these combinations out on this planet. Both portals are not functional. We will need to go back to the first base in Egypt in our timeline."

Dr. Snowden smirked. "I feel like I'm playing timeline ping-pong."

"An apt analogy."

Dr. Snowden nodded.

"Let us head to the command area. V, take us back to the first base in our timeline."

V stood. "Acknowledged."

After they assembled in the command area, V's hands flew over the front console. The Torvatta ascended into space, then popped open a portal to the original timeline. Once through, it flew toward the first base in Egypt.

After landing outside the base, Dr. Snowden noticed a ship nearby. "Looks like we got company."

"Helians," said Lord Vygon. "Must be here to secure it."

"Good. This will save us a trip to Atlantis. We will need two quantum beacons," said Evaran.

"I got 'em," said Lord Vygon as he stood.

Evaran nodded.

After exiting the Torvatta, they walked toward a group of Helian guards around the base entrance. The guards saluted when they saw Evaran.

"Who is in charge here?" asked Evaran.

"Captain Laban," said one of the guards. "He's in the rift room."

"We need to see him."

One of the guards waved for them to follow. Several minutes later, they entered the rift room. A handful of Helians in robes were busy studying the room.

Captain Laban stood at the rift controller, scrutinizing it, along with one of the robed Helians. When he saw Evaran and the others, his face lit up. He walked over and saluted. "Evaran! What brings you back?"

Evaran returned the salute. "We have found the destination codes to the prison planet and the main rift stone. We need to send quantum beacons through in order to determine their location."

"Not a problem." Captain Laban eyed Nanobot Emily, then faced Dr. Snowden. "I see you found your niece."

"Well . . . sorta . . . ," said Dr. Snowden.

Captain Laban cocked his head.

Nanobot Emily extended a hand. "I'm Emily."

"Good to meet you, sorta Emily," said Captain Laban with a grin as he shook Nanobot Emily's hand. He turned halfway around while glancing at Evaran and gestured at the rift controller. "You know how to work these things?"

"It is just the destination code you need. John and Leah showed me how to enter them and some other basic functions."

"I suppose you wouldn't mind leaving us instructions on how to use it."

"Lord Vygon knows the codes. I would suggest destroying these rift controllers and the crystals. However, I leave that up to you and the council."

Captain Laban nodded at Lord Vygon. "Fair enough." He extended a hand toward the rift controller. "All yours."

Evaran walked up to the rift controller and interacted with it. After he entered the destination code needed for the prison planet, the rift door activated, and a red surface appeared. Evaran tossed out an orb that projected an image of V on the bottom right.

"The tracer has been activated," said V.

Evaran dipped his head at Lord Vygon, who then walked up to the rift door and tossed the quantum beacon through.

"Transferring visual," said V.

Dr. Snowden expected to see lines and the beacon zigzagging between them. Instead, there were no vertical lines, just a horizontal line that ended in a hollow oval shape.

"Analysis. Pocket Universe 622 is the destination."

Evaran rubbed his chin. "Interesting." He interacted with the rift controller and shut down the rift door. After entering the prison planet destination code, the rift door activated again with a similar red surface.

Dr. Snowden shook his head. "You sure you entered the right codes?"

"I did. I suspect red indicates a pocket universe destination," said Evaran. He nodded at Lord Vygon.

Lord Vygon walked up to the rift door and tossed the second quantum beacon through.

The projection showed the same journey as the first quantum beacon.

"Analysis. Pocket Universe 23 is the destination."

Evaran shut off the portal and faced Captain Laban. "There is a second base on this planet. I can send you the coordinates. It is partially destroyed."

Captain Laban jerked his head back. "How do you know that?"

"There was another one in the parallel timeline. We visited it here to make sure it existed before telling you about it. There should be no one there, but the front may be a bit . . . scorched."

Captain Laban eyed Evaran. "Pocket universes . . . parallel timelines . . . you've lost me. And you've cleared another base out already?"

Evaran shook his head. "It was abandoned, but we did meet the messengers from the Purifier leader. He left us a gift."

"Nice guy . . ."

"Extend your arm, and I will transfer the coordinates."

Captain Laban wrinkled his eyebrows as he extended his arm.

Evaran placed his UIC on it, which glowed wildly for a moment, then stabilized. He perused his ARI, then tapped at it. After a moment, he pulled his UIC off and put it back on his belt. "You have the coordinates now."

Captain Laban interacted with his forearm. His eyebrows rose. "What is that device?"

Evaran half smiled. "A gift, from a friend, that just gave you the second base coordinates."

Captain Laban narrowed his eyes for a moment, then laughed. "We must be like children to you."

"Not at all. It is a good trait to be inquisitive," said Evaran. He gave a Helian salute. "Nonetheless, we must be off . . . to find the other Emily."

Captain Laban shook his head. "I won't even pretend like I understand, but if you need assistance, let me know."

"Your place is here, on Earth. There is still work to be done in finding the remaining sentinels, and you have the other base to attend to as well as rebuilding Atlantis."

Captain Laban exhaled from his nose. "Yeah . . . there's a lot to do."

Evaran half grinned and placed a hand on Captain Laban's shoulder. "You better get to work."

"You got it."

Evaran nodded and then turned and exited the portal room with everyone in tow. After reaching the Torvatta command area, he pulled up the prison planet destination on the front right screen. "V, take us to the prison planet."

"Acknowledged."

Dr. Snowden gulped as he watched the left screen. The Torvatta lifted off and flew into space. This was the moment he had been waiting for. He glanced at Nanobot Emily and smiled when she gripped his arm. The question of what would Organic Emily think of Nanobot Emily flashed through his mind. His attention focused on the green beam that shot out from the Torvatta. A portal with a gold border and purple rippling surface appeared. He understood now that, like the rift doors the Purifiers used, the colors had meaning.

The Torvatta flew through and exited above a planet.

Dr. Snowden scooted to the edge of his seat as he scrutinized the planet. He flinched when the border of the right front screen pulsed.

"Quantum beacon detected. Time dilation detected. The quantum beacon was sent through ten minutes ago at 5:27 p.m. today. The beacon records a time of 11:27 p.m."

Evaran rubbed his chin. "For every minute in our timeline, it would be ninety minutes here."

Dr. Snowden exhaled sharply. "What? It's been three days since Emily was sent here!"

"I know, and by my calculations, that means it is roughly two hundred seventy days later, or nine months."

Dr. Snowden's heartbeat raced as he struggled to breathe. Gripping the chair did not help as he slid to the ground.

Nanobot Emily knelt beside him and put her arm around him. "If my dreams are insights into what she went through, she was surviving."

"For nine months!" said Dr. Snowden as spittle flew from his mouth. Tingling sensations began to pulse over him.

"Dr. Snowden . . . waves," said Evaran.

Dr. Snowden struggled to produce the mental imagery of the waves, and after a moment, he was able to spread the wave over his body. He stood and then sat back in his chair. "I'm okay. I was . . . close to losing it again."

"But you did not. You are getting better at controlling your anger."

Dr. Snowden shook his head. "Doesn't mean I'm okay with the situation, though."

"I understand," said Evaran. "V, using the calculations on the time difference, take us to the moment Emily arrives."

"Acknowledged."

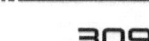

Dr. Snowden's eyes perked up. "So . . . that would mean . . ."

"The last nine months would not have occurred from her perspective."

A big smile crept onto Dr. Snowden's face.

"What about my dreams?" asked Nanobot Emily.

"That will be the price of doing this," said Evaran. "They will remain as just dreams and not a glimpse of reality."

Nanobot Emily nodded and glanced at Dr. Snowden. "I understand. It's worth it. Let's do this."

"Acknowledged."

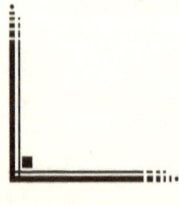

19

Emily frowned as she studied Kal. While the thought that there might be something living here was tantalizing, there was the other thought that they might be hostile. "Do you have an image of them?"

Kal extended his hand. A projection shot up of a small, chubby snakelike creature about a foot in length.

"How many are there?"

"There are three hundred twenty-six."

"Just great. A snake pit."

Kal stared at her.

She sighed. "Show me the layout of this place."

Kal extended his hand and showed a wireframe view of Central Command.

"Indicate the other creatures with a red dot."

Red dots populated in the lower portion of Central Command a bit away from her present location.

"Why haven't the creatures moved to the higher levels?"

"I do not know."

She exhaled from her nose. "Where are the living quarters?"

Kal pointed at several locations in the upper part. "There are multiple living quarter units."

"Take me to the nearest one."

Kal turned and glided across the platform floor.

She followed while scanning the environment. There were other transportation units docked. She figured they were the ones that came when the evacuation order was given. After crossing the platform, they walked up a giant ramp exit. She noticed that like the facilities, the metallic flooring and walls gave an advanced technological look. Screens were embedded in the wall, and the ceiling was a black glass-like material. The strong smell of something rotting assaulted her nose.

Upon exiting the ramp, Kal went down a large hallway and then walked through a small metallic canopy into a large octagonal room. Other hallways branched off to the left and right and opposite them. The slanted sides of the room had long desks in front of them. In the center of the room were various booths with machines.

She wrinkled her eyebrows. "What is this place?"

"Transportation control center."

She looked up and saw that the room was large enough to have a second layer with windows. They continued to the right hallway. As they walked, she peered into the rooms. The medical room was easy to place, but some of the others she had no idea about. At the end of the hallway was a T-split that ended in ramps going in either direction.

Kal gestured to both sides. "The living quarters are the next level up. They are both equally distant. Which one did you want to go to?"

"Whatever one doesn't have those creatures."

Kal took the right ramp, and after going around a bend and up another ramp, they entered the central living quarter area.

She went to the first door, like she had in the other facilities, and checked it out. It was larger than what she was used to, and there were several more rooms. She put her things in the bedroom and faced Kal. "Kal. Deactivate."

Kal shimmered out of view.

She locked the door and made sure there was nothing around. After verifying it was safe, she took a hot shower, which took her mind off the situation for a while. She was not tired, but the massaging water was lulling her to sleep. The bedroom was more and more inviting the longer she was in the shower.

After drying off, she decided to take a nap, and then she would tackle this new environment. She double-checked that the living quarter door was locked and had Kal stand guard to alert her if any of the creatures came near the room.

Her eyes popped open when Kal emitted a high shrieking noise four hours later. She jumped out of bed, put on her suit, and pulled out her PSD. Tingling sensations swept across her. "Kal, what is it?"

"There are three creatures outside your door."

She swallowed hard. "Can they get in?"

"No."

She sighed. "What do you know of these creatures?"

"Everything."

She circled a hand. "How do they attack?"

"They bite and possess a hallucinogenic compound in their venom. When the prey dies, they release a chemical that attracts others."

"Oh, that's just wonderful."

Kal stared at her.

"Would this suit prevent their bites from going through?"

"Only the hardened parts."

"Is there a better suit?"

"Yes."

She shook her head. Talking to Kal was a painful experience. "Where is the clothing adjuster station?"

Kal led her to a separate room.

She jerked her head back as she scanned her surroundings. The room had several cabinets instead of one. On the back of the room was a console embedded in the wall. After fiddling with it, she saw that she could browse the different items that could be made. There was a lot of general clothing, but not much in the way of defensive suits. She faced Kal. "Are there more defensive suits available than what is here?"

"Yes."

"Where can I get them?"

Kal began to walk toward the door.

"Wait! What are you doing?"

"Taking you to the armory."

She sighed. "I need to deal with these creatures first." With her back against the wall facing the door, she aimed her PSD forward. "Kal, open the door."

Kal waved his hand, and the door opened. One of the creatures slithered up to the door. It was green and had what looked like muscles under tight skin instead of scales. The mouth was more like a rat's than a snake's. She hit it with a stun beam, causing it to stop moving. Another creature slithered up. It fell victim to a stun blast. The third creature took off.

She ran to the door, looked out, and could not see where the third one went. "Kal! Show me a layout and red dot that creature!"

Kal complied.

She studied the projection. The creature was moving fast. Looking down at the felled creatures, she could see they were dead. The stun beam was lethal to smaller animals. She grabbed both of them by the tail and tossed them through the waste disposal panel outside the room.

The new goal was to clear this place of these creatures. She knew she would not be able to fully rest with threats around like that. Central Command would need to be secured. She leaned against the wall and smirked at the thought that she was now an unofficial Coraanan guard.

Roughly six months passed with killing the creatures as part of her daily routine. In the mornings, she would clean up, have breakfast, then go up to a balcony she had found on the higher levels. After soaking up the view and relaxing for a bit, she would begin prepping for a cleansing run. Her goal was to secure, section by section, the entirety of Central Command. Areas that were safe got locked up. She had made significant progress, and according to Kal, there were only sixty left.

After her cleansing run, she would rest up. If she had been bitten, then she would have hallucinations for ten to twenty minutes. The hallucinations were potent. It made the creatures seem like people she knew, and they talked. She did not know if it was the creatures talking through the hallucinations, her mind creating them, or a combination of both. Several times they had taken on the form of Dr. Snowden and Evaran, and even her father. Sometimes she even thought the Torvatta was real. The hallucinations did not save the creatures from her killing them. It had been hard for her to do it, but the nanobots kept her coherent to a degree. She could see how others would have fallen for their strategy.

Her afternoons were spent either in the research labs on the upper levels or exploring the rest of the base. She had found that the Coraanan had a vast history. Other aspects such as technology, politics, religion, and the sciences were available to her. It kept her mind busy and was part of the more relaxing part of her day. The rift door system intrigued her, and she studied it in great detail. Central Command used to have one, but the rift controller was destroyed.

After dinner, she would spend her time on the balcony. It was her favorite spot in the base. Central Command had been carved out of a mountain, and the balcony was near the top of it. Looking out, she could see for miles. It made her feel less alone. She still thought about being rescued, but it was more of a fleeting thought. This was her new home.

Her PSD had lost power her second month in. She had extended the morphable matter into a blade and left it out. The PSD had been her constant companion except for a few weeks when she was with Kazaal. Between the suit and PSD blade, she had no issues dealing with the creatures other than finding them. She had food, water, shelter, and access to vast amounts of information. Although the facilities had similar functionality, they always felt cramped to her.

She had plans after securing Central Command to head south. All the stepped pyramids that acted as landing pads were there. She knew she would have to be careful in whom she decided to save, but if people like Ezekial were coming through, she would be able to help them. They could live with her, and she would gain the benefit of having company. The thought of heading south seemed counterintuitive to her, since her goal since she had arrived on this hellhole had been to get to Central Command.

Being alone was not as bad as she had feared. By defining activities and goals, she was able to enjoy her alone time. She still missed being around people, and sometimes, it crushed her. There were times when she thought of Dr. Snowden and Evaran and it devastated her, but the routine was what kept her focused.

At the tail end of the six months, she began her daily routine. She had gotten creative with breakfast and was trying, in sequence, all the varieties of food the replicator could make. After a solid meal, she went to the balcony for her post-breakfast view. She pondered the upcoming cleansing run for the day. She had one section in the lower levels to clear, and that would be another full level secured. Kal had estimated there were ten creatures there. It would be a workout, but nothing she could not handle.

When she got to the section after her break, she had Kal follow her and made him outline the creatures. They would usually try to strike at him, giving her the impression they were more visually oriented than smell or hearing. It was a good combination, and after she had taken down five, she felt the familiar bite of one of the creatures. They typically bit her on the lower leg on the side. She rushed around and killed the others, then leaned against the wall. She knew that the hallucinations were about to begin, and after sealing the door, she braced herself.

"Three living beings detected," said Kal.

Her eyes widened. She had been able to configure Kal to notify her of any living creature that came within twenty feet of her, similar to what she did when she had first arrived.

Kal extended a hand, which had a projection of the layout. It showed three red dots heading down the hallway to the door she had just locked.

She sighed. They would die, just as the others, but first, she needed to ride out the hallucinations. She parked herself in the corner and, with blade in hand, waited.

V interacted with the front console, and the planet shimmered into darkness, then eased back in. "Analysis. The time jump was unsuccessful."

"Elaborate," said Evaran.

"The quantum beacon is present and is still recording the approximate time from when we arrived."

"How's that possible?" asked Lord Vygon.

Evaran rubbed his temples with his left hand and sighed. "I . . . did not expect this. This means only the present exists in this pocket universe. We cannot go to the past or the future."

Dr. Snowden gulped. "How do we fix it?"

"There is nothing the Torvatta can do at this point time-wise," said Evaran. "However, we will proceed with finding where Emily is. V, contact her PSD."

"Acknowledged," said V. After a moment, he faced Evaran. "No contact."

"Hmm," said Evaran. "It is possible the PSD ran out of power. There would be no way for her to charge it."

"Or . . . maybe it was destroyed," said Dr. Snowden.

Nanobot Emily swatted Dr. Snowden's arm. "Uncle Albert! Think positive."

Dr. Snowden looked down, then glanced at Nanobot Emily. He grabbed her hand.

"Approaching the quantum beacon's location," said V.

Dr. Snowden watched the left screen as the Torvatta descended to the planet. It broke cloud cover and then approached a stepped pyramid in a jungle clearing. The right screen showed the quantum beacon just outside the pyramid.

A line appeared from the top of the stepped pyramid to its current location.

After another few minutes, the Torvatta had landed near the pyramid on top of a white strip separating the pyramid from the jungle. Everyone exited the Torvatta, with V in orb mode.

"V, scout mode," said Evaran.

"Acknowledged. Scout mode engaged," said V as he took off flying. After a moment, he shined a beam down near the white strip.

Evaran waved the others forward as he approached it.

Dr. Snowden's mouth was dry. The sky was bright blue, and the temperature was fairly warm. Insects would love it here, something he was sure would drive Organic Emily crazy. He noticed the quantum beacon was still in good shape, almost as if it had been pushed off the pyramid. The white strip made him swallow hard. Upon closer examination, he noted it was bones. He looked around. This place seemed unforgiving.

Evaran picked up the quantum beacon and scanned it with his ring. "The teeth marks would indicate that whatever took the quantum beacon did not find it appetizing."

Lord Vygon smirked. "Yeah, quantum beacons usually—"

Evaran raised a hand as he tilted his head. "V has detected a large number of creatures headed this way. However, there is a podium console nearby I want to look at. Everyone head to the Torvatta."

Lord Vygon looked around. "Ahh . . . I sense them now. Small creatures." He headed back to the Torvatta with Dr. Snowden and Nanobot Emily in tow.

After entering the command area, Dr. Snowden watched Evaran through the left screen, standing in front of a podium console. It seemed different than the ones he had seen with the Purifiers. This one appeared to have a physical touchscreen surface.

Evaran placed his UIC on it and, after a moment, pulled it off and headed back to the ship. When he had returned to the command area, he sat and swiped at his chair console. The front right screen showed an overland map, with a series of dots.

"What the heck is that . . . ," said Dr. Snowden.

Evaran pointed at the blinking yellow dot among hundreds of others in the southern area of the landmass on the map. "That would be our current position. There is a size discrepancy between the dots. I believe that indicates functional level."

"You gathered all that from that thing down there?"

Evaran shook his head. "No. However, the podium showed it was accessed several times nine months ago."

Dr. Snowden sighed. "Okay . . . then which dot do we go to first?"

Nanobot Emily pointed to the first green dot to the north. "She woulda went there."

Dr. Snowden eyed Nanobot Emily.

"It's what I would've done."

"Very well," said Evaran. "V, take us to the first green dot."

"Acknowledged."

The Torvatta lifted off and, after a short flight, landed at the area indicated by the green dot. Dr. Snowden noted that there was a miniature version of the stepped pyramids surrounded by four pillars. He scrutinized the right screen as the Torvatta scanned the pyramid. It showed a facility underground, with a tunnel leading north. He wondered if Organic Emily had gotten this far and maybe even gone through the tunnel. He swallowed hard as the Torvatta landed.

As they exited the Torvatta and walked through its shielding, a beam shot out from the pillar and scanned them. Dr. Snowden jumped as the mini pyramid slid back, revealing a ramp.

"I believe we have found the entrance. Come," said Evaran, motioning forward.

Dr. Snowden's heartbeat incrementally sped up as they descended down the ramp. Nanobot Emily had grabbed his right arm, just like Organic Emily always did. He ran his hand across the smooth metallic walls. This technology seemed very out of place in this environment.

When they reached the base of the ramp, a hologram of a thin beige humanoid with a dinner-plate-shaped head appeared in front of them. Wide black eyes rested on the underside of the head with a small mouth underneath them. It wore a blue jumpsuit with silver lines and black boots. The top of the head looked armored with bumps, and the skin on the rest of the body was smooth. A second beam shot down and encompassed them.

"Translation matrix has been initiated. Welcome to Coraanan research facility number thirty-four. I am the virtual interface, Kal."

Evaran scanned the hologram and looked up at the ceiling.

Dr. Snowden followed his gaze and noticed the black glass-like surface. It reminded him of the strips he had seen on an alien ship long ago when he first met Evaran. His eyes darted around the room, where he noticed two doors on each side.

Evaran stepped forward and pointed at Nanobot Emily. "Have you seen her before?"

Kal tilted his head as he looked at Nanobot Emily. "Not with that clothing."

"I see," said Evaran. "Is there a place to access the systems?"

Kal waved them to follow him into the second door on the left. He stood next to a set of workstations and pointed at one.

"Thank you."

Kal stared at Evaran.

Nanobot Emily smirked. "Yeah . . . that would drive me nuts."

Evaran nodded, then placed his UIC on the workstation console. He tossed out an orb, then swiped his hands around his ARI.

Dr. Snowden swallowed hard as images appeared in the projection from the orb. It showed Organic Emily walking around, studying, watching videos on her PSD, eating, and, in general, living there. He averted his eyes at some of the images showing her naked.

Nanobot Emily's face turned red.

Evaran turned off the projection. "It appears she came here in her second month on the planet. According to these logs, she left after staying for one month. Judging by her attire on her arrival, it appears she underwent something traumatic."

Dr. Snowden circled his hand. "Well . . . show us."

Evaran extended his hand and a projection shot up from his ring. It showed Organic Emily in a rough set of clothing with bone pads.

Dr. Snowden's heart sank when he saw the expression on her face. It looked like she had been through hell. The look in her eyes was not something he had ever seen before.

Nanobot Emily played with a strand of her hair. "She did something that she'd . . . normally never do. I think . . . that creature I saw . . . might be involved."

"Do you remember much about what the creature looked like?"

"No . . . ," said Nanobot Emily. "Just vague characteristics. It was large, strong, and disgusting. I do remember it had brown skin and horns."

Dr. Snowden ran his hand over his mouth as he glanced at Evaran. "Can you show the last picture of her when she was here?"

Evaran tapped at his ARI, and the projection showed Organic Emily in a new suit, with a sad face.

"Well . . . at least she looks a little better," said Dr. Snowden. "Where to next?"

"She entered the transportation hub and took the tunnel north, so my guess is to the next green dot."

"Why don't we just head to the blue dot?" asked Lord Vygon. "We could work our way back if needed, but it's apparent to me that she was headed north, despite whatever might have happened to her."

"That's what I would've done," said Nanobot Emily.

"Very well," said Evaran. "Let us leave."

As they left the facility, Dr. Snowden mused on what Organic Emily must have gone through. It pained him to think that she had probably felt abandoned when they did not show up after two months. What would she be like in nine months? He could feel anger bubbling inside him, but the mental imagery of the waves combined with his tingling sensations kept him levelheaded. The thought of losing control here made no sense to him and answered the question of how would it help the situation.

Once everyone was aboard the Torvatta, they flew north to the blue dot.

After they arrived, Dr. Snowden's eyes popped open as he saw the blue dot looked like an advanced city carved into the mountainside. The city was lit up like a beacon of hope in the darkness. There were two waterfalls to either side of it and a road leading up to an enclosed area before the massive gates at the base. From the angle at which the Torvatta approached, he could see the parapets. There were several platforms at the higher levels that extended out over the city.

After the Torvatta scanned the city, a layout with red dots appeared on the right screen.

"Analysis. Fifty-one life-forms detected."

Evaran rubbed his chin. "Do any match a humanoid?"

"One."

Dr. Snowden half smiled as Nanobot Emily lightly squeezed his right arm.

"Those doors look shut . . . ," said Nanobot Emily.

"Yeah . . . but maybe she took the transportation system in," said Lord Vygon.

Nanobot Emily paused as she tilted her head. "Could be . . . how are we going to get in then?"

Evaran pointed to one of the balconies with an open doorway. "We will go in through the top. V, align the ramp with that balcony and hold position."

"Acknowledged."

Evaran faced Nanobot Emily. "You . . . may want to wait here. I am uncertain of the reaction we might face if—"

"I know, I know," said Nanobot Emily with a half grin. "It would confuse me too. I'll wait here with the V man."

V tilted his head at Nanobot Emily for a moment, then nodded.

The Torvatta aligned with the balcony.

Dr. Snowden gulped as they crossed the semitransparent light-blue ramp that extended from the Torvatta to the balcony. He had never seen the ramp at a thirty-degree angle before. Looking down, he could see the city underneath him.

Once they had assembled on the balcony, Evaran perused his ARI. After a moment, he gestured forward. "This way."

Dr. Snowden soaked in the view as they walked through the various rooms, open areas, and hallways. It reminded him somewhat of Kreagus, the home world of the Kreagan Star Empire they had visited prior to this adventure. The technology was fairly advanced, which made him question why it would be here at all on a prison planet. Maybe this was some type of capital city.

As they entered a hallway deep in the city, Evaran raised his hand. "The humanoid life-form is behind that door. We should proceed with caution."

Lord Vygon narrowed his eyes. "It seems there is this humanoid, with the other life-forms in much lower levels. That doesn't seem coincidental."

"I concur," said Evaran as he walked up to the door. He placed his UIC on the console and, after it connected, tapped at his ARI, causing the door to open.

Dr. Snowden's breathing quickened. His heartbeat ramped up as he stood next to Lord Vygon.

Evaran shot his hand back toward the others. He tilted his head for a moment, then extended his utility handle into a baton. With a final look at the others, he stepped into the room.

Emily's heartbeat skyrocketed as her tingling sensations went into overdrive. The door had opened and a hallucination of Evaran had stepped through. She had seen this one several times. Even been on the Torvatta. These hallucinations were dangerous, and she had been fooled by them a few times.

Each time ended with her fighting her way out of a large group of the creatures.

Evaran snapped his head toward her. "Are you okay?"

Emily lunged forward, striking out with her PSD blade.

Evaran stepped back through the doors, causing her to go flying past him.

Emily looked out the door and saw a startled Dr. Snowden and Lord Vygon. Lord Vygon was a hallucination she had seen only once, early on when she had first arrived. Maybe her mind was playing tricks on her. She stopped her slide, angled herself, then launched through the door.

Evaran took the brunt of the kick in the chest and slid back a few feet. Dr. Snowden stepped back a bit behind Lord Vygon, who had extended blunted blades over his forearms that reached around to his hands.

"Emily . . . what are you doing?" asked Evaran.

Emily laughed. "I won't fall for this again!" She lashed out with her PSD blade.

Evaran stepped back and batted her hand down. "There is no need for this. Something is wrong." He scanned Emily with his ring. "It appears you have something in your system."

Emily scrunched her eyebrows. "You're fighting better. I'll give you that. Sadly for you, I just killed ten of your brothers and sisters."

Evaran looked past Emily into the room. "I see that, but they are not my brothers and sisters. We are real, and you are suffering from some type of delusion."

"Enough!" said Emily. She approached Evaran with blade out. When she got near, she stepped to the left of Evaran and reached in with her left arm to grab his chest.

Evaran reacted by knocking her arm down with his right arm, which Emily then used as an opportunity to step forward and attempt to strike him in the side. The blade tip pierced Evaran's side armor. He stepped to the side and pushed Emily back. He narrowed his eyes and raised a baton-like device with a glowing blue end.

This was the first time Emily had seen this in the hallucination. She paused for a moment.

Evaran reached out and tapped her on the chest with the baton.

Emily fell to the ground. A pang echoed throughout her. Before her eyes closed, she saw the others rushing in. The thought that this must be the end flooded her mind. She could feel the nanobots pushing her to get up. These must be some type of creature she had not encountered before for the venom to be this strong. Her journey would be over, and maybe it was for the best. Living like this for the rest of her life was unappealing to her. Her eyes closed and she passed out.

Thirty minutes later, Emily's eyes fluttered open. She swallowed hard and squinted as she took several deep breaths. The signs of the venom's presence always gave her a queasy feeling, and that was missing. She was still on her back, but the environment had changed. Looking up, she could tell this was the medical lab aboard the Torvatta. Her eyebrows wrinkled. If she was not hallucinating, how could she be here? She tilted her head to the left and saw Dr. Snowden.

"You're awake," said Dr. Snowden with a smile.

Emily's eyes popped open as she rolled off the right side of the slab. Her nanobots kicked in, and she did a quick scan of her surroundings. Was this a new type of venom? She gulped as she raised her hands in a fighting stance.

"Whoa, whoa, whoa," said Dr. Snowden with his hands out. "Emily, it's me. I don't know what you think is going on, but we found you."

Emily's eyes narrowed. "What do you know about Kazaal?"

"Who?" asked Dr. Snowden. He tilted his head. "Is that the . . . bad guy you met before the first research facility? Big, strong guy with brown skin and horns?"

"Hah! I knew it! Uncle Albert wouldn't know anything about that!" said Emily. She stepped farther back into the room. This confirmed to her that this was a new hallucination, one she could not detect as easily.

Evaran walked into the room.

"And you're back," said Emily. She grabbed a syringe from one of the trays on a nearby table. "You won't fool me!"

Evaran extended a hand. "This is no hallucination. The venom in your system has been purged. I suspect you can detect that."

Emily sighed. It was true that the queasy feeling was not present. She swallowed hard.

"Just listen to me . . . for a moment. Would you grant me that?"

Emily bored a hole through Evaran with her eyes.

Evaran sighed. "You were sent to the prison planet by the Purifiers. It took us a while to find where that was, but we did find it. When we arrived, there was a time dilation effect. One minute in our timeline was ninety on the prison planet. Three days for us was . . . nine months for you."

Emily tilted her head. "You're talking like I would expect you to."

"The universal translator works a bit differently for . . . someone like me."

"How did Uncle Albert know about Kazaal?"

Evaran eyed Emily for a moment. "Do you remember when you had some nanobots removed before coming to the prison planet?"

Emily wrinkled her eyebrows. No hallucination had ever mentioned that before. "Yeah . . ."

"The Purifiers tried to weaponize it. They failed. The new nanobots, infused with the rift technology, formed a swarm and killed everyone in the base."

Emily's breathing quickened. She remembered having dreams about that situation.

"After they were done, they formed a new body . . . in your likeness. This new Emily is your duplicate, and she has helped us."

"Where is this . . . new Emily?"

Evaran gestured toward the door.

Organic Emily's eyes popped open as Nanobot Emily entered the room.

"It's true," said Nanobot Emily as she gave a half wave. "I'm . . . you before you went to the prison planet, with a different body."

Organic Emily trembled. No hallucination lasted this long, or was this complex. There was definitely not a version of her in any of them either.

"I'm . . . almost completely made of nanobots," said Nanobot Emily as she stepped forward. "I can . . . share with you what I've seen since I was created. All we need to do is touch hands."

Organic Emily eyed Nanobot Emily. She inched forward with her right hand out and her left hand gripping the syringe in an attack posture. If Nanobot Emily was trying to deceive her, she would get stuck.

Their hands touched, and a rush of memories flooded Organic Emily's mind. She gasped as she stepped back and shook her head. It was real. They had come for her. Finally. She could see how much trouble they went through to find her, and they never stopped. Her arms fell to the side as the syringe dropped to the ground. Her head trembled as tears fell onto her cheeks.

Nanobot Emily's eyes misted as she stepped forward and hugged Organic Emily. "You're safe now."

They hugged for a good while, then Organic Emily turned toward Dr. Snowden. She rushed over to him and hugged him tightly. Her body shuddered, and her breathing staggered. Dr. Snowden never stopped believing she was alive, and that she would survive. He had treated Nanobot Emily just like he would her.

Dr. Snowden pulled back and wiped the tears off Organic Emily's face. "Now what do I do with two nieces?"

Organic Emily half smiled as she hugged Dr. Snowden again. She turned toward Evaran, who had extended his arm. Her eyes watered as she approached him and then gave him a bear hug. Evaran had been her sanity check for as long as the PSD had been active. It had gotten her through some of her roughest times.

"I am glad you are with us once again," said Evaran.

Organic Emily pulled back and swallowed hard. "You were a great teacher."

Evaran tilted his head. "Your combat skills were a surprise to me."

"Your training videos. On the PSD."

"Ahh . . . I see. I have made some more, with V this time."

Organic Emily sniffled. "I look forward to watching them."

Lord Vygon entered the room.

Organic Emily rushed over and hugged a startled Lord Vygon. "Thank you for helping. You are a true friend."

"It was an honor," said Lord Vygon. "You've recovered quickly."

Organic Emily stepped back and crooked a thumb at Nanobot Emily. "I synced memories with her . . . somehow."

Lord Vygon bowed his head.

Evaran nodded at Organic Emily. "Take some time to readjust. We are meeting in the conference room at nine tomorrow morning, but other than that, nothing is scheduled. Clean up, get rested, and welcome back."

"What's the meeting about?" asked Organic Emily.

"We are going to disable the main rift stone that connects all the rift doors. We are headed to the pocket universe it resides in now, and along with the Torvatta's scans, V will assist in any interior scanning should there be shielding. In your condition, it may be best for you to stay aboard the Torvatta and rest."

"I'll be ready to go," said Organic Emily with narrowed eyes. The nightmare was over. A burning fire lit up when she thought of the Purifiers who had done this to her. They would pay. All of them. She glanced at Nanobot Emily, who smiled back at her with knowing eyes.

20

Dr. Snowden enjoyed the rest of the afternoon talking with both Emilys in the main living quarters area. They broke for lunch and dinner, then spent the rest of the day on the roof. He noticed some unusual aspects of Organic Emily, but figured that may have been due to the situation she just came from. Whenever the Purifiers were mentioned, he thought he saw Organic Emily's eyes narrow slightly and her jaw clench. It was a calm rage, something he was learning to master himself. Seeing it on her was unusual.

The journey he had heard described made him cringe. This bone-eating monster had submitted Organic Emily to enslavement and seemed to kill for pleasure and food. Then there was the shadowy presence. Both monsters had been killed, and it was not lost on him that the shadow presence one was a direct kill, and the other an indirect one. She also killed two small humanoids when hallucinating. The hallucination disturbed him in that his image was used to essentially lure her into a false sense of security.

The cleansing at Central Command, as she had called it, was something he could have never seen her do before. He could sense that she was harder now, and less prone to showing emotion. The bubbly nature of Nanobot Emily stood in stark contrast to the more serious Organic Emily. It was like Nanobot Emily was a control group and Organic Emily was an experimental group with nine months on the prison planet as a variable. What bothered him the most was the casualness in which the killings were discussed. It sounded more like her new philosophy on how to handle threats, and something she would repeat if she had to.

The next morning at nine, Evaran and V in robot mode met them in the conference room. Nanobot Emily had taken Dr. Snowden's usual seat next to Organic Emily, so he sat next to her with Lord Vygon and V on the other side. Lord Vygon had his usual drink, and V and Nanobot Emily did not take any breakfast.

Dr. Snowden went light on food since his stomach was twisted around. He tilted his head at Organic Emily's choice of two burgers, a large plate of fries, and a large soda. She usually had something lighter, and if it was a burger, it was half the portion he was seeing and never in the morning. Maybe she was just hungry, but a part of him thought of her as a hungry predator. He could not shake the feeling that there was something horribly wrong with her.

Evaran half smiled at both Emilys. "It is good to see you both here. It makes the place a bit brighter."

Nanobot Emily smiled back while Organic Emily nodded with lips drawn flat.

Evaran tapped at the table console, causing a projection to shoot up of a large pyramid surrounded by an expansive city.

Dr. Snowden noted that the pyramid looked similar to the one he had seen on Earth, but about roughly ten times larger.

There were some landing pads that jutted out at various heights, which suggested they had flying craft. A pulsating red dot appeared in the middle of the pyramid. The projection had wireframe lines inside the pyramid, indicating the various rooms and hallways. A blue line led upward from the ground to about the middle of the pyramid. At the end of that line was a pulsing dot, which Evaran was pointing at.

"That is the main rift stone," said Evaran. "It is not as guarded as I imagined it would be."

Lord Vygon rested his chin on his right hand. "Well . . . this *is* a pocket universe that is only accessible by rift doors, or in our case, the Torvatta. What do they have to defend against here?"

"A good point," said Evaran. "However, with the main rift stone able to open rift doors to other locations, I would think if they came across a hostile location, more security would be needed."

"Maybe. Then again, they could just shield the rift door. This pyramid isn't shielded, so I don't think they have planned too much on it being attacked."

Evaran eyed Lord Vygon. "This is true." He pointed at the blue line that started off at the base of the pyramid and snaked its way up the pulsing dot. "V has defined this as the shortest route to get there." He pointed at a landing pad. "We are stealthed currently and will land there. Once down, we will follow the blue line and disable the main rift stone."

Dr. Snowden cocked his head. "And . . . how are we going to do that?"

"I will use my staff on it."

Dr. Snowden wrinkled his eyebrows. "You're planning to smash it?"

Evaran nodded. "Yes. It may have exotic energy coursing through it, but I can nullify that aspect."

"Like you did with Seeros's armor pads," said Dr. Snowden. He recalled Evaran tossing three orbs against Seeros's exotic-energy-enhanced black armor pads that glowed red. The orbs emitted a white cloud, which nullified the armor's exotic energy component, causing it to stop glowing.

"Correct," said Evaran. "Once the main rift stone is smashed, we will exit the way we came."

Nanobot Emily nodded. "Seems straightforward."

Evaran eased back into his chair and laced his fingers in front of him. "It does. However, we still need to deal with all the guards on the way there. Once we are in, the area will swarm, so we need to be quick. In and out."

"Well . . . I'm wearing the survival suit for this one," said Dr. Snowden.

"I figured as much. I would have suggested you and both Emilys stay behind for this, but I know you will not agree."

Dr. Snowden half smiled.

"So who's in our way?" asked Lord Vygon with a smirk.

"Analysis. Three types of guards were analyzed," said V.

Evaran nodded and swiped his hand across his ARI. The projection changed to a large man around seven feet tall in a golden suit of advanced heavy armor. He wielded a large energy shield with a solid border in his left hand and had a big forearm guard with a crystal embedded in it. Glowing swords hung off his waist and a staff weapon rested on his back. "This was the first type V scanned. I call it a heavy guard. They appear to be heavily armored with melee weapons and a ranged weapon on their forearms. There are not too many of these."

"Uhh . . . that guy is kinda big," said Dr. Snowden.

"Yes . . . I suspect that although they are human, there has been some genetic engineering," said Evaran.

"So much for human purity."

Evaran glanced at Dr. Snowden, then tapped at his ARI, and the projection changed to a normal-sized human male in a black mesh suit with gray pads outlined in silver. His head was covered in a tight-fitting cloth, and goggles with red lenses sat on his face. Small sidearms rested on his thighs and a sword on his back.

Dr. Snowden wrinkled his eyebrows. It reminded him of an advanced ninja.

Evaran gestured at the projection. "This is the second type that V scanned. Although less in number, they seem to reside in areas of higher security along with the heavy guards. I call them strikers. I suspect they can move faster and are more agile."

Dr. Snowden sneaked a look at Organic Emily. She had narrowed eyes and was clenching and unclenching her fist. It seemed that she was looking forward to the prospect of fighting these guards.

Evaran brought up the third projection. Like the second one, it showed a normal-sized human. He wore a leather-like suit with sporadic pieces of silver armor on it and carried a staff weapon with a crystal embedded in one end. A cloth wrapped around the lower part of his face, with a headband containing a crystal on the upper part. "This is the third type. These are the most numerous, and I refer to them as the regular guards. The staff weapon they carry can fire bursts of energy. I am unsure how that is possible, as the scan revealed very few moving parts, but the profile is similar to the ones we saw at the first base. I have not had much time to study this technology."

"So . . . how many we looking at?" asked Lord Vygon.

V tapped at the table console, and dots appeared near the blue line. A legend showing the type of guard and dot color appeared. The locked doors became visible as well. "Analysis.

Base contains a complement of four hundred. The path chosen has twenty-five guards with four doors."

Lord Vygon narrowed his eyes. "I don't like it. Something's off here. I know this is an inaccessible place, but that seems way too weak. Perhaps we can get some help from Atlantis."

Evaran shook his head. "They have already sacrificed a large portion of their groups and need to focus on Earth."

"I guess . . . sure could use more help is all I'm saying."

Evaran studied Lord Vygon for a moment. "Stealth will be to our advantage. That is better achieved with a small group. V, take us to the landing pad."

"Acknowledged."

Evaran faced Dr. Snowden and both Emilys. "Get your survival suits on. You will want your shield deployed and repulsing weapon out."

"I'd like to keep this suit on," said Organic Emily. "I could use an energy shield, though."

Evaran tilted his head. "Are you sure?"

Organic Emily nodded.

"Very well. Meet up at the Torvatta exit in thirty minutes."

Dr. Snowden exited the room with the others. It seemed like the assembled group would be able to handle any threat. Organic Emily's choice to not wear a survival suit intrigued him. While her suit seemed sturdier, it did not have the PSD interface bound to it. Maybe she was more proficient with the PSD than he was aware. It could also be that the PSD had more functionality that he did not know of. He shook his head and went to get his survival suit on.

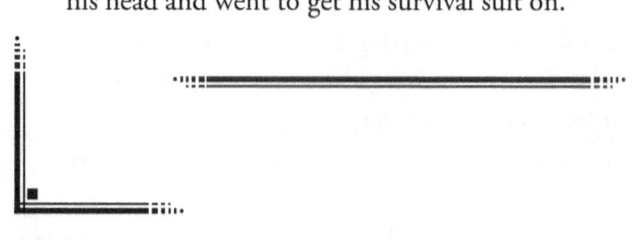

Thirty minutes later, everyone assembled at the Torvatta exit.

Dr. Snowden noted that Organic Emily had a forearm device similar to the survival suit. He did not know if it had been removed from a survival suit or if it was a separate device. Nanobot Emily had on the same suit as he, and Lord Vygon and Evaran had on their regular suits.

"V has landed the Torvatta in stealth mode on the pad," said Evaran. He gestured out. "There is a hallway leading directly out of here with two guards on each side. An enclosed room is off to the right with a worker. V is hovering there now. Lord Vygon is going to rush and take out the worker, and V will place my UIC on the console. The alarm system will be disabled. I am going to rush the guards. Once it is secured, everyone will advance to my position at the door. Understood?"

Everyone nodded.

"Good," said Evaran. He nodded at Lord Vygon and pointed forward. "Go."

Lord Vygon rushed out of the Torvatta.

Evaran waved for the others to follow him to the edge of the Torvatta's shielding. After a moment, he rushed with shield raised toward the startled regular guards. His utility handle had extended into a baton with a glowing white end. He raised it and fired a repulsion blast, knocking both guards down. When Evaran reached them, he interacted with his utility handle, causing the baton end to glow blue. He tapped both guards with his baton, causing them to shudder, then stop moving. He waved for Dr. Snowden and both Emilys to come over.

When Dr. Snowden arrived, he looked to his right and saw Lord Vygon give a nod from the doorway of the enclosed room.

Evaran tapped at his ARI, and the door in front of them slid up. "The alarm system has been disabled." He gestured forward. "This hallway leads to a very large circular room. We will take the corridor on the right side of it once we are there."

Dr. Snowden snorted. This was almost too easy. Then again, what base expected someone like Evaran and his abilities, an ancient vampire, and three people that could stun and repulse from afar?

As they neared the large room, Evaran raised a hand. His eyebrows furrowed. "This was unexpected."

"I don't sense anything," said Lord Vygon, looking around.

Evaran ran his hand over his mouth. "A Hadryn spawn is coming, and I suspect he is not alone." He gestured toward a console inside the room near the right hallway exit. "V, put my UIC on that console."

"Acknowledged," said V as he flew into the room.

Dr. Snowden raised a finger. "And what is a Hadryn spawn exactly?"

"Something not of this plane. They are ancient and powerful. I was not expecting one to be here."

"Oh . . . well . . . that's just great."

"I will draw the Hadryn spawn over to the other side of the base. It will come for me," said Evaran. He swept his finger out. "Everyone else will head to the main rift stone."

"I'm not leaving you to fight this thing alone!" said Lord Vygon with an intent gaze.

Evaran looked down for a moment. He sighed as he looked back up. "I do not make this decision lightly. If this Hadryn spawn were to interfere, I do not think we would prevail. At best, I can stall him until we can disable the main rift stone."

Organic Emily waved a finger between Dr. Snowden and Nanobot Emily. "We will be okay if Lord Vygon wants to go with you. V can guide us to the main rift stone, and we can deal with any guards. Three people who can stun and repulse them should be more than enough. Most will be focused on trying to get to this room anyways."

"I cannot allow—"

"Trust me. Take Lord Vygon with you."

Evaran eyed Organic Emily. "Very well. You can use the PSD to morph hammers to break the stone." He handed three orbs to her, which she put in a pouch on her belt. "These will nullify the exotic energy coursing through them." He tapped at his ARI. "I have opened all the doors there. Once you leave this room, I am going to seal off the hallway behind us and the one you are taking."

Organic Emily nodded. "We can do this."

Dr. Snowden's stomach twisted. It went from easy to hard in a matter of minutes. This Hadryn spawn must be dangerous enough for Evaran to make the decision to accept help in fighting it. Dr. Snowden knew Evaran did not want the Hadryn spawn to involve either Emily or himself.

Evaran pointed off to the right hallway inside the room. "Stay along the walls. Go."

Dr. Snowden followed Nanobot Emily, who followed Organic Emily. V flew ahead of them and waited for them at the exit. When they reached it and stepped inside the corridor, a door began to slide down. Before it shut down, he saw the other door in the room begin to close and Evaran and Lord Vygon head to the opposite doorway from where they all had initially entered the room.

Nanobot Emily tugged on his arm. "C'mon!"

Dr. Snowden nodded and turned. He waved his wrist around and studied the HUD where he could see not only where they were headed, but any life-sign scans V was showing.

At the first T-junction, they turned left. A patrol of eight regular guards had rushed into the hallway they just entered but were immediately bowled over by Organic Emily's repulsion blast. Nanobot Emily and Dr. Snowden fired their stun beams on the fallen guards. When they reached a large room, several entrenched positions with a small cannon faced their direction. A complement of heavy guards along with several strikers guarded each cannon. Regular guards were scattered around the room.

Dr. Snowden shook his head. "This is a trap."

Organic Emily smiled. "I know." She faced V. "Generate a distraction at the back of the room. We're going to take one of those cannons and turn it on the others."

"Acknowledged."

Dr. Snowden jerked his head back. "Uhh . . . are you serious?"

"Of course."

Dr. Snowden sighed. "Great."

Nanobot Emily squeezed his right arm. "We can do this."

Organic Emily pointed forward. "V, go!"

"Acknowledged," said V. He flew to the back of the room and projected a mass of Helians entering the room and firing.

The startled guards began to rotate the cannons toward the back. The regular guards rushed toward the distraction.

"Now!" said Organic Emily. She rushed along the left wall, with Dr. Snowden and Nanobot Emily behind her. When she reached the first cannon, she stunned the striker and two heavy guards. As they fell to the ground, she got behind the cannon and began to fire on the other cannons.

The confused guards began cross-firing on themselves.

Dr. Snowden crouched behind the left cannon mount's raised sides. He used it to peek out and shoot a mix of stun and repulsion blasts.

Nanobot Emily did the same, except on the right side.

Dr. Snowden's blood chilled when he saw one of the strikers fade away. "The strikers have stealth!"

Organic Emily smirked. "To the visual senses maybe."

Dr. Snowden raised his eyebrows as his palms sweat. Organic Emily was enjoying this. He watched as the remaining guards fell one by one. He relaxed a bit as the last one crumpled. Organic Emily had jumped off the cannon and ran to the middle of the room. She struck what he thought was just air, but the hit connected with a stealthed striker.

As the striker fell, Organic Emily extended her PSD into a staff and raised it to bash the striker's head in.

Dr. Snowden ran out. "What are you doing!"

"Ending the threat."

"You . . . want to kill him?"

Organic Emily stared at Dr. Snowden for a moment, then sighed and retracted her staff. She shot the striker with a stun beam. "Look around. What do you think the cannon I was firing did to those guards?"

Dr. Snowden's blood ran cold. "What did that prison planet do to you?"

Organic Emily snorted and glanced at Nanobot Emily, then back at Dr. Snowden. "You weren't there. I'm the same Emily you've always known. I just refuse to be prey anymore." Her voice rose. "Not to these animals, or anyone else! *Never again!*" Her eyes smoldered.

Dr. Snowden saw Nanobot Emily look down. He sighed. "Let's just get this over with."

Organic Emily exhaled from her nose. She looked away. "Fine. Let's go."

They exited the room.

Dr. Snowden's mind went over the discussion they just had. He understood that there would be some impact, just not this severe. While he only knew the highlights, he figured the close brushes with death caused Organic Emily to reevaluate her thinking. He wondered if he would do the same; then again, his anger had ballooned out of control in just two outings with Evaran. With a sigh, he focused on the rest of the journey. He appreciated the narrow confines of the hallway when they ran into other groups of guards. Between V's distraction and their repulsion and stun blast combinations, they were unstoppable, and more importantly, no more had to die. His eyes had popped open when a guard hit Nanobot Emily. Her wound shimmered for a moment, then disappeared.

They reached the main rift crystal room after ten more minutes of traversing. Once there, they disabled the few guards present and removed them from the room. V placed the UIC on the console door, and after he contacted Evaran, the doors sealed. In the center of the room was a cylindrical light-blue shield. Inside it was a large, smooth stone in an oblong shape floating in midair. Around the shield at both the top and bottom of the room were circular golden stepped bases. To their right along the wall was a raised platform with two advanced workstations. A large rift controller sat between them.

Dr. Snowden walked over to the first workstation. "So . . . I guess we need to disable that shield somehow."

Organic Emily tossed one of the orbs Evaran had given her at the shield.

The shield fluctuated for a moment, then changed to a light-yellow color.

"What was that about?" asked Dr. Snowden.

"The shield had an exotic energy component. Couldn't you sense it?" asked Organic Emily.

Dr. Snowden shook his head. He had been so distracted by the previous discussion that he found it hard to focus.

"Well . . . now we just need to disable this shield. V?"

V flew over and placed Evaran's UIC on the workstation. "I will inform Evaran the shield needs to be removed."

After a moment, the shield dissipated.

Organic Emily tossed another orb at the floating stone, causing it to vibrate. She tossed the last one.

The stone's vibrations shook the room.

After it stopped, Organic Emily morphed her PSD end into a hammer. "Now we need to smash it. C'mon."

Dr. Snowden and Nanobot Emily complied. When they all tried to smash the stone, it had no effect.

"We might have a problem . . . ," said Dr. Snowden.

Nanobot Emily placed her hands on the main rift stone. "We won't be able to smash this. It's pretty resilient. There's . . . something odd mixed in with it."

"So . . . what do we do then?"

"I guess we wait for Evaran," said Nanobot Emily. "Until then, I'm going to see if I can interface with it somehow."

Dr. Snowden nodded and then slumped against the wall. The main rift stone was unbreakable, and Organic Emily had changed. His fear that the prison planet had altered who Organic Emily was seemed to be coming true. He wondered what Evaran would think of this. With a sigh, he hung his head in his hands.

After several minutes, V flew over to Dr. Snowden and then projected a hologram. "This is the composite view from the visual feeds of the landing pad on the other side of the base. The Hadryn spawn has arrived."

Dr. Snowden studied the projection. The landing pad it showed was similar to the one that they had landed on earlier. A ship he had never seen before sat in it. The landing pad door was closed, and in the middle of the room was Evaran and Lord Vygon. They faced a seven-foot-tall muscular male humanoid wearing only sandals, a kilt-like metallic covering hanging off his waist, and an elaborate golden headband with a large crystal in the center. The cobra mane structure on his head reminded Dr. Snowden of an Egyptian striped head cloth. The man held a black staff that ended in an oval shape with a crystal held in place by silver strands. It was the overlord he had seen from the South American base hologram.

Surrounding the overlord were four heavily armored guards in black and gold that were different than any of the guards he had seen. The main difference was their size. Standing around nine to ten feet tall, they towered over the overlord and wore black face masks with holes for their eyes and noses. The mouth area had a grill appearance, and the red Purifier symbol stood out around the eyeholes. Another difference from the heavy guards was their weapon load out. They had the same forearm weapons, just much larger. On their shoulders sat two rectangular crystals with a steel-like mount.

Dr. Snowden gulped at the swords they carried on their backs. They were at least as big as he was. He figured these four must be the overlord's personal guards. Around the bodyguards were five heavy guards, two strikers, and ten regular guards. He shook his head. Although Evaran had sealed off the landing pad to just that ship, it carried a formidable force. He exhaled through his nose as Nanobot Emily and Organic Emily crowded around to watch Evaran speak.

21

"**Y**ou must be the overlord," said Evaran.

The overlord smirked and in a deep, purposeful voice said, "And you, the foolish Evaran . . ." He gestured at the closed landing door. "I see you have gained control of my systems here. Quite unexpected." He glanced at Lord Vygon. "However, I do appreciate you bringing me a snack."

Lord Vygon narrowed his eyes and scowled.

Evaran raised a finger. "Hadryn spawn should not be able to come here."

"Things have changed, plane traveler."

Evaran wrinkled his eyebrows. "Even so, the plane would not have allowed your passage."

"And yet, here I am," said the overlord. He tilted his head. "I don't suppose you've come to accept my offer . . ."

Evaran shook his head. "No. I cannot allow you to exist here. Your use of the rift doors to enact genocide on nonhumans is unacceptable. You must be removed."

The overlord laughed. "So righteous! You never change, no matter what form you're in." He waved a finger at Evaran. "You know, the last Evaran I met failed miserably. Oh . . . she put up a good fight, but in the end, she learned what you will today." He gestured outward. "You may be godlike in the plane system void, but here," he said, pointing downward and with a raised voice, "in this plane, you are my *equal*."

"I do not know of this other Evaran that you speak of."

The overlord smirked. "You don't . . . need to worry about her anymore. Thanks to her, I could sense you the moment you stepped out of your ship." He raised his right arm at a ninety-degree angle. "No matter. Your time has come, and I will consume you and your abilities, whether you're dead or alive." He waved his hand forward. "Kill them."

The four bodyguards rushed forward and began to fire heavy bursts of energy fire. The other guards moved to the left and right behind the overlord and began to fire. The overlord angled his staff at Evaran and fired a purple beam.

Evaran stepped back and raised his forearm shield. The impact of the incoming fire sent him sliding backward. He snapped his head at Lord Vygon. "Guards, go!"

Lord Vygon streaked out to the right side. With his blunted blades, he struck both strikers before they could stealth and five of the regular guards, sending them flying. Two of the heavy guards peeled off from firing at Evaran to focus on Lord Vygon. Lord Vygon rushed the first heavy guard, and after a flurry of blows, the guard crumpled to the ground.

The overlord turned toward Lord Vygon. He stepped forward and knocked Lord Vygon back.

Lord Vygon flew into the second heavy guard. He crumpled against the wall along with the unconscious second heavy guard.

The overlord looked at the remaining three heavy guards and five regular guards, then pointed at Lord Vygon. "Finish him."

Evaran pulled out his utility handle and extended it into a baton with a glowing white end. He swept it in front of him and to the left. *Boom!* The five remaining regular guards went flying back and slammed against the wall. Several of them hit the heavy guards that were advancing on Lord Vygon. Evaran's repulsion blast only knocked the overlord's staff away. Other than that, it had no impact on the overlord and his bodyguards, as they had leaned forward and braced themselves.

Lord Vygon crawled under the unconscious heavy guard nearest him as the other heavy guards stood up and opened fire. The body took the brunt of the incoming fire. Lord Vygon tilted the now-dead heavy guard's head. After sinking his fangs into the heavy guard's neck, he began to drink. After a moment, he reared his head back and let out a loud growl. With red eyes and fangs extended, he tossed the body he had fed on at the other heavy guards, bowling them over. He streaked over to the regular guards who were just beginning to stand up and knocked them out with his blunted blades. He then proceeded to do the same to the three prone heavy guards.

Evaran tapped at his utility handle, causing the baton to extend into a staff, with glowing blue ends. He stepped into the first personal bodyguard and swept his legs. With a tap on the chest as he fell forward, the bodyguard stopped moving. Blue arcs danced around the unconscious bodyguard. Evaran rolled to the side as the second bodyguard did an overhead swing with his massive sword. As the sword embedded itself into the floor, Evaran hit the midsection of the second bodyguard. The bodyguard fell to the ground as blue arcs washed over him.

"Hold him!" said the overlord.

The third bodyguard tackled Evaran on the ground, sending his staff skipping along the floor. With the third bodyguard's arms wrapped around Evaran, the fourth body-guard rushed in and held Evaran's legs.

Lord Vygon rushed toward the overlord. When he came within striking distance, his speed slowed down.

The overlord watched as Lord Vygon approached, then sidestepped and grabbed a startled Lord Vygon. With a toss, he sent him bouncing off Evaran and then into the wall.

Lord Vygon struggled to get up.

Evaran broke one arm out and tried to reach for his staff.

The overlord rushed over and placed his knee on Evaran's free arm. With a hand on each side of Evaran's head, the overlord moved his face close. The crystal in his headband began to glow a light yellow. "Time to feed." Glowing tendrils reached out from the crystal toward Evaran. When the first one reached Evaran's face, Evaran cried out in pain.

Lord Vygon stood up and shook his head. His eyes popped open and head snapped toward Evaran upon hearing him cry out. He charged the overlord. When he got near, he anticipated the slowdown and grabbed the overlord under the armpits, then threw him into the air. He slammed his blades into the head of the bodyguard wrapped around Evaran's legs. The bodyguard released his grip and stopped moving. He jabbed his hand into the neck of the one holding Evaran's arms.

The bodyguard grunted as blood spurted out, then went limp.

Lord Vygon pulled Evaran out.

Evaran coughed as he squinted.

Lord Vygon extended a hand and helped Evaran stand.

Evaran picked up his staff, and with Lord Vygon, they faced the overlord.

The overlord sneered as he looked at his hands. "Ahh . . . your power . . . it's . . . it's . . . so much . . ." His eyes widened. "I want more!" He charged forward.

Lord Vygon glanced at Evaran, then down at the overlord's legs, then back at Evaran.

Evaran nodded.

Lord Vygon streaked forward.

The overlord aimed a strike at Lord Vygon as he approached.

When Lord Vygon was within striking distance, he slid into the overlord's legs, launching the overlord forward.

Evaran ran and jumped into the air. When he flew near the overlord, he knocked the overlord down with a strike from his staff.

Lord Vygon streaked to the overlord. He grabbed his legs, then raised them, leaving him on his back.

Evaran landed and rushed to the overlord. He placed his foot and staff end on the overlord's chest.

The overlord placed both hands on the staff, but could not remove it. "You're not a murderer!"

Evaran raised his head a bit. "You are a Hadryn spawn, and I banish you from this plane." He pressed down on his staff, which went through the overlord's chest.

The overlord cried out as a glow erupted on his face. After a moment, his body went limp and the glow dissipated.

Lord Vygon walked up next to Evaran and put a hand on his shoulder. "Glad I came now?"

Evaran winced as he turned his head toward Lord Vygon. "You are quite formidable."

Lord Vygon smirked. "Don't I know it."

Evaran half smiled, then turned toward the hallway leading out of the room. "To the main rift room."

Dr. Snowden watched as the projection faded. Hearing Evaran cry out had sent shivers down his spine. It was a first for Dr. Snowden. He could not fathom what the glowing tendrils did to make Evaran do that. The overlord was dead, as were multiple guards.

He glanced at Organic Emily. A chill went through him as he realized that she had made the same decision as Evaran in regards to ending a threat. He rationalized that the overlord was different due to the power discrepancy, a menace that had to be ended. The striker Organic Emily had hit was not a danger that needed to end in a death. He did not want to argue with Organic Emily about it. Maybe that was more of him not wanting to see her as someone who could kill. He sighed as he stood. His eyes popped open when he felt Organic Emily give him a bear hug.

"Let's not fight," said Organic Emily.

Dr. Snowden swallowed hard as he returned the hug.

After thirty-five minutes, Evaran and Lord Vygon entered the room.

Dr. Snowden calculated that they had made good time, even with any guards that might have woken up.

Nanobot Emily rushed over and bear-hugged Evaran, then Lord Vygon. "You two were amazing!"

Lord Vygon bobbed his head. "Can't let Evaran have all the fun."

Evaran eyed Lord Vygon.

Dr. Snowden nodded at Evaran and Lord Vygon. "That was quite a fight." He looked at Lord Vygon. "I noticed you . . . had a drink."

"Yeah . . . and I know Evaran doesn't like it, but in that fight, I needed the boost."

"I wasn't judg—"

Lord Vygon smiled and slapped Dr. Snowden on the back. "I know."

Evaran looked at Organic Emily. "You did well getting here."

"You didn't do so bad yourself," said Organic Emily.

Evaran bowed and then walked up to the main rift stone. He scanned it with his ring and tilted his head. His eyes narrowed after he placed a hand on it.

Dr. Snowden cocked his head. "Evaran?"

Evaran swallowed hard as he staggered back. He looked down while flexing his hand. After a moment, he faced the group. "The . . . other Evaran . . . that the overlord mentioned. Her being was . . . absorbed by the stone. I can feel her. The absorption was not pleasant."

Dr. Snowden glanced at Lord Vygon. "A future Evaran?"

Lord Vygon looked down. "I can't say either way."

Evaran shook his head. "No. This one is not the same as me, past or future. She was unique, like me. I do not know how that is possible. It would explain why we cannot smash it. The orbs would not nullify that energy. Due to the intermingled nature of the stone now, we would need something made of the stone to affect it."

"So . . . uhh . . . what do we do then?" asked Dr. Snowden.

Evaran snapped his head toward the entrance.

In the room preceding the hallway of the room they were in, a large, dark-skinned male appeared. Behind him were three of the overlord's bodyguards and a small army of heavy guards, strikers, and regular guards. Dr. Snowden noted that the man wore the same clothing as the overlord but had a beard and was physically bigger. The man's smile made Dr. Snowden rub the goose bumps on his arm.

"The overlord," said Evaran. His hands were a blur as they flew over his ARI. A semitransparent light-blue shield flew up on the other end of the hallway that the overlord was approaching.

The overlord paused in front of the shield. He shook his head. "I understand how you have control of my systems now." He cocked his head. "Surprised to see me?"

"Actually . . . yes," said Evaran. "You were dead."

The overlord laughed. "I was. However . . . ," he said, gazing at his hand as he flipped it back and forth in front of him, "not before getting a piece of your essence. Like my new form?"

"Not particularly," said Evaran. "I see you brought your friends."

"Ahh . . . yes," said the overlord, gesturing around him. "Another ability I obtained a while back. Resurrection of others, as long as it is within one hour. Never thought I would use it, but it came in quite handy here. Just like the ability to re-form I have now thanks to you. You're quite tough. Nonetheless, I have a new proposal."

"Go on," said Evaran.

"I'm willing to let you and your little friends go . . . if you give me more of your essence. I would ask for it all but . . . ," said the overlord as he waved dismissively, "you would never accept that. A personal sacrifice, though, to save your friends . . ." He put his hands together in front of him. "If you're thinking of fighting your way out, think again. Your ship's landing pad is now heavily guarded. Not to mention, everyone you fought is now back up and between you and your ship."

Evaran looked down. After a moment, he responded. "I need some time to think about it."

"Go on . . . go on . . . It's not like you're going anywhere anytime soon."

Evaran motioned at V, who flew over the entrance on their side.

V shot a wide solid beam over the door.

"V has put up a visual and audio barrier. We can talk freely."

"You're not seriously taking this into consideration, are you?" asked Dr. Snowden.

"I do not want to. However, since we cannot disable the stone, the only other option is this, or to fight our way out," said Evaran. He clenched and unclenched his jaw. "I do not think we would all make it."

Organic Emily stepped forward. "Well . . . I think we fight our way out. There's no guarantee that he'll keep his word. What if he decides to take all of you? Then what?"

Dr. Snowden glanced at Organic Emily. "I agree. I wouldn't trust anything he says."

Organic Emily half smiled at Dr. Snowden.

Evaran faced Lord Vygon.

"I think we stand a chance if we fight. However, he just had a taste of your essence. He will be stronger now, but like an addict, he will want more. You think he would stop at half? And what happens to us while he is doing it?"

"A fair point," said Evaran. He turned toward Nanobot Emily, who had her hands on the main rift stone. "Your thoughts?"

Nanobot Emily crumpled to the ground.

Everyone rushed over to her.

Nanobot Emily raised a hand as she stood. "Sorry . . . I'm okay now."

Evaran scanned Nanobot Emily with his ring. "You have lost roughly sixty percent of your mass."

"I know . . . and I am giving you another option," said Nanobot Emily. She grimaced and grunted. "After five minutes, release the shield on their end and have V drop the barrier. I'm destabilizing into my base nanobot swarm form. I'll clear a path to the Torvatta, and you'll all leave. Once you're clear, the crystal will break down at that time."

"Why are you doing this?" asked Evaran.

Nanobot Emily smiled. "Three things. One, the crystal needs to be destroyed, and I have begun that process. We needed something made of the crystal." She tapped her head. "I have it here. When the crystal goes, you need to be out of this pocket universe. A rift will form from its destruction, at least that's what I understand from my interaction with it."

Dr. Snowden let out a measured breath. "Oh, no . . ."

"Two," said Nanobot Emily, facing Evaran, "you're too important. I can't allow you to sacrifice yourself like this."

"That is my choice," said Evaran.

"And this is my choice," said Nanobot Emily. She faced Organic Emily. "Three, I now understand my purpose. The nanobots made a copy of you. Me. I was the backup. There should only be one Emily, and now that you're back, you have my memories. We are synced. All that is left is my deletion."

Organic Emily looked at the ground as a tear ran down her cheek.

Nanobot Emily swept away Organic Emily's tear and raised her head. "You always wanted a sister." She swallowed hard and squinted her eyes as she placed a hand on her chest. "And for a short while, you had one."

Organic Emily let her tears flow as she hugged Nanobot Emily.

Evaran shook his head. "I do not agree with this."

Nanobot Emily smiled through a pained face. "I've made my decision, and you know my reasons. Please respect it."

Evaran looked away.

Nanobot Emily walked up to Lord Vygon and hugged him. After stepping back, she said, "You've proven yourself to be a true friend. You came and helped when you didn't have to. Just like Evaran would've. I wish I would've had more time to get to know you better. I'm honored to have known you."

Lord Vygon bowed. "The honor was mine."

Nanobot Emily walked over to Evaran and gave him a bear hug. She laid her face on his chest. With a quivering voice, she said, "Thank you for accepting me." Her body trembled. "You're truly unique." After a moment, she stepped back and smiled at him while wiping away tears.

Evaran's face showed a slight hint of a frown.

"You may not show emotion well, but I know how you feel inside."

Evaran looked up and away and then exhaled from his mouth.

Nanobot Emily walked up to Dr. Snowden, who shook with tears flowing down his cheeks. "Uncle Albert . . ."

Dr. Snowden stepped forward and hugged her tightly as his breathing shuddered. With a cracked voice, he said, "I don't want you to go."

"I know," said Nanobot Emily in a hushed tone. She stepped back and pointed at Organic Emily. "I'll always be here."

Dr. Snowden hugged her again and then let her go.

Nanobot Emily walked up to Organic Emily. "You'll have to keep them in line."

Organic Emily chuckled and hugged Nanobot Emily. "I'll try. I'ma miss you."

"Kinda weird to miss ourselves, isn't it?"

Organic Emily chuckled again as tears fell, and in a weak voice, she said, "Yep."

Dr. Snowden's throat constricted as he watched them hug. He had gotten used to both Emilys, and he did not want to lose either of them.

Nanobot Emily pulled away from Organic Emily, then faced V. "V, thank you for being my friend. Although my existence was brief, I feel like I've known you for much longer. Keep everyone safe."

"Acknowledged," said V as his lights dimmed.

"I better get going," said Nanobot Emily. She extended a hand to Dr. Snowden and Organic Emily. "Before I go, I want to give my nanobots a boost." She glanced at Dr. Snowden. "Let your rage go unfiltered. No waves." She glanced at Organic Emily. "Let your vengeance flow."

Dr. Snowden grabbed Nanobot Emily's hand and began to think about the situation. The Purifiers had hurt Emily and condemned her to die. His face turned red. Nanobot Emily was being taken from him due to the Purifiers' genocidal tendencies. He gritted his teeth. Evaran had a piece of him taken by the overlord. His breathing staggered. He thought of how difficult it was trying to be normal when everything around him was not. His tingling sensations had begun to intensify, but he did not picture waves.

Nanobot Emily gasped. "Your rage . . . I never knew . . ."

Organic Emily grabbed Nanobot Emily's hand. She raised her head after a moment, then clenched her jaw and narrowed her eyes.

"You're so strong . . . well, I guess by extension, I am too," said Nanobot Emily. Her eyes glowed as she nodded at Evaran and V. "Let's do this."

Evaran exhaled from his nose as he interacted with his ARI. The shielding on the opposite end of the hallway dissipated at the same time V dropped the barrier.

Nanobot Emily rushed forward into the hallway.

The overlord smiled big as he entered the hallway when the shield dropped. "What's this? A little entertainment." His smile wound down as Nanobot Emily's head began to disassemble into a swirling cloud. His eyes widened as he stepped back out and pointed at the rapid disintegration occurring before him. "Guards! Kill that thing!"

The guards opened fire. Nanobot Emily disappeared, and in her place was a loud buzzing cloud of nanobots. The ground under the nanobots rippled forward to the guards. When the first guard was impaled by a spike from the ground, the other guards tried to run. The bodyguards screamed as the cloud ripped through them, impaling them and ripping chunks of their flesh off.

Dr. Snowden felt Organic Emily's death grip on his right arm.

Evaran waved forward. "We need to go!" He rushed ahead with everyone in tow.

Dr. Snowden surveyed the impaled corpses as he passed them. The overlord had not been spiked. Instead, two giant hands that looked like they had burst from the floor held the lower and upper halves of the separated overlord's corpse. He wondered if it was his rage that made these nanobots more violent.

After thirty minutes, they reached the landing pad door.

Evaran tapped at his ARI, and the door slid up.

Dr. Snowden noticed the dead guards ringing the Torvatta. The guards had brought in cannons and pointed them at the door, but there was no one alive to man them. He hated the sight of death. The fact that Nanobot Emily decided to change back into the murderous swarm made him nauseous. She gave her life to save theirs, at the expense of the Purifiers. The main rift stone had to be destroyed, and she was the only one who could do it. He understood her reasoning, and in the grand scheme of things, if she had not done what she did, Earth could be attacked again. Maybe she weighed that fact into her logic. He sighed as he continued on.

They rushed into the Torvatta and assembled in the command area.

"V, take us out," said Evaran.

"Acknowledged."

The Torvatta's middle spun around, and then the Torvatta flew off of the landing pad. After a moment, it ascended, broke cloud cover, and proceeded into space.

Dr. Snowden watched the left screen as it showed a view of the planet. An explosion appeared to move impossibly fast across the surface, and after a moment, the planet began to be sucked into where the main rift stone had been.

Evaran tapped at his chair console.

The Torvatta shot out a green beam and formed a portal, but the Torvatta was pulled away from it.

"V, disengage portal, rotate one hundred eighty degrees, fire reverse thrusters, then reestablish the portal."

"Acknowledged," said V. His hands flew like a hurricane over the front console.

Dr. Snowden watched as the portal disappeared. When the Torvatta spun around, he could see that they were accelerating toward the planet. Once V fired the reverse thrusters, the Torvatta moved forward at a crawl. It fired a green beam, and when the gold bordered portal with a purple surface appeared, the Torvatta inched toward it.

"Cut the thrusters!" said Evaran.

"Acknowledged."

The Torvatta burst forward and through the portal.

22

Dr. Snowden looked around at the assembled nonhumans in the Helian grand chamber. It had been four days since they arrived back on Earth, and this was the inaugural meeting of the new United Nonhuman General Assembly, or UNGA, as Lord Vygon had called it. Every pantheon and nonhuman group with any political clout had a representative here. Dr. Snowden glanced at the empty seat to his left.

Evaran, seated to Dr. Snowden's right, put a hand on Dr. Snowden's shoulder. "She will be okay."

Dr. Snowden sighed. "I know . . . just . . . odd to have her back, yet not have her back." He swiveled his head. "Know what I mean?"

"I do," said Evaran. "Give it time."

Dr. Snowden rubbed his temples for a moment, then looked forward. Delia Everoak had taken front stage and stood at a podium, facing out toward the assembled crowd seated in front of her. He had talked with her and Lord Noskov some prior to this assembly, and although he was glad for them, his heart was still heavy. He swallowed hard as he focused on Delia.

"I call to order the first United Nonhuman General Assembly meeting!" said Delia with a booming voice that bounced around the room.

A raucous clapping echoed throughout the room.

"I am Delia Everoak, matriarch of the Ollikrin and first president of this assembly. Our world was under attack by a sinister threat. With the aid of those who shall remain nameless," said Delia, glancing at Dr. Snowden and Evaran, "the threat has been neutralized. Our world is safe, for now, but we must stand, united, to face any future threat. This assembly will ensure that your voices are heard, your issues are tended to, and, more importantly, that we stand together, as one."

Another round of cheering and clapping rang out.

"I'll keep this brief, as there are others here who represent the senior council of this assembly and wish to speak. Getting organized will not be easy, but I have no doubt that we will overcome these obstacles. Over the coming months, we will establish new policies, procedures, and protocols and structure ourselves in a manner that lends itself to efficiency. The Ollikrin Nation is dedicated to supporting this, and we hope everyone here will partake in this new journey together. I would like to introduce Lord Vygon as our next speaker. Thank you."

Dr. Snowden listened with interest over the next four hours as Lord Vygon, Lord Noskov, Elder Cyrus and Ira, Captain Laban, and various other high-ranking nonhumans spoke. Being a time traveler now, he could not tell anyone what he knew of the future. He understood Lord Vygon's refusal to disclose any information. Telling the founding members that the only major organized group he knew of that made deals for Earth were the Helians would not help things.

One thing Dr. Snowden was sure of was that Delia Everoak would be a powerful figure, more than she was already, for the foreseeable future. He knew she was long-lived and wondered if she was around in his time period. Lord Noskov's speech was short, but he made the same vague nod to Dr. Snowden and Evaran. Dr. Snowden chuckled, thinking Lord Noskov, while enjoying the power this would confer, did not like bureaucracy, yet here there he was.

The Helians intrigued Dr. Snowden. Captain Laban had given them an identification device that would allow entry to Atlantis at any point. He also mentioned that it was part of an Evaran protocol that would grant full clearance for any interaction in the future. Dr. Snowden wondered if they would ever use it. He liked Captain Laban. He was tough and blunt in his assessments, but had a kindness about him. Dr. Snowden could not say the same about Ira. If anyone were to disrupt this assembly from reaching its full potential, it would be him. Cyrus had become a strong supporter, and with his and Captain Laban's support, most Helians were okay with the new arrangement.

After the meeting was over, Lord Vygon met them outside. "Long meeting . . ."

Dr. Snowden chuckled. "You did well. Everyone did, it's an exciting time."

"Maybe . . . but I supposed you and Evaran are off. Don't want to leave too big of a footprint in time. Minimize it and all that."

Evaran extended his arm. "You know me too well."

"You better believe it," said Lord Vygon with misted eyes. He grabbed Evaran's forearm and shook it.

Evaran eyed Lord Vygon. "I suspect something bad happens to me. You seem surprised or sad when you see me come and go."

Lord Vygon frowned.

"I understand. My rules."

Lord Vygon exhaled, then faced Dr. Snowden. "We will meet again, except I suspect you will have the advantage of knowing who I am."

Dr. Snowden extended a hand. "You never know. This time-travel business makes my head spin sometimes."

Lord Vygon chuckled and shook Dr. Snowden's hand. "Take care of Emily. What her other self did was nothing short of heroic. I understand why she isn't here."

"I will."

Lord Vygon took a step back and smirked. "You know . . . I had all mention of any involvement by you, Evaran, and Emily struck from the historical records. However, in order to recognize your contributions, the senior council recorded your interactions as a trio of adventurers, the noble traveler, the great tactician, and the heroic warrior."

A chill swept across Dr. Snowden as he glanced at Evaran.

Evaran shook his head slightly.

"You sure you can't stay a bit longer?" asked Lord Vygon.

Evaran raised his eyebrows.

Lord Vygon sighed. "Fine . . . fine. At least you know you will meet me again in your personal futures."

Evaran nodded and wheeled around after another forearm shake.

Dr. Snowden shook Lord Vygon's hand again and followed Evaran.

When they were a few feet away, Lord Vygon cleared his throat. "Oh . . . before I forget . . ."

Evaran stopped and turned around.

Lord Vygon exhaled from his mouth, and then shook his head. "Never mind. Good luck on your journeys."

Evaran studied Lord Vygon for a moment and then headed off to the Torvatta with Dr. Snowden behind him.

After Dr. Snowden and Evaran got back to the Torvatta, Evaran went to the roof while Dr. Snowden met Emily in the conference room.

Dr. Snowden noted that Emily was wearing the same suit she had on when she was found at Central Command. He got his usual burger and fries lunch and sat at the table. Emily sat across from him with an orange drink that she had said was full of vitamins. She had joined him for breakfast, lunch, and dinner over the last few days, but due to the meeting he had just come from, lunch today was a bit later.

"How was the meeting?" asked Emily as she took a sip from her drink.

"It was good. Lot of speaking, but we know what happens in the future."

Emily nodded. "Yeah . . . sorry about not coming. I just . . . don't really want to be around others right now."

"I know. Lord Vygon sends his well wishes to you."

"I said good-bye to him yesterday."

Dr. Snowden jerked his head back. "You did?"

"Yeah. He joined me in my morning training session after leaving you in the cartography lab. Showed me how to use the blades on his arms. Was pretty cool."

"Oh . . . he didn't mention that."

Emily smirked. "He said I was the Emily he knew from his past."

Dr. Snowden swallowed hard.

"You miss her . . . the other me . . . the old me," said Emily.

Dr. Snowden gestured outward. "It was her decision. She wanted to go. I respect it, but it doesn't mean I like it or understand it. She *was* you."

"Yeah," said Emily as a lump formed in her throat. "I just . . . need some time to sort all this out. I hope you understand."

Dr. Snowden's eyes softened. "Always."

Emily reached across the table and laid her hand flat on the table.

Dr. Snowden grabbed it and forced a smile. "You're not too old for an airplane ride."

Emily chuckled as a tear ran down her cheek. "I learned on that planet . . . that life is precious. It's also fragile, and I wasn't ready for what happened to me. I won't let that happen again. *Ever.*"

"It'll never happen again. I promise."

"Traveling with Evaran, do you think you could keep that promise?"

Dr. Snowden looked down. "Probably not. Maybe . . . we should go back home."

Emily gulped. "This is the only place I feel safe. I'm not ready to leave."

Dr. Snowden sighed.

Emily got up and walked around the table.

Dr. Snowden stood and hugged her tightly. "I wish this never happened."

"I know," said Emily. "But it has. I'll deal with it."

"I'm here if you need me."

Emily's body shuddered for a moment. "I know." She stepped back and wiped her eyes, then laughed. "Look at us, crying like babies. Dad would say . . . well, hell."

Dr. Snowden chuckled, then nodded. "He would."

Emily half smiled, then exited the conference room.

Dr. Snowden put a hand on his temple and squinted. A pit had formed in his stomach. The vibrant, bubbly, full-of-life Emily he knew was gone, and in her place was a more serious and guarded version. Nanobot Emily had said she synced up memories, so maybe this change would not be permanent, or he could just be wishing it were not. He decided to visit Evaran on the roof.

Once there, he looked around and realized they were back at the rings of Saturn. Evaran was leaning against the light-blue guardrail on the roof edge. With a sigh, he joined Evaran. "So where, or rather, when are we?"

Evaran glanced at Dr. Snowden. "We are one hour past when we went back in time. It is now 10:00 a.m. on the third of June, two thousand twelve."

Dr. Snowden shook his head. "If someone had seen us at nine, it would appear to them that we disappeared, then reappeared an hour later, right?"

Evaran nodded. "Correct. How is Emily?"

"She's okay . . . I guess," said Dr. Snowden, glancing at Evaran. "Thought I would never hear myself saying this, but she wants to be alone a lot."

"Understandable. She went through a life-changing event. It will take her time to sort things out."

Dr. Snowden nodded. "That's what she said. I guess I just need to give her space." His voice wavered. "No need for me to get in her way."

Evaran scrutinized Dr. Snowden for a moment and then put a hand on his shoulder. "No. She needs you now more than ever, even if she does not realize it. You need to be her anchor."

"How?"

"Be there for her. If she is training, go watch her. Suggest activities you can do together. Whatever brings her happiness, you need to support it," said Evaran. He raised a finger. "She has expressed an interest in engineering."

"What?"

"I suspect it is to understand and build things that she believes will make her safer."

Dr. Snowden hung his head in his hands. "Go figure."

"I am helping her learn. You should sit in."

Dr. Snowden looked at Evaran. "I will." He cleared his throat. "On another note, I have some questions if you have time."

"I would not have it any other way," said Evaran with a smile. "Go ahead."

"That overlord," said Dr. Snowden, "what exactly did he do to you?"

Evaran leaned against the guardrail again and looked over the rings. "He took a part of what constitutes me. As a consequence, I am not as physically capable as I was before."

"Oh," said Dr. Snowden. "Did he take some of your three-L?"

Evaran shook his head. "No."

Dr. Snowden narrowed his eyes. "Okay . . . what did he mean then when he said he could re-form himself, thanks to you?"

Evaran paused for a moment. "Hopefully, you will never need to understand that. What's important is that he is no longer in this plane."

Dr. Snowden looked out for a moment. Evaran was keeping these answers close to his chest. He sighed and then faced Evaran. "So the overlord was a Hadryn spawn. Old friend of yours?"

"Not quite," said Evaran. "The Hadryn are a humanoid race with immense power. They reside in their own plane system, but have somehow crossed over into this one, and more specifically, this plane and this universe. I am not sure what has changed."

"That guy was crazy. If he's from outside this plane, why does he care about human supremacy?"

Evaran glanced at Dr. Snowden, then looked out. "The Hadryn form, which you know as humanoid, is one they promote. To them, it is a symbol that even evolution bows to their will. It would appear they fixated on the closest match."

"Lucky us," said Dr. Snowden with a smirk.

"Indeed. Their true form is more akin to what you would refer to as a titan, just made of a type of energy instead of flesh and blood. However, when they came to this plane, they had to spawn a form, as I have. Plane's rules."

Dr. Snowden narrowed his eyes. "The plane has rules?"

Evaran's eyes twinkled as he cast a sidelong glance at Dr. Snowden.

"Okay . . . so if this Hadryn race has a different form outside the plane, what's yours?"

Evaran smiled. "Not something you would recognize."

"I feel like I'm playing the question lottery," said Dr. Snowden with a chuckle. "Just trying to wrap my head around all this. One thing that still puzzles me is that the overlord talked about a female Evaran."

Evaran nodded. "Your curious nature continues to be a defining trait I like about this evolution of humanity. I am unsure who this other Evaran was, but it was not a past or future version of this form. Something to investigate at a later time." He looked down and swallowed hard. "I sensed that she suffered horribly at the hands of the overlord before dying."

Dr. Snowden's eyes widened slightly. The thought of Evaran dying was a foreign concept to him. Evaran was eternal to Dr. Snowden. He knew Evaran could be hurt, but in the short time he had known Evaran, it just seemed unimaginable. "I suppose we couldn't go back in time and save her."

Evaran shook his head. "We cannot. It has been established that she dies, and I must respect that. Time is fluid, like a river. However, I try to avoid making ripples unless absolutely necessary."

Dr. Snowden smirked. "Paradoxes."

"Yes."

Dr. Snowden sighed. "Nothing can ever be easy."

Evaran nodded.

"I'm just glad Emily's back, but I do miss Nanobot Emily. She gave her life to save us," said Dr. Snowden as a lump formed in his throat.

Evaran raised a finger toward Dr. Snowden. "She did, and remember, she was a version of Emily. The one with us now would most likely have made the same decision."

Dr. Snowden exhaled hard from his mouth as his eyes misted. "I know." He rubbed his eyes. "Can we choose some place for our next visit that doesn't involve genocidal maniacs?"

Evaran half grinned. "Of course. Everything is as—"

"I know . . . I know . . . as it should be," said Dr. Snowden, tossing his hand out at Evaran.

Evaran cast a sidelong glance at Dr. Snowden, and then they shared a laugh.

THE END

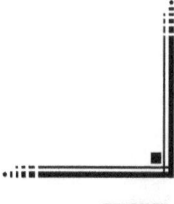

I hope you enjoyed the third book in the Evaran Chronicles! It had some major events for the series and was fun to write! If you enjoyed the book, and have the time and inclination, a review would go a long way in helping out this new indie author. If you do submit a review, I'll put in a word to Evaran to rescue you from a prison planet in a pocket universe should you find yourself stranded on one! Want to be notified about new book releases? If so, you can sign up below.

www.AdairHart.com/MailingList.aspx

I will only send you email about new book releases, major updates, and the occasional newsletter. I dislike getting spammed too, so I will use this sparingly to keep you in the loop.

ABOUT
THE AUTHOR

I have been dreaming about fictional worlds since I was a kid. I devoured anything related to fantasy and science fiction. I developed a setting over the last twenty years and struggled to find a medium I could express it in. Several years ago I discovered I enjoyed writing. It is a passion of mine now, and exploring my setting with it has been an awesome journey.

I work in the information technology field and have my bachelor's and master's degrees in it. It has helped me to shape some of the concepts I write about. I also enjoy keeping up on futurology and science in general.

I live in central Ohio and enjoy walking, reading, gaming, learning, listening to music, and trying to keep up on my never-ending list of TV shows and movies to watch. If you want to contact me, you can do so on my website at

www.AdairHart.com

YOU CAN ALSO REACH ME ON

Facebook............................fb.com/AdairHart
Goodreads.....www.goodreads.com/AdairHart
Email..............Adair.Hart.Author@gmail.com

DEDICATION

To my grandmother who passed away on March 6, 2016. The world is a bit darker without your light. I will forever treasure the impact you have had on my life and strive to live in a manner that would make you proud.

ACKNOWLEDGMENTS

This was a great journey for me, but I wouldn't be here without the help of others. I would like to thank, in no particular order,

My great editor, Laura Petrella. It is through her that I continue to fine-tune my craft. She is an excellent mentor who guides me in the right direction. I am honored to have her along with me on my journey. Her involvement helps me shape my voice, and we have great synergy together.

My cover artist, Tom Edwards (tomedwardsconcepts@gmail.com), for doing yet another fantastic cover. This cover was a bit different, but thanks to his incredible skill, he created another masterpiece.

My family and friends who helped encourage me along the way.

My proofreader, Red Adept Publishing, for providing a great service. They are quick, efficient, and professional.

My formatter and interior designer, Colleen Sheehan (www.wdrbookdesign.com/), for being a great person. Oh, and she makes my book interior look great!

BOOKS

You can see all the books in the Evaran Chronicles at

www.AdairHart.com/Books/Books.aspx

Below are the books in the series:

PREQUEL:
THE
ARRIVAL

BOOK 1:
THE
AWAKENING

BOOK 2:
THE FREDORIAN
DESTINY

BOOK 3:
THE
PURIFICATION

www.ingramcontent.com/pod-product-compliance
Lightning Source LLC
Chambersburg PA
CBHW051319250626
47155CB00007B/2384